Also by Sara Wolf

the Lovely Vicious series

Love Me Never
Forget Me Always
Remember Me Forever

SARA WOLF

Entangled Publishing, LLC
2614 South Timberline Road
Suite 105, PMB 159
Fort Collins, CO 80525
rights@entangledpublishing.com

Entangled Teen is an imprint of Entangled Publishing, LLC.

Visit our website at www.entangledpublishing.com.

Edited by Stacy Cantor Abrams & Lydia Sharp
Cover design by Yin Yuming
Interior design by Toni Kerr

ISBN 978-1-64063-146-5
Ebook ISBN 978-1-64063-147-2

Manufactured in the United States of America

First Edition June 2018

10 9 8 7 6 5 4 3 2 1

For those who have lost their own hearts,
and who struggle with their own hunger.

*"Darkness is only in the mortal eye,
that thinks it sees, but sees not."*

—Ursula K. LeGuin, *The Left Hand of Darkness*

1

THE STARVING WOLF AND THE BLACK ROSE

KING SREF OF CAVANOS WATCHES me with the deadened eyes of a raven circling a corpse—patient, waiting to devour me the second I let my guard down. I briefly debate telling him humans don't taste all that good, until I remember normal girls don't eat people. Or fake their way into royal courts.

Normal, I think to myself. *Completely and utterly normal. Bat your eyelashes. Laugh like you've got nothing in your head. Old God's teeth, what in the flaming afterlife do normal girls do again?*

The other girls would know. There are three of us, three girls in cake-pink dresses, kneeling before King Sref's throne. We wear veils to hide our faces. I'd ask them, but we're currently busy drowning in expensive lace and the silent stares of every gilded noble in the room. Well, the other two girls are. I'm doing more of a *laughing internally at the way they carefully tilt their gorgeous heads and purse their pouts* thing. Look More Attractive Than the Girl Next to You is the name of the game their mothers have been teaching them from birth.

Mine taught me how to die, and not much else.

"You are all as lovely as rose blooms," the king says finally. His face is weathered with a handsome age. Dignity carves lines around his steel-colored eyes. The smile in them doesn't reach those eyes, though, a sure sign it's only half sincere. He is old, he is powerful, and he is bored—the most dangerous combination I can think of.

"Thank you, Your Majesty," the two girls echo, and I quickly mimic them. I've nicknamed them in my head—Charm and Grace. Charm and Grace don't dare look at anything but the marble floor, while my eyes dart about, thirsty for the rich silks of the nobles' clothes and the gold serpents carved into the majestic stone columns. Three years stuck in the woods serving a witch makes your eyes hungry for anything that isn't a tree or deer droppings. I can't raise my head for fear I'll be singled out, but I can look just high enough to see the feet of Queen Kolissa and her son. Crown Prince Lucien d'Malvane, Archduke of Tollmount-Kilstead, Fireborn, the Black Eagle—he has a dozen names, all of them eye-roll worthy. If there's one thing I've learned from my single day at the royal court, it's that the more names someone has, the less he actually does.

I haven't seen more than the prince's booted toes, and I already know he's useless.

And soon, if I have my way, he'll be heartless.

"I welcome you, the newest additions to our illustrious court," King Sref says. His voice booms, but out of decorum, not of passion.

"Thank you, Your Majesty," Charm and Grace say, and I echo. I'm starting to get the hang of this—thank everyone a lot and look pretty. Infiltrating the palace might not be so hard after all.

Queen Kolissa's saccharine voice rings out after the king's. "I hope you will bring honor to your families and uphold the ideals of this great nation," she says.

"Thank you, Your Majesty," we respond.

I hear the queen murmur something. A deep voice softly says something back, and then her voice gets an inch louder— but still so quiet only the three of us, kneeling at the foot of the throne, can hear it.

"Say something, please, Lucien."

"That would be pointless, Mother, and I tend to avoid doing pointless things."

"Lucien—"

"You know I hate this outdated ceremony. Look at them—they're here only for their families. No girl in her right mind would subject herself to this humiliating display." The prince's voice is laced with dark venom, and I flinch. It's nothing like his father's carefully emotionless tone or his mother's sickly sweet one. Unlike the rest of these restrained nobles, his emotions burn hot just beneath the surface. He hasn't learned how to hide them completely, not yet.

"It's a tradition," the queen insists. "Now say something to them, or so help me—"

The screech of a chair across marble resounds, and the prince demands of us: "Rise."

The two girls, graceful as swans, lift their skirts and stand. I bite back a swear as I do the same and nearly trip over my ornate shoes. Note to past self: four days of training isn't nearly enough time to teach someone to walk in a pair of ribboned death traps. How Charm and Grace do it so effortlessly is beyond me, but the blushes on their faces aren't.

I look up to the prince now standing on the top step before us. Even without the advantage of elevation, I can see he's tall—a warrior's height, his silver-vested torso lean and his velvet-caped shoulders broad. A year? No, he's maybe two years or so older than my ageless teenage form of sixteen; the corded muscles tell me that much. Why they call him the Black Eagle is obvious now: his hair is blacker than a raven's, windswept about his face and long in the back, kept in a single braid that traces his spine. His face is his father's in its prime: a proud, hawkish nose, cheekbones so high and dignified they border arrogance. His skin is his father's, too, sun-kissed oakwood, and yet his eyes are his mother's—piercing dark iron sharpened to a fine, angry blade point. He is all pride and sable darkness, and every part of me hates it—hates the fact that someone who's to inherit so much power and wealth is striking as well. I want him hunched and covered in warts. I want him weak-chinned and watery-eyed. But the world is unfair, always. I learned that the day my parents were killed.

The day I was made into a monster.

The girls beside me all but salivate, and I do my best to look bored. On my way here I saw much better-looking boys. Dozens. Hundreds. All right, fine—there was only the one, and he was a painter's model in the streets of the artists' district, but none of that matters, because the way Prince Lucien sneers his next question wipes every ounce of attraction from my mind.

"A lady isn't merely a decoration," he says, words rumbling like thunder. "She is the mother of our future, the teacher of our progeny. A lady must have a brain between her ears, as must we all. For what is beauty without purpose? Nothing more than a vase of flowers, to wither and be thrown away."

Books written by the smartest polymaths have told me the planet is round, that it rotates about the sun, and that there are magnetic poles to our east and west at the coldest parts, and I believe them, yet in no way can I believe there's someone who exists who's *this* arrogant.

The nobles titter among themselves, but it quickly dies down when King Sref holds up a hand. "These are the Spring Brides, my prince," the king says patiently. "They're of noble lineage. They've studied and practiced much to be here. They deserve more respect than this."

Someone's getting scolded, I think with a singsong tone. Prince Lucien throws his sharp gaze to the king.

"Of course, Your Majesty." His disdain at calling his father "Your Majesty" is obvious. *Consider yourself lucky, Prince*, I think. *That you have a father at all in this cruel world.*

"But"—the prince turns to the noble audience—"all too often do we equate nobleness of blood for soundness of mind and goodness of judgment."

His eyes sweep the room, and this time, the nobles are dead silent. The shuffling of feet and cough-clearing of throats is deafeningly uncomfortable. I haven't been here long, but I recognize his stance. It's the same one young forest wolves take with their elders; he's challenging the nobles, and by the looks of the king's white knuckles and the queen's terrified face, I'd guess it's a dangerous game he's playing.

"Let us welcome the Spring Brides as the kings of the Old God did." The prince sweeps his hands out. "With a question of character."

The nobles murmur, perturbed. The silver half circles with three spokes through them dripping from every building in the city weren't exactly subtle; the New God, Kavar, rules here in Vetris. The Sunless War was fought for Kavar thirty years ago, and the Old God's followers were slaughtered and driven out of Vetris. His statues were torn down, his temples demolished. Now, carrying on an Old God tradition is a death sentence. The king knows this—and covers for his son quickly.

"The kings of the Old God were misguided, but they built the foundation upon which this country thrives. The roads, the walls, the dams—all of them were built by the Old Kings. To erase them from existence would be a crime to history, to truth. Let us have one last Old tradition here, today, and shed such outdated formalities with grace."

It's a good save. You don't have to be a noble to see that. Prince Lucien looks miffed at his father's attempts to assuage the nobles, but he hides it and turns back to the three of us.

"Answer this question to the best of your abilities as you raise your veils. What is the king's worth?"

There's a long moment of quiet. I can practically hear the brain-cogs of the girls churning madly beside me. The nobles murmur to one another, laughing and giggling and raising eyebrows in our direction. The king is immeasurable in his worth. To say anything less would be madness. A swamp-thick layer of scorn and amusement makes the air reek and my skin crawl.

Finally, Charm lifts her veil and clears her throat to speak.

"The king is worth…a million—no! A trillion gold coins. No—seven trillion!" The nobles' laughter gets louder. Charm blushes beet-red. "I'm sorry, Your Majesty. My father never taught me numbers. Just sewing and things."

King Sref smiles good-naturedly. "It's quite all right. That was a lovely answer."

The prince says nothing, face unimpressed, and points to Grace. She curtsies and lifts her veil.

"The king's worth cannot be measured," she says clearly. "It is as high as the highest peak of the Tollmount-Kilstead Mountains, as wide as the Endless Bog in the south. His worth is deeper than the darkest depths of the Twisted Ocean."

This time, the nobles don't laugh. Someone starts a quiet applause, and it spreads.

"A very eloquent answer," the king says. The girl looks pleased with herself, curtsying again and glancing hopefully at Prince Lucien. His grimace only deepens.

"You, the ungainly one." The prince finally points to me. "What say you?"

His insult stings, but for only a moment. Of course I'm ungainly compared to him. Anyone would be. I'm sure the only one he doesn't think ungainly is the mirror in his room.

I hold his gaze, though it burns like sunfire on my skin. His distaste for me, for the girls beside me, for every noble in this room, is palpable. He expects nothing from me, from anyone—I can see that in the way his eyes prematurely cloud with disdain the moment I open my mouth.

He expects nothing new. I must be everything new.

I lift my veil slowly as I say, "The king's worth is exactly one potato."

There's a silence, and then a shock wave ripples through the room, carrying gasps and frenzied whispers with it. The celeon guards grip their halberds and narrow their catlike eyes, their tails swishing madly. Any one of them could rip me in half as easily as paper, though it wouldn't kill me. It'd just betray me as a Heartless—a witch's servant—to the entire noble court, which is considerably worse than having your insides spilled on the marble. Witches are Old God worshippers and fought against humans in the Sunless

War. We are the enemy.

I'm the enemy, wearing the mask of a noble girl who's just said something very insulting about her king in the foolish hopes of catching the prince's attention.

The queen clutches her handkerchief to her chest, clearly offended at my words. The king raises one eyebrow. The prince, on the other hand, smiles. It's so slow and luxurious I barely see it form, and then all at once his face is practically gleeful. *He's handsome*, I think to myself—*handsome enough when he isn't being a hateful dog turd*. He tames his expression and clears his throat.

"Are you going to elaborate, or should I have you thrown in the dungeons for slandering the king right here and now?"

The celeon advance, and my unheart quivers. The prince is enjoying the idea of throwing me in the dungeon a little too much for my taste. I raise my chin, carefully keeping my shoulders wide and my face passive. Strong. I will make an impression here, or I will die for my loose tongue. It's that simple.

Except it isn't that simple.

Because I can't die.

Because unlike the girls next to me, I'm not here to impress the king and win a royal's hand in marriage or a court position for my father.

I'm here for Prince Lucien's heart.

Literally, not figuratively. Although figuratively would be easier, wouldn't it? Making boys fall in love is easy, from what little I remember of my human life before—all it takes are compliments and batting eyelashes and a low-cut dress or five and they're clay putty in your hands. But I'm here for the organ beating in his chest, and it will be mine, by gambit or by force. In order to get that close, I must earn his trust.

The prince expects idiots and sycophants. I must give him the opposite. I must be brilliance itself, a diamond dagger between the flesh of his stagnant noble life.

"To the common people of this country," I press on, "one potato can mean the difference between starving in winter and making it through to spring. A single potato means life. A single potato is a saving grace. To the king's people living in his villages, in his kingdom, nothing is more precious than one potato."

The murmur that goes around the room is hushed, confusion written on the nobles' faces. They have no idea, I'm sure, of what it's like to starve. But it's all I've ever known.

I lock eyes with the prince once more. His face, too, is confused, but in a different way from the crowd's. He looks at me like he's never seen a person before, as if I'm some odd specimen kept in a cool cellar for later study by a polymath. The boredom in his gaze is gone, replaced with a strange, stiff sort of shock. I should look away, act modest or shy, but I don't. I make my eyes sing the determined words my mouth can't say.

I am no flower to be ravaged at your whim, angry wolf—I am your hunter, bow cocked and ready. I am a Heartless, one of the creatures your people fled from in terror thirty years ago.

I let the smallest, hungriest smirk of mine loose on him.

If you were smart, you'd start running, too.

The queen smiles, squeezing the king's arm, and the king laughs. Nothing about it is bland or subdued; it leaks with the hoarse edges of unbridled amusement. For the briefest moment as he smiles at me, he looks ten years younger.

"What is your name, clever little Bride?"

My mind says, *Zera, no last name, daughter of a merchant couple whose faces I'm starting to forget: Orphan, Thief,*

Lover of bad novels and good cake, and indentured servant of the witch Nightsinger, who sent me here to rip your son's heart from his chest.

I dip into a wobbly curtsy instead and spill my lie with a smile. "Zera Y'shennria, Your Majesty; niece of Quin Y'shennria, Lady of the House of Y'shennria and Ravenshaunt. Thank you for having me here today."

Thank you, and I'm sorry.

As sorry as a monster can be.

*F*ive *days earlier*

I've been stabbed.

This is, unfortunately, nothing new to me.

"Kavar's teeth." I swear the New God's name, twisting my arm behind me and fingering the dagger's handle. "This was my favorite dress."

One moment I'm walking on the forest road back home, and the next I'm skewered like a village pig. I make a mental note to mark this night in my nonexistent diary as the best one ever.

The willowy figure that stabbed me stands in front of me, a dark, hooded cloak obscuring his face and body. I have no idea who he is—but he moved too fast to be human, and he's too tall to be one of the pale Beneather race that lives underground. The swishing blue tail tipped with fur is a dead giveaway—definitely a celeon assassin, a member of a catlike race that thinks quick and strikes quicker.

"Are you just going to stand there?" I pant, my fingers meeting the slick river of blood running down the laces of my bodice. "If you want to kill me, I'd prefer you make it quicker than this."

"You aren't dead," the celeon growls—their voices always sound sleek yet rough, like a banner of silk dragged across gravel. His eyes glint golden from the darkness of his hood.

"A master of observation *and* a master of stabbing young girls walking alone at night!" I force a pained smile. "It's an honor. I'd bow, but the knife you so graciously gifted me is making that a tad difficult."

"I hit your heart," he asserts. "You should be dead."

"I'd love to tell you you're the first man to say such romantic things to me." I stretch enough to grasp the handle of the dagger, and wrench it out with a great pull. The searing pain dulls to a hideous ache. "But alas—I'm a career thief, not a career liar." I point the bloody dagger at him. "You have ten seconds to tell me who sent you. Celeon assassins aren't cheap, so it had to have been a noble. Which one did I piss off this time?"

His tail twitches—a sure sign he's thinking of ways to close the gap between us and end it.

"Nine," I start.

The triplet moons are full above us, the red twins connected by a spray of stardust and the blue giant bloated like a firefly's abdomen. They shed gloriously bright light on the woods and the Bone Road cutting through it, and I have all the time in the world to admire it, since the celeon chooses to remain silent.

"Eight," I count down. "Was it the lady with the gryphon banners and fancy carriage who came by? She should be *thanking* me for relieving her of that emerald tiara. It clashed hideously with her complexion."

Still, he says nothing. A flock of white crows flies

overhead, settling in the pine trees to watch the showdown with their relentless red eyes. I suppress the urge to throw a fit. The last thing I need right now is a murder of witches watching this. I don't like an audience when I work.

"Listen, my good celeon." I toss the dagger from one palm to the other, inspecting the wicked tip. "You stabbed me. But I can forgive that. Lots of people stab me, and half of them I end up being great friends with! I even attend their funerals. Of course, I'm also the one holding their funerals. Alone. In the woods. With just me and their body and a shovel. But those are minor details. Five, by the way. The timer doesn't stop just for my elegant soliloquies."

The celeon lowers his hood, his pronounced blue brow wrinkling as he frowns. His ears are long and slender and straight and have no visible holes. The celeon look like big cats, if cats were also lizards and stretched out thin and walked on backward-bent legs.

"I don't reveal my employers," he finally rasps.

"Wrong answer!" I chime, throwing the dagger between his legs and pinning his tail to the ground. He howls and collapses on the dirt, the pain of being stabbed in his most sensitive area all but paralyzing him. The celeon might be five times stronger and faster than any human, but they have their weak spots. As he struggles to free himself, I walk over, stepping carefully between his splayed legs and squatting to his eye level. I see my reflection in his fearful gold eyes as big as coins, his slit pupils dilating as I lean in and flick his furry forehead with my fingers.

"And that's why you should wear tail armor like everyone else, silly."

"How?" He pants, his muzzle parted, so I can barely see his wicked incisors. "A throw like that—who are you?"

"Your employer didn't tell you? *Tsk-tsk*, it's almost like they want you dead. And I'd just hate to live up to their expectations."

I reach down and pull the dagger from his tail. Unpinned, the celeon scuttles away from me and down the road faster than I can register, cradling his purple-bleeding appendage.

"I'm Zera!" I call. "Second Heartless of the witch Nightsinger. A bit of life advice: never come to the Bone Road ever again." I pause. "But if you do, bring a new dress! You owe me one!"

The white crows in the trees start to cackle, a storm of noise. The celeon looks from them to me, his pointed face snarling as he hobbles away. He knows what those crows are, and he hates them as all celeon do. When he's gone, I wipe the dagger free of mixed red and purple blood, the pain in my back radiating sharply.

"Kavardammit, this hurts!" Every movement is agony now that the adrenaline's gone.

"What have I said about using the New God's name in front of me, Zera?" One of the crows alights at my feet, speaking with a human woman's voice.

"Just heal me," I gasp. "No lectures. Please."

"Humor me," the crow says.

"Don't I always? That's why you keep my heart in that awful jar—so I can't leave you humorless for a single second."

The crow is patient. She always is. Finally, I exhale.

"Fine. Kavar stinks. Amen."

"Zera."

"I will write you a ten-page essay on how much the Old God rules more than him, just after you heal me. Please. I'm dying here."

"For the third time this week," the crow drawls.

"And the forty-seventh time overall! Did you know the

humans think that number is unlucky? It brings all sorts of nasty diseases to their grain, I guess?"

"Have you been spying on the human village again? I told you not to get too close—"

"Quick!" I exclaim. "Before I start to mold!"

With a bird's version of a sigh, she hops around my body. Usually when I smartly try to climb a very tall tree and break my legs, or cleverly stumble onto a wolf mother den and get torn to shreds, I heal on my own. Well, if you call my heart encased in a jar over my witch's fireplace siphoning magic from said witch to heal me "on my own." But tonight my witch is right here. I feel the sting of a feather's edge in my raw wound, and I bite back another swear. The crow says words, but I can't understand them. No one can, save for her and the Old God, who responds by gifting her magic. Or something. The workings of a witch's magic are beyond me, but the results aren't. The pain fades instantly, followed by the strange sensation of my wound closing up like a stitched blouse in a seamstress's hand. My fingers dart to it, finding only smooth skin and scraps of fabric.

"Would it kill you to ask the Old God to fix my dress, too?" I struggle to my feet.

The crow fluffs her chest out. "Perhaps."

"Ask him right away, then." When the crow just blinks at me, I clap my hands. "Let's go! Hurry now!"

"My death means your death. You're bound to me as my Heartless," she says. "You know that."

I groan and collapse on the grass next to the muddy road. "Life isn't worth living if I don't have a fabulous pile of silk and satin to strut about in."

"It wasn't even your dress. You stole it," the crow says.

"Why do you think I liked it so much!"

The crow lets out an exasperated sigh again. Her brethren wait for her in the trees, and I wave to them.

"It's an honor, sirs and madams! I hope your witchery is well tonight!"

The crow on the ground hops to my shoulder, talons digging into my skin. "Did you determine who sent that Waveborn to kill you?"

Waveborn—what the witches call celeon. A witch's magic spell went awry a long time ago, and the wave of it washed over a small continent to the north. It transformed the celeon from feral beasts into sentient creatures. Most celeon consider their sentience a curse, a deviation from their intended nature, and so they hate witches with a fiery passion.

"Here in the third era we call them celeon, Nightsinger. It's less ragingly offensive to them," I insist. "And no. Not a peep."

"Firewalker"—Nightsinger motions with one wing to another witch-crow—"tells me his Heartless are being attacked in much the same way. Anonymous assassins sent to kill without being told who the target is."

"*What* the target is," I correct.

"Precisely."

"They're not after witches?"

"For once, no."

I cradle my chin in my hand. "So someone is paying a lot of assassins to kill Heartless. Without telling them their targets are Heartless."

"Yes."

"Why? And who can afford to waste that much money in this economy?"

Nightsinger fixes a single red eye on me; I know that look. It's the *let's be cryptic and vague about important issues for an infuriatingly long amount of time* look. Witches love that look. I love that look—love to hate it. Silently, of course, because what magical thrall in her right mind would hate it out loud to the witch in total control of her fate?

"I should return to the meeting," she says finally. "And you should return home. Have you the herbs for dinner?"

I motion to the basket I'd long discarded behind me, brimming with snowdrops and basil.

"Good." Nightsinger ascends, wings beating hard. "I left you dinner. Try not to slop it everywhere this time."

"No promises," I say, watching as she rejoins the flock. They rise as one, eerily coordinated in their every swoop and glide. Nightsinger tried to explain witch meetings to me once, and thanks to my awe-inspiring intelligence I understood a whopping none of it. It's apparently only safe for covens to gather during the Diamond Moon—when all three moons are full. They exchange information and magic, but since witches live isolated and hidden to keep away from humans, they gather as crows—able to fly long distances and connected wordlessly by their minds. It's a small mercy witches who transform into animals are always an unnatural white, or none of us would know when they were around.

With the murder finally gone, I breathe a sigh of relief. No matter how long I've lived around it, the thought of magic still makes me ill. It's bound me to this life of Heartlessness, after all.

I put my hand over my unheart and listen to the emptiness in my chest. After three years, I can barely remember what it feels like to have a heart anymore. I recall warmth and a tugging sensation, and if I reach far enough back in my memory, I find pain. Pain like lightning, sudden and sharp and devastating. Pain like the end of the world. If I pay attention to it, the pain only grows. So I don't. I wander the woods. And when wandering stops working, I don my cloak and a ragged mask and steal from the nobles who travel the Bone Road—jewels, dresses, anything. Anything beautiful. Anything that, when I wear it, makes me feel like a human again.

I pick up the basket of herbs and turn back to the woods, letting the shadows of the trees devour me. They are pretty, in their own sable, pine-scented way, but they're still very much the bars of my prison. That's one of the less-than-ideal perks of being a Heartless—I can't go very far from where my witch keeps my heart: a mile and a half at most. If I try, the pain rips me apart and reduces me to a useless, screaming mess.

A fox watches me from a ridge nearby, curious and fire-colored. I wave. It doesn't move, fixed on me. What an attentive audience! Those are so rare these days. I clear my throat.

"At this point, I'm sure you want to ask—I hate Nightsinger, don't I? I mean, anyone sensible would hate the person who has her life in the palm of her hand. That's reasonable—expected, even!"

The fox blinks blankly at me.

"The answer…" I raise a finger like I'm a polymath and the fox is my student. "Is yes. And no. Because nothing in life is simple. It's all utter maddening chaos and contradicting emotions."

The fox blinks again. I throw my hands up.

"Don't look at me! Take it up with the gods if you're so mad about it!"

The fox is, understandably, not as incensed as I am. It slinks away over the ridgeline without so much as a thank-you for my gracious life lessons.

I adjust the basket higher on my hip and sigh. "Talking to animals like they're *people* who can *understand* you was last year, Zera. Let's try to think of something new and more rewarding to pass the rest of our immortal life with, all right? Maybe something that doesn't make you seem mad."

I start walking again. The answer to the fox's question—*my question*—is this: I don't blame Nightsinger for taking my heart, no matter how it's twisted my body and soul. How could I? She saved my life from the bandits who murdered my family, from the darkness of death itself, and so I serve her. I'm a monster, not a complete arsehole. I know that one good turn deserves another. It's just been a very, *very* long turn. This palatial forest, this empty chest of mine, these memories of what I've done—I've been stuck with them all for three years. I can't remember much about my life before my death—no Heartless can. Those memories fade when our hearts are ripped from our chests. But I remember every second of what happened during my death. And after.

I wait, and wait. And like a faithful, awful dog, the dark voice in my head comes out to play.

Five, it hisses at me, like a snake's scales sliding against midnight grass. *You killed five of them. One old, one young, one with no left eye, one who never screamed (not once), and one with a bad smile that didn't last long. You wish he lasted longer. You wish Nightsinger turned him into a Heartless, too, unkillable like you, suffering forever like you—*

I might not have a heart, but I still have a stomach, and it churns violently. I hurry my steps like I can leave what I did behind, the trees leaning away and into me, creating a path otherwise inaccessible to the outside world. Their branches shudder, roots trembling and bark groaning with the effort.

They conceal Nightsinger willingly—unlike me, they had a choice to join her.

Somewhere between the shifting trees and my own self-pity walks a beautiful young boy in an orange tunic. "You didn't kill the celeon, Zera," he accuses.

Just seeing the boy's outline makes the awful voice dim, lessen. Finally, something other than the past to focus on. I flip my hair haughtily.

"Yes, well, I don't do a lot of things. Wear the color puce, for instance, or obsess over swords. Also, kill perfectly innocent assassins."

The boy snorts, unimpressed. He's younger than me, and he'll always look that way, until Nightsinger releases his heart back to him and he can start growing again. His curly black hair falls in his moss eyes, his skin a deep umber and smooth with baby fat. His full name is Crav il'Terin Maldhinna, born of Mald the Ironfist. He's a Warprince of the Endless Bog, and the third and final Heartless of the witch Nightsinger, but I have my own nickname for him that he appreciates and cherishes.

"Look at you, Crabby." I walk up to him, measuring the top of his head against my shoulder. "You're permanently almost as tall as I am."

"Fall into a pit," he retorts.

"Gladly." I pat his arm. "Just as soon as I've had something to eat. Nightsinger said she left food—did you have some?"

He wipes his mouth on his arm, his sleeve coming away a bit red. "A little. I'm not that hungry."

"Nonsense. We're always hungry."

"Well, I'm not." He thrusts his proud chin forward. He became a Heartless only a year ago—he still fights it in the most childish of ways, in ways I used to. "Now answer me.

Why didn't you kill that celeon? He attacked you."

We walk together, the trees parting one last time. In a violently purple thicket of foxgloves and nightshade sits a round stone house no bigger than any village house nor any fancier. The roof of the cottage is magic-touched canvas to keep heavy rains and snows off our heads. A tin chimney puffs smoke into the air. The few windows of the cottage glow warm with buttery candlelight. I don't know what it is about this clearing, but fireflies adore it like no other place in the forest—hanging in the air as gently pulsing clusters of turquoise glimmers.

"Not everything that attacks me has to die, Crav," I say patiently. I don't expect him to understand—the people of the Endless Bog decide everything in their lives by a strict code of martial rules.

"*The number of my wounds is the number of my enemies dead.*" He recites his favorite Endless Bog saying. I laugh and gather my bloodstained skirts to walk up the few steps to the covered door.

"He wasn't my enemy."

"He tried to kill you!" Crav argues.

"That's because he didn't know what I was. Being ignorant isn't a crime, Crabby, it's a curable ailment."

I pull the tapestry back from the door. The air of the cottage is always thick with the scent of herbs and spices, a fireplace dancing with flames against one wall. In the center of the room is a pit lined with river stone, in which the body of a deer torn open rests, glassy eyes staring at nothing and everything at once. The first time I came into the cottage and saw a similar deer, I just thought Nightsinger had terrible taste in decor. But I learned very quickly that it was a terrible taste in decor that served a purpose—eating raw meat is necessary for a Heartless to live. And by "live," I mean "continue to function as a sentient being with control over our own actions." We're monsters, to be sure. But as long as we eat raw meat, we can be...*lesser* monsters. There's a hunger that comes with our empty chests, settles there like a diseased pustule. It can never be satiated, and it never goes away. But as long as we keep eating raw flesh regularly, the hunger can't grow, can't spread its darkness through our veins and cloud our minds, turning us into something far worse.

Beasts. Berserkers. Abominations. So as much as I enjoy rebelling against any and all traditions, I eat disgusting deer organs like a good Heartless, every day, at the same time. Because I relish my sanity.

Because I've seen the beast inside me once. And I swore that day I'd never let it out again.

Five men dead because of you, you repulsive creature—

I shut up the dark voice by picking a strip of flesh off the deer and sprinkling a few herbs from my basket on it. I down it in one swallow and try to make my grimace as pretty as possible. Even if the hunger can't be fully satiated with food, it does get quieter, much to my relief.

I wash my hands in the stone basin in the corner and settle on a cushion with Crav.

"So, how was your day?"

He pouts mightily. "You could've at least crippled the celeon for life."

"My day was great, thanks for asking," I chime and get up. "Where's Peligli?"

"Sleeping? I'm not her babysitter."

"Peligli!" I stand and shout up the stairs. "Dinner's ready!"

The rustling of blankets precedes the slapping of tiny feet

on the wood floor and a high-pitched chant of *"Zera, Zera, Zera, Zera."* A mass of carrot-red hair rockets down the steps and into me. Peligli—the first Heartless of Nightsinger—looks up, her round four-year-old face pale and flushed, her eyes midnight black and sparkling. She's excited to eat—all her teeth growing slowly into their pointed, jagged, razor-sharp state over her little lips. We can control the emergence of our monstrous teeth, but it gets harder the hungrier we are.

"Zera! You back! Did you get any shinies today?" she asks.

"No shinies. But I did do several terrible things, so it wasn't a total loss." I smile and thumb a sleep booger from her eye. Peligli squirms her hands in a way that means "pick me up," and I hoist her on my hip and approach the deer.

"I like terrible things," she announces.

"No you don't."

"Yes I do!" she insists, kicking her feet to be let down immediately. I comply and watch her fly toward dinner. She picks out the deer's eyes with her chubby fingers and pops them into her mouth like cherries, chewing happily as she chimes, "Terrible things are interdasting!"

"Interesting," Crav corrects dully.

She smiles with bloodstained teeth at him. "Yeah!"

Peligli's full name is Peligli, no more and no less. While Nightsinger turned Crav and me into Heartless because we hung on the verge of death, Peligli was turned of her own free will. She'd been an orphan on the streets of Vetris before the Sunless War, and when she saw Nightsinger she followed her, never leaving her side. Though she looks the youngest of us, she's been a Heartless for almost forty years. She insists Nightsinger didn't let her fight in the War, which is a small blessing. I can't imagine war would be good for a kid's mind—especially because she would've had to fight.

That's what Heartless did in the Sunless War—killed. That's what we do, what we exist for. A witch is just that—a witch, a singular person with magical power. And as it turns out, conjuring giant fireballs from thin air and turning into any animal shape you please tends to make you enemies. Or at the very least, it makes humans afraid of you. Because humans are afraid of everything—especially giant fireballs. Babies, the lot of them.

I look to the rows of ragged books on Nightsinger's shelves—witch books, detailing their history and such. I've read them each a thousand times, because watching mud dry on a tree root gets surprisingly boring after the first month of doing it. The books told me Heartless exist to be soldiers for witches. Bodyguards. Cannon fodder, if we're being generous. But cannons exist only in Pendron and they backfire all the time and—ugh, basically, we're just meat puppets. Padding between a witch and her enemies. Why kill your enemy yourself if you can get an undying, magical thrall to do it?

Watching Crav and Peligli together reminds me just how close they hover to becoming killers. They love Nightsinger more than I do—too young to understand a kind captor is still a captor. They'd do anything for her—but I can't let them become what I've become. I can't let those small hands drip red. Every mercenary who comes looking for a witch's bounty, I drive off. Every curious hunter who strays too far into the woods, I scare away, so Crav and Peligli never have to. And I'll keep doing it, until Nightsinger dies and takes all of us with her, or until she gives me back my heart.

Because she can—a witch can give her Heartless back their hearts, and they return to their human bodies and lives. Their memories of their life before their Heartlessness come back. Except Nightsinger's told me she needs us (me) here to defend her from the human world that's hunting her. This doesn't stop me from begging her to let us go. I've begged on my knees, bargained pieces of my soul away to her every whim, asked if there's anything at all I can do to change her mind, but she simply, softly refuses.

And I get it. I might not be able to go outside the forest, but I hear the merchants and lesser nobles in their carriages talk before I rob them blind. I know the world hates witches. I know the Sunless War killed nearly all of them, and the survivors remain in woods, caves, isolated in dark places to hide from hunting human eyes.

But even if it's impossible—even if it feels like it will never happen in this lifetime—I hold on to the tiny shard of hope that someday, I'll own my life again, that it will be mine to do whatever I please with once more. I envy the celeon assassin, I blaze with jealousy at every human I watch pass on the Bone Road—wrapped up in their problems, yet still very much free to do whatever, go wherever they want. The world is theirs, if only they'd stop and realize it; they hold the greatest gift of all in their hands—their own destinies.

Mine was ripped from me the day I died, and I've been chasing it ever since. I'm a bit of a tragic figure that way.

I stick out my tongue, the taste of my own thoughts bitter and ridiculous. Tragic? Me? Impeccably fashionable and intensely witty are much better adjectives. With the added bonus of sounding far less self-pitying.

Crav always knows what I'm thinking. He's got an uncanny ability to read faces—maybe it comes with the territory of being a Warprince, constantly compared to his dozens of brothers and sisters. He sits beside me, both of us watching the deer carcass.

"Nightsinger will clean it up with magic," he says.

"Thank the Old God." I sigh. "Can you imagine the stains?"

There's a long silence, the sound of crickets echoing outside.

"Did you ask her yet?" Crav inquires softly. "About our hearts?"

I shoot him a sharp look. "How do you know about that? Have you been listening in?"

"She always leaves her door open," he grumbles. "And you always ask around this time. I stay up and listen."

"Well, you can't," I say sternly. "Starting now."

"It's my heart, too!" he protests. "I want to know when I'm getting it back."

I thought I was the only one having my hopes crushed over and over. I asked Nightsinger when we were alone specifically so Crav and Peligli wouldn't get their feelings pulverized, too. But my efforts were for nothing—he's been listening all along.

"You should ask her again," Crav insists. "I think this time she'll really give them back—"

"She won't!" I snap. "We're never getting them back, okay? Not now, not ever." Peligli squeaks at my tone. Crav flinches, his eyes suddenly welling with tears, and I regret everything instantly. "Crav—oh no. I'm sorry, I—"

He jumps to his feet and dashes out the door. I lurch a few steps after him, but Crav is the fastest of us—if he doesn't want to be caught, he won't easily be, and I don't have the stamina to attempt a chase through the woods right now; that dagger wound drained me more than usual.

Peligli tugs at my hand, her own eyes tearful. "That... that's a lie, right? We get them back...someday?"

She was turned willingly, but even her young mind's

been strained by the decades of Heartlessness. No matter how young, how willing, every Heartless gets tired. Tired of eating raw organs. Tired of seeing the same small circle of space over and over. Tired of listening to the hunger etch its toxic words into our brains. Tired of feeling empty, imperfect, unwhole. Tired of waking up and knowing all it takes is a few missed meals to become monsters. Tired of not remembering how we lived or who we loved.

I walk through the garden with her, rocking her back and forth, the swarm of fireflies lighting her tear-stained face as she sobs until she hiccups, until she exhausts her little body into the pale imitation of sleep we go through as Heartless. We don't *need* sleep, what with our bodies always magically regenerating, but our human brains sometimes forget that and lapse into the old habit. I walk back into the cottage and place Peligli gently on the flax-stuffed sheepskin she calls her bed.

"I'm sorry," I murmur, tucking a blanket over her. "I'm sorry for being terrible."

Terrible doesn't begin to cut it, the hunger sneers faintly. *Look at her—you broke her heart; human or Heartless, it doesn't matter what you are, you're still a hideous—*

"The fire looks very nice tonight, doesn't it?" I mutter to drown out the voice. "Very...hot. Full of...flames." I pause, then say to no one in particular, "Remind me to never become a poet."

I get up and wander over to the hearth, warming my palms on it. It's strange fire—colored blue-black, like a bad bruise, but Nightsinger's never clarified why, and I've never bothered to ask, because frankly her explanations of magical things tend to make no sense. My fingers flit to the iron cage set just above the fire. It's sturdy, the bars thick, but not thick enough to hide the view of the three jars within and the three hearts beating inside. I asked Nightsinger once why she puts them above the fire, and she smiled and told me they need to be kept warm, either by spell or flame. There are dents on the iron cage from when I was younger—when the anger consumed me and I bashed it with my father's sword until my hands bled and my legs gave out. I'd been trying to destroy my heart, to end it all. I learned later the books call that "shattering" a Heartless, and it's the only way to kill us besides killing our witch.

As mundane as the cage looks, it's magic. Even slipping something between the bars is impossible—some invisible barrier is woven there. Nightsinger won't even let us kill ourselves.

Like I told the fox. It's complicated.

Peligli's heart is the smallest. Her jar is old, scratched, and fogged with age. Crav's jar is sea glass, etched with ivy vines. His heart is a little bigger than hers, and currently beating fast like it's exerted. Probably from all the running he's doing. I'll apologize to him in the morning with a long, uninterrupted sparring session. He'll like that.

My heart is in the middle of the two. Elizera—or Zera for short—no family name I can remember, second Heartless of the witch Nightsinger. Sixteen years old at the time of her death. Her heart is the largest, and rests on the bottom of a curved red jar. The books say witches make the jars themselves, though some prefer bags or boxes. It's a magic they practice from a young age, becoming progressively better as they grow older. Nightsinger's progress—from Peligli's simple jar to Crav's elegant one—shows her prowess clearly. Ten, twenty years from now, how many more jars will sit beside ours? I pray to any god listening that my heart won't be there at all by then. I dread the thought of seeing a jar more beautiful than Crav's.

The door at the top of the rickety stairs creaks open just then, a beam of light shafting across my face.

"Zera?" Nightsinger's voice calls. "Could you come up for a moment?"

"I could," I lilt. "Or I could stay down here and not get stuck with a chore."

She laughs. "Scaring off mercenaries is hardly a chore for you."

"You're right. It's a breeze. But it's a breezy pain in my arse."

"No mercenaries, I promise."

"It's a hunter, isn't it?" I groan. "Hunters are way harder to chase off. And they all have stories about starving kids they need to feed. Remember that one you tried to give the boar to, and he almost shot you in the head for being a 'heathen'—"

"No hunters, either," she interrupts smoothly. "Just a talk between you and me."

I heave a sigh and ascend the stairs, my stomach dancing. I always get nervous when I near her room—it's something about the smell of it, lilies and sandalwood—that puts me on edge. Or maybe it's the magic emanating from it; it turns the air heavy, as if I'm breathing fog.

I push the door open and adjust my eyes to the thousands of glass flowers throwing light around the room. It's Nightsinger's favorite hobby—crafting plants from glass. She keeps them in dozens of vases, in baskets, while some of them simply float in midair. Delicate, impossibly detailed orchids and roses glitter with transparent petals, capturing the candlelight and fracturing it into a thousand points of diamond brilliance. There are flowers I don't know the names of, flowers that glow of their own accord or spiral slowly in on themselves and back out. Some exhale and inhale as if they're alive, spreading crystal pollen on the wooden floor like snow. I've seen her use them to "see," sometimes—the flowers showing her images of certain areas in the forest. My best guess? They're attached to the trees that hide us, somehow, but that's as far as my magic theory-crafting goes.

Nightsinger sits in the middle of the flowers, on a simple wooden chair. The room is empty save for her crystal creations—no bed, no dresser, not even a desk. Out of her crow form, she cuts an impressive figure; a full bosom all but bursts from her usual white dress, her waist and arms strong and thick. She's so tall she has to duck beneath the doorways of the cottage, and though she could easily change the height of them with magic, she doesn't. A mane of tawny hair descends along her back, always glossy and curled just so at the ends. Her lips are sensuous, her fair, plump face decorated with hazel eyes sharper and full of more wild secrets than that fox's.

She stands from the chair and sweeps over. It's her movements that mesmerize me the most—fluid, as if her feet don't really touch the ground. While Heartless can still pass for human, anyone looking at her would know instantly she's not human in the slightest. She was born a witch—raised to believe making Heartless was as natural as breathing. And she isn't the worst of them by far; I've read enough to know Nightsinger turns only children killed too early, children who deserve another chance at life. There are—or rather, *were*—some lovely witches in history who turned just to see humans suffer. Some even did it as a status symbol; only witches with powerful magic could sustain many Heartless at a time; the more you had, the stronger you looked. Most of them died in the Sunless War. Nowadays, the few left choose their Heartless carefully and less often.

"There's some news, Zera, that we must share with you," Nightsinger starts. In that moment, I see the two white crows sitting on the far corner windowsill. "If you would, my friends."

The crows fly onto the floor, glowing. The brightness shifts, unfolds into two large human shapes, then fades. Two witches stand before us, radiating power; a pale, bald man in an immaculately pressed gold-threaded suit and a woman with short, impossibly blue hair and a flowing, gauzy dress that hides little of her midnight skin. Both of them are so tall— though not as tall as Nightsinger—and with that same eeriness about them that gives me goose bumps.

"Zera, this is Firewalker"—Nightsinger points to the man, who nods at me stiffly—"and Seawhisper. They've come for you."

"Little old me?" I ask nervously. "And here I am, without a single cup of tea to offer."

"Silence." Firewalker steps forward, thin eyes sharp and on me. "You will listen, not speak."

Oh good. One of *these* sorts of men. Seawhisper chides him for me.

"Come now, have an ounce of patience, will you?" She turns to me. "I'm sorry about him. He's a bit of a...*relic* when it comes to treating Heartless decently."

"We don't have time to waste," he snaps, "on coddling our puppets. We need her in Vetris *now*. The Spring Welcoming—"

"Is in four days," Nightsinger interrupts him patiently. "We have time at least to explain what's going on. A confused Heartless helps no one."

Firewalker opens his mouth to argue, then closes it. "Fine. Then you explain it. But do it now. Her carriage is waiting, and humans are known for their impatience."

"Vetris? Carriage? Spring Welcoming?" I start. "Does he always spout nonsense or is tonight a special occasion?"

Firewalker glowers at me in a way I assume is supposed to be *very* intimidating, but it just makes him look constipated. Seawhisper kneels so she's eye level with me, her gaze lighthearted, sparkling despite the seriousness of her next words.

"We think the humans are on the verge of starting another war, Zera," she says. I shoot a look at Nightsinger, who remains expressionless. "That assassin who attacked you tonight—do you still have his dagger?"

I fish around in my bloodstained dress and hand it to her. With skilled fingers she opens the handle by a little latch, revealing that it's hollow on the inside, a tube of white fluid there. The smell of it is acrid and bitter.

"Is that stuff why it hurt more than the usual stab?" I ask. Seawhisper nods.

"White mercury. It's a chemical the humans discovered during the Sunless War."

"They *invented* it to kill us with," Firewalker corrects coldly. "It's the entire reason we were weakened during the final battle at the Moonlight Keep. If we ingest even the smallest amount, our magic is suppressed for hours, making us easy targets."

Seawhisper nods. "A human—we don't know who—has been equipping assassins with these sorts of weapons and sending them to suspected witch haunts. We believe it's to test the effectiveness of white mercury against Heartless, in preparation for war."

I frown. "It didn't kill me, or even incapacitate me."

"It's not meant to harm *you*." Firewalker narrows his eyes at me. "White mercury suppresses magic—that includes the magical connection between witch and Heartless—so it takes more magic to heal a mercury-infected Heartless. Use your puppet brain—stab all of a witch's Heartless, force her to heal them, and what do you have left?"

"Well that one's easy—a weakened witch."

He nods. "A simple kill for even the most battle-green human."

"Clever. And nasty." I put my hand to my mouth. "But what does this have to do with me?"

The two witches look to Nightsinger, who puts a gentle hand on my shoulder. "The High Witches have devised a plan, Zera, to delay the war. Do you know what the Spring Welcoming is?"

"Some old Vetrisian ceremony full of pomp and glitter and sweetrounds, I'm guessing."

"Enough with the stalling," Firewalker barks. "You're going to Vetris. You will pose as a noble intending to marry the prince, and when you have the opportunity, you will take his heart and turn him into Nightsinger's Heartless."

There's a stretched silence. I snort. "Your jokes are almost as bad as mine. Almost."

"We need the prince as a captive," he insists. "A ransom—a bargaining chip against the humans."

I look at Nightsinger, but she's quiet. Seawhisper is, too, as if they're both waiting for my reaction. The whole idea is so absurd I can barely keep myself from laughing.

"Even if I wanted to play dress-up and commit treason, you're forgetting I can't go a mile and a half from my heart without becoming a useless, screaming lump. A witch would be better off doing it."

"We cannot," Nightsinger says softly. "The humans have erected a tower called the Crimson Lady. We aren't sure how it works, but it can detect magical energy within the city of Vetris almost instantly. We lost all of our witches in Vetris within a matter of days."

"They were drowned," Seawhisper says solemnly, her smile absent this once.

"But—" I grasp at something, anything, as I start to realize they're serious about this. "Me? I'm kept alive by your magic. That tower will detect me—"

"You aren't a conduit of magic as we are." Firewalker rolls his eyes. "You are simply tethered to this world by it. That infernal tower can no more detect a Heartless than the naked eye can see the wind."

"And you decided *I* was best for this job? Don't the other witches have a Heartless who knows how to dance and kiss copious amounts of noble arse better than me?"

"There are few who fit the age bracket for the Spring Welcoming," Nightsinger says. "It's a ceremony in Vetris that welcomes marriage candidates for royal children into the Vetrisian court. The prince has rejected so many potential brides that the humans have grown desperate. It's the perfect opportunity. And it was decided among the High Witches that you are the most outwardly pleasing of our Heartless."

Seawhisper chimes in. "If we want the prince as our Heartless, we'll need to set a very pretty trap. And you're the perfect bait!"

"*P-Pretty*," I sputter. "As in, pretty irritating? Or pretty loudmouthed?"

"Pretty as in… Well, you've got a nice face," Seawhisper says, eyes nearing my chest. "Among…other things."

"You've got to be kidding me. You chose me because of my—"

"According to our information, he has a type, all right?" Seawhisper throws her hands up. "And you fit it!"

"Listen, I'm flattered, but—"

"Ugh. Spare me your modesty," Firewalker snarls. "I have little patience for it."

"Fire," Seawhisper says sternly. "That's enough. She's overwhelmed."

"I do wish you'd stop making excuses for her," he insists coldly. "She's a Heartless. Her duty is to obey, not question."

"My duty is to Nightsinger." I straighten my shoulders. "No one else has my loyalty—least of all an irritating slimeball like you."

Firewalker's face darkens, but Seawhisper comes between us with a cheery smile. "Then you'll do it, won't you?"

"You haven't explained what I'm doing, except for seducing this prince and taking his heart. We're talking about the same prince, right?"

"Eighteen-year-old Lucien Drevenis d'Malvane," Nightsinger's soft voice cuts in. "Heir to all of Cavanos and the Higher Reach, Archduke of Tollmount-Kilstead. Also known as the Black Eagle of the West."

"That's a very impressive list of titles and all, but I still can't leave these woods—"

Seawhisper shoves something in front of my nose—a delicate gold heart-shaped locket etched with stars and the three moons. Mystified, I take it, and she smiles brilliantly.

"Go on, open it."

I carefully pry open the locket, only to see a scrap of pink flesh resting within. Beating, in a very familiar rhythm.

"Is this…?"

"A piece of your heart!" Seawhisper chimes. "I made the locket myself. It will let you go much, much farther from your heart than normal. Far enough to get to Vetris, for certain."

"She fails to mention the magic to make something like this was lost in the War," Firewalker drones. "And that four other witches died attempting the same spell."

"Oh, don't be macabre." Seawhisper punches his arm lightly. "It's all for the cause, right? I'm sure it'll be worth it. That is, if Zera agrees to go."

"Do you *have* to turn him into a Heartless? Why can't you just kidnap him?" I ask.

Firewalker snorts. "Because a Heartless can be told what to do. They can be ordered."

"Ordered?" I wrinkle my nose. Firewalker's face lightens, and he looks to Nightsinger.

"Don't tell me—you've never ordered them?" he asks. Nightsinger can't meet his eyes. Firewalker laughs, for what's the first and probably last time. He turns his gaze back to me. "Hilarious. But then again, I should've expected it. Nightsinger's always been a soft touch."

"What do you mean—"

"A witch can give a command to a Heartless with enough magical force behind it to make them obey. That's why we need the prince Heartless—he'd escape, otherwise, or try to kill us. Maybe send messages to his father. When the prince is Heartless, Nightsinger will command him to be utterly silent, utterly pliable. Won't she?"

Firewalker looks to Nightsinger, but she won't look back at him. I had no idea. The books never talked about that. I thought being forced to eat organs was bad, or chasing off intruders in the woods. But this? She has total control over us, even though she's never used it? She focuses her green eyes on me, a deep sadness in them.

"Will you do it, Zera? Will you take Prince Lucien's heart?"

She's asking me, not ordering me. She's different from Firewalker, from every other witch who apparently commands their Heartless. A pressure settles on my chest, suffocating me. Nightsinger called the humans desperate, but the witches must be equally desperate if they want the prince as their captive this badly. Badly enough to rest all their hopes on an unproven wild card like me? Badly enough to throw any girl his way and hope for the best? I feel like a piece of meat all of a sudden. Nightsinger comes up wordlessly behind me and takes the locket from my hands, circling its chain around my neck and fastening it for me.

"Won't the Crimson Lady detect this magic necklace?" I ask.

"I told you." Firewalker bristles. "They can't detect the tether—"

"Fine, fine. Say I go to Vetris," I interrupt him. "And what then? I just walk up to the prince and say, 'Hello, handsome, I do hope you enjoy bodily injury,' and take his heart?"

"If only it were that easy." Seawhisper shakes her head. "There's a noble within the court—she's the one waiting in the carriage outside the forest for you. Her family is one of the rare human families who still worship the Old God. She'll claim you're a long-lost niece and help ingratiate you into the court."

"How can you be so sure she won't betray—"

"I tire of this," Firewalker snaps. "Your questions are meaningless. We've arranged it all—you must go, *now*. Nightsinger, if she won't agree, order her—"

"Will you give us a moment?" Nightsinger's voice rings clear. Firewalker looks disgruntled, but Seawhisper tactfully pulls him away. The two of them transform into white crows in a blinding light and fly out the window. Nightsinger turns to me with a soft smile.

"I'm sorry about them. They're...on edge. We all are, ever since we learned of another impending war."

"Are they really willing to place the fate of a war in my grubby little hands?" I hold up my palms, forest dirt under my bitten nails. She folds her hands over mine, encompassing them gently.

"No. But we are outnumbered. And these white mercury weapons the humans are making—" She exhales. "I will be frank with you, Zera; we won't survive another war, unless we act before the humans do, and quickly. You aren't our only plan, but you are one of the few that may buy us enough time to prepare others—we suspect the king will be eager to save his only heir and refrain from striking out at us as long as the prince is ours."

I stare at a floating glass rose, my own face distorted in it. Nightsinger's skin is cool and soft, her nails long and ladylike.

"Nightsinger, I—"

"I won't ask you to defend us for nothing in return," she says quickly. "I've done that for too long. If you do this, I'll give you your heart back. And Peligli's, and Crav's—all of your hearts returned. You'll have that freedom you ask after so often, if you succeed."

Hope floods my chest cavity like a searing light. To be whole again? To be human, to go where I please, to eat real food, to be the only voice in my own head? To regain my memories of my mother, my father, their love for me before they died? It's everything I've wanted for so long, for three years of wallowing in dim woods and my shattered past. A tiny regret pulls me the other way; if I say yes, it'll mean another jar on Nightsinger's caged shelf. But if I say yes, it'll be the *only* jar there.

"I'll do it," I say finally.

"It'll be difficult, and dangerous."

"It doesn't matter." I straighten my spine. "If you asked me to go underground and kill a hundred fire-breathing valkerax for my heart, I'd do it. But you haven't. You've asked me to take some stuck-up noble's heart. And that's much easier."

Nightsinger flashes me a smile, a rare and gentle thing. She and I walk down the stairs. Crav is back, sleeping on his sheepskin right next to Peligli. I move to pack my clothes, but Nightsinger stops me with a whisper.

"Lady Y'shennria will provide you with new garments. Come—I'll take you to her."

I look at Crav's sleeping face. "Can I say good-bye?"

She nods. "Meet me outside when you're ready."

I kneel as quietly as I can at their sides. Crav's dark lashes flicker over his cheeks. His eyelids are slightly red and swollen, his boots a little muddy. He probably ran to the head of the creek. It's peaceful there, and I know he cries only when he's sure he's alone, like I do. We're both prideful like that—refusing to let others see us in our moments of weakness.

"Don't worry, Crabby." I stroke his cheek. "I'll get your heart back."

If I squint, they look like human children. Children with hearts and freedom, growing and changing, never trapped by magic stasis. If I look at them sleeping peacefully, I start to believe I can make up for killing those men by freeing them, no matter how little it truly is.

I leave the cottage, my hands empty of anything but my

father's old relic of a sword—rusted at the hilt and dented in the blade, but still bearing a semblance of dignity. It's all I have of him, of my old life. The three witches stand tall in the foxgloves discussing something, the fireflies dancing among them. When I approach, they quiet.

"It's been decided." Firewalker straightens his suit lapels as I approach. "If the humans discover your true identity, they'll most likely torture you for information. And we can't have you revealing anything about us. Lady Y'shennria will send word if your position is compromised, and Nightsinger will perform your shattering."

I make my eyes the sweetest of daggers at Firewalker. "I've been ripped apart by wildcats, stabbed through by humans. I've fallen off a cliff and broken every bone in my body. It's hilarious that you think a little torture will be enough to make me talk."

"It's not a matter of a 'little' torture." He sneers. "We have no forces to send into Vetris to free you. A caught spy is never treated well. It would be years of pain the likes of which you can't even imagine—the humans would pump your veins full of white mercury and burn you from the inside out, repeatedly. *Slowly.* And that's the best-case scenario."

My face goes cold, but I don't give him the satisfaction of flinching.

Nightsinger can't meet my eyes as she murmurs, "I'd rather you not suffer more than you have already, Zera. I hope you understand why it must be this way."

Of course I understand. I understand my life is hers to do with it what she will, that I'm powerless to resist, or decide, or even change. That is the fate of a Heartless, the price of our eternal life—chains heavier than iron.

But I can break them. I know exactly how to break them

now—with Prince Lucien's spoiled little heart.

"Are you two done?" Firewalker demands. "The carriage awaits."

I spare a glance at him. Underneath his shortness and anger, the moonlight reveals fear in the lines of his face. Even Seawhisper's smiles now look paper-thin to me, her lips trembling, as if she's holding something in. For all their power and majesty, they're still afraid of war—of death. Of being unwritten from this world—a fear all living things have. A fear I have once again.

"Yeah." I straighten. "I'm ready."

"Good." He looks pleased with me for once. "Then stand in the center of us. We'll send you there—it's faster than walking, and you're on a bit of a time restraint."

The three witches form a triangle. Seawhisper looks to Nightsinger with concern in her eyes.

"Are you sure you still remember the spell, Night? You've been away from the Tree for so long—"

"I remember," Nightsinger answers immediately. They fall silent and still. One second their eyes are normal, and the next they're jet black, from lid to lid, corner to corner. Their fingertips hanging at their sides grow black, nails stretching long and sharp like claws, and equally dark. Nothing about the growing darkness is natural—it's cold and void-like, a black deeper than the night itself, as if the magic is eating away at the very reality of color. It consumes their skin all the way up to their wrists. The stronger a spell, the higher the void grows up a witch's extremities. I've only ever seen Nightsinger turn her tear ducts black, or the very tips of her nails. This spell, though, is something far more powerful. Their mouths form the same words in sync, but all I hear is the roaring silence of the woods. They speak the Old God's tongue—an inaudible prayer to him. The foxgloves around me sway with a sudden wind, the fireflies scattering.

In a flash, Nightsinger opens her eyes—no longer black, but green and white again—and smiles at me, her voice audible once more.

"Be safe, Zera."

"You—" I blink, and get to finish my sentence to a whole new vista, one with a muddy road and a misty midnight horizon. The forest is to one side, vast grassy plains on the other, the Bone Road stretching beneath my feet. "—too."

I haven't seen the world on this side of the forest in three years, and I drink it in greedily. The tall grass of the plains sways gently in the midnight breeze. Everything looks so huge, the sky pressing down on me; the three moons seem even bigger without a canopy to hide their faces. I take a moment to breathe in—not the damp, molded pine smells of the woods but the bright, alive smell of earth warmed to its bones by the sun and cooled by the moons each and every day.

A carriage waits not far ahead, covered in slate gray silks and drawn by two roan mares. The driver waves his hat. I begin toward him at a trot, looking back once at the velvet woods. I'd forgotten how strange the feeling of leaving was, like a bittersweet snowflake on the tongue. It's a bare taste of the freedom I've lusted after for three years—a freedom that waits for me in the chest of Lucien Drevenis d'Malvane.

Stupid girl. You'll never be free. The hunger rasps a laugh, clinging like a spider to the dark corners of my mind. *No matter how much you squirm, no matter how far you try to run, those men are still dead because of you. The shadows of what you've done are long and eternal.*

I don't make a habit of responding to the hunger, that darkness that lingers inside me, reminding me always of my mistakes. I like to ignore it, push it away with my own voice, with whatever joke or thought comes to mind. But tonight, standing on a precipice, I stride forward and answer it with a whisper.

"Then maybe it's time to build a brighter fire."

2

THE IRON LADY

I APPROACH THE CARRIAGE at a jaunty pace, plumes of hot air from the horses' noses floating up into the cold night.

"You're my new partners in crime, then?" I ask the man who waved his hat at me. He descends the carriage, all lanky limbs and long face and nut-brown wrinkles. He's so thin and tall he looks like a scarecrow without all the stuffing. His warm smile is much heartier than his body.

"Indeed, miss. I'm Fisher Jell, Lady Y'shennria's driver." He extends his hand in greeting but retracts it suddenly, wiping it on his trousers and flashing an apologetic smile at me. "S-Sorry."

"For what?" I blink.

"You're a— Well." He clambers over himself to finish his sentence.

"Don't force yourself, Fisher," a clipped voice comes from the carriage window. "She's a Heartless, not a human. There's no need to be terribly polite."

A woman leans out of the window ever so slightly, her

dark, fluffy hair amassed atop her head and pinned back discreetly with amethyst jewelry. The purple lace dress she wears accents her dark skin beautifully, the high neck of the collar somehow making her sharp hazel gaze look even more imperious. Her face is smooth, yet so well taken care of that you can barely see the creases of age at her eyes and mouth.

She looks me up and down appraisingly. Her nose wrinkles at my bloodstained dress, my scuffed and many-times-mended boots. This is definitely the Lady Y'shennria the witches mentioned. She oozes regality so much I'm almost intimidated. Almost. I lay awake at night for three years vowing I'd do anything for my heart when the time came—I can't back down now.

I clear my throat and say, "I'm Zera. Second Heartless of the witch Nightsinger—"

"I'm aware," Y'shennria sighs. "Why else would I be here?" She opens the door with one gloved hand and raps it. "Get in. There's much work to be done and little time in which to accomplish it."

I climb in and settle on the plush seat across from her. She immediately tucks herself in one corner like she's afraid of catching something from me.

"Haven't you heard? Heartless can't carry diseases." I flash her a smile. She ignores me.

"Take us home, Fisher," she says out the window. Fisher tuts at the horses, and the carriage lurches into motion, the steel-plated wheels cutting through the muddy road with little effort. This is the first time I've been inside a carriage since I was human, and the first time ever being in one so fancy. The whole cart smells like cinnamon and roses, though maybe it's just her.

"In public, you will address me as Lady Y'shennria," the

noblewoman says abruptly, eyes glued to the passing woods. "In private, you will address me as Lady Y'shennria—"

"That'll be a tough one to remember," I drawl.

She breezes on without acknowledging anything. "You are, from this moment forward, Lady Zera Y'shennria, my stepbrother's bastard daughter and the last living relative I have."

The last living relative? I study her face—up close she looks even more elegant and refined, yet now I can see the massive scar reaching down her jaw and to her throat: three distinct slashes that her high collar barely hides. I'd recognize those anywhere. Jagged teeth marks. A Heartless tried to kill her a long time ago. There's a tense, stretched-out silence.

"What—" I swallow. "What happened to them? Your family?"

"They were killed," she says curtly. "Do you see that castle in the distance?"

I squint at where she points—a dim shadow lurking on the horizon my mile-and-a-half radius never let me see before. She rummages in a silken bag at her hip and shoves a brass tube at me. I lamely stare at it.

"Do you want me to swallow that, or…?"

"Try again." She holds the brass tube away from my grasping hand. "Politer, this time. I know it isn't so in those lawless woods of yours, but in Vetris we respect our elders."

"All right. Let's give uppity a go." I inhale and put on my best haughty air. "Pray tell, what is that thing, Lady Y'shennria?"

"I didn't say mock nobility, I said try to emulate it." She narrows her eyes to thin slits. Not angry, just thin. Anger threatens on her face, but she doesn't let it show through.

"I'm sorry, aren't they the same thing?" I smile.

Y'shennria's having none of it as she draws herself to her full height.

"Do you want your heart or not?"

We stare at each other, neither of us even daring to blink. If willpower were an animal, it'd be a tiger, and there'd be a cacophony of wicked snarling between us. I'm not used to losing, but Y'shennria has me cornered, naked in front of the truth. I back off and hold my hands up.

"All right, you win. I want my heart."

"You'll ask to see this tube politely, like a noble might. Or the best approximation of one your feral mind can conjure."

I inhale and put on a lighter voice. "May I please see that object, Lady Y'shennria? It interests me greatly."

She watches me, those hazel eyes like green-gold slits of agate. Finally, she relents.

"You may have a kernel of potential after all. But that is all it is. From this moment forward, the only armor that will reliably disguise you in the Vetrisian court is hard work and effort. Remember that." She hands the tube to me, and though she seems perfectly calm and collected, the hand she holds it out with is trembling. I get it, suddenly, why she keeps careful space between my boots and her skirts. She isn't worried about catching something. She's afraid of touching me. My stomach squirms. Disappointment. Shame. A hundred things claw at my insides, the hunger laughing at me.

Of course she's afraid. You're a monster. There's blood on your hands.

I take the tube, careful not to let our fingers meet.

"Hold it to your eye," she instructs. "Close the other, and point it at where you wish to look."

With clumsy fingers and facial muscles, I do as she asks.

What a delightful little human machine—I can suddenly see the castle in the distance with perfect clarity. It's a crumbling, blackened mess of stone parapets and iron gates, but the sheer size of it is impressive. Crows darken the air above the ruins, and a tattered banner flaps in the wind, the sigil and color too worn by time to discern.

"Thirty years ago, that was my home," Lady Y'shennria says. "Ravenshaunt. It was where my family and I lived for generations. Until the Sunless War took even that from us, too."

Her eyes are distant, her voice unnervingly even.

"You must know the Y'shennria family history if you are to pass in court. Our family worshipped the Old God for centuries, but none of that mattered to the witches. We were human. We were the enemy."

I swallow hard, words failing me. They don't fail her, though, her voice strong, unwavering, as if anything less would be a crime to her family's memory.

"I learned, that night, that you can outrun a witch. It's their Heartless you can't hope to escape. They never stop. They never rest. They hunger and they hunger, until there's nothing left for them to devour."

I suppress my flinch. "Why are you still an Old God believer, if the witches killed your family?"

"Why do you drink water, if a fouled stream poisons you once?" she snaps. "Because you must, to survive."

"But—"

"Enough." Her words strike like falling icicles in the dead of winter. "Let us begin your tutoring immediately." She points at my wide legs. "A lady always sits with her knees together. Otherwise you distort your skirts, and the bulkiness is unsightly." She watches me expectantly. I press my knees together. "That's a start. Now, there are three types of nobility in Vetris—the Firstblood, Secondblood, and Goldblood. Care to guess which is the highest rank among them?"

"Goldblood." I know how much humans love their precious metals. Mercenaries came into the woods willing to risk their lives to kill Nightsinger and collect a witch's bounty. The bandits killed my parents for their gold.

"Goldbloods are the last on the social ladder," she corrects. "They're nobles who paid the courts for a position and title—merchants, mostly. Secondbloods have lineage, though they have no great claim to extraordinary wealth or power. Firstbloods are the highest ranking, with considerable history, land, and wealth. They are often assigned important political roles, such as the nine ministers of the king's cabinet, and very commonly Firstbloods rise to power as kings and queens. It is the Firstblood family, the d'Malvanes, who've been ruling for five hundred years now."

"Which are the Y'shennrias?" I inquire.

"Firstbloods." Her back straightens. "But in name only. The war ruined Ravenshaunt, our only ancestral land, and because of our ties to the Old God, most families have shunned us. In thirty years, I haven't been able to drum up a single offer to help us rebuild."

"And so now you're helping the witches," I say. "To, what? Get back at the nobles?"

She looks me up and down, lip curling. "You are so *young*."

I bristle instantly. "And yet here I am, apparently old enough to turn a prince Heartless for you."

Y'shennria falls quiet, and then she speaks, voice cold iron. "I agreed to tutor you so I could aid in preventing another war." Her hand flits up to her scarred jaw, where it rests on mangled skin. "This world has seen enough suffering.

I have seen enough suffering. And I do not wish it on anyone else."

The three heart jars over Nightsinger's fireplace flash in my mind. *Not another jar. Not another heart.*

"I understand that much," I say. "Not wishing your suffering on anyone else."

Y'shennria finally turns her gaze to me. It's guarded and thorny, a rosebush without a single bloom. I'm suddenly keenly aware of my Heartlessness—of the fact that someone like me destroyed her family and likely gave her that scar. She's brave for even agreeing to this, for being in the same small carriage as the same thing that killed her loved ones.

Y'shennria inhales. "The most important thing you must know is this: I need your obedience. If you don't do exactly as I say, all of this will be for naught."

"I'm not very...*good* at obedience."

I might imagine it, but Y'shennria's mouth quirks up in the smallest of sardonic smiles as she says, "That makes two of us." She pulls out a glass jar from beneath her seat and hands it to me. It's a gorgeous work of art—pale purple glass, etched with a coiled snake and scattered stars. "The jar. For the prince's heart. You will keep it until the time comes."

I never wanted to see it, and yet here it rests, in my hands.

"How long do I have?" I ask hoarsely.

"His heart must be put inside within the hour, or so the witches told me."

"No, I mean—" I swallow. "How long do I have to get his heart?"

"The Spring Welcoming requires the prince to choose a wife by Verdance Day—the summer equinox. Which means you have roughly—"

"Two weeks," I mutter. Y'shennria nods.

"After that, whether he is engaged or not, all potential suitors will be sent home. This is the prince's last Welcoming—he's stymied the other three, and the king's patience wears thin. There is talk that if he doesn't choose a bride this time, the king will arrange a marriage for him." Her eyes grow weary, her age suddenly showing in the hairline cracks around her eyes. "You could very well be the last chance we have."

"And certainly not the best," I chime, my voice quavering with my nerves. Fourteen days. That's all I have to earn back my heart.

"I hope you realize how much is at stake," Y'shennria insists. "If you fail, war is inevitable. If you get caught and die, I have no doubt the humans will find some way to twist your infiltration into an aggressive gesture on the witches' behalf, and declare war."

"I think war will be the least of my concerns if I'm dead."

"Typical Heartless, thinking of yourself." She scoffs. "If you fail, every man, woman, and child in Cavanos will be plunged into—"

"I get it," I interrupt her. "I get that people will die, all right? I know this is important. The only reason I joke about it at least once a minute is because if I don't, I might start puking."

She says nothing to that, but the silence doesn't last. It's a half-day's ride to Vetris from Nightsinger's forest, and in that time she has me memorize the Secondblood and Firstblood families (Himentell, d'Malvane, Y'shennria, d'Goliev, Steelrun, Priceless), how to greet them as a peer (a half bow, not too deep, with only one hand behind my back instead of two). She gives me stock phrases to use when I'm unsure of what to say—things that are harmless and polite. She asks how my digestion works, though she clearly hates every word of my explanation: Alcohol and water are digestible, though anything other than that has to come out. When Heartless consume something that isn't raw flesh, it's digested instantly and painfully by the magic inside us, and our bodies purge the contamination the only way they know how—with tears of blood. The first time it happened to me was very soon after I was turned; so sick of deer, I tried eating one of Nightsinger's wheat cakes. The agony was blinding, but the tears—my fingers reaching up to touch them and coming away bloody—were far worse.

Y'shennria assures me most of my "meals" will be for show, but I'll have to eat publicly (and discreetly visit the restroom when it becomes too much to bear) at the banquet the king puts on for select nobles. Banquets are a way of maintaining loyalty, Y'shennria explains. Feed them and they'll have little time to plot rebellion, and even less inclination to do so when their bellies are full of cream and honey. It makes a twisted sort of sense. Even one's clothes, Y'shennria explains, are picked for hidden reasons—a gaudy belt or low bodice, for example, take the eye away from the face. The more distracted people are by what you wear, the less they notice what you do or say. The more impressed they are by your clothes, the less they question you. She points out that I never once asked if she was Lady Y'shennria—I discerned it unconsciously from the way she's dressed. And she's right. Until that moment, I never realized how much power clothing had, and it's terrifying.

Vetris sounds completely different from the relative simplicity of my life in the woods. I ate, I talked, I practiced the sword. In Vetris I'll do all that, but in silks, and with a dozen variations for each action depending on who's around and how high their rank is. I absorb as much information as I can, repeating Y'shennria's every word after she says it. It's impossible. It's impossible to learn all of this in four days, before the Spring Welcoming. But I'll do it, and I'll do it perfectly.

Because if I don't, my freedom slips from me like sand through my fingers.

I'm so bent on learning I don't notice the sun rising until it shafts directly into my face through the carriage window. I flinch, adjusting to the gorgeous melon-greens and blush-pinks of the sky. The sun is a golden disc peeking over the horizon, incandescent in its shy beauty.

"—as for the prince, our goal is clear. The girls of the Spring Welcoming are called Spring Brides, and they..." Y'shennria's voice grows cross. "Are you listening?"

"S-Sorry." I tear my eyes away. "I've— This is the first time I've seen the sunrise since I was turned." The sun rises in the south, and that direction was always impossible to see through the dense trees of Nightsinger's forest. Y'shennria doesn't demand I ignore it like I expect her to.

"How long ago was that?" she asks.

"Three years." The sunrays blossoming through the clouds hypnotize me again, my voice hoarse. "How did I ever forget how beautiful it is?"

There's a long silence. Finally, she asks, "How old would you be this year, if you were human?"

"Nineteen."

"You were sixteen, then, when it happened?"

Memory clouds my awe of the sunrise. I stare at the carriage floor, working my fingers in a knot of fabric on the seat. I haven't told anyone what happened. It's been a dark shadow of a secret, threaded between only Nightsinger and me. But Y'shennria offered her own painful past. The least

I can do is be honest in return.

"It was bandits," I say slowly. "My mother and father were traders. We were poor, but happy. We traveled all over— Cavanos, Avel, even the desolate peaks of Helkyris. Or at least, I think we did. Becoming Heartless takes away your human memories—"

"And they reside in your heart," she finishes for me. I don't ask how she knows that. I just wade on through the cold, bitter waters of my past.

"There was a boy on the road. He was crying out in pain, begging for help. Father tried to go around. He was suspicious, but I made him stop. The bandits were hiding in the woods nearby."

I don't tell her how the bandits riddled Father with arrows, bits of his brain on the steel tips, or how they split me open from navel to throat and left me to die, to watch, as they did the same to Mother. The hunger gnaws at my edges, the memories like blackened catnip for it. *Your fault,* it whispers. *You killed your own parents with your weakness.* I shake it off.

"Nightsinger found me and turned me. And she was even so nice as to bring me the bandits, too."

I don't tell her about the blinding fury, the dark tidal wave of anger and pain and hunger that pulled me under, drove me to rip the bandits to nothing more than pieces. I don't tell her about the monster inside that burst forth from me, killing everything in its path, relishing in the blood and death.

"Do you know what she told me," I continue, "when I asked her why she brought me the bandits? She said, 'Because I thought that's what all humans want. Revenge.'"

I put my hands between my knees, then pull them out.

That's not how a lady sits. I press my knees together instead, holding my head high and my shoulders wide in a pale mockery of Y'shennria's perfect posture. Her hazel gaze is fixed on me, and I stare back, the old, bitter glaze of regret settling. I try a smile, because I know I must look terrible. It's hollow on my lips.

"And she was right."

3

WATER FOR
A WITCH

WE STOP TO REST the horses two hours out from Vetris. A sudden fog rolls in on the grasslands, turning everything gray and dreary, but I don't mind. The scenery is still brand new. My eyes absorb every gray blade of grass, every ripple of wind among the reeds, every ghostly outline of the rabbits and hawks whirling together in the dance of death. Y'shennria and I get out to stretch our legs, and she has Fisher pull down a trunk from the top of the carriage. She rummages through it before handing me a sleek green silk dress, braided with silver threads. It's gorgeous—the sort of thing I'd only dreamt about in the woods.

"Old God's tit!" I plunge my hands into the smooth silk, rubbing it against my cheek. "Did you really get this for me, Auntie?"

"A lady doesn't swear." Y'shennria sniffs. "And she certainly doesn't call me 'auntie.'"

"But that's what you are, right? My auntie. Auntie, auntie, auntie." I hold the dress up to my bust, watching the skirt billow. "It's kinda fun to say."

She flinches minutely at each repetition. "Enough. Change into that before we enter the city. Those rags of yours will convince no one."

"Hey!" I look down at my tattered, faded blue dress, the lace bodice stained with old blood and dirt and the back ripped to shreds by the celeon assassin's dagger just today. "This rag served me well. And before I stole it from a carriage's trunk, it served some noble lady well. It deserves a proper dress funeral."

Y'shennria quirks a dark brow. "You've stolen from nobles?"

"'Stolen' is such an ugly word." I wrinkle my nose. "I prefer 'long-term donation.'"

"The witches never informed me of this."

"The witches are a little desperate," I say. "In case you haven't noticed. And desperate people get sloppy about details."

She looks nervous, her stone mask cracking for the first time. "Did any of the nobles see your face?"

I sigh. "I know it's sometimes hard to tell through my impeccable acting—"

"Did they or did they not?" she barks imperiously. Fisher looks up from petting the horses. I breathe out.

"No. Of course I covered my face. I'm sort of very good at making myself hard to see. Comes with the territory of being hunted by every human in the country."

Y'shennria's cracks slowly fill in, her mask cementing itself again. "All I can do is take your word for that. And I despise relying on words alone. You will tell me any and all secrets of yours that might hinder our goal—"

"I've told you everything."

There's a tense silence between us, her eyes prying into my own cracks, as if she's deciding whether she can trust me. She doesn't have a choice—she *has* to trust me as much as I have to trust her. Finally, she turns and retreats into the carriage.

When she's gone, I feel the weight that's settled on my chest since I left the forest lift a little. I press the dress to my body, whirling around with the skirts. It's a thousand times nicer than anything I've worn in my life. I didn't used to like dresses—I remember that much about my human life—but becoming a Heartless shifts your priorities around drastically. I went from wearing breeches every day to stealing beautiful dresses—the prettier the things I wore, the less I felt like a freakish monster removed from her humanity. A good skirt became better than any armor for me.

I dress quickly behind a far line of heavy bushes, cradling my old bloodstained dress in my arms. When I return to the carriage, Y'shennria snatches the dress from me.

"We're discarding this."

"But that was my favorite—"

"Your life as a Heartless is over," she asserts. "From now on, you are my niece. You are an Y'shennria. And an Y'shennria would never be caught hanging on to such an ugly garment."

I swallow, any witty words lost in the realization that she's right. Who I was doesn't matter. Who I have to become is the only thing I can focus on now. Y'shennria tosses the ragged dress into the bottom of the trunk.

"Now, let us see you." She turns, walking around me in slow circles. She muses, "You wear it well, even if your posture is hideous. You may be coarse-tongued, but you have a voluptuous body, and this will serve you in catching the prince's eye."

"I'm to seduce him, then?" I chirp. "And here I thought it was an aunt's job to be *against* allowing her niece to have any fun."

Y'shennria's face is solemn. "We will do anything to have the prince's heart—you must do *anything*. Do you understand that?"

I swallow her words like lead. Anything beyond mild flirting is a huge blank in my repertoire of experience. It's been three years since I've *seen* a boy my age. There was that one mercenary who came to the woods to kill Nightsinger, only a year older than I, but cutting his left pinky off hardly qualified as "flirting." The woods never made me stop to consider my body as anything more than something to be fed and cleaned, yet Vetris demands I think of men, of women, of anyone who'd desire me. And desire is a strange, foreign game to a murderous monster.

Five men, their tortured screams like honey to your ears as you ripped their tongues out—

I breathe in deeply. "I'll do anything. You have my word."

"A Heartless's word means nothing," Y'shennria says. "I can do nothing but hope you stay true."

That disappointment gnaws at me again, but I can't refute what I am. Y'shennria looks me up and down, rummages in the trunk, and hands me an ivory hairbrush and a leather thong.

"Do something about the mess on your head. We'll have to cut it when we get home."

"You don't like it? I was hoping forest-grown split ends were in style in Vetris."

"It's not the split ends, it's the length. Long hair is a symbol of rank in the Vetrisian courts, and it always has been," she insists. "Men, women, it doesn't matter—the longer it is, the more powerful your family. Only the royal family has hair as long as yours. Firstblood families keep their hair shorter than that as a show of respect."

"So only they get to look amazing? Bit selfish, don't you think?" I grunt, and begrudgingly pull my gold hair back into a ponytail. Y'shennria looks mildly satisfied, for once.

"What about that rusted old thing?" She points to the sword on my hip. "There'll be lawguards everywhere—you'll hardly need to defend yourself. Physically, at least. Socially, however, is another story."

I grip the hilt. "I keep the sword."

"A sword is fine on a lady," she agrees. "But one as ugly as that? No. Impossible. Discard it, and I'll buy you a new one in Vetris."

"I said no."

"You will get rid of that unsightly thing, or I will—"

"I'll do anything. Wear any dress, seduce any prince. But the sword stays."

"At least tell me why you're so intent on it."

I clutch the blade closer. "It was my father's."

She's quiet, and then finally she sighs. "Fine. Keep your rust. If it drives the prince away, it's you who will be apologizing to the witches in the afterlife."

"If a simple sword drives the prince away," I fire back, "I can't imagine what my personality might do."

Fisher leads the horses by to hook them back up to the carriage. They're healthy, well fed. The smell of their warm flesh makes my mouth water, though I shake it off. No. There'll be a thousand horses in Vetris—I can't look at every one as if it's a delicious feast. As if reading my mind, Y'shennria hands me a paper parcel.

"Hurry and eat," she demands. "We leave soon, and I won't have you making a mess in the carriage." I unwrap it to see a boar's heart inside.

It looks like his heart, doesn't it? the hunger hisses. *That old man you tore limb from limb.*

Burning, and desperate to stop burning, I look up at Y'shennria and ask, "How will I eat in Vetris?"

"I'll be the one providing you with food," she says. "Discreetly, of course. The witches informed me hearts and livers satiate you easier. But they didn't tell me how—" She swallows, the second outward sign of nervousness from her, but she tames it quickly. "How often must you eat?"

"Every hour on the hour," I drawl. "A thousand infants' hearts."

A shadow passes over her face, and I quickly remember she lost her family to us. Too close. Too real.

"Sorry. I do this thing where I joke before I think, and it's terrible sometimes." I clear my throat quickly. "We eat twice. Morning and night. Livestock or wild game."

"Not so different from us, then," she murmurs. "Very well. I'll arrange this. I'll have someone I can trust deliver meals to your room, where you can eat"—she tamps down a flinch—"privately."

With that being settled, she returns to the carriage. Eating near Y'shennria seems almost cruel, especially after I ran my mouth like an idiot, so I walk off the road a little ways and sit down, the long grass hiding me from view. When I'm done, I wash my hands in a puddle and head back to the carriage. Y'shennria refuses to look at me, preferring to read a book as Fisher urges the horses into a trot. I, on the other hand, casually and constructively pass the time by dwelling in my head on every moment I've ever been horrible to someone. Eventually we crest a hill, and Fisher calls out, "The city is in sight, mum!"

The city! *A* city! Y'shennria doesn't move, but I eagerly stick my head out the window. There, in all its glory, is Vetris—a halo of whitestone spires ringed by emerald farmland. A sea of windblown grass all around us looks like crushed velvet from this height, swaying in time with the jade-green banners strung atop the intimidating wall that cradles the city proper. It's so much more massive than I thought it'd be. Stone buildings and brass machines crowd inside, blowing out great buffets of smoke and steam. A giant building that must be the royal palace Y'shennria talked about lords over it all, tower upon tower glittering white in the high noon sun, the grounds around it latticed with an intricate pattern of sapphire waterways.

"Put your head back in this instant," Y'shennria barks. "Before someone sees you."

I retreat. "Please tell me using my eyes isn't considered unladylike."

"We aren't here for your sightseeing. We're here to do a job. A job which we will speak of no more, unless we are alone and in private. The court has ears and eyes everywhere. Caution is paramount to our success. If you're unsure whether you should say something—"

"'Don't say it at all. Silence is better than chance,'" I finish for her. "Yeah, I remember that one."

I fold my arms over my chest until Y'shennria quirks a brow at me. Right. Unladylike. I put my hands at my sides and crane my head, desperate for a good angle that'll let me see the city again. Finally it comes into view. There's another building, almost as big as the palace itself, coated with iron spikes along its edges. The tallest spire has a very familiar metal symbol on it—the Eye of Kavar. Three lines, angled through one oval, forming a sort of pupil where they meet. It's strange seeing it so big—I'm used to very small versions as pendants around the necks of mercenaries and hunters. No doubt that's the Temple of Kavar, the New God. Right next to the temple is the Crimson Lady the witches were talking about—an obelisk of redstone, but not as bright a red as I imagined. It's a rusty color, almost dull, and it stretches tall, barely shy of the temple's tallest spire. The top is flat, and nothing about it seems unusual save for its color. Whatever magic-detecting force it's emitting is utterly invisible.

I say a moment's prayer for the Lady to pass me over.

The road becomes busy around us, then busier, and then we're in the very middle of an undulating crowd of humans and celeons alike: merchant carts, dust-weary travelers, farmers hauling their meats and vegetables into town, and lawguards. *Lawguards.* The chainmail armor they wear and the sword-shaped badges on their chests feel familiar, even if I can't remember them from my human life.

"Sit up straight," Y'shennria says. "We're here."

The shadow of the imposing main gate plunges over us. Fisher brings the carriage to a stop, his conversation with someone else barely audible above the crowd's din. My ears ache—I haven't heard so many people, so much noise compounded on itself, in so long. A celeon lawguard's plumed helmet is suddenly in our carriage window, and I start back. His feline face is a rouge-ish purple-red, furred in some spots and smooth with iridescent scales in others. His tendril-like whiskers are far shorter than the assassin's were.

"Good morning, officer." Lady Y'shennria smiles. She never once smiled on our way here, but now she turns it on full-force.

"Milady." The lawguard bows. "And who might this be?"

His golden eyes are on me. This is practice—if I can't make eye contact with a lawguard as if I'm nobility, how will I ever look another noble in the eye? I force myself to gaze at him, burying the lies behind my irises with a sweet grin.

"This is my niece." Y'shennria turns her smile to me, and I feel somehow itchy under it. "My stepbrother's bastard, but of Y'shennria lineage nonetheless. The Minister of the Blood found her only recently—and I'm simply overjoyed."

The lawguard smiles wanly, all his sharp teeth showing. "If you don't mind my saying, milady, I'm glad of this. Kavar knows you deserve a bit of happiness in your life."

"That's very kind of you to say."

The lawguard pats the carriage with his clawed hand, and Fisher takes that as a signal to trot the horses through. I glance up at the Crimson Lady, at the lawguards I can see now standing in the windows at the very top, but Y'shennria frowns.

"Fret not. If it had sensed anything, we'd be in the process of being arrested right now."

"How? How would those guards up there tell the ones down here so quickly?"

Y'shennria motions to the side of the gate, where two or three strange copper tubes no higher than my waist stick up from the cobblestones. "The watertells."

A popping noise bursts through the crowd's cacophony, and I jump—one of the copper tubes expunges water wildly, then goes silent again. The lawguard nearby thumps his fist on top of the tube, and it opens like a lid. He reaches inside, pulling out yet another copper tube, smaller. This one holds a piece of parchment, perfectly dry. He reads its contents and searches over the heads of the crowd, pointing at a woman with a cart of eggplants. The other lawguards close in on the woman.

"Don't stare," Y'shennria mutters. I have no choice either way—Fisher presses the carriage onward, and I lose sight of the woman and her lawguard accosters in the crowd.

The ominousness of it all lingers, but soon the city takes my breath away. At first that's a good thing, because the stench of horse excrement is everywhere, mixing with the smell of roasting meats and a very human smell—hot metal. The breeze is merciful, wicking away most of the smoke and steam from the machines and houses, but a strange acrid scent still hangs in the air. I look to the watertells—a copper tube on every block, it seems. But they can't be making that smell, unless the water is rancid.

"White mercury," Y'shennria answers my unspoken question when I wrinkle my nose. "That's the scent it gives off as it's converted to energy. The majority of the machines in Vetris are power sources for the Crimson Lady. The other half are water pumps for the sewage and watertell systems."

I only half absorb what she says as my eyes drink in everything. We pass by stalls selling rainbow silks and jewels, and I do a double take when I see a celeon leading what looks like a massive insect through the streets. It has a thick, chitinous yellow body that gleams in the sun and six powerful legs tipped with hairs. Its two long antennae twitch this way and that, and its four eyes are black and bulbous, imprinted with a pattern of interlocked hexagons.

"Mirtas," Y'shennria answers me yet again before I can ask. "An animal native to the celeon homeland. The celeon tame them for riding, as horses tend to dislike the celeon. They didn't used to be so big, but the Wave that gave the celeon sentience also increased the mirtas's size."

"They're amazing." I gape. "Like nothing I've ever seen."

She points past the giant insects to a passing few people in plain brown hemp robes, the only thing gaudy about them their heavy belts hanging with all sorts of complicated tools I've never seen before.

"Polymaths. Of those you know, I assume."

"Scientists, doctors of the mind and body—philosophers and scholars. The most intelligent people in Cavanos."

"The most intelligent," she agrees. "And the most dangerous."

"Is writing books and papers considered dangerous now?"

"Who do you think invented the Crimson Lady?" she asks. "The watertells, the pumps that make them possible? Who do you think truly won the war for the humans against tens of thousands of witches with omnipotent magic and hordes of Heartless on their side?"

I watch the brown-robed figures as they pass, a new wariness growing in me. She has a very good, and very terrifying, point.

As we pass through to a quieter district lined with shops, I notice more and more iron over the doorways. Every house, every shop, every baked goods stall—all of them have the iron eye of Kavar hanging from somewhere. The people of Vetris are clearly very devout. Or very scared. Perhaps both, considering one feeds the other.

The carriage halts suddenly, and Y'shennria looks around. "Why have we stopped?" she asks. "This isn't the tailor."

"There's a purge blocking the way, milady," Fisher calls. Y'shennria looks to me grimly.

"Well. I suppose now is a better time than none to see the state of the city for yourself. Get out."

"Gladly." I disembark on unsteady legs to a thundering

crowd. It chokes the street, blocking off the horses. I see something tall and metal poking above the heads of the crowd, and it's too silvery to be a giant watertell. Fisher jumps down from the driver's seat, Y'shennria instructing him to watch the carriage. She leads me away, through a dim alley, then two. She finally pushes into a bar with dark wooden countertops and stained glass windows.

"Lady Y'shennria!" The woman at the bar bows deep. "It's an honor."

"We're here for the purge," Y'shennria says, clipped. "No need for drinks."

"Very well then, milady."

Y'shennria pulls me toward a set of stairs in the back. It leads to an upper level spaced evenly with tables, but it's the balcony she walks toward. There are a few other nobles (and I can tell they're nobles because their clothes are equally as fancy as Y'shennria's) standing at the railing, watching the center of the crowd from this perfect height, where a strange contraption that looks like an oversize metal coffin sits ominously.

"Baron d'Goliev!" Y'shennria smiles at a portly man in black silk. "How nice to see you."

The baron turns from the railing, grinning. "Oh, Lady Y'shennria! What a pleasure. I happened to be in Butcher's Alley when I heard a purge was happening. Distasteful, the whole lot of it, but better to free ourselves of these threats now than wish we'd done it later, don't you agree?"

"Absolutely." Y'shennria's smile is tight, but then she motions to me. "Baron, this is my niece, Zera. She'll be a Bride at the Welcoming in a few days."

"Ah!" The baron's ruddy face creases with a grin. "Finally went and got her, did you? Welcome, milady. It's good to have you with us."

"Thank you, Baron d'Goliev. It's an honor." I recite the canned phrase Y'shennria told me to and bow, too deep, because she clears her throat and nudges my boot with her own. When I straighten, the baron squints at me.

"That's quite the sword you have there. It's rare to see a lady carrying one these days. Do you fence, then?"

"When I can get away with it," I admit. He nods and turns to Y'shennria.

"She's pretty enough, isn't she? Her hair's a little long, though."

"We're cutting that before the Welcoming, rest assured," she says. I bite back the urge to remind them I'm standing right here. Y'shennria told me hours ago to expect this sort of treatment, but it's still irritating.

"Of course, of course. Speak true, milady—do you think you'll catch the prince with her?" He talks to Y'shennria like I'm bait for a fishing rod. I can't stand it one second more.

"If we do catch him," I say, "I very much hope someone will clean his scales before we roast him."

The baron blinks, and Y'shennria's expression is deadly cold before she smiles at him sweetly.

"I'm sorry, Baron. She's a little rough around the edges."

"Being raised on a farm will do that to you." The baron chuckles nervously.

"It would be lovely, though, wouldn't it? If such coarseness could somehow catch his finicky eye?" Y'shennria presses.

"Indeed. Just think of it—the Y'shennria family on the Crown Princess's side! Why, you'd give the whole Steelrun family a fit! They have their own girl in the Spring Brides this season, you know."

"So I've heard. Lady Steelrun hasn't been quiet for

months about it."

"Well, this is our last chance to keep the d'Malvane bloodline in Cavanos, so I'll be rooting for both of you. Kavar forbid Prince Lucien marries some servile, tower-kept thing from Avel."

They laugh in tandem. I don't get the joke, and I'm more than a little glad for it, because it sounds like a terrible one. The other nobles must not be worth talking to—either that or they're one of the many families who don't associate themselves with the Y'shennrias because of their Old God ties. By the snide looks I'm getting, it must be the latter. I focus on the crowd instead. A few people position themselves by the strange metal coffin—one of them a man in an impressive white robe with long silver hair. I wish I had that little brass seeing tube, but Y'shennria is deeply immersed in conversation with the baron, and I don't dare interrupt.

"People of Vetris!" The silver-haired man's voice booms, startling me. He holds a copper stick to his mouth, and it somehow amplifies his voice—another strange yet useful human machine. "I bring to you today a purging of our hidden wickedness, an enemy of Kavar, and a threat to the safety of our great nation!"

The crowd roars. One of the nobles beside me waves a handkerchief like a flag. Y'shennria leans in to me, murmuring, "That man in white is the Minister of the Blade—Archduke Gavik Himintell. He's the leader of all the lawguards in Cavanos, and he oversees Vetris's army."

"Sounds like a man with a lot of power," I say. Y'shennria nods.

"Too much, some say. He and the king have grown close in the last six years, and he has the king's ear in all matters.

He's dangerous and clever. Stay away from him if you can."

I watch the archduke in the distance, his voice still booming.

"By the grace of our king, the guidance of our High Priest, and the workings of our Crimson Lady, we have discovered a witch traitor in our midst, plotting even now to kill and maim your children, your husbands, your wives!"

The crowd roars again, fire on their tongues. The man raises a pale sword high, sweeping it around the throng.

"They would take the hearts from your chests!"

Another roar. The hunger whispers in agreement with him: *Gladly*.

"They would curse you with magic enough to turn your blood to ash, your crops to stone!"

Another cheer.

"They would taint the holiness of our great and honorable city with their Old God filth, and for this, they must die!" Archduke Gavik motions for someone. Two lawguards lead a young boy forward, no older than me. He looks underfed, afraid. He's gagged with a wad of cloth and bound at the wrists. The crowd goes absolutely wild at the sight of him. People chant *drown the witch*; others throw rotting fruit. I clutch the railing, a sick feeling rising in my throat. That's what the coffin is for. That's why it's suddenly filling with water from a long tube attached to it at the side. The silver-haired man lets the crowd work itself up with every inch of water that seeps in. More fruit, stones, sticks. The boy flinches as a rotting peach hits his feet. I look to Y'shennria, her head held high, her eyes never leaving the sight.

"Y'shennria—"

"No," she says simply, quietly, so the baron watching next to her can't hear. My unheart sinks. Am I to be forced to sit here and watch someone die? If I do nothing to stop this, it's as if I killed him myself—another body to the pile of my cruelty.

The lawguards bring a stepping ladder, placing it against the now-full metal coffin. They open the lid, and the silver-haired archduke points at the boy.

"Drown the witch, in the name of the New God, in the name of peace!"

The lawguards muscle the boy onto the stepladder, his thin body flailing madly in a last attempt at freedom. Celeon, human—it doesn't matter. Everyone is cheering. And if they aren't outright cheering, they're grimly watching everything unfold before them. Baron d'Goliev makes a gesture, touching his eyelids, then his heart.

"Water for a witch," he mutters, as if it's a prayer that will protect him. "Fire for their thralls."

Y'shennria's face is grim, granite. No one moves. No one even tries. I grip the hilt of my sword tight. If I do nothing, he dies—but how can I do *something*? I'd put myself at risk, get thrown into the dungeons. Nightsinger would shatter my heart, and that would be it. I would never be free.

And it's then I realize with crystal clarity just how selfish, just how monstrous, I really am.

I have to let him die.

I can't watch. I squeeze my eyes shut as the boy takes his last forced step up the ladder. There's silence, the slamming of something metal. Time moves so long and slow, until cheering bursts from the crowd like a grim punctuation mark on the end of the boy's life.

I run back into the bar and vomit into the nearest vase.

4

A MEETING OF THIEVES

"THIS CITY IS ROTTEN," I hiss, wiping at my mouth with a handkerchief Y'shennria's offered me.

"This city is afraid," she corrects. "And fear turns the wisest and kindest men stupid and cruel."

"Then Archduke Gavik is the cruelest and stupidest of all," I snarl. Her eyes dart around, as if fearful someone heard that, but she doesn't disagree. "Why does he do these purges? How often?"

"It started as once every few weeks, then became once every few days. He claims it's for the city's sake," Y'shennria says. "Though I've known him since we were young—he's always held a burning hate for witches and their kind. His father was killed in the Sunless War, and his mother wasted away slowly before she took her own life."

"That's no excuse to drown a living being like that!"

"I never said it was an excuse," she says softly. "Simply that our pain breeds hate, and our hate makes us all do terrible things."

"There aren't any witches left in Vetris," I murmur. "They told me that themselves. So who was that boy?"

"A human, no doubt. A drifter, or a starseed addict, or a refugee from Pendron and its civil war. The archduke isn't picky about his scapegoats."

"Can't the king stop him?"

"The king knows about it, undoubtedly sanctions it."

"Why?"

"To keep Cavanos in line, of course. He's not his father— he doesn't have the love of his people. But he has their fear."

A hard pit of hate begins to burn in me. It's an old hate, a familiar hate—the same hate that drove me to tear the bandits apart. Hate is dangerous. This city's reminded me of that much.

Mercifully, Y'shennria ushers me out of the bar and back into the carriage. She lectures me on how to wear the colors of spring correctly—pinks and greens and oranges, no reds or yellows, ribbons appreciated and chiffon a requirement, but I can barely parse it all. She knows that, presses hard on these lessons as if they'll distract me from what I just saw. But I can't banish the lingering sick in my throat, at both the city and at myself for how ready I was to sacrifice that boy for my freedom.

Y'shennria stops the carriage at a tailor shop, and numbly I go in. I can't even muster excitement about the endless rows of gorgeous, ruffle-drenched dresses in the window. I let the bug-eyed old man measure my every body part. He croons about how lovely velvet would look on me or some such nonsense. Y'shennria urges me to thank him, but when I don't, she pulls me aside.

"You must put what happened behind you, if you want your heart," she mutters. "You are a lady, and a lady always hides her true feelings behind an impenetrable mask of politeness."

"They killed someone," I hiss. "In front of everyone."

"And they will kill many more," Y'shennria hisses back, "if you don't take the first step and impress the prince and the court with these dresses."

I swallow, and when she steps away, I smile at the tailor.

"I'm sorry, good sir. You'd be surprised how quickly traveling turns one into a grumpy wreck."

The tailor grins, bobbing his wizened head and resuming his measurements. When it's over, and Y'shennria and the tailor are talking of what fabrics to use for my extensive wardrobe, I bow out of the shop and breathe the mercury-tinged air of Vetris deeply. A shout rings out just then in the square, a welcome distraction.

"*Thief!* Lawguards, a thief just stole from my pockets!"

I whirl to see a noble in distress, fishing about lamely at his gilded vest. A dark figure speeds away from the noble, something golden clutched in his hand. Clanking armor resounds as the lawguards dash after the figure, swords drawn.

I might not be able to stop a purge, but I can definitely catch a thief.

I gather my skirts and dash madly after the thief before Fisher can stop me. He ducked into a side alley—how predictable. Except when I round the alley, he isn't there. I hear lawguards shouting, their armor clanking in other directions. The thief won't be near any noise if he's smart. He looked tall and strapping, so climbing the fence to my right wouldn't have been a problem. I pull myself up with some struggle, landing on the other side. It's another alley. A dead end.

"I'm guessing you don't want a gold watch because you need to tell the time," I say loudly. A dark shadow straightens from behind a pile of trash, the sunlight shafting through the buildings barely illuminating the dark leather armor he's wearing. Silent boots, silent gloves. A hood and mask obscure his face; the only things showing are two eyes so dark they hum with shadow, like the deepest parts of a midnight sky. He's tall and lean and moves achingly slowly with suspicious tension.

"It's all right, I won't snitch. Yet." I hold my hands up. "I wake up on the marginally more criminal side of the bed, too, some days."

"How did you know where I was?" he asks, voice low. I laugh, then stop when he doesn't.

"Oh, I'm sorry. Was that a serious question? This alley is the only one small enough to lose a cadre of sword-chests trying to throw you in jail. Dungeon? Dungeon-jail. Not the happiest place, really."

"I could've taken any other alley," he insists, the gold watch spinning by its chain in his hand.

"Ah, see, that's where you're wrong. The southern alley has too much sun this time of day—that'd give you away. The alley by the grilled fish stall does have a great cover of smoke, but it's full of lawguards. So that leaves this one."

"You talk like you know this city," he scoffs.

"I know thieves," I correct. "And I know a smart thief doesn't pick the most expensive item on a noble. The gold pieces are always hardest—around necks, in breast pockets. So either you're a stupid thief, or you're after the thrill of the challenge, not the treasure."

His eyes narrow to dangerous onyx slits. "Now that you have me all figured out, why don't you turn me in?"

"Where's the fun in that?" I smile.

There's a tense, fleeting second of silence. Neither of us moves, some invisible string pulled taut between us. An unquiet challenge courses through the air, audible only to those who deal in shadow, only to him and me.

And then it snaps, and the thief runs, and I tear after him. He vaults over a stack of boxes with catlike grace, and I leap with all the forest muscle I have. He is water moving over stones with every turn of his body around street corners and through surprised crowds, over copper watertells and below stone arches. I don't move in beautiful ways, not like he does. But my brute force is enough to keep up with him—to pivot hard and run harder.

A flock of sunbirds takes off as he runs through them. Red feathers fall like bloodied snowflakes, blinding me momentarily. I spot the thief's dark figure as he ducks into an alley. At the end of it, a magnificent waterway cuts through the streets. A massive serpent carved in solid marble sits at the head of it, spewing water from its mouth. Children and laborers and the homeless gather to play in its waters, cleaning themselves of the grime and dirt of the hot day. The water-slick ground throws off my footing, but it doesn't throw off his—he runs up a set of slippery stairs with ease. I can't lose him now. I clutch the railing and drag myself up. At the top, I spot him standing still, debating between two roads.

This second hangs in the air, the sound of my panting mixed with the joyful cries of the children. Water dances up from the snake's mouth in quartz fragments, splashing cool against my sweating skin. I haven't run this hard in so long. I haven't seen this many new things in so long. Molten excitement courses through my veins—this is what it's like to be free. To be human. I remember now.

The thief turns his head my way. The moment he locks his dark eyes on me, life kicks up its speed, and he takes off again. As I follow him, out of breath and half in stitches, I realize this is a path with a very specific pattern. He runs it often—and he knows this city like it's his limb. I can't cut him off, but I can catch up at the very least. I shove all my energy left into my legs and double my speed. I reach my fingertips out to his shoulder, so very close—

He spins away at the last second, and I stumble. When I look up again, he's gone. There are at *least* four paths he could've disappeared down. My brain says he went to the next alley, but my gut tells me he's stopped, just over the wall to my left. I grab the pipe system grafted into the wall and pull myself up and over with the last of my strength. I land on shaky legs and see him standing there, poised in a fighting stance.

"You," he hisses, panting.

"M-Me!" I exclaim, fully out of breath. "Now that the introductions are out of the way, maybe you can stop the whole 'being a criminal' thing and return what you stole."

He snorts. "I've met some self-righteous hypocrites in my time, but you take the cake."

"Thank the New God. It'd be a waste of good baking otherwise."

"Whisper?" A tiny voice interrupts us. We both whirl around to see a little girl standing there, her dark hair tangled and her dress worn through with holes. She looks the same age as Crav—no more than ten or eleven—and she's barefoot. The thief goes to her instantly, kneeling in front of her and offering the watch.

"Here. I got it. You can sell this to the pawners for a good amount."

She looks over the thief's shoulder and points to me.

"Who's that, Whisper? A friend?"

"A stalker," he corrects.

I make a bow with flourish. The girl giggles at it. The sound reminds me so much of Peligli it makes my unheart ache. She starts to walk over to me, but "Whisper" holds her back.

"Don't," he says. "She could hurt you."

"He's right," I agree lightly. "Never trust strangers. They're sometimes mean and oftentimes smelly. And occasionally, they'll even call you a hypocrite."

"You *are* one," he insists.

"Oh, I know. But that doesn't mean it didn't hurt to hear."

He turns to the girl and says something softly. She looks to me, then walks off with the watch in her hand. When she's gone, I speak.

"You stole it for her, huh? I misjudged you, *Whisper.*"

His black eyes turn hard, like the edges of knives. "Why did you follow me?"

"I was bored, and you were making quite the ruckus."

"The real reason," Whisper insists, cutting through my lie. I smile.

"When I see people do the things I do, and do them better, I get curious. Offended, but also curious. I had no choice but to follow you!"

I circle him once, looking him up and down for any indication of who he really is. But there's only black leather, gloved hands clenched, a lean frame, and those narrow midnight eyes.

"There's always a choice," he says. He wears the heavy words with ease, as if someone's said them to him a hundred times before. Practiced. Resigned. They aren't his words, nor are they his experience, and it shows.

I laugh, the sound scaring a nearby sunbird from its perch on a laundry line.

"The only people who say that"—I manage to catch my breath—"are the people who never have to make hard choices. People with luxury. People in power, who are never well and truly backed against the hard wall of life."

...one young, one old, one with no left eye, one who never screamed...

I can smell Mother's blood, see Father's insides, hear the bandit's screams, even when I close my eyes.

"Sometimes, Sir Whisper, the choices are made for you, and there's nothing you can do except make up for them."

The emptiness in my chest is proof of that. But I don't say any of this. His eyes glare out from beneath his hood—I had no idea obsidian could burn so hot.

"You speak as if you're much older than you look," he says finally.

"And you steal in broad daylight from a Goldblood. Either you're a madman or desperate."

"You're the one going to court to become one of those repulsive, gossip-stuffed morons." He scoffs, a sudden venom in his words. "If anyone's desperate here, it's you."

It wouldn't take a polymath to figure out I'm a noble from the terribly fancy silk I'm wearing. First he steals from a noble, now he insults them. I'm beginning to think this is personal. I make a bow.

"A noble girl, at your service. I'd curtsy at you, but I assume you get enough of that already."

He glowers. "You think me noble?"

"I know you to be noble."

"You know nothing about me."

Angry. Imperious. So quick, too. Defensive—like he's hiding the truth I got far too close to. He might be a good thief, but he's a terrible liar.

"Listen to that tone. You really *are* a noble," I marvel. "Let me guess—a lord's son? No, something higher, something so high you have to slip out of the court and steal in the streets just to breathe. A duke's son."

As I inch closer to the truth, his eyes get narrower. "He doesn't like girls like you," he says.

"Who?" I blink.

"Prince Lucien."

"You're friends with him, then? He's told you gold-haired girls with little in the way of modesty aren't his type?"

"A dozen girls just like you have pined after his looks, his power, his riches. Or all three. You're no different—he's an object to you, a symbol. Something you can obtain for your own selfish ends."

"And what if I told you I'm not after any of those things?" I ask.

"Then what *are* you after?"

I put a hand over my empty chest. "I might be a thief, but I'm also a romantic. I'm after his heart."

He scoffs. "You're a liar is what you are. The court isn't the playground you think it is—if you underestimate it, it will rip you apart, leave you in scraps for the dogs. The prince isn't worth the pain. Leave, while you still can."

I ponder this deeply for a half second before smiling.

"I'd love to, but I can't. I've got something to do. And if I left now, I'd hate myself. There are lots of things in life I can live with—world hunger, plagues, my terrible bedhead, the inevitable end of civilization as we know it—but I just can't *stand* hating myself."

I saunter toward him, all smiles, until we're nearly touching. Ever since leaving the woods, the scents of the world assault me; he is all leather and rainwater and sweat. He's a noble—one of the many I need to fool. He's also a boy. If I can't soften this one up, what chance do I have with the prince?

Whisper's frozen in place, dark gaze never leaving my face.

"Aren't you the same way?" I ask, tracing the leather over his broad chest with one finger. "You're a noble, and yet here you are, stealing from your peers and giving to the poor. As if that will make up for the fact you live in an overly gilded cage while the common people starve and get purged by that madman of an archduke." I laugh. "And you had the gall to call *me* a hypocrite."

Through the gap in his cowl I watch his eyes. Nothing. He doesn't so much as blink or swallow. He's stone. If he's affected by my touch at all, he's very good at not showing it. There's some halfway decent willpower in this one. I stretch my hand up to his jaw, cupping it, and he makes no move to stop me.

"Poor thing," I croon. "Trying so hard to be good in a world that's bad."

It feels strange to touch someone new for the first time in a long time. Someone tall, someone with eyes that bore beneath the silk of my dress, down to my very skin. This close I can see his strict brows knotted beneath his cowl, the faintest outline of his lips. His frozen state breaks at my fingertips against his cheek. His gaze turns livid, and he slaps away my hand as if swatting a fly.

"How dare you touch me?" he growls. Such an indignant tone! If I was unsure of his lineage before, I am no longer—he sounded almost exactly like Y'shennria.

"You'll quickly discover I dare a lot of things." I smile. "Including the court. Your warning is pointless—you won't stop me."

"You're so determined to suffer," Whisper scoffs. I can't help the giggle that escapes me, born of despair. Of irony. He knows so little. About me, about the world. About what's coming for his precious friend the prince.

"Have you considered that maybe I deserve it, milord?" I ask.

Deserve every painful grain of it, the hunger snarls.

There's a beat of utter silence. This time, he's the one to approach me—two long strides and we're barely grazing chests again, the warmth from beneath his leather armor pouring into me like a heady brandy. The hunger all but goes wild, clawing at me to tear his throat out. I've been close to humans before, but not this close. His voice is low, his will behind it iron.

"And what, pray tell, did you do to deserve it?"

I giggle again, this time lighter, and twirl away. "Now, now—a lady must keep her secrets, or she's not very interesting."

"A lady who chases down a thief so stubbornly would be interesting no matter the number of secrets she kept under her skirt."

It's a sideways compliment and a taunting trap all at once, and it sends a strange electric thrill through my spine.

"How do you know I keep my secrets under my skirts?" I ask.

"You're right, I don't know. I could check if you'd like, but something tells me your secrets aren't the only things you want to keep intact."

This time, my own laugh catches me by surprise. "You're

going to have to do better than maidenhead jokes if you want to get anything out of me, milord."

"Not all of us are born with razor wits such as yours, *milady*," he counters. I put on a halfhearted imperious air.

"Then get practicing. I expect you to be fluent by the time we meet again at the Welcoming. You *will* be at the Welcoming, won't you?"

"Unfortunately."

"Miss?" A shout echoes then, the voice undoubtedly Fisher's. "Miss, where are you?"

As entertaining as this is, Y'shennria will have my head if I linger. I turn to Whisper one last time, and curtsy facetiously at him before walking out of the alley.

To say Y'shennria is upset with my "reckless behavior and thoughtless cavorting" would be like stating there are three moons—painfully obvious and undeniably true.

"I said I'm sorry," I remind her in the carriage. "I also said I *didn't* undress myself in front of a bunch of nobles and dance in a fountain. So I really see no reason for you to be mad at me."

Y'shennria's lips purse tight. "Your lack of respect for what I'm—what *we're*—trying to do is unacceptable. That heart locket of yours alone cost us four—"

"Witch lives," I finish for her. "I know."

"And then there's the intelligence, the amount of paperwork and right bribes at the right time to get you declared as my kin—" She kneads her forehead and snaps, "Fisher, take us home."

Fisher cracks the reins of the horses. "Right away, mum."

"Don't take it out on him," I say. "I was the one who did all the 'thoughtless cavorting.'"

"He let you," she says. "It must not happen again."

"No one 'lets' me do anything. I do what I want."

"You do what I tell you to, or you don't get your freedom."

There's silence in the carriage. I bite back helpless, angry words. She's right. She's right, but that doesn't mean I have to like it. All I can do is watch the world change from modest buildings and storefronts to vast emerald lawns and perfectly manicured gardens. Like a gemstone in a crown, the noble quarter rests in the center of the city, gorgeous sandstone chateaus half hidden by greenery and grand statues.

"The Firstbloods reside here," Y'shennria says, chilly. "Along with the Ministers. There is the Minister of the Brick, who deals in Cavanos's construction of roads and ships and buildings of import. The Minister of the Blood is the one in charge of overseeing the Firstblood and Secondblood family trees. He allocates funds and ensures the proper inheritances go to the proper inheritors. He's the one who 'found' you and granted your title back to you."

"What did you bribe him with? It must've been something utterly mind-blowing."

"The Minister of the Coin keeps tabs on Cavanos's wealth." She ignores me, speaking louder as if to cover the stain of my words. "And he's also in charge of overseeing all trade routes in and out of the country."

As we pass, I pluck a radiant geranium flower from a bush, burying my nose in its orange petals and breathing deep. The carriage comes to a stop not before one of the cream-bricked mansions but at a much smaller, more modest darkstone house. Hard iron spikes decorate the eaves and parapets, looking every part the spines of an angry animal. Unlike the bare, crisp green terraces of the other houses, this terrace is kept in careful chaos with black rosebushes and long, wispy swathes of translucent ghostgrass. Thorns and black petals litter the ground, rotten crimson berries spread and mush in the dirt like trodden hearts of tiny things. Never in my wildest dreams did I think I'd find somewhere gloomier than even Nightsinger's forest.

When we pull up, three people in dark uniforms line up before the carriage. Fisher helps Y'shennria and me out, and Y'shennria dismisses him and a shy-looking boy to take care of the horses. The only ones left are an older woman practically folded in two with her ancient posture and a slightly less old man with a dapper white beard and mustache.

"Maeve, Reginall, may I introduce Zera Y'shennria, my niece." Y'shennria extends her hand to me, and they bow, though Maeve does more of a stiff nod. The urge to insist these formalities aren't necessary nags at me, but then I spot the mansion next to ours over the hedge. A very well-dressed man and woman taking a walk watch us with eagle-eyed interest from beneath the woman's parasol. Of course the formalities are necessary, if I'm going to fool these nobles.

"Maeve is our masterful cook," Y'shennria says. "And Reginall handles the housekeeping. Reginall, if you'd help Zera bring her luggage in—"

"I don't have anything." I show him. "Don't worry about it."

"On the contrary, miss." Reginall points to the top of the carriage, where several trunks wait. "You look as if you brought quite a bit."

My eyes go wide, and I turn to Y'shennria. "How much did you buy at the tailor's?"

"Just some underthings and shawls," Y'shennria insists. "Reginall, please be sure to burn the old dress at the bottom of the blue trunk when you get a chance."

Reginall bows. He pulls a trunk down with surprising speed, but I hurry to catch the second one.

"Milady, I will take these. Please rest inside," he insists.

"Nonsense. I've got two working arms, don't I? I can help carry my own underpants at the very least."

Maeve blinks her bleary eyes, as if she doesn't quite believe what I've said. The noble couple at the hedge laughs, the sound carrying over.

"Are the Y'shennrias so poor they have to lift things themselves, now?"

"Oh don't be crude. They can hear you!"

"Look at their manor—it's barely standing! Let the last one slander me. No one believes the word of Old God worshippers, anyhow."

Their words are so cold I practically shiver. I knew nobles were cruel, but this is stepping over the line. Y'shennria looks to them, then to me, and grasps my arm, leading me through the darkwood doors of the house. I try to yank away, but she's deceptively strong. She leads me to a drawing room, plopping me down on a slate-gray sofa. She sits opposite me in a high-backed chair, posture regal.

"You will not offer aid to the hired help."

"Your hired help are ancient!" I protest. "You can't make them haul stuff that heavy!"

"Reginall is more than capable of hard labor."

"That doesn't mean you can—"

"My household is not the royal court," she says fluidly. "I employ wages, freedoms. The royal court holds no such tradition—their servants are to be seen and not heard, in every sense. What if you help, and a noble sees? They might say that servant is incapable of doing their job. They'll be let go, to the streets of this cruel city, shunned by all other employers because of an incompetence rumor."

"That's…*mad*." My stomach churns, a tornado nestled in a hurricane. Y'shennria fixes me with her impassive hazel stare.

"That is how Vetris turns, and how you will turn. You will train with me in this room every day until sundown. Breakfast is at seven sharp. Cake is at noon, and we take dinner at eight. You will dress in one of the garments provided for all three occasions."

"Three different—but that's absurd!"

She doesn't miss a beat. "Your room is up the stairs, fourth door on the left. Meet me in this room tomorrow morning at seven thirty. Any later, and we will have problems. Is that clear?"

"Clearer than the ice on your heart," I mutter. Y'shennria's lips form the barest of smiles as she stands, her dark, fluffy hair flouncing. It's the first time I've seen her cold mask of composure truly loosen, truly warm, but something in the weak way it peters off seems deeply hopeless.

Her gaze fixes on an impressive oil portrait in the hall of a very handsome man, his skin dark and his smile white. We blazed past it when she dragged me in here, but now I can get a good look at him. He's young, much younger than Y'shennria is now. The artist's talent is great, but it's not strictly the art that makes the piece startling—it's the subject. Something about him is so comforting; his gray-black eyes hold infinite wisdom, shards of precious diamond suspended in a space we can never reach. The regal gold-trimmed coat he's wearing marks him a noble, and with the tender way

Y'shennria looks at him—he must be Lord Y'shennria. The husband she lost to the Heartless. To the war.

"That's a nice sentiment, isn't it, Ruberion?" she asks the painting softly. "That my heart could still be clear, after all this time."

The painting is quiet, and I'm quieter.

5

HUNGER LIKE A BLADE

IF I WERE HUMAN, I would've entered my modest room and collapsed on the four-poster bed immediately. We'd spent almost a day on the road, by my count. But I'm not human, so instead of wasting time sleeping, I count the diamond pattern on the ceiling and productively reflect on my impending doom.

Eighteen. Nineteen. Twenty.

I should be scared. I was brave in front of Whisper, but he's right. The court waits, vicious. My goal waits, precarious. I should be terrified.

Twenty-one. Twenty-two.

But I'm not. All I feel is queasy. Fear is so distant, a howl of a wolf too far to reach me. I haven't been truly afraid for three years, but it feels like a hundred. A hundred years, deathless and ageless and roaming the woods, flirting with starving wildcats and hell-bent mercenaries just for a change of pace.

No, I'm not afraid. Not yet. But I'm sure I will be.

Twenty-four, twenty-five, twenty-six. One tilt of my head, and the dark diamond pattern on the ceiling becomes eyes, the same ruthless birdlike tilt as Whisper's. I'd been stealing alone for so long, it was comforting to see someone just as skilled as me. To know that the world moves like me, outside of me, whether or not I'm free.

I throw the window open and watch the sun ooze across the sky. Unlike Nightsinger's forest, Vetris moves, visibly and always. It changes with the sun—noon painting it a stark white, while the shadows of afternoon carve out deep crevices between buildings and roads, like dark veins. Sunset makes the city blush. Nobles in frilly clothes and crested hats stroll by, in pairs or alone, bowing to one another, smoking long cigarettes, checking their pocket sandwatches. The trees mute the bustle of the city, but the sound of the temple clock tower hitting high noon is a clear, powerful bellow, even here. Sunbirds and cranes swoop around one another, and I drink in their bright plumage. Not a crow in sight.

A knock on my door pulls me from the sunset. I open it to see a silver tray waiting, covered and faintly warm. I look for Reginall or Maeve, but the hall is empty. I pull the tray in and lift the lid—a hearty stew of beans and lamb, with a fluffy side of bread. The smell is incredible. There's a small note next to the bowl: *Practice makes perfect.*

Y'shennria's handwriting is flawless. I grip a silver spoon by the bowl. She's right—if I have to eat human food for weeks, I'll need a refresher course. I take one bite, the taste just like I remember, warm and tangy. It's incredible—I shovel another spoonful in my mouth, and another. It's almost delicious enough to justify what's coming.

I last ten minutes, and then the pain grips me like hot iron. I cry. I cry blood like rivers, my Heartless body rejecting the slightest bit of normalcy, humanity. When the worst is over I lie on the cool wood floor, breathing through the residual spasms and counting the black diamonds again.

Twenty-seven, twenty-eight, twenty-nine. Whisper is a noble. A thief. An obsidian spark in my mind, shrouded in mystery.

Thirty, thirty-one. I'm a noble now, too. I clutch my gold locket, open it, and watch the piece of my heart beat there, powerful and pitiful all at once. It's so small. Incomplete. I've been incomplete for a long time. *Thirty-two. Thirty-three.*

Right here, right now, even if it hurts—I can pretend to be perfect, human, free. Whole.

I pick up my spoon again.

It turns out, even as an immortal magical thrall, staying awake for an entire night is the worst.

I suppose that's partly why Heartless sleep—because there are precious few other ways to kill time, or turn off our brains. The day's events parse through my mind in a messy jumble. Whisper—so full of himself, so broad in the shoulders and lean in the torso. Crav, Peligli. I hope they're safe. I hope I'm safe. Gods, I hope this place doesn't kill me. Or if it does I'd like a fair warning, at the very least. Something around a day—enough time to scamper off with all these pretty dresses Y'shennria just bought me, yet not nearly enough time to leave the guilt behind.

Dawn peeks through the windows and alerts me that I've wasted an entire night worrying. I sit up and watch the sunrise again, this one more glorious than yesterday's. I'll never get tired of these. How many do I have left, I wonder? How many will I get to see before my hunger drives me to kill someone? Before I make a single mistake in this place and die for it?

"Don't be maudlin," I murmur to my doubtful self. "You've done enough of that in the woods already."

I'll have a thousand sunrises. I'll control my hunger, say all the right things, catch the prince's eye and heart, and be done with this place.

I wait until I hear movement in the kitchens before I get out of bed. I dress in a cool white linen dress, tucking my locket beneath the collar. I venture downstairs, the rampantly delicious smell of buttery fresh bread greeting me. Gods— how long has it been since I smelled fresh-baked bread? Nightsinger never ate anything but vegetables and wheat cake.

The dining room has an impressive winged table at the center. Y'shennria sits on one end in a mauve dress with ruffles up to her chin, neck scars hidden, and she motions for me to sit on the other. It's so large, and our bodies so distant, I can't help but burst out laughing.

"Something funny?" Y'shennria inquires with one eyebrow arched.

"I'm just very tickled by the idea Vetrisians have to apparently scream across the table at one another."

"They don't," Y'shennria says coldly. "I simply don't feel the need to sit close in order to instruct you."

Of course she doesn't. What human in her right mind would want to eat next to a Heartless? No matter how composed and regal she is, no matter how good her ladylike mask, she's still afraid. It goes unsaid, but I hear it clear as day.

Maeve comes in and ladles spoonfuls of warm corn

porridge into my bowl, shaved chocolate and berries presented prettily on top. Y'shennria places a handkerchief next to me and says until I finish that bowl, I can't leave the table. My tongue tingles, eager for the delightful taste of human food again, and yet my body screams dissent. I spoon sweet, thin porridge into my mouth, knowing every bite will only inflict more pain. I try to find the smallest scrap of pleasure in the way it tastes, but almost immediately the gnawing begins. My hunger begs for something raw, something flesh, but I force it silent and spoon every last bit into my mouth, my stomach aching.

I clutch at my chair, desperate for some outlet, Y'shennria grilling me on noble family names, dancing etiquette, the history of the d'Malvane rule. The grilling gives my agonized brain something else to focus on, but my attention wavers between the pulses of pain. This is the most human food I've ever eaten at once, and my body despises me for it. I can't let Maeve see me cry—Y'shennria keeps her around as some sort of test, as if daring me to let the pain overwhelm me and reveal my true, hideous nature to her. Maeve asks me what's wrong, kindly, but Y'shennria makes some excuse of sickness for me.

Finally, Y'shennria orders Maeve to leave, and when she closes the door behind her I gasp and reach for the handkerchief, desperately wiping at my face, the inferno of pain siphoning off slowly with my tears.

"Seven minutes," Y'shennria announces, looking at the sandclock in the corner of the room. "Tomorrow, we aim for ten. The longer you can hold it before you must excuse yourself, the less suspicious you become. Your mask slips too often—you will learn to endure the pain without nearly so much squirming."

"If there's one thing I love, it's repeated agony," I drawl, and hold up the vibrantly red handkerchief. "I hope you've got a good excuse about this for whoever does the laundry."

We go to the sitting room, where she has Reginall move all the furniture so I can practice bowing in thin-heeled boots and curtsying (one for men, one for women, and a special version for greeting both at once). I bend until my knees ache, bow until my back cries out, practice the simplest of motions—turning doorknobs silently with only two fingers, walking up stairs with skirts, holding myself high enough to keep two decorative crystal orbs nestled firmly on my shoulders—until the sun kisses the drawing room windows good-bye. Reginall passes by as he cleans the house, always careful not to meet my eyes but watching us nonetheless. When it's dark out, he raps on the wood of the doorframe. At the sudden noise I slip carrying the crystal orbs, and both of them fall to the floor with heavy *thunk*s.

"Not again!" Y'shennria exclaims. "Pick them up and start from the beginning of the room."

"These shoes are awful," I pant. "And my shoulder—"

"Again," she insists harder, then turns to Reginall. "What is it?"

"Pardon my intrusion, milady, but it's been thirteen hours by the sand. Perhaps a break for the young miss is in order."

Y'shennria looks to me, then to my chest, her eyes lingering on the space where my heart should be.

"No," Y'shennria finally says. "She will continue."

"Milady—"

"Please assist Maeve in preparing dinner, Reginall." Y'shennria's words are clipped. He bows and leaves.

"Auntie dearest," I grit out. "I need to stop for a second—"

"*Lady Y'shennria*. And there's no time." She ushers me

forward, signaling me to walk. "You've barely scratched the surface of what you need to know, and poorly, might I add. You have no inherent grace, and your sense of balance is nonexistent. Add on the fact you seem to have never walked a straight line in your life, and—"

My legs quaver violently. I manage three steps before I slip and collapse.

"Why is this so difficult for you?" she barks. "It's a simple matter of walking correctly."

Rip her throat out, the hunger lashes against my thoughts. I can feel all my teeth growing sharp and jagged into my lips—exhaustion isn't a good look on me. I need to eat. Y'shennria's throat looks too appetizing.

"Believe it or not," I pant, "monsters get tired, too."

Y'shennria picks up the crystal orb from the carpet. She turns to a shelf, where seven orbs are lined up, the first of plain glass, the second of stone, the third of copper and embedded with little needleheads. One orb for each level of posture training for noble children, she'd told me. She reaches for the orb on the very end—black iron, razor-sharp ridges adorning its surface.

She places the orb next to me.

"No—no more. I need to eat," I manage through my gritted teeth. "Now."

"And I will feed you," she agrees. "After you walk without dropping this orb."

The razor edges of the orb glint maliciously back at me.

"I'm fairly certain I told you in the carriage," I pant. "That I become…*unmanageable* if I'm not fed."

Fear glances briefly behind her eyes, but she straightens her spine. "And I told you—there will be times you are forced to go without for a little longer. You must endure."

And you must die, the hunger retorts at her, flaring like a tongue of flame against oil-soaked wood. I fight the sudden urge to lunge at her. My eyes blur—her skin all I can see, the heat beneath it a siren song to my gnawing insides. The hunger can smell her fear, her flesh.

"You are a Heartless second, Zera," Y'shennria says. I hear her voice as if she's far away, underwater. "You are a lady first. Put those fangs away."

"I...can't..."

"You can," she asserts. "Prove to me you are more than your hunger. Prove to me an ounce of human still remains in your bones."

I've clutched at my humanity—kept what little was left of it safe and dry beneath my skirts, behind my jokes. I kept hope, but there's a deep, yawning pit in me where the hunger resides. And it laughs at the thought of hope.

You are nothing, it whispers. *Nothing but an animal consumed by hunger. You can never escape what you've done.*

Father's sword digs into my side. I can barely remember his face, Mother's face. I can't recall their voices anymore. What's the point of becoming human again, if I have nothing left in the world but scant memories?

Wherever they are in the afterlife, they must hate you for causing their deaths.

"Zera!" Y'shennria barks. "You are my niece. I expect you to oblige my requests."

Through the fog of my hunger, my unheart gives a pang. *Niece.* Family. She isn't my true family, but she's willing to pretend. She's willing to call me her family, even if I'm the thing that destroyed it. Three years of suffering is nothing compared to her decades. Compared to Y'shennria, I'm so weak. She's counting on me. Crav, Peligli. Nightsinger. All of them, counting on me.

My own heart, counting on me.

I squeeze my eyes shut, and with a great internal wrench I force the hunger back inside, my jagged teeth filing into human stubs, the hunger's voice dwindling.

I throw myself to my feet and pick up the orb gently to avoid the razors, nestling it in the crook of my shoulder. I'm a human. I'm an Y'shennria. The razors bite down, just hard enough. One misstep, a single stumble, and they'll pierce through my skin. Carefully, I walk ten steps. Eleven, twelve— my ankles protest, wavering, and the orb's razors gnaw at me. Warm blood oozes down my skin. It's not the pain that's the worst part—it's my mind. It's exhausted, crammed full of gestures and rules. I haven't eaten. My thoughts swim like a heat haze in summer. Every step must be perfect. Still the hunger claws at my insides, like the bars of a cage.

Thirteen steps. Fourteen. The razors eat away at me, every instinct screaming to shuck the orb off once and for all. I'm almost to the end of the room. Sixteen. Sixteen years of my humanity, forgotten, lost. Eighteen, nineteen—I let out a gasp as the razors press down deeper. I should be nineteen years old. One last step.

Twenty.

My twentieth year of life, spent free. That's all I've ever wanted.

I reach for the bookshelf, clutching at the lip of it to stabilize myself. My knees shake so hard I can barely keep standing. The sound of Y'shennria's footsteps resounds, and then the bite of the razors subsides as someone pulls them out of my skin. She looks me over, the bloodied iron orb in her hand. Her eyes hold the barest wisp of softness.

"Well done, Zera."

Coming from her after hours of relentless *not good enough*s, the words are sweeter than clover honey. I drink them in greedily, forcing what's left of my energy into a grin. She leaves to bring me food, and I collapse on a nearby settee to nurse my aches. Reginall comes in then, a duster in one hand.

"Perhaps a bit of bedrest is in order, miss?"

The hunger leers at him, eager to consume. Forcing my brain to order words and sentiments into coherent jokes makes it easier to ignore, but just barely.

"I-If I were the lazy, slovenly type, I might just take you up on that offer," I manage weakly.

He bows. "Of course, miss. I could discern that by the way you upended your entire closet onto your bed this morning."

I laugh, the tight knot in my chest undoing itself bit by bit. He and I are quiet, the triplet moons outside the window all but dwarfed by the haze of Vetris's lights, each window a square of gold burning bright. For all their hate and suspicion, the humans are so very good at making beautiful things.

I can feel my flesh mending, my shoulders and the razor cuts there bared for Reginall to see. Panic grabs me by the throat, but I do my best to make my voice even.

"Could you fetch me a shawl, Reginall?"

He obliges, returning with a silken one. I wrap it around my shoulders, and he smiles.

"It looks lovely on you," he says. I squirm on the settee.

"Is it weird that when people say I'm lovely, or pretty, I get itchy?"

"We all get a little uncomfortable when our value is reduced to our physical appearance," he says patiently.

"Clever," I admire.

"I'm afraid not, miss. I'm simply old."

The same tiredness as Y'shennria's works its way into his eyes. How much has he seen? He must've been alive during the Sunless War, too.

"Where were you, Reginall," I ask, "during the war?"

"Fighting, miss."

"On whose side?"

Wordlessly, he peels down a portion of his suit collar. Tendrils of a flowerlike scar on his chest crawl up his neck. I recognize it—how could I not? I'd seen it only once before, on another witch's Heartless. *Former* Heartless. That flowerlike scar blooms over our chests when our hearts are returned to us and we're made human again. That's the shape I've longed to see over my own chest for so many years now.

"You're a—"

"I was." His gaze is steady. "Thirty years ago, I was human, and then I was not. So I fought. And at the end of it all, when the graves outnumbered the children in the streets, my witch gave me back my heart as she said she would, and then took her own life."

It's hard to breathe all of a sudden. "Why?"

"I'm not sure, miss. But she killed many during the war, and it ate at her, until the only release she could find was in death."

My own guilt flares. ***Five men. One young, one old—*** I shake it off quickly, before it can burrow. "I'm Heartless, too."

"I know." He smiles. "Lady Y'shennria told me, and none of the others."

"Why did she hire you, if you were Heartless? She hates us."

He thins his lips, speaking carefully. "I believe she's

been trying these past thirty years to understand the things that killed her family. Trying to find meaning in it, meaning in the war. When one loses much, one tries desperately to understand why."

I'm quiet, the ticking of the sandclock hollow between us, until: "So you're free. You could go anywhere—why stay here? They hate witches in Vetris. If you're found out—"

"Have you ever killed a human, miss?"

The bandits' silent screams pierce my ears. I can't move. Reginall just smiles, kinder now.

"You have. So then you must know the horror of it. You know the hunger reveled in the blood, and the carnage, and the light in their eyes as it faded."

My memories are sudden and blinding; blood slick on my hands, I licked it off, laughing, a skull beneath my palm, a hard rock I slammed it into, shards of stone and bone—

Reginall puts a hand on my shoulder, pulling me out of the darkness.

"And you must know, too, that the hunger isn't you. You must never confuse its evil for your own thoughts and feelings. I remember vividly that was the worst part of being Heartless—thinking that shadow was part of my own soul."

"What is it?" I ask quickly. "The hunger."

"I don't know. We spoke of it together, in the war. Some of us thought it the magic's curse. Others thought it man's darkest instincts made undeniable. I can't say for sure what it is—only that it exists, and is cruel." He moves to the mantelpiece, absently dusting the sandclock there. "I will aid Y'shennria in preventing this looming war, down to my last breath. That is all I can do to make up for what I've done—that is why I'm here. Why are you here, miss?"

"For my heart."

"And?"

"To stop a war."

"Is that all?" He smiles, and I can tell he knows. He knows my words are half truth, and only saying them just now do I realize that, too. I want my heart, my friends' hearts, and freedom. I want all those things. But none of them will be enough. None of them will fill the emptiness, the gaping chasm, the cold void of the girl I used to be. A happy girl, an innocent girl. A girl with family. A girl who believed in the goodness of the world, once.

A girl with love.

Reginall moves to leave, bowing at the threshold of the room. "I do hope you find what you're looking for, miss."

6

THE SERPENT'S NEST

THREE DAYS isn't enough.

But Y'shennria tries her hardest to ensure it is.

We train throughout the night—Y'shennria sacrificing sleep to stay up with me. As I practice with the razor orb, I injure myself less and less. One day I come away without any cuts at all, giving a fist pump she calls "unladylike" even as she smiles. Y'shennria keeps my hunger fed, so it's a bare murmur as she teaches me dancing—too nervous to touch me, instead having Reginall be my partner. She sits at the key harp, playing beautiful melodies I have to learn every twist and turn to. I'd be lying if I said I'm graceful, but I am fairly good at moving my body in a rhythm—one upside of doing nothing in the forest but practicing swordplay with Crav—which means I can string the moves together, but they have no charm or fluidity to them. *Like watching an oak tree flail in a storm*, Y'shennria snorts.

She's infinitely more refined at art, and music, and dancing. She invites several nobles to have dinner with us, including Baron d'Goliev, as a chance for me to learn how to conduct myself properly without the pressure of the entire court's eyes. They ask me questions I clumsily respond to, my fingers slipping over the four spoons laid out for soups alone. After dinner, they linger over chocolate and tea in the sitting room, taking turns at the key harp or showing off their latest sketches of nature. Compared to Y'shennria's sketches, though, they're like children's scrawls. Even her conversation skills are more refined, quicker, sharper, keeping everyone entertained. She's the pinnacle of what a noble should be, what a noble was in my mind before coming here.

I start to realize just how much she's lost when the others tell fond stories of Ravenshaunt's beauty and grandeur, of Lord Y'shennria, stories of how the two of them fit together so well, how gallant and good he was. Y'shennria listens to them all patiently, her eyes in those moments softer than I've ever seen them. I can only stare at my hands with shame. Shame that what I am—things like me—took so much from her.

It makes me want to learn. To make her proud, no matter how impossible that might be.

Slowly, with her excellence as my teacher, the dinners get less and less awkward. I speak clearer, and some people even laugh at the things I say. I start to correctly pick the small spoons for cold soups, the big spoons for hot ones. Instead of waiting for Nightsinger to heal me, impatient and suffering loudly, I now understand my pain threshold with perfect clarity, a silent knife's edge I dance on just before the tears are about to spill from my eyes. I time my excuses to the bathroom—between courses being set out but before dessert. I can't play an instrument or draw, but Y'shennria has me sing after dinner. She asked me if I had any talents, and I told her I sometimes sing. I showed her, and she must've considered it passable enough. I get scattered applause, and Baron d'Goliev insists I have the sweetest voice he's heard since Queen Kolissa was my age, but no one takes it seriously, considering he likes his Avellish brandy after dinner far too much.

I drown my doubts, my fears, my confusion in the lake of learning. In the strange, vast lake of becoming Zera Y'shennria, niece of Lady Y'shennria.

The morning of the Spring Welcoming comes too fast. Dawn breaks through the window, crimson and ice-blue bleeding together, but even the beauty can't distract me from the truth—I'm not ready. None of that matters now. Time has a way of disappearing on me, and then reappearing with horrifying punctuality. The time is now. I have to be ready. At the very least, I have to fake it, if not for the court, then for the witches whose lives hang in the balance, and for my heart.

I've died dozens of times. I know—I'm getting sick of hearing myself even think it. But in the end, that's the only advantage I have in this quiet war between the court and myself. They can't kill me. They can belittle me, they can mock me, they can tear me apart. But they can't kill me. Only my own mistakes can do that.

Only *I* can do that.

It's a small comfort, to have a bit of control in the dizzying madness of this dance.

I watch my reflection in the window, my straw gold hair freshly cut to my shoulders, and lift my chin. Everything comes down to this day, these next few hours. If I don't successfully debut, it's over.

My one chance at freedom—gone.

Maeve draws me a bath, sprinkling whole black roses

and sticks of cinnamon in the tub. I ease myself into the water, the smell soothing my frayed nerves. It's a familiar smell—Y'shennria's hair and clothes smell the same, and I feel a little honored that I'm allowed to carry the scent, too. When I'm dry, Maeve dresses me in an effervescent, cherry-blossom pink dress, and it's so beautiful my nerves part for a brief moment as I stroke the silken ruffles. Next she fixes my hair, her slow, gnarled fingers catching on tangles. She's been doing this for longer than I've lived, and it shows; she forms dozens of plaits into a rose, elegantly nestled halfway into a bun. She tries to fasten the whole thing with a lattice of quartz pins, but she must get tired, because the pins keep falling out loosely.

"That's quite enough effort on your part, Maeve," Y'shennria says as she sweeps into the room. "I'll handle it from here."

Maeve makes a little bow and closes the door behind her. It's just me and Y'shennria and the glint of the sun off the quartz pins.

"You don't have to," I say. Her hands aren't shaking, but her lips are tight.

"Don't be ridiculous. It's simple enough." She arranges the pins, sliding them in tight against my skull. Touching me out of necessity, of course—she'd never do it otherwise. Y'shennria pulls the last few strands of hair free from behind my ears and looks at me in the mirror. "Have you eaten?"

"Those perfectly uncooked livers downstairs? Yes."

She jumps right in to a refresher course. "Never take the hand of a man if offered to you—"

"—in the evening," I finish. "When sitting at tables, it's women first."

"In what order?" she interjects quickly.

"Noble rank, modified by age. Highest in both categories sits first, but only if she's married. The unmarried sit last."

"Which means an unmarried lady of sixteen such as yourself will always sit last."

She hands me a waxy tube of pink lip tint and watches me put it on. Not too much, always in the very center of the lips.

"Much better than your first try," Y'shennria claims. Her lips are tinted purple, her scarce few wrinkles disguised by powder. She may look cool and composed, but her knuckles are white on the back of my chair. Lives hang in the balance. I know it. She knows it better than I. We both know it in the silence of the mirror and the brightness of our war paint.

"I still remember my Spring Welcoming," Y'shennria says softly.

"I'm not ready," I confess. She smiles grimly.

"I'll let you in on a secret; no one is ever really ready."

"Milady!" Reginall announces from behind my bedroom door. "The carriage has arrived!"

My face tinges a ghastly green in the mirror. Y'shennria sees it, and I brace myself for an order to apply more rouge or to get ahold of myself, but instead I feel a soft, strong hand on my shoulder. Hers.

"They will ignore you. They will try to tell you that you aren't good enough. This is a lie. You are an Y'shennria. You have always been good enough."

The words are strong and true—so strong they don't feel as if they belong to me. Perhaps she meant to say it to her own children, once upon a time. Her own daughter, at her own Spring Welcoming.

I take one final look in the mirror. A girl with paper skin and blond hair looks back at me. She wears a heart-shaped locket of gold. Her too-thin lips are pink in the center. Her blue eyes are bolded with dark kohl, two lines tracing down her cheekbones as is the current Vetrisian style. She has a blemish beneath her bangs she's worried about, but she's worried more about her teeth, the sharp ones that come out when she's hungry.

She is young. She is terrified. She is playing dress-up. She is playing a very dangerous game.

She is Heartless.

Y'shennria helps me up, her hands strong beneath my elbow. I faintly realize how much effort it must take her to swallow her own fear and touch me not once, not twice, but three times. She leads me through the house, down the stairs, past the painting of handsome Lord Y'shennria, and out to the carriage. This one's much fancier than the travel carriage that brought me to Vetris—black velvet tassels hanging from the horses and copper accenting the wheels. Fisher's in the driver's seat, looking much older in a black suit and feathered cap. The dignity of his clothes can't disguise his shy grin, though.

"You're looking sharp, miss."

"With any luck I'll gouge someone's eye out," I agree through my locked-up throat. Y'shennria opens the door of the carriage, and I get in. I poke my head out the window, my voice tingeing desperate.

"I was under the impression you weren't going to abandon me to the wolves."

"The Spring Brides and Grooms arrive on their own." Y'shennria holds my gaze. "Remember what I taught you. Follow what the Headkeeper says. Do your best to stand out in a polite way. I'll try to visit you after it's over."

Her words are so clipped, so final-sounding. An unsaid condition lingers after her every sentence: *If you don't fail horribly.*

If you aren't discovered and promptly killed for what you are.

I force a smile, but it hangs crooked on my lips. "If I'm shattered, will you at least come to the memorial service? I can't promise any drinks, or good food, or even other people, really. But I'd appreciate it."

"You'll be fine," Y'shennria says sternly.

Fisher nicks the horses into a trot, the carriage wheels crackling over the gravel path. I watch Y'shennria and Maeve and Reginall grow smaller behind me. Soon I'm left with only the serene cries of the sunbirds in the trees that line the road and the constant high-pitched scream of my anxious mind. The nobles striding about with their lovers and pets stop and stare at my carriage, pointing and whispering. I remember the nobles gossiping over the hedge the first day I came and fight the urge to slink down in my seat. My Y'shennria lineage might be only a cover, but I won't let her family name go sour in my hands.

It's a relief when the royal palace finally comes into view. Like the rest of the city, it's made of whitestone, but the elegant, barely clothed women carrying spears carved into every buttress and tower make it much more intimidating. The watertells of the palace are made of silver, not copper, and it seems each one is nigh constantly in use—expulsing water accompanied by loud popping noises as lawguards and servants fetch and send the little tubes with messages in them. Watertells are a luxury, clearly—I've never seen a single commoner use one. The man-made rivers dug into the palace's landscape weave fluid, mesmerizing patterns, and we pass over them on a dozen bridges. At the head of every river is a fountain shaped like a coiled viper spewing water from its mouth, much like the one I chased Whisper through the other day.

Whisper. Will I recognize him? The thought of him waiting at the Welcoming—tall and lithe and dark-eyed— has my body in mysterious, slightly irritating jitters. I force myself still; a lady doesn't jitter.

A Heartless doesn't listen to a Whisper, the hunger sneers. *We eat him.*

A pale-blue carriage passes me, then another of green. Curious nobles gather on the sides of the road, watching the carriages come in one by one. The pale-blue carriage is getting a lot of attention, a pretty girl smiling and waving out the window. Another girl in an ostentatious gold carriage waves, too. The nobles applaud, throwing flowers they'd picked from the lawn—red carnations and stalks of shellflowers.

"Don't they look lovely?" a noble's voice leaks into my window.

"Quite pretty indeed, but nowhere as beautiful as last year's batch. If the prince didn't take to last year's, these stand no chance."

"These." "Last year's batch." If I didn't know better, I'd say these idiots thought of us as sacks of marriageable meat rather than actual people. It's brutal to hear, but I'm just a passerby, a fake. I can't imagine how much worse it is for the real children of these nobles who treat them like commodities. Like race dogs to be gossiped over, betted upon, bred to the proper dame and sire.

Fisher slows the carriage to a crawl, stopping it just before the massive pool and the front steps of the palace. Nobles flood the stairs, standing on either side in ritual tandem. The palace guards—differentiated from city lawguards by the four jade-green feathers in their helmets—stand sternly before the crowd, not so much holding them back as marking the appropriate area for them to be. Fisher opens the carriage door, letting in light and the sounds of commotion: cheers, whistles, shouting. Among the well-dressed nobles are polymaths in their plain brown robes and tool belts. Everyone in court is here to see the spectacle. Fisher doesn't offer me his hand—that's only for suitors—but he does hover in case I need help descending.

My copper-toed boots hit the ground. Everyone's watching; even the cold, blank eyes of the statues stare down at me and add an extra layer of pressure to my chest.

"You'll be all right, won't you, miss?" Fisher asks, but I can barely hear him over the crowd's din. Miss. He's one of the few who calls me that, instead of milady. Milady is sharp, full of expectations, but miss is much softer. I somehow feel comforted, knowing at least one person in the world doesn't expect much from me.

"No," I admit. "But as Y'shennria would say, that hardly matters, does it?"

A red carnation catches in my hair, swinging on loose strands and batting my face. I pick it out, bewildered. I should be happy to be here, happy to be picked as a potential bride for the prince, but with every cheer of the nobles I feel more and more like a cow lined up for slaughter. All I can think of is how quickly they'd turn on me if they knew what I really was. I force my lips into a grin. The other girls getting out of their carriages smile so easily, like they were born to it, and flit through the crowd and up the stairs. Shakily, I follow.

"Head high," I mutter Y'shennria's words. "Square chest. Always look up and forward, and never down or back. And don't forget: if you're found out, you're dead."

I catch up to a girl in a gold dress on the stairs, and she shoots me a look from under her long eyelashes. Her face is made up as much as mine—lip tint, dark symmetrical lines drawn in wax from her eyes, though hers are laced with curlicues.

"Your necklace is very nice," she says. I look down at my glittering locket. My first urge is to say thank you, but Y'shennria taught me better than that. Accepting compliments in court is seen as a weakness to flattery.

"As is yours," I say.

"Oh, this old thing?" The girl laughs and picks at her garnet necklace. "It's nothing much. Papa sent me in hand-me-downs, really. My sister's old jewels, her old dress, her old carriage—ugly things."

Her carriage was the golden one, velvet-lined and diced with tassels, the fanciest one for miles around. She's definitely part of a Firstblood family. She shoots me a pitying smile.

"Is your dress hand-me-down, too? What a shame—you should've asked me for one! I'd be more than happy to buy you something that doesn't make you look as if you're a Snowsum Eve's duck!"

Snowsum Eve ducks are always packed to bursting with fruits before roasting. She's calling me fat, and she isn't being subtle about it. She may as well have slapped me in the face with how overt she's being, yet she can easily pawn the insult off as politeness. So that's how they play it here in the royal court, hm? Fine by me.

"You flatter me, milady." I smile. "I can see the prince being very happy with your kindness and consideration for others."

It's a two-faced insult, and we both know it. The girl goes five shades of angry red and loses her concentration, tripping on a stair. The crowd watches her with a bevy of hushed whispers.

"Is she all right? Poor thing had so many fevers as a child, it's a wonder she's strong enough to be at the Spring Welcoming—"

"The Steelrun are sickly children, after all, runs on the father's side—"

"—can't have a royal generation of bedridden princes, now can we?"

Steelrun—a Firstblood family. I was right. But Whisper is more right—these nobles really *are* gossip-stuffed morons. Their willingness to tear someone down in front of them chills me to the marrow. I extend my hand to her. She glares at it, hoisting herself to her feet and brushing past me with a disgruntled mutter.

"As if I'd let you look good at my expense."

I watch her go for a moment, sighing. "Right, how could I forget? Basic decency is illegal here."

Finally, I make it to the top step—out of the sun and into the cool shade of the entrance. Two celeon guards in silver armor engraved with snakes bow and open the massive gilded doors for me. The main hall is a feast for the senses—marble banisters polished so well they shine like full moonlight. The intoxicating, lush perfume of plant life wafts from every basket and ceramic vase, the hall overflowing with bouquets of orchids and lime flowers. White ivy drips from the railings of the second and third and fourth floors like natural streamers, heavy and ripe with pale star-shaped flowers. The sound of water beneath my feet makes me look down; the floor of the main hall isn't a floor at all—it's an iron grate woven in a delicate pattern and overlaid with glass, a shallow lake of turquoise water below. It scatters sunlight into diamond shards around the vaulted hall, making it look as if the room glows from within.

To contrast all the opulence, a woman with a strict bun and sharp gaze stands before a regal statue of some very important dead man. Her dress is a sensible black, but she wears a gold-threaded mantle over her shoulders, hanging long past her waist. All court servants wear a mantle, and all of them are different colors to indicate their rank and job. A gold mantle marks her as Headkeeper—the overseer of every servant in the palace. If there's anyone who knows the court's dirty little secrets, it's her. At her sides are other keepers in similar clothes, though their mantles are much less gaudy.

"Welcome, Bride," she says, and bows. I almost bow in return but catch myself. "I am Ulla, Palace Headkeeper. We will wait for your fellows to reach us before entering the Hall of Time. Please make yourself comfortable."

"Thank you. I'll try my best. Comfort is a far dream in these shoes." I sigh.

Ulla immediately claps her hands and barks, "Fetch the Bride a chair, quickly."

Two men branch off, returning with a heavy ironwood chair. My eyebrows skyrocket at how fast they put it down just behind me.

"I didn't mean— You didn't have to—"

Ulla raises her own brow. Having the Headkeeper suspicious of me would be *very* bad. I put on a haughty face and sit, fighting my urge to thank the men as they retreat to Ulla's side. The Steelrun girl is already here in a similar chair, her eyes avoiding mine. We wait. And by that I mean I stare at everything in the hall like a drooling newborn fascinated by the slightest glimmer, and the very obviously bored Steelrun girl taps her foot on the floor, impatient to meet her royal husband. I don't have the heart—literally—to break the bad news to her, so I just smile when our eyes meet instead.

Ulla welcomes a well-dressed boy in a sea-green tunic, his shy smile ruddy. Two slender boys enter after him, twins by the look of their identical blond coifs and sallow skin and blue eyes. The boys are here as Spring Grooms—a much more celebrated title when a Princess is in line for the throne, but today they'll simply be introduced to the court so they can begin their social life. Finally, a girl in a luxurious deer-hide dress joins us, panting and looking around happily, as if she's thrilled to be here. All of the noble children have fine features and soft-looking, well-fed skin. They've never seen a day of work, let alone a day of hunger, and half of me pities them. How helpless would they be outside this mechanical city of extravagance?

How helpless would they be beneath your fangs? The hunger slithers around in my skull.

"Now that we've all assembled," Ulla begins, "I will walk the Spring Grooms to the hall to be introduced first. Brides, please wait here until I fetch you. I'd ask you all to be on your best behavior, as this is your first introduction to the people you will call peers for the rest of your lives."

"We know, old woman," one of the twins drawls. "Our parents gave us this same talk, and much quicker than you."

I can't stand his tone, or the way Ulla simply takes his insult without so much as blinking.

"Someone woke up on the wrong side of the baby's crib," I drawl. The boy's brother shoots me a venomous glare.

"I wasn't aware gloomy little paupers like the Y'shennrias were allowed to speak," he snarls.

"Shouldn't you be at home, praying to your heretic god?" The first twin sneers at me.

"It looks like you two need to do a little praying of your own." I smile. "First order of business: ask Kavar for some better insults."

The smiley, deer-dress girl chokes on her laughter. The twins throw her a nasty glance and turn on me.

"You'll watch yourself," one of them says. "The Priseless have long memories."

I look to Ulla, but she doesn't move to interfere or stop us. Maybe she isn't allowed to.

"Longer than your temper, I'd hope," I say.

The other twin narrows his eyes. "You—"

"What's all this ruckus?" a new voice booms down the hall. All of us turn to it, and everyone bows. Not wanting to look disrespectful to whomever this is, I quickly bow with them.

"Milord," Ulla starts. "I was just about to take the Spring Grooms into the hall for introduction."

"And they can't manage to control themselves for even that long?" The man who steps forward is tall, nowhere near a witch's height, but the way he carries himself makes it seem that way. He's clean-shaven, a long mane of silver hair trailing down his back. I recognize that hair, and my stomach goes cold. It's Archduke Gavik Himintell, the man who led the purge the other day. His eyes are blue and watery, yet his smile is harder than ice. Everything about him screams precision and calculation. He wears a white tunic with long sleeves, a mantle on his shoulders much like Ulla's—though his is gray and encrusted with quartz flakes: a Minister's mantle. On his hip is the same sword he pointed at the crowd.

"Sir," the Priseless twins bark a greeting. The archduke smiles at them.

"We've always spoken of manners, haven't we boys? Show a pleasant face, even to your worst enemy. Decorum is—"

"The demolisher of opposition!" the twins echo, their expressions enraptured. They clearly admire the archduke, to the point that all their anger at me is left by the wayside. The archduke chuckles, and then fixes his blue gaze on me.

"Now here's a fresh face I'm unfamiliar with."

I make a small bow. He might be the Minster of the Blade and an archduke leagues above my lady status, but Himintell is a Firstblood family equal with the Y'shennrias.

"Archduke Himintell," I say. "It's a pleasure to meet you. I'm Zera Y'shennria, Lady Y'shennria's niece."

"So you know who I am? How is that, considering this is your first time at court?"

A mistake. Of course I wouldn't know who he is if I've never seen him before. But I have. Y'shennria warned me to stay on my toes at all times around him. If I play the stupid little girl act, I might be able to hide my real intentions from him.

"My aunt told me to look for the handsomest man at court." I pepper my words with an eyelash bat or twelve. He's quiet, and for a second I think I've offended him.

"Of course." His smile is just as bright as mine. We're both forcing ourselves. "Lady Y'shennria spoke of your discovery with such happiness the last time I saw her. It's good she retrieved you safely. Let us hope you merit her joy."

"I plan to, milord."

He doesn't blink, and neither do I. It feels like he's sizing me up, trying to see into my inner workings. It's all I can do to keep my face clean of the rage I've bottled up at him ever since the purge. Thankfully, he breaks our stare-down first and turns to the others.

"I hope you are all prepared to meet the court," he says. "The Brides especially."

"Ready as we can be, milord." The Steelrun girl curtsies.

Gavik nods. "You need all the readiness you can muster if you're to be dealing with Prince Lucien." The way he says it is touched with just enough disdain. He clearly doesn't like the prince much. "If you would excuse me, then, I should've been gathered in the Hall with the rest of the court long ago."

"Of course," Ulla says, and bows deeply. "Good day, milord."

We all bow with her, my eyes lingering on the Minister as he passes me. Ulla leaves with the Spring Grooms. And finally it comes our time to enter the Hall. As I follow Ulla with the rest of the girls, I try not to ogle the gold filigree on the doors, the luscious oil portraits of hounds and lions, of Kavar himself, depicted as a young man with eye symbols all over his skin, holding a scale of justice in one hand and a sword in the other. He's both sinister and awe-inducing at once. Nightsinger's books were insistent a witch should never presume to know what the Old God's physical form might look like, and yet here the humans are, painting their New God with abandon. Banners of jade-green silk waterfall from the tops of the spotless windows, the silver serpent logo stitched there catching the sun. The palace's pure grandeur makes Y'shennria's manor look small and modest.

Ulla takes us down a vast hall with walls made entirely of colored glass. The sun shafts through, dyeing our skin all colors of sunset and twilight. It takes me a shameful few seconds to understand that the colors depict scenes from history—the humans first building Vetris, important polymaths inventing things like watertells and sandclocks, the Eight Winters' War when Helkyris was our bitter enemy fighting for control of the Tollmount-Kilstead mountains, and finally, in the most recent section, the Sunless War. It stretches on all around me—armored battalions of celeons and humans viciously fighting tall, dark-eyed figures with darkened hands and nails—witches. And in front of them, a horde of fanged monsters, each depicted with a red chasm where their hearts should be.

Heartless.

I clench my fists. Is that how they really see us? Is this how terrifying we look to them? We're hunched and wild-eyed, moving like animals instead of people. During the War, Heartless were on the front lines, making up the bulk of the witch army, whether they wanted to fight or not. I don't doubt the witches commanded their Heartless to protect them. And on top of being surrounded by all those humans? Their hungers probably ran rampant, transforming them into bestial monsters that cared little for human behavior. I've felt it sometimes, deep down; the darkest part of the hunger waits for me to weaken, to lose. And this mural reminds me, painfully and vibrantly, exactly what losing means.

It would be so easy, the hunger insists. ***Just a moment, and it would be all over. You'd never have to worry about anything again—***

Orange and yellow glass engulfs the Heartless. Flames. The humans learned, early on, that there weren't many ways to slow Heartless down save for burning them. It takes a witch much longer to heal charred flesh. It's their preferred way of dealing with us. *Water for a witch, fire for their thralls,* the baron had said. I shudder at the thought of the pain, of enduring that much agony for so long. Pain is bearable only when you know with absolute certainty it'll end quickly. And that's how I spent the last three years—certain. Now? Now nothing at all is certain.

"What are you staring at?" the deer-dress girl asks me quietly. I skitter my eyes away.

"N-Nothing."

She doesn't seem to believe me, staring at the Heartless over my shoulder.

"It's okay," she leans in and whispers. "I feel sorry for them, too, sometimes."

She turns her back to me quickly. Her admission is so hushed, so forbidden in these halls. But it tugs at my chest regardless. To think a human could pity me—us—after everything we've done, everything I've done. I shake my head. If she knew what I really was, she'd run far and fast from me. She'd cheer as I was burned and my witch purged on the archduke's stage.

Ulla stops us before a door of glass and knocks twice. Uptight-looking guards open it. The sound of a crowd carries on the chilly air coming from the entrance. Ulla turns to us, proffering several silken veils attached to filigree headbands.

"You will wear these, and walk down the center of the Hall, abreast one another. Do not take them off until instructed to do so by the royal family. In addition, you will speak only when you are addressed by the royal family."

"We aren't children, Ulla. We've seen this done for years now. We know how it goes," the Steelrun girl says, breaking her silence for the first time. Her back is so ramrod-straight, her every step graceful. I don't know her first name, but Grace will do in my head.

"I'm simply repeating it, milady. Some of us"—Ulla's eyes flicker to me—"are newer here than others."

"And some of us don't have the patience to babysit country bumpkins." Grace holds her head high and steps through the door. The other girl follows, timid, flashing me a charming smile nonetheless. Charm. That's a good head-name for her. Ulla ushers me after Grace and Charm, and I take my first steps into the dark hall. It's narrow and low, my scalp almost scraping the stonework, but then it opens up into a vaulted cavern. Whoever made this carved it straight out of the stone, stately pillars as big as ancient trees punctuating the otherwise airy space. Light spills from a perfectly round glass-covered hole in the cavern's ceiling. It shines bright sunlight on a stone platform in the center of the room, upon which an ostentatious glass throne sits. And the people are, regrettably, *everywhere.* A crowd hangs at the sides of our walkway, tittering softly and melding with the shadows of the cavern. I can't see their faces, but their dresses and tunics stand out in all colors. Their voices, though soft, echo eerily off the high ceiling.

We approach the throne. It isn't glass at all, but crystal shimmering with rainbow opalescence. How clever! Make the throne shine, and all your subjects will be in awe of you. No gold or jewels can compare to the light the king's seat gives off. No human lawguard can compare to the intimidating celeon guards standing at the foot of the throne. They're the tallest celeons I've ever seen, armed to the teeth with razor-sharp halberds. Grace waltzes right through their parted weapons, and Charm and I scrabble as gracefully as we can to catch up with her. My mouth goes dry when one of the celeon looks at me too long—I know they have good noses; can she smell my Heartlessness? *No, Zera, that would be stupid. If they could do that, Vetris would've won the Sunless War much earlier.*

We line up before the throne and curtsy deeply to the man on it.

King Sref of Cavanos watches me with the deadened eyes of a raven circling a corpse.

It's just one analogy about the king's worth being equal to a single potato. But it has the entire court gaping at me. Either these nobles are easily impressed, or they just don't get out much. If I wasn't a penniless monster in the midst of committing treason, I'd put money on the latter.

With the Brides presented, the ceremony draws to a close, and the king and queen leave the Hall of Time, their guards leaving with them. Prince Lucien stays, though. I watch the prince's profile now that I'm not so nervous, the proud hawkishness of it striking. He isn't as handsome as I first thought, not in the traditional sense, but he's nothing if not arresting. His sharp features demand that you look, but only gently, for fear of cutting yourself on them. It's then I notice with some rampant disgust that I'm not the only one staring at him—practically every woman in the crowd titters and coos at his every sigh of his, every motion of his hand. Did I somehow fall into a hole of vapid unreality between leaving Y'shennria's manor and coming here? It's almost absurd, laughable how much attention he's getting, but then I remember he's the heir to the largest country on the Mist Continent. If this is his everyday life, if he's constantly watched and simpered over to this extent, it's no wonder he harbors such distaste for the court. It reminds me of Whisper, almost. *Whisper.* He's here somewhere, isn't he? Excitement like static runs through me at the thought that he could be looking at me right now, but common sense dampens it. I'm here for the prince, not him.

I tear my eyes away from Prince Lucien promptly; I can't afford to act like just another girl in the crowd. Charm and Grace, however, have no such compunctions as they try to parse the bored look on his face.

"Do you think he liked what I said?" Charm whimpers. Grace turns to me, face twisted.

"You think you're clever, do you?"

"No." I purse my lips and tilt my head. "I *know* I'm clever."

"I thought she was wonderful." Charm smiles at me. Grace scoffs.

"Oh, yes, wonderful. If you think insulting our king is a form of merriment, like some drunken commoner."

"You clearly missed the point of my riveting analogy," I say. "Which I will forgive. Subtlety isn't for everyone. And neither is losing gracefully."

"You arrogant little—" Grace begins to curl her lip, but a noblewoman approaches her with a smile, engaging her in conversation. Soon more nobles cluster around her, then Charm, then me, all of them complimenting us over one another.

"However did you come up with something so prescient, Lady Zera?" A lady fans herself, wafting the smell of her my way. The hunger licks its lips, but I force it silent.

"Did you see how hard the king laughed?" A nobleman shakes his head. "I haven't seen him so amused in years! Not since before the princess died."

"Princess?" I start. The nobleman lowers his voice.

"Were you not told? Princess Varia died five years ago now."

"That's awful. How did she pass?"

The nobles look to one another before the nobleman

leans in to whisper, "Heartless, milady. She was touring the provinces when a band of them ripped her entourage to shreds. It was a great tragedy. We mourned for months. The king never stopped, I think. He used to be so full of life, and yet that all faded when Princess Varia died. She'd always been his favorite. And don't even get me started on poor Prince Lucien. He's been devastated ever since."

Prince Lucien lost his sister to Heartless? Something like pity tries to sprout in me, but I refuse to let it. He can't be a person to me—only a goal.

"Indeed," a noblewoman speaks from behind her gloved hand. "That's why the prince goes on hunts so often."

"Hunts?" I furrow my brows, but the nobles don't say anything more, making some convenient excuse to drift off. The new information swirls in my brain. I only vaguely see Y'shennria come up beside me, face tense.

"You very nearly sabotaged yourself," she murmurs.

"I took a chance," I agree. Y'shennria's icy mask doesn't crack.

"Perhaps next time you'll think twice before 'taking a chance' and stick to the stock phrases we rehearsed instead of spouting something terribly risky."

"Where's the fun in seducing a nation's hope for the future if you can't be a little risky about it?"

Y'shennria gives something like a little groan. There's a beat, and we watch the nobles flitter around one another, spewing compliments and pleasantries with no real staying power. Of course she isn't complimenting me. I'm not expecting to be lauded by her of all people, but a "good job on not immediately being burned alive" would be awfully nice.

"An overly perfumed little bird sang me a fascinating

song," I press. "About Princess Varia being killed by Heartless."

Y'shennria's lips tighten. "I suppose it was only a matter of time before you learned."

"Another little bird, this one with even worse perfume, told me the prince goes on 'hunts.' What did she mean?"

Y'shennria is suddenly solid steel, unreadable. She straightens her back as a noble calls her name, quickly drawing her into a conversation about my performance. Avoiding me? Maybe. Avoiding the question? Most definitely. No one wants to talk about the hunts, and because the gods shaped me out of the curious part of the clay puddle, that only makes me want to talk about them more.

Over the heads of the milling crowd I spot Prince Lucien leaning languidly against a far pillar. If I were a painter or a poet, I'd probably make art about him. Not some sappy love sonnet or romantic watercolor portrait, but a stanza or seven about the way he stands—arrogant, like he's in his own little bubble where nothing can touch him. And the most infuriating part is nothing can; decorum dictates the prince approaches if he wishes to speak, not the other way around. I'd paint his silver vest glinting in the light of the cavern, his sable eyes shadowed by his dark, mussed bangs as he scans the crowd, and I'd point out that his silver vest could feed a thousand, and that too much of his country's future is riding on him to have that much hair in his eyes. I'd flambé him alive in an acid bath of criticisms, and I'm sure he wouldn't care one bit. He's the Crown Prince, after all. He looks like he's above it all, immune to the court's relentless attentions, and certainly immune to the likes of a single loudmouthed Spring Bride.

Beside him stands a pale boy, his skin a bloodless

paper-white color, no pink to be seen. He's perhaps a little older than the prince, with short gray hair from which his pointed, bladelike ears peek out. The size of them startles me—longer than two handspans. That's surely the prince's Beneather bodyguard Y'shennria warned me of. Beneathers are a rare sight aboveground—I've never seen one in the flesh until now. They typically stay underground, beating the fire-breathing valkerax back into the depths. The claymore strapped to his spine is nearly as big as he is—certainly too big to be wielded by anyone his size, and yet he carries it and his heavy ceremonial armor with practiced ease. I've fought enough mercenaries to know the posture of a skilled fighter, and this Beneather is certainly one such fighter. If I'm to get anywhere near taking the prince's heart, his bodyguard has to be removed from the equation. And experience tells me I won't be able to do it by force. Trickery, then. Perhaps seduction will work twice—once for him, and once for his prince.

The Beneather's eyes catch mine. His pupils are so strange—so much larger than any human's. They almost eclipse his bloodred irises, leaving only faint rings around the black. He puts a long-fingered hand on the prince's shoulder and nods toward me without a word. The piece of my heart in my locket gives an anticipatory shudder as the prince looks to me, his face absent of any smile. I'm almost jealous. He doesn't have to force a smile, while that's all I've been doing today.

Prince Lucien hefts off the pillar and begins to move. The crowd parts for him, his bodyguard following in his steps. He approaches Charm and speaks to her, her face reddening. Y'shennria elbows me sharply.

"Don't stare," she whispers. I skitter my eyes away, but I'm not the only curious one. The crowd of nobles continues conversing with one another. Occasionally they glance over to the prince and the girl. It's subtle but effective. I mimic them, stealing a peek every few seconds. One moment Prince Lucien and the girl are talking, the next he's making her giggle.

"They're...*flirting,*" I mutter to Y'shennria. "That's what that is, right? The reddened cheeks, the high-pitched laughter, the crooked smiles. Flirting."

"Obviously," she drones.

"Trees and animal droppings don't tend to flirt, so you'll have to forgive my slowness."

"Could you refrain from being witty for perhaps a *single* minute?" Y'shennria inquires.

"I'd rather eat gravel," I say. She gives me a look. "Sugared gravel, preferably."

Back in Flirt Kingdom, the prince bids Charm farewell, then moves to Grace, who smiles with all her teeth at him. She has very many teeth, and I marvel at the fact no one has slapped any of them out yet. Then I remember they don't slap faces around these parts. If someone comes for you in court, it'll be a dagger from behind.

They talk, laughing together. His smile is so bright and different from his past scowls it strikes me half blind. Is that what it means to be a prince—smiling at nobles you clearly dislike?

"Prepare yourself," Y'shennria murmurs to me. "He's undoubtedly coming your way next."

I watch him tuck a strand of hair behind Grace's ear tenderly. Just a moment ago he looked at her like she wasn't worth his time, and now he's touching her? Is he fickle or simply short of memory? I watch his expression more closely, and the edges of it look worn thin—an expression I saw on my own face in the mirror as I trained with Y'shennria. He isn't fickle at all. He's faking it. The crowd murmurs:

"He always does this—"

"—pays them all special attention, then never settles on one—"

"—what I wouldn't give to have him look at me that way—"

"—a criminal flirt, if you ask me—"

Prince Lucien bids Grace farewell and walks toward us. I lift my chin and tense my shoulders, ready for him to fake interest in me, too. When he's an arm's length away, close enough to touch, the hunger beings to growl madly.

Take his heart, it thunders. **Feast on him. Take him, right here and right now, and you have your freedom.**

Images flash—images of blood and teeth and Father's and Mother's bodies. The pain that's in my every breath, haunting me even now below my bodice—in one fell swoop I'd be free of it. His shoulder brushes against mine ever so slightly as he passes me by without a word. My teeth grow long and sharp instantly, ready to lunge at him, to end our suffering here and now, but I fight it desperately. Amid the raging inferno in my chest is a single moment of cold, clear silence; the smell of rainwater and leather follows him. That scent is unique. The sight of his dark eyes up close; the curve of them, the shadowed corners, the anger within—something about them is familiar. The crowd reacts immediately.

"—slighted—"

"—the first time I've seen him ignore a girl—"

"Is something wrong with her?"

"—the girl of an Old God family—"

"—must've truly displeased him—"

"Now that you mention it, she isn't very pretty at all—"

The words lodge like that celeon assassin's dagger did,

square in my back and burning. They're all watching me for some reaction—but I give them nothing. A snub from a prince is nothing compared to what they'd do if they knew my chest beats empty. I must never forget—no matter the compliments, the smiles, every single person in this room is my enemy.

All of humanity, the hunger whispers. *Our enemy.*

Prince Lucien's gaze lingers in my mind. Those eyes. *Those eyes.* Where have I seen them before? And then it hits me, and I feel like an absolute moron for not realizing the moment I first saw him.

The gods must be playing a joke on me. They played one before, when they allowed me to be born into this world. And now they've turned to pure cruelty.

The thief Whisper, Prince Lucien d'Malvane. They're the same godsdamn person. His dislike for nobles, his voice. The boy I chased gleefully through the streets of Vetris. The boy who, for one fleeting moment, made me feel human again. He's the Crown Prince of Cavanos, the one I'm destined to rip the heart from. I was too nervous, too bent on not failing, to see it before.

With a great internal wrench, I suppress my teeth and whirl around, saying clearly to his back: "Do you enjoy walks about the city, Your Highness?"

The crowd goes deathly still. Y'shennria stiffens beside me, and her ingrained lessons echo—I shouldn't be speaking to him first. It's a breach of etiquette. But etiquette isn't who I'm here to impress. The prince freezes, his bodyguard fixing me with his crimson eyes. Only Whisper and I know what I'm really asking. My stomach churns; maybe this was a mistake. Maybe he doesn't remember me as vividly as I remember him.

"Occasionally," his voice rings out, though he doesn't turn around. "Though I prefer to walk with a lady who knows her manners."

Relief spreads through me like molten honey. A half insult. He *does* recognize me.

"I'll be sure to bring Your Highness one such lady, then, as tribute." I swear I hear him snort at that. He strides away, bodyguard following, and the crowd breathes only when he's gone.

I'm still smirking as Y'shennria yanks on my elbow (is it getting easier for her to touch a monster, I wonder?) and hisses, "Do you have any idea—"

"I can explain," I insist. "But only somewhere without a thousand prying eyes."

Her hazel irises look me up and down for truth. "The carriage, then. We leave, now, and you pray to the Old God your reasons for breaching the most important rule I taught you are sound enough."

We leave the Hall of Time, leave the decadent halls of gold and marble behind. The prince is Whisper—Whisper is the prince. Two very different presentations of the same personality. How did a prince learn to steal so well? How does a thief sneak in and out of the palace grounds regularly? I'm so lost in my questions I barely hear the deep voice on the way out to our carriage.

"You will tell no one."

Y'shennria ducks into a bow instantly, and I look to my side to see Prince Lucien, waiting just outside the door. He nods once to acknowledge Y'shennria, but his dark eyes are narrowed squarely on me. His bodyguard lingers at his side, bloodred eyes lazily fixed on a butterfly settled on his long finger. I know I should bow to the Crown Prince, but the idea of bowing to the snarky thief Whisper is intolerable. My pride makes my back stiff. Y'shennria's sideways glances demand I do, but as I bend my ankle, Prince Lucien scoffs.

"Don't. You didn't do it the first time we met, and if you do it now, I'll start to dislike you."

"I'm sorry." I laugh. "Do you not dislike me already? I couldn't tell with the way you shunned me and left the entire court to dogpile on my good name."

"I warned you about the court, and you ignored it like a fool." He breathes, tired and long, and runs his hands through his hair.

"I'm not in the habit of taking advice from strangers in dark alleys," I retort. His eyes snap to Y'shennria, but she betrays nothing on her face. I press. "I haven't told anyone about you. Yet."

"And you will continue to remain silent on the matter," he says imperiously. "I've worked *very* hard to keep it quiet. I won't have you ruining all those years of effort."

I can't help my laugh. "All right. Say I keep your secret; what's in it for me?"

"Zera," Y'shennria says sharply. "You will speak to the prince with respect."

Prince Lucien waves one hand at her. "I'm taking no offense, Lady Y'shennria. This girl is a…" He narrows his eyes further at me. "*Special* case. And an especially annoying one."

"Don't try to change the subject by flattering me," I sing-song. "Do you know how hard it is for me to keep my mouth shut? Spectacular compensation is the minimal requirement."

Y'shennria watches in absolute stillness, coiled tight, as if she's ready to pounce the moment the conversation turns sour. The Beneather bodyguard chuckles, the sound sending the butterfly on his finger into the air.

"She's not afraid of you, Luc."

"I'm aware," the prince drawls without taking his eyes from me. "And I hope *you're* aware you're blackmailing the prince of Cavanos."

I sigh greatly. "And here I was, thinking of calling this the beginning of a beautiful friendship."

"Your Highness, I—" Y'shennria jumps in, but the prince holds up a hand and silences her. Silencing stern, to-be-obeyed Y'shennria? I hardly believed it possible until this moment. He leans in to me then, so close it's breaking at least a hundred thousand rules of decorum.

"I could run you out of this court with nothing but a single slipped rumor to my bedchamber servant," Prince Lucien says softly. My hand twitches toward my sword—my usual reaction to men threatening me. If this were Nightsinger's forest and he a witch-hunting mercenary, I would've sliced part of his ear off already. I preferred him as Whisper, not this arrogant, insincere royal pain in my ass. At least I could fantasize about punching Whisper without the fantasy immediately being ruined by the threat of dungeon-jail.

"You could," I ponder. "Except then I would stalk the streets, wait for you. Don't you think the lawguards will appreciate a citizen pointing out every fish barrel and shadowy alley a *person*"—I refrain from saying "thief" with Y'shennria right here—"of your caliber would hide in?"

Now his eyes narrow to deadly cold obsidian slits. "You wouldn't."

I smile sweetly. "Of course I wouldn't. Just like you wouldn't run me out of the court with a rumor, right?"

"What do you want from me, Lady Zera?" He snarls. "Gold? Gems? A position of power?"

And now I finally see it—real emotion. I'm getting to him, peeling away a bit of that princely shell. No more arrogance or faked smiles. Something about the way he looks at me—so intently, like a starving hawk on the hunt—makes it near impossible to lie to him. And I lie to everyone. But now my mouth and mind refuse to. Is it deep-seated pity for what I'm going to do to him? Is it pity because I know his fate, and he doesn't? Pity is dangerous. A wildcat doesn't pity its prey.

It's a small mercy that my lie is also a truth. I throw on my best genuine smile.

"I simply want your heart, my prince."

Y'shennria goes terribly stiff and pale beside me. The Beneather raises one blade-thin gray eyebrow. Prince Lucien doesn't so much as blink as he studies my face. The naked truth hangs in the air, too bright. I have to shade it.

"Oh!" I clap my hands. "And perhaps a dress or two along the way. I'm awfully fond of pretty dresses."

"I hate to disappoint you," Lucien starts finally. "But I have no heart to give."

"That's strange. I could've sworn princes who give golden watches to beggar girls qualify for at least one whole heart."

Y'shennria's eyes dart between us, and the prince scoffs. The heart that pumps his blood, moves his breath—that heart that lets him scoff so is exactly the one I need. Something like bewildered amusement melts the stone in his eyes, that bitter, thorny exterior he keeps up, but it's cut short by the newcomer who exits the door just then. In a blur, Lucien separates from me, his courtly reflexes quicker than mine.

"What's the meaning of this, Your Highness?" Archduke Gavik approaches, Y'shennria and I bowing to him only slightly. The prince refuses to bow at all. "A nigh-private rendezvous with Lady Zera? Have you already chosen which Bride will be yours? Impressive. I counted you more particular than that."

It's a sly insult to both of us, but I do my best to look stupid and unaware of it. The dumber Gavik thinks I am, the more I can get away with. Prince Lucien's whole face changes in an instant at Gavik's words. The slight warmth and humor in his expression fade rapidly, until all that's left is the princely mask.

"I don't recall asking your opinion on the subject of my future wife, Archduke," Lucien says.

"Of course not. But your father asked me to oversee this Welcoming," Gavik interjects, smoothing his silvery mantle between two fingers. "Considering the last three have been such...*disappointments* for you."

The prince and the archduke stare each other down in a moment of utter stillness. I know I'm supposed to be polite to Gavik, but I can't get out of my head the image of him ordering that boy to be purged. It's all I can do not to sneer at him constantly.

"Your Graces, please," Y'shennria slides her words in sideways, smooth as fresh cream. "My niece would be heartbroken if you gave her false hope as to the prince's affections. Let us remain on neutral ground until the Verdance Day announcement, shall we?"

Gavik reluctantly pulls his veiled glare from Lucien's more outward one and glances at Y'shennria with white-hot venom. "Indeed. Does your ladyship plan to attend the blessing this week? I didn't see you at the temple last time."

Y'shennria's eyebrow gives a little twitch. It's the same twitch I've seen the last few days every time I've done something to irritate her.

"I was traveling to retrieve my niece then, Your Grace."

"So you were. Yet my lawguards in Northgrove tell me you came and went through the town without joining in the midweek blessing."

Y'shennria's brow grows sharper. "I'm sure Kavar, in His infinite kindness and wisdom, would forgive a woman who's lost her family some urgency in retrieving her last living relative."

"Perhaps He would," Gavik agrees. "But a mortal such as myself, who knows your family's proclivity for heresy, wouldn't."

"You've forgotten far too soon what it's like to lose someone dear to you, Archduke," the prince says coldly. Gavik fixes him with a look.

"I've never forgotten, Your Highness. Not once in fifty-eight years."

There's a taut sinew among the three of them, dangerous and barbed and heavy with history I'm not privy to. Fisher pulls the carriage up to the bottom of the stairs then, and I grab for it as an escape route.

"Auntie, I'm terribly fatigued." I put on my best whiny noble voice. "Can we go home now?"

The tension fractures as Y'shennria excuses us, and we bow. I sneak one last smirk at Prince Lucien over my shoulder, the carriage a welcome rest from pretending to be oh-so ignorant and empty-headed. Y'shennria is quiet as the carriage rolls away from the palace, and I look upon the grand fountains, thoughts swirling in me as the water of the man-made rivers swirls.

Of all the nobles Whisper could have been, it had to be the prince. Of course it was. Fate has never once shied away from the opportunity to take a massive shit on my life, and this time is no exception. Whisper could've been anyone—

someone harmless, someone without a target painted on his back. Someone I could've been friends with, instead of enemies. Equals, instead of predator and prey.

When the palace is just a distant white glow behind the trees, Y'shennria lets out a breath.

"I never thought I'd say this." She looks at me. "But I'm grateful to you, Zera."

"For what?"

"Pulling me away from that man," she says. I gasp.

"You don't like the archduke? Is it the rancid attitude or the genocidal tendencies?"

Y'shennria scoffs. "Both, and more. No one in court likes him. They simply pretend to because they must."

"And Gavik doesn't like you, either."

"Me, particularly." Y'shennria fusses with her sleeve, almost nervously. "Because my family once worshipped a god he hates."

"Is that all? It seemed like a little more than religious differences."

She's quiet, and then she chuckles. "I've taught you *too* well, haven't I?"

Y'shennria doesn't speak again until we reach her manor, and I don't press her. The far-off look in her eyes is the same she gets when she looks at the portrait of her husband in the hall—reminiscent. And I'm not so cruel as to pull a woman who's been through so much out of her last kind haven—her memories.

"Why did you call out to the prince?" she finally asks as Reginall helps us shed our coats. "What secret do you have of his?"

"I was going to tell you, but you heard him—I can't tell anyone."

"I'm very good at hiding secrets," Y'shennria insists. I laugh.

"Don't I know it."

"You *must* tell me. For the good of our goal."

"Trust me when I say I'd love to. But if he finds out, he'll hate me, and that's the last thing we want."

"There's no possible way he'll find out."

"Are you willing to take that chance?" I tilt my head. "Because I'm not. Not after you've done so much to get me this far."

Y'shennria thins her lips. "You must not blackmail him, at the very least. Such a thing will never endear you to him."

"I know it seems odd, but I think it might work to our advantage."

"How? It's a negative thing, a terrible thing—"

"I don't know how, but it's different. You've seen the way the other Brides look at him, the way the court looks at him. All they do is try to get on his good side. He expects me to."

"That doesn't make any sense," she snaps. "If you stick to what we discussed earlier, you will surely succeed. I've poured months of thought into this, all of my years of noble upbringing. But this? This is just a gamble! And we can't afford to gamble!"

"Now that I've met him, now that I've seen him in the flesh—" I swallow at the memory of his proud shoulders, his bitter eyes. "Your plan is good. Thorough. I'm going to stick to it. But that plan is tailor-made for the Crown Prince, the Black Eagle of the West, the archduke of the Tollmount-Kilstead mountains. Not Lucien. Just Lucien."

There's a beat as she considers this.

"What are you saying?" she asks carefully.

"I'm saying..." I clear my throat. "That to be young

and lonely is a terrible thing." She doesn't speak for a long moment, and I press. "I trust you, Lady Y'shennria. You've taught me so much, given much to get me here. But you have to trust me, too."

"I cannot. You're a Heart—" She swallows. "You're inexperienced with this sort of intrigue."

I pull the quartz pins from my hair. "I'm a Heartless."

Reginall and Y'shennria share a look before Reginall bows out and leaves us there in the hall, with only the grand sandclock's ticking daring to break the silence. The disappointment is so bitter in my mouth it burns. Even after everything, all my training, all my effort, I'm still just a Heartless to her.

"If I were human," I manage, "would it be easier for you?"

She doesn't look at me. "Yes."

I walk up the stairs to my bedroom, and she doesn't follow or call for me. And I'm glad. I did everything right. I followed her every teaching, I pleased the king, I gambled with risky moves, earning us the upper hand. I caught the prince's eye, so much so that he waited outside the palace doors for me. *I did everything right.*

But it's still not enough.

Of course it's not enough. Y'shennria's fear is a clear, rational reminder that I'll never be anything but a monster until the day I have my heart returned to my empty chest.

So long as this hunger infects my mind, my body, no human can fully trust me.

I bury my selfish sadness in cleaning Father's sword with an oiled rag. The indents in the faded brass handle, the scratches on the blade—at this moment they feel like the only friends I have. I'd give anything to spar with Crav right now or sing to little Peligli, anything to ease this gnawing emptiness. Father's blade reflects my face back at me—a flash of sunlight over my eyes, and my teeth are long and jagged, my eyes blackened completely, my chin stained with blood...

How delightful those five men tasted, but their screams were more delicious.

ours later, when the three moons are cold gemstones against the black sky, Reginall knocks on my door with a tray of fresh livers, from Y'shennria no doubt, and a strange note on fine parchment paper.

"This message came for you, milady, from the watertell." I thank him and move to close the door, but he clears his throat. "Are you all right?"

"No," I say shortly. "But I didn't come here to be all right, did I?" I hear myself, and I sound awful. Angry. But I can't stop it. "At least in the forest, I could be a monster in peace."

"Could you?" he asks. "Forgive me, milady—I simply find it so very hard to imagine. Never once was I able to live peacefully as a Heartless."

His words aren't a salve over my open wound, but they're a splash of cool water. Of reality. Of the difference between him and me—one a former soldier in a long-ago bloody war, the other a spy in a bloodless court. He makes a little bow and leaves me with my food and my note. I read it once I'm full, once the hunger is muffled.

There, in sharp, curled handwriting and rich ink reads a sentence: *What is your price?*

Prince Lucien sent this, no doubt. Insistent, isn't he? I go to my desk and begin writing with a quill, only to see blood smearing across the paper. Red on white. White like the bandits' skin stained with their own blood, like Mother's neck as she gasped for air, her torn lungs never giving it to her.

My hands are still dirty from the livers. Cursing my clumsiness and my memory that insists on keeping only the nightmarish things, I wash in the basin nearby and return to the desk with fresh hands.

Fresh as they can be, anyway, when I've killed five men.

But as I write this letter, I'm not a murderer. I'm a human girl. That's what Prince Lucien thinks I am. No matter how fleeting, I can pretend for a moment I haven't done terrible things. I can pretend, in so many delightfully illusory steps, that I'm a coy lady writing a letter to the object of her affection and nothing more. It's easier to be her than it is to be me.

I ink my response on a new sheet of paper.

Time. I want your time, Your Highness, and nothing more.

I think back to today. I told him the honest truth. I told him I wanted his heart. He said he warned me about the court.

But I warned him, too.

7

FIRE FOR THEIR THRALLS

SEND THE LETTER out in the morning, before breakfast training. Reginall takes it with a smile and assures me he'll deliver it to the watertell. I'm positive Y'shennria knows the prince sent me a letter, and that I sent one back, but she doesn't mention it at the long table over our plates of perfectly poached eggs and seared ham hock. Unlike my first time eating human breakfast, I can hold my tears in for a good twenty minutes before the pain becomes unbearable. It's a new milestone. But Y'shennria doesn't comment on it, strangely quiet as she sips her tea and I wipe the blood from my face.

"We're going to court, aren't we?" I ask.

"Not today," she finally says.

"But—"

"Today is for blessing," Y'shennria clarifies, getting up from the table. "Be sure to wear white and keep the makeup simple."

She's acting strange, but before I can comment on it she disappears upstairs. Was it what I said yesterday? Feeling somehow responsible, I return to my room and riffle through my wardrobe. I find the pure white dress, modest and yet achingly delicate in its lace hem and ruffled collar. I'd wondered what this was for—it stuck out like a sore thumb among so many gold-threaded, complicated court garments.

Blessing. How long has it been since I've gone? Four years? Five? My gap-filled memory insists Father and Mother and I used to go, to get our yearly blessing for Father's trading business. Was it yearly? Or biannually? I can't remember. But I do recall that before I was turned into an Old God's servant, I was just as faithful as anyone else.

I prayed as hard as anyone else.

Did Kavar know my fate? When I knelt in His temples and listened to His priest's songs, did He know that little girl was doomed to become a monster? Did He know my parents were going to be murdered?

If He did, He never told me. And I hate Him all the more for it.

In the carriage to the temple, I study Y'shennria. She's in a similar white dress, though hers covers her entire neck and the scars there.

"Are we going because Gavik threatened you yesterday?" I ask. Y'shennria straightens but doesn't say anything. In her right hand, half hidden by her sleeve, she carries a rosary of some sort—made of wood, a pendant shaped like a naked tree hanging from it. She rubs the tree over and over, almost nervously. Going to the temple like this means she's being forced to worship a god she doesn't believe in, just to keep up appearances.

To keep Gavik off her scent.

"Why are we trying so hard to please Gavik?" I ask.

"I've told you time and time again—he's the most powerful

man in Vetris," Y'shennria snaps, then falls quiet. "And he hates me very much."

"Why?"

She doesn't say anything more. Noble carriages gather at the steps of the intimidating stone temple. The faint strumming of a dozen key harps wafts out of the main doors. Nobles filter in, all wearing varying shades of white, with only modest jewelry. Some—the more devout, I imagine—carry an iron eye of Kavar clutched in their hands, Gavik included. He ushers people through the doors, greeting them all warmly, or as warmly as an ice-eyed man can. When it comes to Y'shennria and me, though, he doesn't bother hiding his disdain.

"There you are, Lady Y'shennria. I was beginning to think you'd never show."

Next to me, in a motion too small for anyone but me to see, Y'shennria grips her rosary as if for strength, her whole hand covering it easily. She bows to Gavik and walks in without a word and I do the same, hurrying after her. I half expect to be smote by some bolt of god-light the second I walk over the threshold, but nothing happens. Perhaps Kavar's taken pity on me.

I might not remember how often I went to blessing, but the temple's shape is as familiar as an old scar; everything is made of stone, and in the very center is a massive pit, each level of it carved so as to make rings of seats. Even though all the nobles of Cavanos have seemingly gathered, it could seat so many more. Y'shennria takes the opportunity to pick a seat away from anyone else, and I sit beside her.

"It's been years since I've been in one of these," I whisper to her. Her face is so tense. "One time, when I was sick, I remember Mother brought me into a temple to pray for a

cure, but I just ended up vomiting all over the eye." I motion
to the center point of the pit, where a huge eye of Kavar
symbol rests, molded out of pure gold.

Y'shennria shoots me a look. "You lie."

"Of course—I don't have most of my old memories." I
smirk. "But you have to admit, it was an entertaining lie."

She wrinkles her nose, a good change from tensed, at the
very least. But as the final few nobles filter in with the priests,
her anxiety returns, her fingers working over her rosary
faster, and yet more hidden than before. The key harps stop,
and the head priest enters with the royal family—King Sref
and Queen Kolissa in fitted white garments. Prince Lucien
lags behind them in a crisp white overcoat, his dark hair and
eyes contrasting violently, his Beneather bodyguard in dark
chainmail armor, grayish hair pale and short. They're two
perfectly inverted monochrome figures of each other. The
prince and I meet gazes for a brief moment, the locket on
my chest giving a start, but he quickly looks away to situate
himself with his parents at the bottom ring of the pit. Did he
get my letter, I wonder? He looks just as happy to be here as
Y'shennria, but I'm certain that has more to do with who's
leading the sermon than religion itself. Gavik steps up to the
eye altar with the high priest, and they speak in unison, their
voices booming among the vaulted stone ceilings.

"Among friends and among foes."

"Among friends and among foes," the gathered nobles
echo, Y'shennria's voice only a bare murmur.

"From within and from without." Gavik and the high
priest leave a pause for the crowd to echo their every sentence.
"His light of knowledge touches all who are true, his light of
knowledge smites all who are false. In this law we pray, in
this law we ask enlightenment."

I glance at Y'shennria—I've never seen her worship. I never saw Nightsinger outwardly worship, either. I wonder how this compares to worship of the Old God, if there is any at all.

"Lifter of man and lighter of minds, may his enemies part before him as stone before copper, as flesh before blade. Let darkness of the unknown be chased into far corners by His light. In His name, Kavar."

"In His name, Kavar." The crowd finishes strong. Gavik clears his throat, the high priest seemingly deferring to him.

"Ladies and gentlemen of the court, I am heartened to see how few of these seats remain empty. I still remember thirty years ago, when I was but one of a handful to attend blessing. And yet now the temple's bounty is full." He smiles broadly. "This is just proof of how light can be found even in the darkness—that light can be born from war."

A murmur goes around the temple, much softer than any palace whispering. It's strange to think that the city of Vetris held both Old and New God worshippers before the Sunless War. You wouldn't guess that from the state of things now.

"There may come a time when such light is needed," Gavik continues. "Even now, the witches beat on our doors. I'm infinitely pleased to report our Crimson Lady has stopped five witches from entering Vetris just this fortnight. To think they would've been let loose on the streets if not for the polymaths and their invention—" He gives a theatrical shudder. "I quiver with fear at the possibility."

"His bigotry might be strong," I mutter, "but his acting is weak."

Y'shennria doesn't even reprimand me with an elbow to the side or a harsh look. And that's how I know she's really upset.

"But it is this fear that makes us strong." Gavik makes a fist, touching it gently to the gold eye of Kavar. "It is by His knowledge that we endure—we've *endured* the witches. It was five witches this fortnight, but two the fortnight before, and one before that."

The murmurs turn anxious, rapid. The Crimson Lady works perfectly, and yet here he is lying to them, for what purpose? To incite panic?

"Despite our best efforts, they are rising again, their foul magics returning them from the brink!" Gavik thunders. "My lawguards and the polymaths work night and day to ensure your safety from them. Many of you have attended my purges and seen this yourself—so many heathens must be purged, from within even our great wall. True peace is only an illusion, so long as a single witch remains alive in Cavanos!"

It turns my stomach to hear some nobles cheer at this. King Sref's face remains emotionless, the queen's likewise, but Lucien's face brews with anger. Gavik, on the other hand, looks infinitely pleased.

"It is my hope Kavar will aid us and wipe them from the country with His swift justice!"

A louder cheer, but this time it dies down rapidly as Gavik gives center stage to the high priest, a tottering old man in white robes and a split hat with strings of crystal chimes on each end. He raises his liver-spotted hand and the key harps begin to play again. The priests all around the room join in song, in such specific and odd locations I can't help but think it's for acoustics. The head priest raises to his lips one of those copper volume-enhancing sticks I saw Gavik use at the purge and begins to sing, his voice powerful and rich despite his age. I can't deny the song is beautiful, but it's equal parts gorgeous and eerie. It's so different from the witches—they don't sing to their god, only speak.

"I don't recognize the language," I whisper to Y'shennria. She tears her eyes from the altar.

"It's Old Vetrisian," she answers softly. "From when the first d'Malvane king ascended to the throne. With the help of the witches, of course."

"Witches?"

Y'shennria lowers her voice, so much so it's hard to hear her over the priests. "It's Vetris's best kept secret that the d'Malvanes are witches themselves."

"But not anymore?"

"Surely you know how a witch becomes."

And that's all she says, turning back to pretend reverence at the high priest's song. Of course I know—I read Nightsinger's books. Witchblood is a requirement—passed down from parent to child. A witch baby grows but never comes into magic of their own accord. It must be given to them by something the books called "the Tree." The same Tree Y'shennria clings to as a rosary even now, perhaps? But that's where the books became hazy—never detailing exactly how a humble forest sapling could bestow magical power on a witch. It's undoubtedly a metaphor for some sort of magical ceremony.

I watch Lucien, his dark eyes boring a hole into the altar he's fixated on. If Y'shennria knows the d'Malvanes were a witch family once, then surely he knows. Surely King Sref knows, and yet still he sanctions Gavik's purges of his own people.

The song surrounds me, and despite the atrocities Gavik promotes through Kavar, I find myself praying. Not to the New God, but to the dead. To my parents.

This city will kill me if I so much as show my teeth. If that happens, when I come to see you in the afterlife, I hope you can forgive me for what I did. To you. To those bandits. To even this twisted prince I have to drag into the darkness with me.

"Fire!"

The serenity inside the temple shatters. Shouts filter in through the open doors, panicked shouts of *magic* and *fire*. Gavik goes on point immediately, ordering several of his guards to come with him. When he's gone, the nobles begin to titter nervously, King Sref the only one looking calm. Queen Kolissa seems utterly lost, as does Lucien. Y'shennria's knuckles are white.

"It's today? That bastard," she murmurs.

"What's today?" I ask. "What's going on?"

Some of the nobles let curiosity win out over their fear, and they move toward the temple exit. Their exclamations of shock and horror only incite others to leave and see what's going on, too, Prince Lucien included. I get up, but Y'shennria's hand on my sleeve stops me.

"Be careful," she manages.

I approach the crowd at the mouth of the temple, craning to see over their heads. I hear it before I see it—the roar of an enormous fire, guttural and furious. But these flames aren't red; they're a deep black, like shadow come to life. The dark fire consumes everything around the temple in a perfect ring—wagons of hay, abandoned food stalls, stocks of barrels and boxes. I start—it's the same color of fire I saw in Nightsinger's hearth every day for the past three years. Gavik and his lawguards are desperately trying to put out the flames with buckets of water from a nearby pump, but the blaze doesn't diminish in the slightest.

The nobles mutter frantically:

"Black fire, immune to water? It can't be—"

"—witchfire used in the war against us—"

"—the very same that scorched Ravenshaunt—"

Ravenshaunt. The ruined castle Y'shennria showed me on the way to Vetris: her ancestral home. Is that why she isn't out here with me, because it's too scarring to see these flames again? How in the afterlife did she know this black fire was going to happen?

Gavik raises his sword. "Fear not! I've called for the polymaths. Surely they will know how to put this cursed witchfire out!"

I glance around the crowd, only to find Prince Lucien missing. I see the tail end of a white suit flit around a cornerstone of the temple, and I start after it. Sure enough, Lucien's there, searching for something in the western side of the ring of flames. His posture, usually so straight and perfect, is totally different away from the eyes of the court—limber and easy. Whisper's posture. He spots me and glowers.

"Go back to the crowd."

"Is that concern I hear in your voice?" I tease. He rolls the sleeves of his suit up, wrists strong, the slight tendon there rising against his skin beautiful in a way.

Delicious, in a way, the hunger hisses.

"You're awfully cheery, considering we're under attack by the witches."

"We're not. It's not witchfire," I say. Lucien quirks a brow.

"It's black fire that can't be extinguished. That's the very definition of witchfire."

I knit my lips. I can't exactly tell him the witches themselves told me they aren't able to get into Vetris, let alone spell a fire.

"It's just—the Crimson Lady detects all magic, right? So no witch could've gotten through to do this."

"The polymaths' inventions are fallible," Lucien insists. The Crimson Lady isn't, but I still can't say that. "A witch could've slipped through. Or five, according to Gavik."

"Do you really trust the word of a man whose guts you hate?"

Lucien's dark eyes flash. "Are you here to remind me of my enemies at court or to actually help?"

"You doubt I can do both at once? I'll have you know I'm very talented."

"Talented at stalking me," he groans.

"What can I say?" I shrug. "You're an eye-catching person. Very...*visible*. All that dark hair, I suppose. Oh, and the palpable aura of bitterness helps, too."

"And you prefer bitterness in your men? Or just the ones you blackmail for something as vague as their time?"

He's referring to the note I sent this morning. I smirk. Before I can get a word out, a patch of black fire near us spits sparks, the wooden wagon it consumes giving a resounding crack that startles me out of my skin. Lucien looks me up and down.

"You're lucky it didn't get you."

"I'm lucky it didn't get *you*," I say when my breathing resumes. "The other Spring Brides would have my head for not jumping between you and certain fire scarring."

He rolls his hawk eyes, then points into the distance.

"Before we entered the temple, I saw someone suspicious kneeling at a wagon in that direction."

"And what about them was suspicious?"

"When you've patrolled these streets as long as I have, you know when someone doesn't fit into the usual crowd. This was one such person. A robe, hood covering their face."

"Like them?" I point over his shoulder, to where the outline of a hooded person wavers through the fire. It must be the same person, because in an instant Lucien starts running in that direction. I don't even blink before chasing after him, the heat of the fire growing hotter the closer we near, the crackle deafening as it consumes every inch of fuel its dark tendrils can reach. The hooded person bolts when Lucien gets close, and he stops, frantically looking up and down the wall of fire.

"You're not seriously trying to find a way over that?" I yell. He ignores me, eyes settling on the low, still-untouched roof of a stable. Faintly, I hear lawguard voices shouting *"Prince!"* and *"Secure the prince!"* They've figured out he's missing.

"Your Highness," I insist. "I'm not one to give good advice, so let me give you a good idea instead—don't scale the wall of fiery death! Let the lawguards handle it!"

"So Gavik can boast to my father about arresting yet another witch?" Lucien scoffs. He bends his knees and in one remarkable leap clears the fire and reaches the roof of the stable, pulling himself onto it. He looks down at me, lit from the dark flames below. "I think it's time I took matters into my own hands."

He whirls, and I lose sight of him.

"Prince Lucien!" I call. No answer. I try more creative names. "Unimpressive daredevil!" Silence. "Hey, you arrogant horse-arse!"

No response. Whoever set this fire is doing it to make it seem like the witches' fault. Caution tells me to stay. The hunger tells me to go after the prince—he's escaped. He's away from his bodyguard. Now's my chance to take his heart. Or back him up. Back him up? No—if this robed mystery wants to kill him, I just have to be there to take the heart before his body goes too cold.

I get a strange, sick feeling thinking about Prince Lucien dead, the same feeling I got seeing that boy purged by Gavik—disgust at myself, at my thoughts.

Perhaps death would be kinder. The hunger slithers into the forefront of my mind. ***Than what you have planned for Lucien.***

I plant my feet and jump for the edge of the stable's roof, scrabbling desperately to pull myself up. The black fire licks my boots, eager to feed on the white leather, but I push all my strength into my arms and heave. From the roof I can see the robed figure running a few alleyways down, Lucien close on their heels. This city isn't so different from the forest, if you consider the buildings as trees. I've been chased—by man and beast alike—through the woods many times. I leap for the flattest nearby roof I can find, and wait. I listen carefully—the sound of panting is close. The hunger in me smells the robed figure—the warmth below their flesh faint but very much there. The figure tips barrels into the street behind them, Lucien staggering to avoid being run over. He's losing ground, and fast. But I'm still here. When the robed figure turns into an alley below me, I jump down and cut them off, Lucien coming up behind them. The figure looks between both of us, a visible quiver in their shoulders.

"Remove your hood," the prince commands, long braid whipping as he comes to a stop. The figure looks to me like I'll be easier to get past, but I draw Father's blade and smile.

"Try me."

Prince Lucien advances, and so do I, the two of us closing in. The figure throws off their hood suddenly, revealing the terrified face of a young man a little older than Lucien, with hair like spun sunrise and freckles crowding his skin.

"P-Please!" He gasps. "Please, don't hurt me! I was doing

only as they asked!"

"You." Lucien frowns. "I've seen you before. You're one of the apprentice polymaths for the palace."

"Y-Yes, Your Highness!" The man bends one knee to him.

"Who is 'they,' and what did they ask of you?" Lucien demands. The apprentice darts his eyes around.

"Please, Your Highness. If they know I told you, they'd have me run out of the city! Or worse!"

"The Crown Prince can just as easily run you out if you *don't* tell him," I say lightly. "You're in the pits either way."

The man flinches. Lucien flickers his gaze up at me, then back down to the man.

"If you tell me, I promise you it will never get back to your superiors."

"It will!" the man insists. "It always does!"

He's too fearful—it binds him like iron shackles. I hold my sword higher, inspecting the rusty blade. This could be the perfect way to gain a bit of the prince's favor. The man needs more pressure, and I'm in a perfect position to act dangerous, in the same way I always did to scare off Nightsinger's hunters.

"In my experience, Your Highness, cutting someone usually makes them sing the sweetest songs. Say the word, and I'll try to make it only slightly painful."

The man's eyes go wide, and he scrabbles back from me.

"No," Lucien suddenly thunders, obsidian eyes tearing into me. "You will not touch one of my citizens as long as I draw breath."

The full force of his shadows press inexorably on me, and for a moment I feel paralyzed in the same way as when I stumbled into a starving bear in the woods. His protection is fierce, instant. I may not be facing one ton of muscle and claws this time, but it certainly feels like it. I back down quickly.

"As you wish."

Lucien relents, pulling his gaze from mine. He kneels so he's eye level with the man and fishes a gold pouch from his belt, handing it to him. His eyes—so furious before—are now oddly soft, the same softness he had with the little girl. He keeps it so well hidden from the court, but here in the streets with the common people, he lets it shine.

"With this, you can leave the city—the country—before they find you. Now tell me—who are you so afraid of?"

The man swallows, clutching at the purse like it's a lifeline. "The royal polymaths, Your Highness. They—they gave me this powder." He holds up an empty pouch, a bit of green-tinted dust spilling from it. "They told me to come here before dawn, told me to sprinkle it around the temple in a ring, and then to set it ablaze once I heard Kavar's songs!"

"And what were you to get in exchange for this?" Prince Lucien asks. "No—don't tell me. A full position as a royal polymath."

The apprentice nods frantically. "The money, the experiments I could do with their equipment, the prestige—it seemed such a huge reward for as small a thing as starting a fire."

Lucien dips a fingertip into the green powdery remnants on the ground, bringing it to his nose. He recoils violently at the smell.

"*Gods*, what is this stuff?"

"I don't know—they wouldn't tell me. But it smells like bearingbud to me, Your Highness, thrice-refined with copper and tar. Though I've never seen bearingbud produce such dark flames."

"Dark flames," Lucien mutters to himself, then stands. "Go. While you have a head start. The caravans leave from the west gate around this time. You can still catch one if you're lucky."

The man staggers to his feet and bows a dozen clumsy times before tearing through the streets. Soon it's just a thoughtful prince and me, the sound of the roaring flames distant.

"It seems I was right," I drawl, never sheathing my sword. Now would be the perfect time to run him through. "You have a heart after all."

But not for long, the hunger cackles. I can't let him know what I'm planning, so I make my posture relaxed, my steps light as I near him. So close. Just a bit more, and I'll be within striking distance.

"He was simply a tool being used by someone else," Lucien says, dusting his hands free of the green powder. "A tool is blameless. Your eagerness to break him was unfounded."

"There's a handy little something called a bluff, Your Highness." I flush, feeling somehow chastised.

"There's also a handy little something called empathy," he fires back.

"I-I was trying to help."

"That man feared for his life. You told me yourself that sometimes the choices are made for us."

I'm struck silent for once, not a single joke or comeback on my lips. Lucien fixes me with every piercing arrow in his gaze.

"If I ever see you threatening my people again, I will show you no mercy."

"That man started a fire," I insist. "He could've killed people—"

"He was a tool. You break the wielder, not the tool itself."

I freeze in place, all thoughts of taking his heart

momentarily blown out of my head. Break the wielder, not the tool? A tool. I've felt like Nightsinger's tool more than once. I've felt like a thing to be used ever since my heart was taken. Even now, dressed in these silks and lying my way through the day, I'm her tool. *A tool is blameless.* Is it? Is it truly blameless, when it will take a human's heart just to secure its own freedom? Is it truly blameless, even when it took pleasure in killing five men?

"Regardless of your missteps, I owe you, Lady Zera," Lucien interrupts my rigor. "That polymath was on the cusp of getting away before you stopped him."

I swallow hard, my voice cracking. "Don't be modest. You would've caught him eventually."

"Eventually. That's time I don't have. The lawguards and Gavik are looking for me. I'm the prince, after all—I should be cloistered and protected, not learning about what nefarious deeds my royal polymaths have committed." He scoffs.

I watch the black fire burn and, beyond it, the cadre of royal polymaths on gilded horses approaching the flames. Gavik yells something to them, and they descend from their steeds and pull out a nozzle-like tool from their belts, spraying down the black flames with an oily yellow substance. It kills the fire remarkably well, leaving behind the scent of something like old yeast. More important, the royal polymaths make their way toward us as they spray, ensuring I can't take Prince Lucien's heart easily anymore. *Godsdammit!* I squandered my chance. The prince threw me off-balance once. But he won't do it again.

"That stuff works fast on the fire." I struggle to turn his attention from my blade, from me.

"Of course it does." Lucien snorts. "The polymaths, for all their scheming, are geniuses first and foremost. If they invent a weapon, they invent a suppressor for that weapon at the same time. *Pe deresas, in deresas*."

The foreign accent sounds like the Old Vetrisian songs of Kavar I just heard. "What is that?"

"Their motto. Create the power, control the power."

"Why would they do something like this on blessing day?" I muse. Lucien's quiet, staring at Gavik, and it's then I put it all together. "Because the nobles are here."

"They control the land of Cavanos, its resources, and its soldiers," Lucien agrees.

"Make them think witches are attacking again," I say. "Make them afraid."

"Eager for another war," he adds. My stomach twists uneasily. Then the witches were right about an impending war and someone in the city egging it on.

And that someone is most certainly Gavik.

The dark flames are all but dead now, only embers on the cobblestones. The archduke is doing his best to calm the frantic nobles on the steps. The panic is over. Without the firewall, the guards will find us soon. The royal polymaths are finished with their firefighting, returning to Gavik, their backs to me. I have to strike now. Just as I gather the willpower to approach Prince Lucien with my sword again, there's a sudden crack above me, and I look up too late—the fire-weakened beam of a nearby house topples at breakneck speed toward my skull. Time slows, every sound coming into my ears dulled and muted.

"Lady Zera!" I hear the prince shout faintly. My body is suddenly assailed by a brute force knocking me to the ground, hard cobblestones digging into my back and something very warm and heavy pressing on top of me. The smell of rainwater and ash.

I blink, time catching up with me all at once. There, just above, is Lucien's face. Dark, velvet eyes, looking more startled than I feel, his hair like a raven's wing around his face. His striking features might be intimidating from afar, but up close they're enough to knock the wind from me, if it hadn't been already. A thrill runs through me—a soft terror at its heels, like a rabbit frozen by a hawk's attention. His sharp hips are against mine, his legs tangled between my own. He cradles the back of my head, cushioning it from our fall against the cobblestone. No one has ever been this close to me before, this entangled in me. My sword lies utterly forgotten at my side.

The moment breaks, and he pushes off quickly, pulling me to my stunned feet by my hand.

"The wood," he grunts roughly, pointing at the smoldering beam just inches from us. It would've definitely left a dent in me, if not killed me outright. And coming back from death in front of him—in front of anyone other than Y'shennria—would've been more than a little messy. He might think he just saved my life, but he doesn't know the half of it.

Lucien can't meet my eyes, and strangely neither can I meet his. Being killed a dozen times doesn't make my body react any less violently to near-death experiences; my heart races fast and my hands shake. Or is it because of him? Both. I can't tell.

"Th-Thank you," I manage finally. "I would've—"

"It's nothing," he says quickly, dusting off his coat with a sudden zeal.

"Luc! Where did you go?" Prince Lucien's Beneather bodyguard lopes up to us. "You made me walk through the fire to look for you. Scared the humans terribly." The bodyguard spots me with his crimson eyes and bows. "Lady

Zera! We haven't been introduced; I'm Malachite. I didn't expect you to walk through the fire after the prince, too."

"As if I'd dare such a thing with my frail human body!" I act offended. "I scaled the same stable the prince did."

The bodyguard, despite saying he walked through the fire, has no sign of fire damage on him, not even a single singed hair.

Malachite whistles, impressed. "And that's no small jump. Well, well, she isn't afraid of you *and* she can keep up with you. You're in deeper trouble than I thought, Luc."

Lucien ignores him and turns to me. "You were right, Lady Zera. It wasn't witchfire. I'm starting to learn that doubting you has its consequences."

And I'm starting to learn taking your heart might be harder than I thought. I pick up my blade and force a smile. "Let this be a lesson to you—never underestimate a woman with impeccable taste."

"You're choosing to spend time with Luc," Malachite says. "I wouldn't exactly call it *impeccable.*"

Lucien shoots him a sardonic glare. Malachite ushers us back to the crowd on the temple steps, the queen running to Lucien and looking him up and down for any sign of a wound. She sees a scrape on the back of his hand, flustering over it. Lucien insists he's fine, and a guilty blush rises in me when I realize that scrape is on the same hand that cradled my head against the fall. Malachite gives me a sly wink, the cocky bastard. Did he see what happened? He clearly has no sense of decorum—he calls the prince by just "Luc" and talks to him as if they were equals, rather than bodyguard and royal. And strangely, some deep part of me envies him for that, envies how easy it is for him to be around the prince when my every move is calculated and overthought.

If it were that easy for *me*, I'd have his heart a dozen times over by now.

"The witch's evil has been contained!" Gavik exclaims, only to receive thunderous applause from the very impressed nobles. Gavik motions to the royal polymaths, who take generous bows. "A round of applause for these brave men of the mind."

I retreat to Y'shennria, who's tucked away in a corner near the door of the temple, looking glad to be out. The carriages start coming around one by one, the nobles departing with relieved looks on their faces. Y'shennria and I get into Fisher's carriage, silent and weary after our separate trials. I watch the misery outside the window—merchants peeking from their houses only to see their barrels of goods burned, their stalls ruined. They mourn with stiff hands of shock and faces of utter loss. We pass a pair arguing over an open barrel of charred spices, one of the men nearly in tears.

"—do we do, Marix? The taxes—we promised to pay the taxes this month! They'll put us on the street—"

"I'll find something," the other man replies. "I promise you, I'll do anything I can to keep this roof over our heads—"

Our carriage passes, their words petering off. We pass other carriages—the nobles leaving the scene of the fire without a scratch. But the people of Vetris? They're the ones who're going to suffer the most from this little stunt. If Gavik is responsible for this fire, I hate him all the more for it. The color slowly comes back to Y'shennria's stern, graceful face. She openly fidgets with her rosary, stroking the tree pendant's every branch, though her motions are calmer now. She fixes me with her hazel gaze and says only one thing: "I think it's time you met my spy."

8

THE LAUGHING DAUGHTER

I'VE LEARNED BY NOW that Y'shennria doesn't answer any questions she doesn't want to until she's good and ready. I'd call it a lesson in patience from her, but she looks entirely too drained to even consider lessons at the moment. When we're finally inside the sitting room of her manor, sipping on lavender tea and in much more colorful clothes, I dare to say: "Either you're a witch who read the future with magic, or someone told you the black fire was going to happen."

"And which do you consider more likely?" She sips her tea calmly.

"The witch."

"Your manners might be getting better, but your jokes are getting worse."

I laugh, and it catches me by surprise. I didn't realize how good it would be to see her back to her usual exacting, critical self.

"I have a spy inside Archduke Gavik's home," she clarifies. "She joined me of her own volition a year ago. She's quick, quiet, efficient, and most importantly she knows where the archduke keeps his important documents. In fact, I'd be confident saying she knows the archduke best out of anyone in Vetris."

"Do I ever get to meet this girl, or are we going to praise her into eternity?"

"In a few minutes."

We wait, both of us paging through the volumes on the sitting room's massive bookshelves. I leaf through a tome on rare animals—the inked fangs of a mighty valkerax gaping open at me. Its long, sinewy body is drawn next to a human —the human barely bigger than one of its claws. I've read about them in Nightsinger's books, but those never had sketches. They resemble snakes, if snakes also had manes of fur and powerful lionlike legs. Their heads are like a wolf's—feral and yet dignified, with a mouth entirely crowded with razor-sharp fangs. Fangs that almost look like my own in the throes of hunger—jagged and pervasive. They have six eyes, each below the next, and each white as snow. Are they blind, maybe? Seeing this sketch, I'm glad they remain underground, kept there by the Beneathers. They're beautiful but fearsome.

"Miladies." Reginall bows in the entryway, someone on his heels. "Lady Himintell."

A girl in a rose-pink dress and overly curled, mousy brown hair walks in. Her gait is uneven, a limp to her left leg, yet despite that she practically flounces as she walks. She carries a cane made of some sort of ivory, a six-eyed creature's head I recognize now carved into the handle—a valkerax. She flashes a bright smile at Y'shennria and curtsies, then curtsies to me. We curtsy back, and Y'shennria motions for her to sit. Lady Himintell rests her cane against a table and sits right next to Y'shennria, gleefully clapping her hands at the sight of the honeycomb cookies on the tea tray. Their elbows nearly touch, the girl taking a cookie offered by Y'shennria.

"My favorite! Oh, you shouldn't have, Y'shennria."

"Nonsense. It's the least I could do," Y'shennria insists, smiling brightly. Not once does she pull away from the girl, make space between them. Neither is she trembling. I frown as I watch the girl consume a cookie with almost childlike happiness, rocking side to side on the sofa. Reginall said "Lady." But Gavik has no children, and she's far too young to be his wife.

"Hello." Lady Himintell smiles at me. "You can just call me Fione."

"Zera." I return her smile, though mine isn't nearly as sincere. *This* cheerful girl is the spy Y'shennria praises so highly? I was expecting a servant, not a noble. How much does she know about who I am? "Though I was under the impression using first names is strictly forbidden in court."

Fione waves a dainty hand, crumbs flying from it. "I think formality is a little silly considering we're risking our lives together."

"Only *our* lives?" I smile with all my human teeth. "I happen to be risking many more than that."

Fione blinks, a wounded look to her eyes, but Y'shennria snaps.

"That's enough, Zera. She's done more than you have to stem the war, and with much less training required."

I glower into my tea, but Fione's laugh pulls me out of it.

"That really isn't necessary, Y'shennria. I'm sure Zera's trying her best. We all are. We have to." Her last few words grow soft, and her smile wanes sadly.

"Fione told me about Gavik's plan with the royal polymaths," Y'shennria says. "Apparently he commissioned them months ago to create a powder that produced flames identical in appearance to witchfire."

"Witchfire. What exactly is it?" I ask. Fione shoots a look to Y'shennria, who suddenly becomes very quiet.

"It's black fire," Fione blurts. "It burns hotter than normal fire and never stops burning. It can't be put out unless the witch wills it or is killed. It was used…um. A lot. In the war."

Her eyes dart nervously to Y'shennria. Witchfire decimated Ravenshaunt. Maybe it even burned her family alive. No wonder she stayed inside the temple. Just the sight of the stuff that consumed her home would've been too much to bear. It's strange to think the little black flames that constantly warmed my heart on Nightsinger's hearth were capable of so much destruction.

"It's my belief Gavik intended to use this powder to imitate a witch attack," Y'shennria recovers. "He's been doing nothing but sowing unrest and unease toward witches and the Old God since he rose to his position as Minister. When Fione informed me of his request to the royal polymaths, I knew he was going to use it for that purpose alone. I just didn't know when. But I should've seen the signs that it was soon—Gavik was encouraging the nobles to attend blessing more fiercely than usual."

So Gavik really was behind the fire. That bastard! The fire was a show, an act—a ruse to manipulate the nobles and devastate the common people.

"Why doesn't King Sref do anything to stop him?" I ask.

Fione blurts a laugh, then looks to me wide-eyed. "Oh. Sorry. You were being serious."

I quell the irritation rising in my throat. "I haven't been here long."

"Right. Sorry, again. I've spent my whole life in Vetris— it's hard to remember some people haven't."

"King Sref encourages Gavik's behavior," Y'shennria interrupts our tension. "Half because they've been friends for a very long time, and half because King Sref rules with fear. And the more Gavik feeds that fear, the more control King Sref has."

"Queen Kolissa—" I start.

"The queen is powerless," Fione says with surprising force. "Gavik's made sure she is."

"Powerless? She's the godsdamn *queen*."

"Gavik convinced the other Ministers to revoke old traditions granting the queen influence in political matters." Y'shennria stirs her tea delicately. "She was once active in politics, but when Princess Varia died, her priorities shifted dramatically to ensuring her only remaining child stayed safe. From everything—but especially from magic."

"My uncle is just feeding more fear into her about the witches." Fione clears her throat. "Effectively paralyzing her."

"Your uncle," I repeat. "So you're Archduke Gavik's niece?"

There's a pause, and then she nods, curls bouncing. No wonder Y'shennria recruited her. But why would Fione risk betraying such a powerful family member? From what I've seen so far of the nobility, I wouldn't put it past her to be doing it for the thrill, for a change of pace from the stagnant, bloated life of the Vetrisian upper crust. Or, since she's Gavik's niece, she could be a traitor, a double spy, ready to spill our secrets to Gavik at any time.

As if hearing my thoughts, Y'shennria speaks up. "I trust

her wholeheartedly, Zera. And you will do the same."

"You can't tell me what to think," I mutter quietly.

"You aren't here to *think*," Y'shennria fires back coolly, every word like icy razors. "You're here to look pretty, to say the phrases I told you, and to win the prince's *affection*."

How dare she? How dare she treat me like a tool and yet praise Fione so lavishly? I'm risking just as much as Fione—*more*! Fury wells up in me, the hunger begging for me to lunge at her.

She's already lost most of her neck flesh, it taunts. **She wouldn't miss an eye.**

"You will work with Lady Himintell," Y'shennria insists. "She knows much about the court and can help us in our goal."

The imperiousness of it all—the way Y'shennria talks to me and the way she talks to Fione. Two different ways for two different things—a human and a monster. My eyes flash from Fione's faintly smiling face to my own hands—hands that ripped the flesh from five men. She sits like a noble, I sit like a pale imitation of one. Her ladylike mask is impenetrable, and I can feel mine failing as we speak.

I bolt from my chair and march up to my room, slamming the door behind me as loudly as I can. *Immature.* I hear Y'shennria's voice saying that downstairs, faintly. Apologizing for me, like I was the one who did something wrong. I didn't. Nightsinger did, by turning me into this instead of letting me die.

You killed those men in cold blood. Men who were once babies. Men who were once alive. You killed them slowly. Painfully. You played God. You paid death and suffering back with more death and suffering.

You did everything wrong.

Minutes drag on, until I hear Fione's saccharine voice excusing herself and the front door close. From between the lace curtains of my window I watch her get into her silver carriage, willing my despair to burn her as it's burning me alive.

I dream furiously. I dream like a storm—flashes and howling. Darkness and coldness, and then it fades into a precise, perfect view.

I know this place. I'm in the Hall of Time at the palace, the stained glass all around me. But in this dream the glass moves, the battles depicted in the walls carrying on as if they're happening all over again. Red glass blooms as blood flies, humans and celeons spearing witches through and Heartless splitting people open with their fangs and claws. Black witchfire glass flares, burning humans alive. Human fire, orange, charring the skin of the bestial Heartless.

And every glass figure is screaming as they die, a thousand tortured voices ricocheting in my head at once. The Hall of Time shatters with the force of the sound, clouds of glass shards twinkling brightly as they fall all around me, like rainbows made into a deadly snow.

Through the glittering, I see something made of wood. Two somethings. I begin to walk toward them, but pieces of the glass impale me, the pain somehow a thousand times worse in a dream. I know, with aching clarity, that this is a dream. But I don't care. Something in me demands I reach those wooden things. I struggle, pulling my leg flesh free of the glass, pulling my arms from their rainbow spikes. My feet are bare, the glass snow litters the ground and slashes the bottoms of my feet, blood and agony. Still I walk. In shreds, in tatters, leaving a trail of blood behind, I reach for the wooden things—so close I can make out their shapes now.

Two rosaries, each with a tree pendant on the end. So simple. So small. And yet I know of their importance with a terrible certainty.

I reach for them with bloodied fingers, but just as I'm about to touch them, sleep leaves me, and I'm yanked into the darkness of my room again, cold sweat beading my aching body.

The memory of that dream—or should I call it a nightmare?—is quickly drowned by my reality. I spend the next morning trying on dresses in an attempt to avoid Y'shennria, to avoid my childish feelings of jealousy over Fione and her. Ruffles hide so much of my anger. Silk gloves do a perfect job of making my hands look clean, instead of the bloodstained sinners I know them to be. The mirror whispers I'm beautiful, even though all I can see is the twisted, malformed darkness of my unheart bleeding out of my every pore. I refuse to let Maeve in to bathe me, the old woman eventually tottering off with a tired sigh.

There's a banquet this afternoon—I remember Y'shennria telling me about it. And instead of preparing for it, I'm locking myself in. I emerge from my room only to eat the livers in the kitchen, but Y'shennria doesn't once acknowledge me or say hello. She remains in the sitting room, reading. But as I make my way back up from the kitchen, I spot her in the hall. She's affixing something to the wall—a fire-calendar. A slab of rich mahogany wood, thin and yet sturdy, with the dates of the month carved into it in orderly rows. She raises a candle to a date on the wood, the flame barely licking the surface. The heat reveals a mark on the date, dark and implying that day is over. She goes down the line, eliminating the days that've already passed. All that's left between today and Verdance Day is a measly week and a half.

When she's finished, Y'shennria looks pointedly at me without saying a word and returns to her reading. Each dark mark seems as if it's laughing at me, a deafening cacophony of my impending failure. I don't have much time left, and Y'shennria is making that abundantly clear.

What am I doing? There are more important things than my tangled web of emotions. Crav, Peligli. They're relying on me. My own freedom is relying on me. I can be a mopey sack all I want once I'm human again.

I arm myself with a dress worthy of court—red velvet and orange taffeta, like the most violent sunset. A knock at my door brings me out of my thoughts. I call for them to come in, Reginall entering with a sheepish look on his face.

"Milady."

I sigh. "I'm done throwing a tantrum. There's no need to convince me to come out."

Reginall opens his mouth, then closes it. "I am glad to hear it, milady."

I'm quiet. Y'shennria sent him instead of coming herself because he's an ex-Heartless. She thinks he knows me better than she does. Or maybe she's too scared of me to approach herself. I slide on a pearl bracelet, marveling quietly at the rainbow sheen it gives off in the sunlight.

"I can't let anything get in the way of taking the prince's

heart," I say finally. "Not my emotions, not the hunger. Nothing."

"Are you having trouble, milady?" Reginall asks. "With controlling the hunger?"

"You've clearly forgotten how hard it is to control to begin with."

Reginall is quiet, and then: "Perhaps I have. It's been many years."

"You are impeccable with a duster, and a fearsome force of nature with a polishing cloth," I say. "But your burning questions face could use work."

"There was a way long ago, milady—a way we found in the war to suppress the hunger."

"Oh, I know how to suppress it," I assure him. "Devouring a hundred or so still-bleeding things usually does the trick."

"I apologize, I misspoke." Reginall strokes his mustache patiently. "I meant suppress the hunger entirely. Completely."

I swallow. The sky is blue. The Twisted Ocean is made of crystal. The hunger cannot be suppressed entirely. These are all true and clear realities. The hunger is so powerful and pervasive, always. It haunts my dreams, my waking hours. But if that's true—if there is such a way to subdue it—I could feel human again. Whole.

"How?" I demand.

"It takes much practice, milady. And the results—" His voice catches. "There are unintended side effects."

"Like what?"

"The hunger doesn't...*prefer* being subdued. You bleed from your eyes until you lose control, and the hunger resurfaces."

I breathe out. "Bleeding? Like when we eat human food?"

"Yes. Both are such cases of the hunger rebelling against

our actions. Eating human food, suppressing it. The pain feels as though it's meant to break us, doesn't it? As if it's a warning to stop what we're doing."

"You speak of it as if it's a living thing."

"I don't know if it is, milady. I know only what I have felt and seen. For brief moments, those Heartless who learned to suppress the hunger had minds running clearer than a winter stream. No matter how hard a witch commanded them to fight, no matter how hungry they were, they could resist. Not for long, but for long enough. It was a sight to behold, milady." Reginall's eyes light up from within. "Seeing them on the battlefield weeping, resisting—they instilled a great hope in the rest of us that we could fight our fate. Hope that we were still worth saving, no matter what we'd done under the banner of war."

My breath comes shallow. The mere idea of it—of living for one moment free, free of this gaping emptiness as I haven't been in three years, has my head reeling.

"You can teach me." I stand from my chair and grab his weathered hands. "You can teach me to weep as they did!"

"You'll have your heart soon enough," Reginall insists. "And your freedom. I'm sorry to say—but taking the prince's heart would be much easier than learning the ways of Weeping."

It takes a moment for the all-consuming lust for freedom to cool, but when it does, his words ring true. Weeping sounds like a bare shard of freedom, but I can have the whole gem if I do what I came here for. Reginall pulls his hands gently from mine.

"It's better that you don't learn anyway, milady. There are certain...dangers associated with it."

"Dangers?"

He knits his lips beneath his white mustache. "The witches didn't take kindly to the Weeping gaining independence, no matter how fleeting. If they were discovered, if another Heartless betrayed them, their hearts were shattered."

Shattering. Shattering without a hope of ever becoming human again. Dying as a tool, with only the hunger at your side as you leave this world. It's my worst nightmare, second only to living forever Heartless. I shudder, Reginall's faint voice as he bids me good night barely registering. The thought haunts me as I get ready, haunts me even as I descend the stairs, my makeup arranged just so for tonight's banquet. Y'shennria quirks a brow.

"Where's your corset?"

"I tried it on," I assure her. "Five minutes of not being able to breathe was enough, thank you."

"It's the fashion," she insists. "From Helkyris."

"Well now it's the fashion from Helkyris that's in the garbage can."

Y'shennria snorts. "You're being difficult again."

"And unless you'd like me to pass out in my bowl of soup instead of getting any socializing with the prince done, I suggest you let me continue being *difficult*."

She takes in my face and the makeup on it—a red lip tint, and a three-line black pattern beneath my eyes, the little triangles like the fangs of a wolf. Y'shennria wears a deadly sleek black dress, her voluminous dark hair netted down with an intricate nest of silver cords. In the sunset light of the hall I can see exactly how breathtakingly beautiful she was, and is. Her own midnight lines drawn on her cheekbones are small yet elegant, like the tips of tiny bird wings. She wordlessly turns and walks out of the manor to the carriage.

I've made her angry again. This seems to be a trend. I

follow her, pausing at the painting of Lord Y'shennria.

"You've got a beautiful wife, sir," I murmur. "But she's awfully stubborn."

His wry, handsome smile seems to say, *As equally as you.*

I toy with the red ribbons woven in my fishtail braids as the carriage drives. The lack of a sword at my hip eats away at me, but Y'shennria insisted weapons were forbidden during a banquet.

"Have you told Lady Himintell what I am?" I ask Y'shennria. She quirks a perfectly sculpted brow.

"Do you think me mad? As far as she's concerned, you're a farmer girl I've hired to pose as my niece to steal the prince's heart. Figuratively, of course."

"So she thinks you just want to raise the Y'shennria family to power by making me queen."

"Precisely."

There's a beat in which the sunbirds cry to one another, forlorn and melodious.

"Why didn't you? Hire a farm girl, I mean."

"Because you can't control a farm girl." Y'shennria exhales like I'm asking the simplest question in the world. "Humans are...*unpredictable*. Unreliable. They become blinded. They can fall in love—it doesn't matter with what— noble boys, lovely dresses, power, luxury. A Heartless only ever burns for one thing—their own heart. And those who burn don't easily blind."

For some strange reason, that moment Lucien "saved" me flashes through my mind. The weight of him against me, the feel of his warm breath on my skin; it blew every thought of taking his heart out of my head. I was blind then—blind to anything but him.

He's nothing but a means to an end, the hunger hisses.

As we arrive at the palace, the facade of whitestone absorbs the blaze of the peach sunset, setting it aflame. Y'shennria leads me through the doors and into the main hall, the water beneath the floor ruby-laced with sunset beams. The hall is crowded with extravagantly dressed nobles, clothes of mauve and emerald green and seastorm blue, gold and silver threads so entwined and delicate it looks as if the fabrics just sprouted them naturally. I'm nearly blinded by the flashes of the sunset off their precious gems—the nobles clearly saved their best dresses and baubles for tonight. On the opposite spectrum are the modestly dressed servants in black, offering wine and iced fruit on silver trays.

"Why is everyone waiting?" I ask Y'shennria.

"The dinner is still being prepared," she explains. "And lingering in the hall is a type of...tradition. We gather here and watch one another filter in, critique everyone's presentation."

I groan. "That sounds *riveting*."

"It's more for the adults. Not much else is expected of you other than to sit there and look beautiful."

"Do I? Look beautiful?" I bat my eyelashes at her as a joke, but her face remains serious as ever.

"Very much so."

I'm taken aback by the sincerity in her words, but before I can say anything she disappears into the crowd. Knowing her, she'd just been stating a fact. Seawhisper said it herself; I'm the prince's type. That's why they chose me in the first place.

I exhale and lean against a marble pillar in a less busy spot of the bustling hall. If everything goes as planned, the prince will develop real feelings for me, feelings enough to blind him to his own safety. But how genuine can his feelings be, if my entire personality is faked? If I'm just carefully curated bait in a steel trap?

I shake my head and take a wine flute from a passing tray. Why do I care? If I deceive him, then I win this awful game. And winning is all that matters. What happens after the facade breaks is none of my business.

And yet some tiny voice in me chimes up, hoping the prince—no, Whisper—will be smart enough to not fall for me. Whisper is a thief, and I know a thief's instincts. He can't go soft, lose his cloak of wariness. If he does, I'll be disappointed.

If he does, he loses his humanity.

A laugh born of despair works up to my wine-stained lips. "I really am a monster, aren't I?"

Feeling suddenly uncomfortable in my own skin, convinced every person here can tell how selfish I am just from a glance, I walk out of the hall to the west wing. At least I think it's the west wing. Y'shennria had me study the palace layout, but it'd been so huge and my lesson so brief I've forgotten it already. I let my feet wander; the farther I get from the nobles and their chattering, the easier I can breathe. That's all I want—to get away, to be anywhere but here. The wine buzzes through my veins pleasantly as I waltz the vast, rich, and yet nigh-empty hallways, and I wonder back to Reginall for a moment; did he and the other Heartless drink during the war? It's one of the few human things still left to us. I'm willing to bet they got drunk every night, so drunk they'd forget the blood they'd spilled that day.

I trace my own cheekbones, where blood tears would be by now if this wine was anything else. A celeon guard watches me from his post before a door, his violet eyes narrowed slightly.

"Good evening, sir." I smile at him. "How are you faring tonight?"

The celeon grunts, the tentacle-like protrusions of his whiskers twitching. "Just fine, milady."

"That makes one of us." I giggle. When he doesn't crack a smile, I quiet down. "So, what sort of valuables do they have you guarding? Treasure? Or perhaps stuffy, important documents?"

"Pictures, milady."

"Pictures?" I raise a brow. The guard straightens, holding his halberd a little tighter, a little prouder.

"Behind me is where they keep the private d'Malvane family portraits of their dead. I guard them in case of defacers."

"Who would ever want to deface a d'Malvane portrait?" I frown. The celeon cracks a fanged grin for the first time.

"You'd be surprised, milady."

"Would I? I'm a new arrival in Vetris. I hardly know anything about this place, or the d'Malvanes—you don't learn much about the royal family on a pig farm."

The celeon fixes me with a stare. "You're the Y'shennria Spring Bride, then?"

I curtsy with a smile, the wine nearly unbalancing me. "The one and only."

"Rumor has it the prince doesn't like you much."

I look him up and down; no other servant in the palace would dare to say that to a Firstblood's face. Maybe the palace guards are used to speaking their minds more.

"Well, rumor has it that I don't like him much, either," I say lightly. He blinks his large violet eyes.

"Then why are you here, milady?"

"Why are you here?" I shoot back.

"To make a living in this cruel world," he rasps.

"As am I."

He chuckles at this, the sound somewhere between a purr and a snarl. It's cut off as a familiar bellow vibrates down the hall.

"Is that you, Lady Zera?" Baron d'Goliev waves his sunbird-feathered cap madly at me, several other nobles on his heels. He turns to them. "Come, you must meet her—she's a Spring Bride, and clever at that!"

"Kavar's bloodshot eyeball," I curse. I dart my eyes around for a way out, the door in front of me pushed open all of a sudden by the celeon's paw. He jerks his head inside, ears pricking in the same direction.

"Go on, milady. Hide in here. I'll tell you when they're gone."

I shoot him a grin. "You're a lifesaver."

I duck into the dim room, and the guard closes the door behind me with a heavy thud. The door and walls are so thick I barely hear the baron's and his cadre's footsteps, though their voices demanding to know where I went are louder. The guard fends them off with as many *miladie*s and *milord*s as he can, but the baron won't have it. I slide away from the door, tucking myself in a corner of the room in case they do manage to barge in here.

The room itself is so different from the rest of the palace— no marble walls or floors, only soft, polished wood. The curtains are black, not pale green, and no gold decorations or statues stand in this room. It's kept plain save for the walls, which are lined with stunning oil portraits of people long dead. There's a common thread to them—all wear expensive furs, most of them have Prince Lucien's dark raven-wing hair. A few are much younger than the dead should be. The first paintings are faded, worn by time and air, but as the wall extends and the paintings grow, the brighter the hues and

the fresher the canvas until, at the very end, tucked away in
the same corner I stand, is the most recent painting.

The eyes are what take my breath away—her eyes, like
obsidian daggers. There's no mistaking those eyes; this must
be Princess Varia. Though, unlike her brother's blade-eyes,
forged with anger and seriousness, Varia's eyes glimmer with
mirth, like she's keeping some hilarious secret all to herself.
Her broad lips are twisted in a half smirk, but something
like heartbreak rests in the corners of them. Her black hair
is pulled up into an elaborate bun, her dress bright crimson.
She stands before a chair and holds a sheaf of bellflowers
in one hand and a strange white sword in the other. The
painting is so lifelike and distinct I know instantly it's the
same painter who did Lord Y'shennria's portrait.

"Beautiful, isn't she?"

I start out of my skin at the voice. I turn to see none other
than King Sref rise from a chair in the deep shadows on the
other side of the room. I fold into a curtsy.

"Y-Your Majesty," I start. "I didn't know you were here;
the guard didn't tell me—"

"Be at ease." He smiles, face crinkling. "I loathe to admit
it, but I've been here for many hours, since before his watch
started. He didn't know. I hope you won't hold it against
him—Noran is a good man."

"Not at all," I protest. "I thought him g-good as well. A
little intimidating, but I suppose that comes with the job."

I curse my runaway mouth—this isn't the time to be glib.
But the king just laughs softly.

"Indeed." He turns, his pure gold robe whispering over
the wood floor as he approaches Varia's portrait. His salt-
and-pepper mane is tied in three long braids, which are
twisted together in an intricate pattern at several points down

his back. A gold circlet graces his fierce brows—Lucien's brows, and Varia's too. He takes the portrait in with gray, melancholic eyes, as if searching for something he knows is there but can never grasp. I feel almost awkward at his reverent silence, until he turns to me and smiles.

"Forgive me, Lady Zera. I tend to get lost in this painting, much to the chagrin of my Ministers and the queen. I'd blame the painter for it, but the man was a genius—and you can be angry at genius for only so long."

I knit my lips. The nobles said Varia had been the king's favorite, that he changed so much when she died. It's a delicate subject, and I'm in a far more delicate position. Y'shennria didn't train me for one-on-ones with the king of all Cavanos. But I can't remain mute.

Will he mourn for Lucien when I turn him Heartless, the way his eyes mourn for Varia now?

The king asks suddenly, "What moons were you born under, Lady Zera?"

"Um." I scrabble to make something up—my birthday is a missing memory locked tightly in my heart. "The Flint moons, Your Majesty."

"The Giant one-third waning," he murmurs. "The Twins two-thirds full. Good moons. Dreamer's moons. I thought for certain you were an Onyx. Varia was born under Onyx."

He goes quiet, and then turns to me, smile gone.

"What you said to me at the Welcoming—it was something she would've said. She was always so painfully aware of the common people she was to someday rule, more than even I. If she could've heard your quip, I'm certain she and you would've become fast friends."

I should bow and take the compliment modestly. But instead I look to Varia's smirk, so amused with herself and yet somehow broken deep inside. It's a familiar sight—I see shades of it in the mirror every morning.

"I like to think we would've, too," I finally manage. I burn to ask him a thousand things—why he lets Gavik purge innocents, if he knows they're innocents at all, if he truly hates witches and the Old God enough to turn a blind eye to such carnage. But I can't ask him. It would be beyond impolite—it would be treasonous.

King Sref chuckles, the sound muffled by the darkness of the room pressing in on us. "You're just as bad at hiding a question on your face as she was."

I'm thrown by how easily he sees through me, but I make my voice light. "Just the one, Your Majesty? I have hundreds."

"I'm sure," he agrees. Both of us remain silent, knowing if another word leaves our lips it could cross the unseen line that permeates every noble conversation—the line between our real selves and our court selves. Our masks and our faces beneath. The king clears his throat. "If I could ease the most pressing question in your mind, I'd very much like that."

It would be simple to make up something frivolous, something intrusive about Lucien. It's expected; I'm a Bride, after all. Maybe it's a specialty of the d'Malvanes—to make someone feel as if they must tell the truth—because beneath the king's gentle stare only honesty emerges from my throat.

"Why do you let Archduke Gavik have so much freedom to torment your people?"

The king's smile fades, and I brace myself for the certain anger and indignation I've grown used to from Lucien. But Sref is not Lucien. He doesn't get angry. He gets tired— the same defeated tiredness I saw in his eyes during the Welcoming. He doesn't try to dispute it. He doesn't try to argue. He merely sighs.

"Because, milady—he's made me a promise." I feel my face twist, but he speaks before me. "Have you ever lost someone dear to you?"

I nod. "My parents."

"My condolences. But that means you've also longed to get back at what took them from you—at time, at chance, at death itself, if you must."

At five men, the hunger sneers. My hands shake in my lace gloves, and I quickly hide them behind my back. I won't let the king, of all people, see me weak. Shadows carve deep into the lines around his mouth.

"The archduke will find Varia's killer for me. And until then—he is allowed to do whatever he must."

"But your people—"

"The world can rot, Lady Zera, if it means finding my daughter's killer."

His voice is so even as he says it, so calm, and that scares me more than anything else. My very marrow chills, my skin icy with goose bumps. Reality comes rushing in as the baron's voice outside the door crescendos. King Sref's gaze flickers to the door, then to me.

"I hope you enjoy the banquet as much as I enjoyed our talk, Lady Zera."

And with that perfectly crafted farewell, he sits back in a chair against the wall. Taking the hint that I'm dismissed, I turn and leave through the door, light and sound and the Baron's friends staring at me, and for once I'm grateful for it, for them making me move, respond, think of something other than the horrifying calmness with which the king of Cavanos condemned his people so easily to suffering. The guard smiles at me ruefully, a half apology, before the baron— insisting we're late—whisks me away to the banquet amid a tittering circle of his friends.

I cope with the unease the king's put in me the only way I know how—with beauty. Admiring it, enjoying it, taking it in. The dining hall is filled with orb-like golden oil lamps suspended from the ceiling by impossibly delicate chains. The air carries the mouthwatering smells of roasting meat. A massive blackwood table stretches the whole length of the room, the chairs high-backed and seated with silk cushions. I spot Ulla in a corner, whispering to other servants. Archduke Gavik wears an ornate silver robe—laughing and toasting wine with a bunch of old, bearded men, some of whom I recognize as the royal polymaths who put out the fire. The king and queen are thankfully absent, but I see Charm and Grace talking to each other in pretty, laced-up dresses. When I enter, they shoot me looks and laugh behind their hands.

"They think your lack of corset funny." Y'shennria slides up to me seemingly out of nowhere.

"And I think their lack of manners funny," I lilt. Y'shennria's thin lips break ever so slightly into a ghost of a smile I never thought I'd see again. I start to tell her of my encounter with the king, then think better of it; if she knew I confronted him about Gavik, she'd be furious, and I'd like to have her smiling at me for as long as it lasts.

She takes my arm (for show, of course, what aunt doesn't link arms with her niece?) and introduces me to people she considers important; the Minister of the Blood is a squeaky, portly man whose eyes twinkle when I curtsy before him, and the Duchess Priseless all but sneers at me. She's the mother of those irritating blond twins from the Welcoming—no doubt they told her about our little spat, but she can't be openly rude. All she can do is compliment Y'shennria on her dress and "politely" ignore me.

I spot Fione, her curly hair in a low, modest ponytail and her dress a muted beige. It's a far cry from the bright pink she wore yesterday. She uses the same ivory cane carved with a valkerax head. Yet unlike the visit to Y'shennria's manor, Fione doesn't look cheery at all. Her eyes are downcast, her body posture screaming "scared of my own shadow." A noble says something to her, and Gavik puts a hand on her shoulder, gripping so tightly his knuckles go white. Fione recoils into herself even more at Gavik's touch. Even if she's faking shy, that one motion of hers is too real, too instantaneous to have been faked. Her uncle genuinely disgusts her. I might dislike her for naturally being everything I'm not, but at least we have that much in common.

Finally, Ulla rings the crystal dinner bell and announces the entrance of the royal family.

My stomach clenches as the prince walks in. I've learned the sound of his footsteps by now: quick, tightly wound. He's in a black taffeta hawking suit, with a high collar framing his knife's-edge cheekbones. His black hair is braided in one long, silken cord, and his boots are tipped with wicked-sharp gold edges, as are his pointer fingers—a clawlike gold ring on the end of each. My face grows hot at the sight of the bandage on the back of his hand, covering the scrape he got shielding me from the fall. I wonder if it still hurts? If he's in pain?

He'll be in leagues more pain when I'm finished with him, the hunger slavers. I focus on Malachite at his side, silent and paler than snow, with eyes like crimson fire, his breastplate a magnificent ruby-crusted thing. King Sref and Queen Kolissa follow Lucien and Malachite. The queen and king sit first, followed by the prince, then Archduke Gavik. It goes down the line until finally, *finally*, I sit last, Fione sitting just before me. She must be older than me, then. A New God priest comes in and says a prayer, his voice reedy.

"And from the darkness our God did come to us, and with his love gave us knowledge to light our way. He is called He Who Bore Arathess Anew, He Who Did Bring Us Out of Despair, and we say His name with great thanks and joy before our nourishment in His name."

"In His name," the room echoes to varying degrees. The prince doesn't say it at all, and Y'shennria barely mumbles it, her lady's mask pained ever so slightly. The servants bring wine and a starter course of creamed asparagus soup and almond dumplings, and I try not to look like a complete oaf eating. The king speaks to Archduke Gavik, and the entire table pays silent attention to their every word about trade routes, and how "witch aggression" could see a rise in the prices of grain. Gavik turns to Fione and asks her what she's learned from her polymath tutors about trade routes recently.

"I-I think there was something—" She squirms under the attention of the entire table, and her elbow knocks her fork flying. The gesture is too big to be anything but planned, but why is she playing clumsy? The servants go for the fork but I beat them to it, scooping it up and laughing.

"Whoops! I dropped it." I smile. "These Vetrisian utensils are much more slippery than the ones back home."

This pulls a few chuckles from people, and King Sref's eyes gleam amused. Y'shennria frowns, however, and Lucien only raises a single eyebrow.

Fione looks genuinely relieved, and when the king's drawn the attention away from us with more conversation, she leans in and whispers, "Thank you."

"Anytime you want to pretend to drop a fork for inscrutable reasons, I'm here for you, Lady Himintell," I mutter.

"Or should I still call you Fione?"

"Lady Himintell is a better cover. We aren't supposed to have met."

"Does your uncle always publicly grill you on your studies?" I ask.

"Since I was little he's enjoyed inflicting emotional distress on me," she agrees coolly. "It bothered me only until I built my armor. Now I simply pretend it does to satiate his sadism. But it used to make me want to—"

"Run off and hide in the darkest corner you could find?" I ask.

"How did you know?" She smirks.

I hold up my wineglass. "Great minds drink alike."

She laughs behind her napkin, yet I can't tell if it's a genuine laugh or a polite one. She blurs the two so seamlessly. There's a moment in which I pick at my food and she eats hers delicately. The urge to apologize for the way I acted earlier bubbles up, but what's left of my pride drags it back down into the depths. It's then I notice Grace and Charm watching us across the table with sharp eyes. Us? No—Fione. Just Fione.

"Looks like they aren't fans of yours," I murmur. Fione suddenly becomes very interested in her food.

"It's difficult to have fans when you're me."

"Niece of a warmongering archduke," I muse, stirring my pale green soup. "I can see how that'd be a slight problem."

"As if they care about that." She leans out and taps one of her legs with her napkin. "It's the clubfoot most people can't stand."

"And here I thought you were just trying to start a fantastic new fashion trend with that cane."

Her lips twist in a wry smile, but she quickly douses it to

a more modest quiver when Gavik looks our way. He watches us for a moment with his watery blue eyes, but the queen asks him some question that captures his attention, and we blessedly escape his tyranny for the moment. The servants bring the second course—young geese fried in herb oil and lemon peel, the smells mouthwatering and the presentation incredibly delicate. I do a quick calculation—two bites of this and I can push the rest around on my plate long enough to delay my visit to the bathroom until the third course. Seven courses in total. I heave a sigh. It's going to be a delicious—if very long and painful—night.

But what night hasn't been, since I was made Heartless?

I glance at Fione, who eats her food with ladylike precision, a mirror image of Y'shennria farther down the table. She leans in suddenly.

"He's been staring at you the whole time."

I glance to where she's looking—right at Prince Lucien. He starts when our eyes meet, quickly diverting his gaze to his dish. Fione gives a little snort.

"Don't like him?" I ask with a hush, twisting my locket between my fingers to stop it from beating so fast.

"I debuted at the Welcoming last year," she answers. "Against my will. It's because of him I had to embarrass myself walking up that awful aisle in front of everyone. I'm used to people recoiling, but not so many at once."

My deep-seated resentment for her begins to wilt at the roots. How hard has her life been here at court? I can't begin to muster the arrogance to even imagine. Fione downs more wine, shrugging.

"Though he did criticize their disdain for my leg. Loudly. You should've seen the look on their faces—every noble in court being chastised at once by the Crown Prince. Not that any of it stuck in their heads. But for a single moment, after seventeen years of their jeering behind my back? It was glorious." She cuts her goose delicately and yet with an edge of delighted viciousness. I wrinkle my nose, and she tilts her head. "Is something the matter?"

"Prince Lucien keeps insisting he has no heart," I say. "And then he turns around and does something that directly disproves that."

She laughs again, quietly and into her napkin. "I've known him since we were young. He cried so easily—over silly things like someone squishing a spider or one of the palace cats killing a bird. But then Varia died, and…well—" She struggles with her next words, her next breath. Varia. Not Princess Varia. Just *Varia*. Did she know the princess when she was alive? "Varia was the one who always protected him. He got it in his head he had to be tough like she'd been. I haven't seen him cry since the day they delivered what was left of her body."

I try to imagine it: a young Lucien, watching the guards bring the remains of his sister to the king and queen—to him. The pain in my stomach suddenly cuts through my thoughts and the wine numbness all at once. I've held it long enough. I get up and excuse myself. It's much cooler and quieter in the tile bathroom, but the blood tears burn down my face. It's been getting worse since I started regularly eating human food, and tonight is no exception. It ties me into knots around myself, and I bite my lips to stifle my groans. The hunger begs for something real and raw.

I stare at my reflection, at my fraying braids and twisted face. I carefully wipe away the bloodstains with water and practice a smile. No matter how excruciating it is, I have to keep going. Y'shennria is waiting. The court is waiting.

I push out of the door and make it halfway to the banquet before I feel a strong hand on my wrists. Both wrists. Someone's trying to subdue me. Did the gods just decide tonight wasn't going to be Zera's night? I let out a startled yelp.

"Who in the afterlife—"

"Shut her up!" I hear someone hiss, and immediately a cloth roughly forces itself into my mouth. I curse my lack of sword, my excess of wine. I whip my head around wildly, only to see the Priseless twins wrapping my wrists tightly with twine and pulling me into a nearby room. They throw me to the ground—strong, despite their age. One of the twins locks the door behind him. At that moment I desperately wish all the stories humans make of us were true—super strength, speed enough to dodge any arrow. But I'm only a girl who can't die.

"Now." The other twin squats eye level with me, a wicked smirk on his face. "Where should we start?"

I lash out at him with a kick, but he dances away.

"We told you," the first twin scoffs, "not to insult the Priseless family. But you did anyway. Everyone has their place here. You wouldn't know yours, of course—you're a commoner from a pig farm. But we'll help you."

The twins laugh together at that, and I squirm against my bonds violently. I'll gladly take a hand off if it means freeing myself, but I'm versed in swordplay, not escape techniques or brute strength. A twin kneels at my side.

"I think we'll start by making it so you'll never be able to show your face in court again."

He pulls a dagger from his hip, the honed edge of it glinting in the light. I slide across the floor in fear—not of the injury, not of the pain, but of the thought of them seeing me heal, right before their very eyes. If only I had my sword right now! I knew leaving it behind was a terrible idea. I kick at the first twin, but he orders his brother to sit on my legs, and his weight is enough to staunch my efforts.

I flail wildly—I trained in the sword for three years! I've endured agony the likes of which they could never fathom! I won't sit here and let two arrogant little pups take my one chance at freedom from me!

I head-butt the first twin, and he howls in pain and stumbles back. The second one moves toward me, and I feel my teeth growing—out of fear, or desperation, or simply the smell of human so close, I can't tell.

Two delicious morsels of arrogant. The hunger laughs. *What color will their blood be on our pretty shoes?*

If he moves any closer, I'll bite him through. If I can't use my sword, I'll use my teeth. I'll use anything. But before he ever makes it to me, a deep voice rings out.

"Why in the world wasn't I invited to *this* little get-together? It seems infinitely more fun."

There's a resounding crack, and I look up to see Malachite, his arms crossed over his breastplate and his crimson eyes utterly unamused. The door swings wide open behind him, the lock in shattered slivers on the ground. Did he break it? Are Beneathers really *that* strong? The twins freeze, the first one hiding the dagger behind his back quickly and both their faces draining paler than Malachite's skin.

"We were just— She—" The second twin starts. "We found her like this! Someone must've been kidnapping her!"

"We were just trying to help," the first twin insists, his hands shaking. They might be cruel, but they aren't very smart.

Malachite taps his chin. "I see." He moves in to the

twins, putting one pale arm around each of their shoulders and drawing them close. "Well, if you find the person who did this, please let them know: If I ever catch them, I will disembowel them. Slowly. One inch of intestine at a time."

They nod, fear ripe in both their eyes. Malachite shoves them toward the door.

"Be off with you."

When their panicked footsteps are gone, he turns to me. Gratitude is the last thing on my mind as I struggle to my feet, but he wraps a strong hand around my elbow and helps me up. I've never been this close to him—not close enough to see the way light makes his gray mop of hair look threaded with silver stars. His skin is cooler than a human's, like a shaded creek in summer. I flinch away as he reaches for my gag. He meets my eyes—the pupils of them small, for once, is that how they get at night?—and pulls his hands away.

"I suppose you'd want to do that yourself," he murmurs. He saws at the twine around my wrists with a fanged dagger, huge and hefty, nothing like the smooth little things intended for human hands that the blacksmiths sell in the Vetrisian streets.

"I'd say thank you, but that would imply I didn't have the situation perfectly handled," I pull out my gag and retort.

"If you want to thank anyone, thank Luc," he says. "He's the one who sent me to look for you. Dark Below—" The way he says that sounds like a swear. "He's going to be so pissed when I tell him what the little idiots were up to this time."

"I wasn't aware a bodyguard's job includes stalking."

"It normally doesn't. But Luc was concerned."

"That I'd be unable to find my own way to the godsdamn bathroom?" I say it with more venom than I intend, but Malachite just smirks.

"Most people would be flattered to have the Crown Prince

send his personal bodyguard to ensure their safety."

"I'm not most people," I snap, rubbing the twine imprints on my wrists to ease the pain. "Those little *horseshits*. Who do they think they are?"

"This isn't the first time I've seen the Priseless twins terrorize someone they don't like."

"And the nobles just let them do it?"

"The Priseless family has allied themselves with Archduke Gavik heavily. Apparently in human terms that means they get to do whatever they want."

I scoff. There's a quiet before Malachite makes an *O* with his mouth and fishes for something in his pockets. He holds out a folded paper.

"For you. Luc wanted me to give it to you before you left the banquet, but this seems as good a time as any."

"Bodyguards are watertells as well, then? What a multifaceted role."

"The watertells," Malachite stresses, "are controlled by lawguard hands. Luc's being a worrywart—thinks someone might sneak a look at your correspondences. So from now on, I'll be delivering them."

"You're awfully candid about the prince."

He shrugs. "I've never been one for suffocating Vetrisian decorum. Besides, he likes it; I'm the only one who dares talk bad about him. Well, I was. Until you came along."

I act offended. "I do not talk bad about the prince!"

"No, but you don't mince words around him, either. And you dared to speak to him first during the Welcoming. That took *vachiayis*." I quirk a brow. He clears his throat and translates, "Ox balls."

"Lovely."

"Isn't it? I keep trying to tell these humans swear words

sound much better in Beneather."

The noise of the banquet filters in through the open doors, the conversation getting louder as the wine flows longer. The hunger that gnawed at me is muted to its usual background noise, my teeth dull. Malachite looks to me.

"You know, when we're alone, Luc always says you're wasted here, thrown at his feet as an offering."

I ramrod my spine like I'd seen Y'shennria do so many times before. "I'm no offering, wasted or otherwise."

"Really? Because when I came in here you were bound like a suckling pig to be put over a fire."

"They took me by surprise. Trust me when I say that doesn't happen twice."

His smirk is crooked as he bows. "I'll keep that in mind."

Malachite leaves, and I smooth my skirts and put the note into my pocket before following at a modest lag so the court doesn't get the wrong idea. When we return, the banquet is in full swing, a windlute quartet playing in the corner and conversation erupting. Honey-roasted potatoes and brined shadefish await me, but I'm far from hungry. Fione flashes me a polite smile as I sit back down, and Y'shennria throws me a questioning look, but I shake my head minutely. I'll tell her later.

I manage to down a few bites of food, the aching pain immediate, but Fione provides the perfect excuse not to eat. We talk about her lessons, how her mother and father are always traveling as Cavanos ambassadors and are never home, leaving Archduke Gavik as her guardian. Servants take away our plates, replacing them with paper-thin, translucent slices of chilled lamb and green truffle. Dessert is a fluffy cake of crushed chestnuts topped with sweet cream and gold foil leaves. I savor every bite. I suffer every bite.

As I'm trying to figure out how many people a single gold leaf on this dessert could feed, Fione chimes up.

"Forgive me, Lady Zera, but you've looked terribly angry for a while now. Did I say something wrong?"

"What?" I look up from the cake. "No—as if your ladyship is capable of ever saying something wrong."

It's a biting thing to say, a petty thing to say, my mind crowded with the way Y'shennria praised her so lavishly and treated her so kindly. Fione's face falls minutely, but she plasters on a careful, practiced smile over it. The pain from the food pierces at me, up through my lungs, into my spine, the hunger dragging me into the darkness.

Eat her, the hunger froths. ***Take her eyes, her hands, soak in her blood and just maybe Y'shennria will think you human—***

It takes all the energy I have left to stamp down the hunger and manage civil words in Fione's direction.

"Sorry," I say. "I mean—my apologies. Out of all the garbage things I've said in this city, that one took first prize."

Fione freezes over her wine, a little smile staining her lips. This one is clever, catlike, and somehow more real than the practiced ones she gives so freely.

"It's all right. It's sort of a relief, really, if you are mad at me."

"Relief?" I wrinkle my nose. She nods.

"It means you aren't afraid to show me your emotions, like everyone else here. I don't have to guess, or probe, or bribe, or weasel information from your servants or aunt. You just...show me. No work required on my part, for once." She motions with a flat palm to the nobles at the table around us. "In a court like this, where no one betrays their true feelings, you're a restful, easy oasis."

I rile at being called easy, but the way she says it belies no malice, her blue eyes sparkling intently. Not a shade of shyness or pleasantry dims them. I look up to see Archduke Gavik gazing at us, his older, thinner blue eyes intent. He stares like a mountain lion—never blinking, searching for some weakness, some slowness to pounce on. I won't give him that satisfaction. Fione relents, softening and clutching her napkin anxiously, but I smile and nod at him, forcing him to be polite. He looks momentarily surprised, then smiles back.

The archduke and Fione—I'm beginning to learn the Himintells are schemers at their cores.

The banquet concludes after tea and Avellish brandy coffee, and the king and queen take their leave. The prince follows (looking back only once at me in a single piercing moment, Malachite throwing me a wink), and then the rest of us are free to go. People linger in groups in the hall, speaking in hushed tones as Fione and I pass. For once they aren't staring at me, but at her.

Grace and Charm are a good way down the hall, but even I can see them laughing in our direction. Laughing at Fione's limped gait. Something snaps in me at the sight of Fione's expression—strong and stoic yet clearly upset in the well-hidden tightness of her jaw. The urge to punch Grace and Charm is overwhelming. No matter how nasty they're being, I can't let it show. And neither can Fione. That wouldn't be "proper"—that isn't how the Vetrisian court works. You never show your true feelings, no matter how unfair or wrong something is.

Grace laughs a little louder, the sound like serrated bells.

Screw proper.

"Is there something you'd like to say to Lady Himintell,

miladies?" I ask clearly, aiming my gaze at Grace and Charm. The nobles passing us go still, everyone's attention drawn to them, to me. I keep my gaze ice, steel, trying desperately to imitate Y'shennria's most intimidating stare. The two girls go pale, mouths zipping closed as they dart behind a nearby pillar to avoid the attention. I turn back to Fione, and the crowd begins to move again, whispering bewilderedly to one another as they take the grand steps down the palace's facade.

Fione's blue eyes are shocked. "You—you didn't have to do that."

"I can't stand nasty people like that," I snort. "Which is unfortunate, because it seems that's the only sort of person the king stocks this court with."

Fione is quiet, and then, "Let me repay you with a word of warning; in this place, be careful how much kindness you give others. There are some who can and will use it against you."

"Like you?" I ask lightly. "You could betray Y'shennria and me any time you please."

Fione swallows, her eyes settling on Archduke Gavik as he emerges from the palace. Her face transforms in an instant; shy, tender. Easily frightened. But her whisper is strong.

"If I betray you, Lady Zera, then I lose everything I've been fighting for."

Without another word she turns, her cane tapping out a staccato rhythm against the marble floor as she walks over to Gavik. He barely acknowledges her before he walks down the steps to their silver carriage, never once offering her help inside. I watch them go, cursing the man in that carriage with everything I have in me.

"A whisper on the wind tells me you chastised Lady Steelrun and Lady d'Goliev?" Y'shennria murmurs as she draws aside me. Hearing Grace's and Charm's real names throws me off momentarily.

"'Chastised' is a bit of a strong word choice," I say. "Personally I'd go with 'verbally spanked.'"

"Any particular reason you 'verbally spanked' them, or are you just determined to become as unlikable as possible?"

"They were being terribly—how do I put this—*unladylike* about Fione's leg."

Y'shennria's glare, hard before, softens minutely when I say that, and she doesn't bring up the subject again during the carriage ride home. I tell her about the Priseless twins, about Malachite intervening. She looks pleased.

"Prince Lucien sent his personal bodyguard to check on you. How remarkable."

"I'm fine, thanks for asking."

"Oh, hush. As if those two hellions could've done anything to you."

"They would've seen me heal."

"Not likely—they tend to favor hit-and-run tactics. I have no doubt they were…*encouraged* to target you by Archduke Gavik." Y'shennria frowns. "It wouldn't be the first time he's encouraged them to scare off a Bride or two. He thinks the whole Welcoming tradition pointless—would much rather have Prince Lucien arranged into a marriage and be done with it. Regardless, it's good the prince is so worried about you. If this keeps up, he may even take you on the next hunt."

"I'm thrilled. I love hunting…what? Foxes? Wolves?"

Y'shennria breezes past my question. "If the prince wishes to, he takes a small entourage with him on his hunts. He's never done so before, of course, but if he does now, it's a sign he truly wishes you to be close. It'd be the perfect opportunity to take his heart. You and him, alone in his tent. You could escape so quickly once the deed was done. The more I think about it, the more perfect the opportunity becomes."

"You still haven't answered my question, *Auntie*."

The carriage halts before Y'shennria's dark, looming manor, the shadow of it obscuring her face for a moment. She gets out, saying nothing as she retreats into the house. I open the carriage door to dash after her, the insistent question lingering on my lips, but Fisher's faster to answer from his driver's seat.

"Witches, milady."

I turn slowly, and he tips his hat to me.

"Prince Lucien goes into the woodlands and hunts witches every few months. Keeps trying to find the witch and Heartless who killed his sister, if you ask me."

I go still. Fisher sighs deeply.

"Lotsa people say it's for revenge. I just say it's a godsdamn tragedy—killing only makes more killing. Killing only makes more hate, and the world's got enough of that right now."

Five men. Ended by my hand.

Two parents. Dead and gone by theirs.

I swallow the bitterness suddenly welling in my throat, and hurry inside as if the darkwood walls will shelter me from the memories of the day I lost everything.

9

MONSTERS OF US ALL

VERDANCE DAY LOOMS, closer on the fire-calendar with every sunrise. I struggle to swallow my impending panic attack each time I look at it. Ten days. That's all that stands between me and the end of everything.

The prince's hunts, thankfully, don't last ten days. They last exactly three, according to Y'shennria—one for travel to the suspected area, one for the hunt itself, and one day for the ride back. He prefers to kill witches in their animal shapes. But of course he would. They look too human otherwise. Thinking about him doing such a thing sends waves of nausea through me. How did I ever hold a civil conversation with him—with a murderer? But the hunger taunts me; I'm no better. I'm also a murderer, though I'm sure my body count is much lower. How can he care so much for the poor of his nation and yet ruthlessly hunt witches? How many has he killed? I try to put myself in his shoes, perhaps uselessly; if my mother and father's killers were still out there, would I ever rest? Or would I hunt every bandit I could get my hands on until I found the ones who killed them?

If Nightsinger hadn't brought me the bandits themselves, would I be consumed with as much revenge as Prince Lucien?

Yes.

Undoubtedly, truly, clearly—yes.

Maeve wakes me the next day to a breakfast of chocolate drink and spiced buns. My morbid thoughts are thankfully dulled by the precise ritual of makeup and dresses. She helps me squeeze into a sensible sage-green dress. I remember the note from Lucien suddenly, and rummage in the pockets of last night's dress before Maeve takes it away for cleaning.

Tomorrow night, nine half, at the Tiger's Eye Pub. You can have a portion of my time there, blackmailer.

I find Y'shennria on the balcony of her master bedroom, nursing a cup of tea and a book, her lavender dress robe casual and her voluminous tufts of hair left to shine freely in the afternoon sun. It's the most informal I've seen her. She looks startled as I come in, reaching for a starched jacket.

"Did you barge into my room unannounced for any particular reason?" I show her the note, and she quirks a brow. "In the city? Absolutely not."

"Why not?" I set my fists on my hips. "There are a dozen dark alleys I could take his heart in."

"I can't guarantee your safety outside the noble quarter. Or your escape in one piece. You aren't strong enough to lift his body in secret all the way back here. You'd take his heart, come back to the manor, put it in the jar, and then what?"

"Lead Fisher to Lucien's body," I insist. "And then we put it in the carriage and leave, back to the Bone Road, back to Nightsinger."

"You think it will be that easy? Any lawguard's wandering eye blows that plan to smithereens."

"You've taught me how to be seen," I say slowly. "But I taught myself how to go unseen."

Y'shennria thinks on this, then shakes her head. "No. The Hunt is a much better option. Safer."

"If I fail at the Hunt, there's only one day left after that. Who cares about what's safe?" I throw out my arms.

"I do," she snarls.

"Why? I'm a Heartless. I'm the thing that killed your family."

"Witchfire did that," she corrects, jaw tight. "Not Heartless."

"Then what about those scars on your neck?"

At this she falls silent, staring into her tea.

"You can't fool me. I know the shape of those scars," I press. "Those are Heartless teeth marks. I've seen them before. I've…I've made them before."

She shuts her book with a soft, final note and puts it on the table, moving slowly, as if to avoid startling me. Like I'm some wild animal. Dangerous.

"What does that matter?" she asks.

"It matters." I harden my shoulders. "Because I don't care about what's 'safe.' I just want my heart back." I clench my fist. "That's all I've ever wanted."

Y'shennria doesn't move, doesn't blink. The hunger never relents. ***Heart or no heart, you'll always be a monster***, it sneers. Magma needles of pain run through my chest at its dark words, so abrupt my throat curls around a bitter, dissolving laugh.

"But that's the thing, isn't it? Even if I get my heart back, even if I delay a war, even if I return two hearts to two children's chests—I'll still have blood on my hands. I can't undo what I did." I force myself to look up at her. "So don't. Don't bother trying to keep a monster safe. Throw me to the wolves. Throw me to the lawguards. But don't ask me to wait a moment more, because that's far crueler."

Y'shennria's looking at me differently, in a way I've seen only when she looks at Lord Y'shennria's painting. Tenderness. Heartache. Regret. Fondness. All things that shouldn't be aimed at me.

"I am nothing if not cruel." Her words contradict her expression completely. "The Hunt is safer. You may go to this clandestine meeting with the prince. But you will not take his heart. It will be done at the Hunt."

"Why?" I demand.

"Because I said so." She raises her voice minutely, enough to puncture.

I feel like someone's scooped out my innards, spread them on hot coals. I turn and storm from her room, fury and agony warring like dark gods in my head, in between the gaps of the hunger's mockery.

I try to drown myself in reading a children's storybook from the impressive library in the manor, but even there it haunts me—a picture of a Heartless, all fangs and claws, limbs unnaturally long, tearing through the woods after a child, its eyes wide and feral and blacker than night, no whites to be seen. A Heartless consumed by the hunger. I've lost sight in all the silks and pretending; at the core of it all, this thing on the page is what I am, and they are the children who should be running from me.

To escape this monstrous fate, I have to condemn Lucien to it. Will he mourn, I wonder? Will he rage as I did when I was first turned? Will his life be a hopeless darkness he tries to cover with light words and pretty jokes, as mine is? Will he curse my name?

Will he hate me as I hate me?

Outside my window I watch Y'shennria's stable boy, Perriot, play with two other children; servants from other manors, not starving like street orphans, yet not dressed richly like nobles. They hold hands and circle a leather ball, joyously singing what sounds like a children's rhyme at the top of their lungs;

"One kick, two kick, find the head,
One jump, two jump, hide in bed,
Someday soon we'll end them all,
Bring water for a witch,
And fire for their thralls."

When the triple moons rise, I bathe, and Y'shennria has Reginall dig me something out of her closet from when she was my age—a black cotton outfit, with pants and loose sleeves and a long cloak, perfect for concealment while still enabling one to move quickly. When I ask where she got it, she changes the subject. When she's gone, Reginall tells me with a twinkle in his eye that it's from when service in the Wildwatch was mandatory for noble children, before the Sunless War. She was a scout. Y'shennria in the Wildwatch? I can hardly imagine it—elegant Y'shennria on the cold, rugged island continent—the Feralstorm—where all the world's magical creatures are monitored and maintained by the group of skilled rangers. Her scout outfit fits me barely. I fix my hair back and pull the cloak over my shoulders.

"Do not take his heart. Do not give away your status as a Firstblood," Y'shennria warns me on the steps of the manor as she adjusts my hood. "You can cross the channel between districts without being seen if you follow the watertell pipe system."

"You're awfully knowledgeable about sneaking around Vetris for a proper lady," I drawl. She smiles faintly, a fraction of my dark mood lifting at it.

"I wasn't always an old woman."

She ushers me off, and I venture into the dusk air, the Twins trembling in the sky as they rise red. The Blue Giant is a paler azure tonight, smooth like the surface of honey—a mellivorous moon. The tangled maze of copper watertell pipes that spans the length of the channel separating the noble quarter from the common quarter is difficult to balance on, jump over and under, but it's not unlike navigating through the roots of a thousand metal trees. Shops and stalls are empty, folded over with colorful blankets for the night. The only people who remain working are those in the flesh-houses and the priests and priestesses of Kavar at the temple. The flesh-house assigns a man to hawk their wares outside the building—and tonight he decides to hawk at me.

"Come now, miss—let my pretty boys show you how a real man kisses!"

I call back, "No thank you—I'm saving my first kiss for a dashingly handsome fellow by the name of Success!"

The man chuckles, and I leave him to enter the west square where Kavar's temple looms. The eye of Kavar on the very top spire throws a long moonlit shadow, engulfing my every step. Two priestesses sweep the stairs, gray robes immaculate, necks rimmed with crystal pendants, faces placid and absorbed in their work. They look so...normal. They're fed by the temple, clothed by the temple. The celeon guard who presided over the d'Malvane portraits—Noran?—

his words echo in my head now. *"To make a living in this cruel world."* That was his reason for serving the king. Are these priestesses the same—simply trying to make a living? I know of the demons that lurk beneath their domestic peace—intolerance, hate. Or is that simply Gavik? Are these priestesses taught to hate by their religion or by the archduke's influence? Or do they both combine to create unstoppable machines of war?

How many purges have they swept the stages of? How many songs have they sung of the Old God's worshippers deserving death?

The priestesses see me staring and wave, smiles bright, beckoning. I turn, the tail of my cape whipping behind me as I move on.

The sound of a celebration meets my ears, the edges of a crowd leaking into the streets. I follow, morbidly curious—is it another purge? Soon I'm surrounded by what feels like every person in Vetris—old and young, drunk and sober. I was wrong; this is no purge—this crowd sings, dances, all of them wearing some sort of white mask, the eyeholes outlined by the same symbol of Kavar. Massive waterdrums in horse-drawn carts thunder out a beat, the windlutes sighing a cheery song.

"Here, lady!" a little girl chimes, offering me a mask from a basket of them.

I take it and ask, "What are we celebrating?"

"Verdance Day is almost here!" the little girl insists. "Kavar blesses the water pumps, so we can have a good growin' season and good health! Or at least, that's what Father says."

Take her apart, the hunger lilts seductively. ***She's weak, delicious, and barely able to put up a fight. Look at all***

these humans—distracted by their happiness. Use it against them.

Unnerved by my silence, the little girl trots away. The white mask in my palm seems to cackle at me with its open mouth. I don't want to wear it, but it's a very good disguise—better than the hood around my head. I clip it on and slip into the nearby Tiger's Eye Pub. Music blasts from a trio of key harps in the corner, pipe smoke blurring the high ceiling. The barkeep is a broad celeon, his furred chest bared, his ears studded with long silver chains ending in little bells, and his blue arms stacked with copper bangles. A busty woman smiles and offers me watered beer. I ask for wine, sipping from my tin goblet and watching the polymath in the corner. He's with several others, drinking and laughing.

It hits me then that the metal coffin I saw drown that boy when I first arrived was mechanical—no doubt the polymaths made it. They made the water pumps that give the city plumbing, sewage, and irrigation for their crops outside the wall. They made the watertells the lawguards and nobles use for communication. Half of their inventions seem made to improve killing, the other half made to improve living. The humans' technology is a rather dangerous conundrum. I think of the witchfire that destroyed Ravenshaunt, the Heartless spell that saved my life—I suppose magic is no different.

In the shadows behind the polymath's table sits a young man in a deep hood. His eyes gleam hard, like obsidian freshly polished. Black leather armor, a cowl, ever-confident posture. Prince Lucien. Even pretending his hardest to be a commoner, he doesn't blend in entirely, that noble upbringing still clinging to him. I can't help but think of his hunts, his role in witch death. His heart is my goal, but I must never forget he's taken lives with his hatred.

Does he keep count? Does his number haunt him as my own haunts me?

I get up and walk over, settling in a chair opposite him. The music is just enough to cover our conversation.

"And here I thought you and Malachite were born attached at the hip," I lilt. Lucien looks up at me and snorts.

"I managed to cut the cord this once. He kept insisting he come. Something about how 'watching the two of us is like watching the most entertaining play,' or similar nonsense. I don't doubt he's followed me out here, lurking in the shadows as he likes to do."

Damn! The possibility of that silver-haired, smarmy bastard watching means I can't try anything on Lucien. Y'shennria wins this round, but the idea of holding all our cards for one day is ludicrous with how much we stand to lose. If a good opportunity presents itself tonight, I have to try, bodyguard or no bodyguard.

You can make it sound as noble as you like, the hunger sneers. *But in the end, you're just hurrying for that heart of yours—*

"You don't drink?" I cut off the hunger and motion to his glass of water. Lucien narrows his eyes.

"No. Not anymore." He laces his fingers together on the table, eyeing the mask covering my face. "You look prettier than usual. New makeup?"

"I was so ready to declare you have a heart." I click my tongue. "As it turns out, it's just a lump of coal in there."

At the next table over, a brawl is brewing, two men glaring holes into each other. Lucien leans back in his chair. "You take so many stabs at me, I figured you'd appreciate a stab back once in a while."

"Oh, I do. But only aimed at a nonvital organ."

"Implying your beauty is a vital organ of yours?" He scoffs. "I took you for many things—troublemaker, inscrutable. Not once did I consider vain."

"You forgot selfish," I add. "And demanding of your time."

"This demand of my time is nothing compared to the daily demands you make of my patience."

"One can only hope someday I'll blossom from an awful harridan into an undemanding, demure, boring high lady."

The two men begin to argue, drunk voices steadily rising. Lucien's cowl moves, an eyebrow quirked. "Is high lady a metaphor of some kind?"

"Don't be ridiculous. As if I possess the intelligence to construct metaphors."

"I've seen you do it at least twice," he points out lightly.

"By the New God, the secret's out; I'm fully capable of *thinking*!" I lament. "There goes my courtesan career."

"It was over the moment you blackmailed the Crown Prince of Cavanos," Lucien murmurs as he leans in, eyes gleaming with something like amusement.

"Is the Crown Prince not enjoying the price of my blackmail in the slightest? And here I thought it'd be entertaining for one of us at the very least."

The drunk men at the next table jump to their feet, throwing anything within reach at each other: mugs, bread crusts, their own shoes. Lucien suddenly whirls his cape in one fluid motion, the two of us covered from a wayward splash of beer. Inside the dimness of the cape, he pulls his cowl down, a smirk crooking his lips.

"You know, if you're regretting it, you could always beg my forgiveness."

I laugh too loud—but the fight outside our cloth haven

drowns the sound. I slide up my mask and smile sweetly at him. "The only time you'll ever see me beg, Your Highness, is when my body is cold and dead and on the pyre."

There's a moment, our eyes roving over each other's faces, our grins mirror images of each other. That rainwater scent of his is faint but very much there, a welcome relief from the smells of the tavern. We're so close I've no doubt our eyelashes will tangle any second, but Lucien's expression suddenly hardens, and he puts careful distance between our faces. The locket under my shirt trembles violently. His heart is no doubt still, unmoved. I'm so rooted in the moment I barely register the sounds of the celeon barkeep kicking the drunken men outside. Finally Lucien snorts, pulling his cowl back up and lowering his cape. I quickly put the mask back on, watching as his eyes grow progressively duller.

"A pyre, hmm?" Lucien ponders. Before I can speak, he does. "I've only ever been to one funeral, and I'm not keen to go to any more."

He means Varia. I lace my fingers between one another, determined not to tread this dangerous ground again. Once with the king was enough. Lucien swirls the water around in his glass, the lamplight reflecting as rainbow shards over his skin, over the bandage on the back of his hand.

"Much to my utter disgust, I find myself owing you yet another thank-you," I brave the silence. "For sending Malachite to stalk me."

"He *is* very good at that," Lucien agrees softly. "Just as the Priseless twins are very good at hurting unsuspecting Brides and using their family's influence to make them stay silent about it." His dagger eyes glance up at me. "I warned you about the court."

"Say that one more time and try to act surprised when I explode from it."

"If you exploded here and now, all my problems would be over. Well." He thinks about this. "At least eighty percent of my problems. It's like you don't have ears. Either that, or you don't believe in obeying your Crown Prince."

"I don't believe in obeying anyone, Your Highness." I smile. "Least of all the entitled."

"Entitled," he murmurs. The waitress comes by, offering us more wine, but the prince refuses it brusquely. I take more, eager to drown out the hunger that's slowly crawling its way up my throat.

"I used to drink," Prince Lucien repeats when the waitress is gone. "I was thirteen—angry at the world. I'd spend my days drinking until I couldn't feel anything, let alone the pain."

I'm quiet. He doesn't continue, so I ask the burning question.

"Does it hurt?" I motion to the bandage. Lucien looks surprised.

"I wasn't aware blackmailers cared about the well-being of their victims."

"If you die, I don't get any more of your time." I clear my throat. His surprise dims, a half-cocked smirk replacing it.

"It hurt when it first happened. But I had more pressing matters on my mind then."

"Like saving a beautiful damsel."

"You think so highly of yourself," he says, but unlike Grace, it's without ire. Just a clear, simple, slightly bewildered statement. I take his water cup and raise it to him in a toast.

"If I don't, who will?"

He snorts, a rare almost-laugh. "So unwavering. You're most definitely Lady Y'shennria's niece."

Those words burn in the nest of lies smoldering where my heart should be. I get the fleeting, impossible thought that it'd be nice if I really were related to her. If we really were family. If somehow, someday, she could treat me as one of her own.

But not in this life.

"I don't want you thinking you owe me something just because I pushed you out of the way of some rubble or sent Malachite to guard you," he insists, black eyes razor-sharp once more.

"Fantastic," I agree. "I do prefer not owing anyone anything, ever. Makes things much easier at the inevitable end."

The prince studies me, or rather, my mask. My eyes behind the mask. It feels as if he's trying to peel away the layers of my defenses, my secrets, like a bird of prey peeling back skin and muscle from a kill. To redirect the intensity of his gaze, I point at the sword on his hip. It's of strange make—white metal, and very gracefully wrought, with a basket handle carved like a nest of snakes. It looks somehow familiar.

"Is that yours?"

"No. I stole it," he drawls.

"Aha! I knew it! Your stealing wasn't entirely selfless." He goes quiet, and my sardonic tone flattens. "It's a very pretty sword, is all I meant."

"Varia left me two things—this sword, and the crown. The latter wasn't meant for me. A part of me hates her for giving it to me almost as much as for leaving me alone."

That's why it was familiar; the sword in Varia's painting and his sword are the same. The stone wariness in his usually guarded expression vanishes—eroded by years of mourning, leaving only a young man behind. Not a prince, not an heir, not a target, but a brother. A boy. A human who's lost as I have.

"And so you carry her sword around." I grip the hilt of Father's sword on my hip, tracing the grooves with my thumb. "Hoping beyond hope that maybe someday she'll come back to get it. Hoping someday it'll be gone from your waist because she took it back—because she's as alive as you are."

The prince's eyes move to Father's scabbard, his face unreadable.

"You're not the only one who knows what it's like to lose someone," I say. "Or to desperately, foolishly hold on to whatever tiny scraps you have left of them."

Prince Lucien drinks in the silence that falls after my words. He finally gets up, putting two coppers on the table, and leaves out the door. I follow. The cool night air kisses my flushed cheeks as I look around for him—finding him leaning against a stack of barrels. He looks so empty, despondent, like the first bitter snow of winter, like the first time I saw him—standing imperiously in front of me during the Welcoming. That wine might have been a little *too* strong, because I get all sorts of ridiculous ideas in my head about cheering him up, making him smile.

"If you want, we could be friends," I say. "Instead of blackmailer and blackmailee."

"That's the worst joke I've heard from you yet." He snorts.

"I'm serious," I say. "You saved me. Twice. The least I could do is not force you to spend time with me."

"What if I want to be blackmailed?" he asks. My head shoots up, and he catches my eyes with his own. "A prince can't have friends. He can have subjects, certainly. But he can't consort with those subjects, lest they influence his decisions. Lest they try to manipulate him for their own gain or assassinate him."

His words sound rehearsed again, like they were said

to him instead of independent thoughts he's had. It almost sounds like something King Sref would say.

"But if a prince is blackmailed into spending time with one of his subjects..." Lucien smiles sadly at me. "Then what choice does he have?"

The loneliness in his voice claws at me like a starving wildcat.

"The Welcoming," he continues, staring up at the three moons, the heavenly orbs reflected in his obsidian ones. "After you gave that answer and looked at me—like I was equal to you. I could tell in your eyes; you weren't afraid. Of me. Of anyone. And that's the exact moment I knew you'd be a thorn in my side."

His arm crooks above me against the barrels, his shadow blocking the moonlight from my face as he leans in.

"But now I'm not so sure. Are you a thorn? Or are you a flower?"

The heart locket on my chest thunders against my skin. I'm still, terrified any movement of mine will be uncontrollable. He's still a human, and the hunger is still very much within me, begging to end him where he stands.

He'd open so easily under your fangs.

This is the perfect place—quiet, no onlookers. A short jog to Y'shennria's manor, and I'd have his heart in the jar in no time, despite her overcautious fears. It's his freedom for mine. My freedom, Peligli's and Crav's, and delaying a war on top of all that—for his heart. A prince who's never stepped foot out of Vetris, who lives alone, locked away in the insincere world of the court and his own mourning—shackled to a witch and forced to fight for her. Forced to live somewhere dark and isolated, forced to become one of the very monsters who took his sister from him.

Forced to live with this dark hunger.

It was so easy a week ago. But now he has a face. Now he has a story. Now he stands here, looking at me as if I'm the greatest mystery in the world, his eyes both sad and hungry—starving for something he's never known the name of.

Challenge. An equal. A friend. He's starving for it all.

Starving for *me*.

10

A LIAR'S DANCE

THE VERDANCE PARADE BREAKS the spell over the two of us as it passes our hideaway behind the barrels. Lucien watches it, then reaches out for my hand and tugs me toward the dancing crowd and blaring music. The hunger in his eyes isn't gone, but it's hiding.

"Vetris doesn't celebrate much anymore," he says. "It's all purges, not parades. Join me for this rare occasion, would you?"

I should pull away. I should stab my sword through his chest and take his heart while we're still hidden. But the music, his face lit by the moonlight, that strange thrum in my locket beating relentlessly whenever it's just him and me—I haven't danced in three years. The drums call to me, beg me to revel with them like a girl without a care in the world. Just one dance won't kill me. Just one moment of genuine happiness amid a storm of lies.

I let him lead me into the parade, his hand so warm and broad compared to my cold one.

Dancers in long white skirts line up behind the carts, whirling madly to the music. This celebration feels somehow older—a deeper tradition than the strict temples and blessing days of the New God. The dancers move out, letting parade-goers shuffle into their places and continue the dance. Lucien slides in, his movements perfectly in sync with the others, more lithe and graceful than anyone. When he reaches out to me as the music shifts, I swear I see his dark eyes grinning above his cowl.

"This is the partner sequence of the dance," he calls. "If you'd do me the honor."

"Y'shennria didn't teach me this one," I protest. He shakes his head.

"It's simpler than anything in the court. Just follow my lead."

"All right. But I'm warning you—I'm a terrible student. I ask all sorts of questions and make a thousand mistakes."

"Is that a threat or a promise?"

"Both!"

His steps are light, the crowd moving in the same patterns, their arms raised and their knees bent. Their feet and his move so fast I can barely keep up, but I grasp the basics of it—a quick turn, a joining of hands of the partners, and then they rotate around each other. The world spins with Lucien's face as the center point, his obsidian eyes practically sparkling out of his hood. This is the happiest I've ever seen him—all that wariness, all that bitter armor, cracked and discarded. It's like he's another person entirely out here, among his people, sharing in their traditions and their joy.

The end of the dance demands one of the couple hold the other around the waist from behind. It's then I notice who our dancing neighbors are—young couples, old, but all of them glowing with affection for each other. Lucien snakes his arms around my waist, gingerly, careful not to tighten and truly embrace me. His heat looms behind me, tall and against my spine.

If I were a human girl, perhaps this wouldn't be my first time feeling such a thing. But it is, and it's terrible and terrifying and terrific all at once. The hunger keens for me to whirl around and sink my sword into him, but I can hardly hear it over the rushing of blood in my ears and the frantic beating of my heart locket.

And then, just like that, the dance is over. Lucien is the first to pull away, immediately, like he's touched hot iron. He clears his throat brusquely as we move out of the parade to catch our breath, letting others dance into the center.

"I wasn't expecting a cinfalla ending technique," he grumbles. "I thought they stopped doing that years ago."

"You've done this before, then?" I ask. "Sneak out to a Verdance parade and dance with the world's most alluring woman?"

"Implying that's you, of course," he drawls.

"Who else?" I laugh. "The Crimson Lady doesn't even come close—she's got too many sharp angles and all red is a terrible makeup look."

Behind the mask, his eyes narrow, but in a smiling way. Or at least I think they do. I could be seeing things, or wanting to see things. Both are equally dangerous and equally useless to the looming end point, the goal of all of this. That's what this is, I remind myself. A goal—a means to an end. Not a dance, or a blazing night spent with a darkly handsome boy—but a plot. A ploy. A lie.

We breathe together until we even out, and then he speaks, watching the remnants of the parade pass us.

"When I was younger, Father would disguise me in peasant clothes and wear some himself. And then we'd venture to this parade and dance."

I'm quiet. The dour, serious, witchdeath-bent King Sref, *dancing*? I can hardly imagine it.

"That was before Varia died," Lucien continues. "After that…we stopped. But he was the one who taught me how to blend in with a crowd. He taught Varia, too."

"Did he teach your prodigious stealing skills?" I tease, trying to work some light into his dark memories. He shakes his head.

"I learned those on my own. Varia always talked about it. She read these novels about a thief who stole from the rich and gave to the poor."

"The Midnight Gifter," I blurt. "I read those, too."

He looks surprised. "All of them?"

"All of them. They were my favorite. A little cheesy and over the top, but a good book series is always a little of both, don't you think?"

"Perhaps." Lucien goes quiet, and then, "I think she secretly wanted to abandon her title of Crown Princess and become the Midnight Gifter for the rest of her life. Or at least become someone who could help the common people without consequence. She hated not being able to do anything about our people's suffering more than anyone."

"And you?"

He scoffs. "Before she died, I couldn't have cared less if some orphan I didn't know died in the street from starvation. I was young and selfish."

"You were a child—"

"Ignorance doesn't excuse cruelty." He cuts me off cleanly. "I had my toys, and my puddings, and my horses. I had no care for the outside world."

"But then she died," I say. Lucien nods.

"And when she did, I threw myself to the streets. But unlike before, when I'd get lost in the Verdance parade, Father never came to find me. He was too wrapped up in his own grief to care about me anymore. He hired Malachite, raised him to guard me, afraid he'd lose me to witches, too. But that was the extent of his attention. The more time I spent in the streets, the more I realized there were boys exactly like me who lost sisters every day, but to stupid things—not enough bread, not enough clothes, the common cold. Things that are preventable.

"So I started stealing. Well, it'd be more accurate to say I watched other children steal. And I copied them. And then I started copying the better ones. And then I became one of the better ones." He pushes his sweat-dewed bangs out of his eyes. "What about you? How did you learn?"

There's an urge in me to tell him the truth. But I shrug instead. "My story is much less tragic. There wasn't anything to do where I grew up. Collecting beautiful things made me feel better about life. In short, I learned by being selfish."

"Don't we all," he murmurs. After a moment he holds up a crystal hairpin that's oddly familiar.

"Where did you get that?" I paw at it, but he holds it up high. I step in to him, desperately grasping for it, but he keeps it just out of my reach. I lean in closer, so close I can feel the heat radiating from his chest, his smooth neck.

"From the Welcoming." He smirks down at me. "When I bumped into you."

I jump for it, but he holds it higher, our chests colliding roughly on the way down. Blood rushes to my cheeks and I sputter. "How did you—in front of all those people?"

"I told you—I became one of the better thieves."

"You've clearly never seen Lady Y'shennria angry," I say. "Or you'd wet yourself. And then give that pin back right away."

"Y'shennria has dozens. I'm giving this one to that girl," he insists.

"The one you gave the golden watch to?"

"The one and the same. She might look timid, but she knows how to haggle in Vetris's black market. The gold she makes from my trinkets goes to keeping the younger orphans alive."

"I was wondering why you had such a healthy urchin population in Vetris," I muse. He extends his elbow to me like a nobleman might to a lady.

"One more walk about the city with me, then? I promise we'll be home by curfew."

I laugh. "You're a liar. A very pretty liar, but a liar none-theless."

He rolls his eyes and begins to walk. For one lucid, moonlight-kissed moment, I stroll with Lucien arm in arm, flush with the dance and drunk on my own humanity, drunk on the illusion of freedom I have right now underneath this starry sky, surrounded by this labyrinthine city. The thought of taking his heart surfaces once, twice, but I fight it back down to the depths, refusing to let this moment be ruined. Just one moment of being human—is that too much to ask?

But that's what I said to myself before the parade dance, too. I'm getting greedy. As I admire his hawkish profile, proud and severe, the hunger refuses to be ignored.

If he knew what you were, he'd split you apart with that white sword of his. Hunt you, like he hunts the other monsters.

I pull my arm from his suddenly. It's true. The prince *would* kill me if he knew what I was. His sword gleams cold on his waist as he turns, brow furrowed.

"Is something wrong, Lady Zera?"

"I-I just remembered," I say. "Who we are. You're the Crown Prince, and I'm a lady. It isn't right to act so close."

Lucien's face falls. "Act? Is that what you think this has been? I'm not acting." His gaze turns searing. "Are you?"

Yes.

"No," I start. "It's just—"

He leans in, suddenly close. The smell of him—mixed with sweat and night air now—dizzies me, infects down to my marrow and sets it ablaze. He's so human. So dark and svelte and lean, his lips incredibly close and incredibly alluring. A kiss. What would it feel like, to kiss a prince, a boy, a bird of prey? To be close to someone, gentle with someone, after three years of nothing but regret and pain?

"If I were to kiss you here and now," he murmurs, voice rumbling in my chest, "it would not be an act."

He presses into those last few inches of distance between us, and the hunger ambushes me from nowhere.

MINE! it screams, growing my teeth long and hazing my vision with red. *MINE AT LAST!*

With the fragments of clear sanity I have left, I thrust my arms forward, pushing him away. Lucien staggers back, and the heat between us goes instantly cold.

"I—" I swallow acid regret and relief all at once, thanking the gods for the mask that hides my face, my jagged teeth. "I can't. It's not right."

Prince Lucien looks incredulous—not with me for pushing him away but with himself. He looks down at his hands as though he's unsure whose they are. And then suddenly, before I can scrape up a joke to patch the wound, a shrill scream breaks the air. Lucien's head snaps up to the source—a derelict house we'd been approaching.

"Not the market," he whispers through clenched teeth, and dashes beneath the ruined wood of the doorframe. Flustered and worried, I follow. The whole house is charred black—a victim of a long-ago fire. The screaming emanates from beneath us somehow, and I'm baffled until Lucien yanks open a trapdoor I thought was a scorched pile of wood. He leaps down and I follow into a barely lit tunnel lined with brick. The screams get louder, joined by yelling and rough orders being shouted. The clank of armor.

It's all so sudden and jarring—so surreal as Lucien draws his sword and I draw mine. We were at peace not a minute ago, weren't we? Time stood still in Nightsinger's forest, but here it leaps and bounds forward.

The tunnel opens up into a cavernous room, though it seems small, since the floor is choked with a mass of writhing, panicking people. Ramshackle stalls selling food and cloth are overturned, the crowd itself dressed in nothing more than rags—this must be the black market Lucien was talking about. Between the rags shines silvery lawguard armor as they beat down the crowd with oak batons. Children cry as mothers shield them, men forced to the ground and pinned by their arms, celeons with their furred hackles raised, daring the lawguards—some of them celeon themselves— to come close. And the smell of blood—blood on foreheads, blood dripping from broken noses. Blood in pools beneath motionless bodies. So much chaos and fear sends the hunger salivating within me.

And above it all, standing on a lip of brick flanked by lawguards and oil lamps, stands Archduke Gavik. He watches the chaos with his pitiless watery eyes, watches his lawguards drag off screaming, kicking people, his expression bloated with satisfaction.

"Bastard," Prince Lucien hisses. "This way!" He calls out to the crowd, ushering some of them to the entrance we just came from. I'm frozen, and Lucien barks at me. "What are you doing? Help me get them out!"

The smell of human blood seeps into my nostrils, my teeth growing long. The crowd undulates, panic making their eyes wide like cattle doomed to the chopping block. Lucien slams a hand on my shoulder.

"Now, Lady Zera! Before more die!"

His warm touch chases the hunger away, releasing me from its grasp. There's a fraction of a second in which I marvel at just how clear my head is—the hunger blown out like nothing more than leaves in a storm. The prince is right. These people are in danger, and five men are all I can bear on my conscience.

As soon as the hunger leaves, it surges back like a dark tide.

Selfish, the hunger cackles. *Even saving these pitiful people is just for your own peace of mind.*

I put my arms around an old woman clutching at her headscarf and lead her down the tunnel, her grandchildren sobbing on her heels.

So weak. Soft, weak bones, easy to rip apart. A simple meal.

She can't ascend the ladder—too slow, too frail, people pushing over her in their frenzy to get out. I wait for a break in the crowd and wrap her arms around my neck, ascending the ladder with her clinging to my back, desperately fighting the hunger's desire to consume her. I pass her thin frame off to a young girl with startlingly blue eyes and a long robe.

When I jump down again and make it back through the tunnel, the lawguards are frozen in a perfect circle around Prince Lucien, who's torn his cowl off, revealing his face and long dark braid. Gavik's laughter rings through the cavern, the crowd's moans and cries muffled by its sheer volume.

"And what do you think you're doing here, Your Highness?" Gavik asks.

"Leave these people alone, Gavik," Lucien grits, his white sword drawn and ready to strike whichever lawguard lashes out first. "They've done nothing."

"Nothing but steal and murder," Gavik insists. "Some of them are witches, Your Highness. Surely you want to see these monsters brought to justice?"

"How do you know they're witches?" he snaps.

"The Crimson Lady, of course." Gavik smiles with all his teeth. "Or do you not believe in the veracity of the polymaths' efforts?"

"What I believe means nothing." Lucien's voice is an oil fire—ever burning, ever growing. "These people are trying to survive."

"By selling stolen things in this dilapidated little black market!" Gavik tuts. "I'm doing this for the good of Vetris, Your Highness. They're criminals and witches besides. You'd do well to remember that, before I'm forced to throw you in the dungeons with them for dissenting."

"I'm your Crown Prince." Lucien narrows his eyes. Gavik laughs.

"If you defend a thief, that's forgivable, but defend a witch or Heartless—Crown Prince or not—and you're a traitor to the New God." The archduke inspects his nails lightly. "Punishable by the temple's laws."

"How many of them are witches?" Lucien presses, stalwart amid the bald-faced threat. "What did your red tower tell you?"

"Oh, I can't remember." Gavik thinks. "Seven? Eight? Perhaps ten. It seems my men have killed"—he takes a moment to count the still bodies—"thirteen here, but then again, three of those were thieves, suckling like leeches on the underbelly of Vetris."

"Look around you—these are starving people, people whose livelihoods were ruined by my father's poor economic choices! If anyone should be punished, it's him."

Gavik laughs again. "Are you suggesting I jail your own father? I knew you were rebellious and stubborn, my prince, but I had no idea you were treasonous as well. You're almost starting to sound like Princess Varia—foolish little thing that she was."

Lucien flinches, balling his swordless fist, and I press down the seed of rage that sprouts in me. How dare Gavik talk about Varia like that in front of him? I won't let Lucien's pain go to waste—I motion as many people as I can toward the exit while Gavik and Lucien talk. And then suddenly, Gavik's voice booms.

"Lady Zera! I'd recognize that bosom anywhere. Wave that little hand of yours one more time toward that tunnel and I'll have my men shoot it off."

"Lady Zera," Lucien barks, without turning to look at me. "Leave, now."

"And abandon you to face this rancid dog's anus alone?" I scoff. "Not a chance in the afterlife."

"*Rancid dog's anus,*" Gavik muses. "You're more creative than any Bride we've had thus far, I'll give you that. But I'm quite serious about the shooting."

I swallow my grim laugh. "You don't know me at all, Archduke, if you think the threat of a lost hand will frighten me."

Lucien starts for me, stopped only by the lawguards' swords pointed at him. "Lady Zera, no—"

"Then allow me to test your resolve," Gavik says coolly, and at a flick of his fingers a lawguard archer at his side takes aim with his crossbow and fires faster than I can move. The bolt sears like iron, cracking the bones of my left wrist and leaving behind a bloody, tangled hole of flesh and nerves. The pain is so thunderous and instant it knocks the wind from me, serrated daggers sawing at my skin each time I try to breathe in. A scream runs through the crowd too close to me, my blood splattering on horrified faces. I tear at my midnight shawl with my teeth and wrap the cloth around the hole.

"You—" Lucien's face darkens, looking from my wound to Gavik's face. The fire in his eyes sears, his voice suddenly fierce and hoarse, a force of nature. "It is time you learned just how little forgiveness I give those who've hurt my subjects."

He raises his sword, looking ready to lunge at the lawguards all around him, at Gavik above him. He can't. He's outnumbered, and even if Lucien is the Crown Prince, Gavik of all people wouldn't hesitate to hurt him, jail him—

"Is that all you've got?" I call out to the archduke, hiding the desperate edge to my tone. Desperate to distract Gavik from Lucien. When did I get so protective of a human? "Or do you not have the *vachiayis* to come down and finish the job yourself, milord?"

Gavik frowns at the Beneather word, his confusion buying enough time for another celeon citizen to slip to the exit.

Suddenly he raises his hand, and the archers point not at me but at the people fleeing behind me.

"Stop where you are!" he bellows. "By order of the Vetrisian lawguards, you are under arrest!"

The running crowd freezes. My body moves before my mind does, standing between them and the archers, throwing my arms out to make myself as big as possible.

What are you doing, you pathetic worm? The hunger snarls at me. *What in the gods' name do you think you're doing?* If I get riddled with arrows, I'll be "dead," unable to show my face at court anymore. But I can't stand by again and watch Gavik kill people like he killed that boy at the purge. I'd never be able to live with myself if I sacrificed this whole crowd for my freedom.

"Kill them with impunity, Archduke," I shout. "But kill me, and you'll have killed a Firstblood. And the king's favored Bride."

"You are nothing. You are expendable." Gavik looks down his nose at me, staring, his six icy words ricocheting.

They will try to tell you that you aren't good enough. Y'shennria's words ring in my head. *This is a lie. You are an Y'shennria. You have always been good enough.*

I hold my head a little higher. "Then expend me. But do it quick. I get bored easily."

"Lady Zera!" Lucien shouts—I'm surely imagining the ragged worry in his voice. "Stand down!"

"I'm afraid I can't do that, Your Highness," I say without tearing my eyes from Gavik's unblinking glare.

Gavik mutters something as he looks at me, the crowd nearly too loud to hear him. Lucien takes a step toward me, but the lawguard circle around him tightens, and Gavik sighs as he suddenly turns his attentions to the prince.

"Don't you want to see these witches dead, Your Highness? They killed your beloved Varia, after all. What if one of those escapees was the one who controlled the Heartless that did it? You can't let them flee from their long-overdue justice."

Lucien narrows his eyes to hard, midnight slits. "The justice is mine to dole, not yours. And not with innocents as victims. My father might be all right with such causalities, but rest assured—I am not. And my father's reign is more than half over. Mine will be long, and longer of memory."

It's a not-so-subtle threat. Gavik's eyes dart from Lucien to me, and then he laughs.

"Very well. You may play folk hero this time, Your Highness. But I'd like to remind you that the people of Vetris don't know how to wield swords. They don't know how to kill Heartless. They don't know how to drown witches. They don't own a single scrap of white mercury or the machines that make it. But I do. I do many times over."

His own threat lingering, Gavik turns and leaves through the arch behind him, every lawguard following suit until all that remains are terrified, bleeding people and their darkly furious prince.

Gavik's words linger in my head. Not the angry ones, not the snide ones. But those words I could barely hear, an assertion of my character, his eyes narrowing as he uttered them.

He'd said, *You're not afraid of death.*

It takes a good hour to clean up the bodies and bandage the wounded. In the crowd I spot the little girl Lucien gave the gold watch to, but she fell during the stampede, her left eye ground into a sharp corner. The bandage over her eye quickly stains completely red. Some aren't so lucky—arms broken by reaching for a weapon to defend themselves, a leg or two crushed beneath the panicking stampede. But the people who are untouched come together in a way I've never seen before—fast, prepared. The vendors pitch in their wares—herbs to disinfect, thread for gaping injuries, blankets to rest on. Kettles of hot water are warmed over fires, fresh gauze and blood-soaking wool produced from nowhere. Those good with stitching close wounds, others move bodies dead and alive into quiet, restful places. Young children sing the younger ones to sleep, and I'm hit with an overpowering wave of nostalgia as I'm reminded of the nights I used to sing Peligli to sleep. Celeon hold down those who thrash in pain as tourniquets are applied, passing around flasks of strong celeon liquor to ease nerves.

It's nothing like a purge, nothing like the barbarity I'd come to expect from the people of Vetris.

A celeon woman with a flowing turquoise mane hands me a clay flask, smiling.

"For you, in gratitude. The finest *yolshil* this side of the Tollmount-Kilstead mountains. Very delicious, very strong."

I sip at the flask—the taste of something like ginger and rose apples warming my insides. "Thank you. But I did hardly anything."

"You risked much by putting yourself between the archduke's wrath and us."

"It was no great feat."

The celeon chuckles, though her face is too weary to

move with it. "We have a saying: Modesty kills as a drought does—slowly and from within."

"I'll keep that cheery thought in mind," I croak. The celeon pats me on the back with one clawed paw and drifts off, passing out more clay flasks. A figure in leather-clad armor parts the crowd—Prince Lucien. When he sees me he hurries over, lowering his hood and squatting at my side.

"Lady Zera, there you are! I've been looking everywhere for you." He's winded. Two shards of me fight—one of them happy he's concerned for me, the other dreading it, dreading what it means, what it stirs in me.

"Save your worry for a sweeter girl, Your Highness," I tease, my cheeks burning. The *yolshil* is stronger than I thought it'd be. Lucien doesn't enjoy the joke, frowning.

"I will worry for whom I please. Is your wrist all right? Did you get it looked at?"

I switched my shawl bindings out for clean gauze when no one was looking, just to maintain appearances, though by now the wound is long healed. I tamp my smile down, pretending to wince instead. "If by 'looked at' you mean some lady came along and poured herb watcr in it and sewed it shut with her mercilessly huge needle, then yes."

"It's my turn to ask you; does it hurt?" His expression is strangely soft as he looks me over. *Why?* Why is he looking at me like that? It's tearing me apart. I take a huge swig from the *yolshil*. Maybe booze will lessen the pain.

"Not anymore. Is that girl you give the trinkets to all right?"

"She'll live," Lucien says. "But life isn't kind to girls on the streets of Vetris with only one eye." He falls quiet, golden firelight pooling in his dark irises. "You didn't run when I told you to."

"I might be a lot of things, Your Highness—a joker, a lightweight, a fool—but I'm not a coward."

Lies. A coward by nature—killing unarmed bandits, taking this boy's heart for your own gain, for the easy way out.

"Undoubtedly." Lucien curls his fingers around my uninjured hand, his palm rough. "You're far braver than anyone I've met before."

It stings, coming from him. It soothes, coming from him. Pain and pleasure mixed, as if my brain can't decide which one to embrace. Lucien's serious expression doesn't lift.

"Chin up, Your Highness," I say. "We won this fight."

"Lucien," he exhales. "Call me Lucien."

I start—first names are for friends. He can't be my true friend. I can joke about it, it can be a farce, but it can't come to honest fruition. Not him. Anyone but him.

"Lucien," I whisper. The tavern's wine was water compared to what I'm drinking now. The world blurs, the heart shard in my locket aching strangely as Lucien's dark gaze pierces through me.

"It looks like you two stole my thunder."

The moment breaks, and we look up at the voice—it's the girl in the robe I passed the old woman off to. Her blue eyes glimmer as she lowers her hood to reveal curly, mousy-brown hair and a rosy-cheeked face. Her cane is missing, but her robe hides most of her uneven gait.

"Lady Himintell," Lucien breathes. "What are *you* doing here?"

"I could ask you the same thing, Your Highness." She raises an eyebrow at the gauze around my wrist. No doubt she wants to ask if Y'shennria and I planned for me to be here, but she can't while Lucien is standing right next to us.

Lucien? The hunger slides in. *You mean the target. The prey.*

"I told you to stay out of your uncle's business." Lucien narrows his eyes at her. "But again and again you ignore me. Do you really want to be hurt that badly?"

"If I do, it's none of your concern," Fione snaps, and then as if realizing who she's snapped at, she calms herself. "You shouldn't be here, Your Highness. You know as well as I my uncle will take any chance he gets to lash out at you."

Lucien glowers at her. There's something between them I can't quite put my finger on—some resentment, some history. More history than just Fione being shunned at her Welcoming, that's for certain. Fione turns to me and plasters a smile on her face.

"If nothing else, the two of you make a lovely couple. But this is a *very* poor spot for a date, if you don't mind my saying."

A couple? A fleeting, impossible thought. It's dangerous to say anything to her, to give away even one inkling that I know her outside of formality. Thankfully, Lucien asks the next question for me.

"You knew Gavik was going to be here, didn't you, Lady Fione?"

Her smile doesn't crack. "Of course. He'd been talking about it for weeks with the captain of the guard, taking walks in our lily garden and hashing out all the details. I'd planned to come ahead of time and herd away as many people as I could before the chaos broke, but—" Fione's blue eyes flitter over the injured, exhausted crowd. "But no one would budge. There's a tipping point in one's desperation where the song of food and necessities becomes far louder than one's safety. And these people have perhaps lingered on that point longer than possibly bearable."

Lucien's face grows somber as he looks over the crowd, too. He massages his forehead tiredly, muttering, "I could barely do anything. If she could see this, she'd be so ashamed. Disappointed in me."

She. The weight with which he says it can mean only one person—Varia. Fione hears, her expression souring even through her actor's smile.

"Don't flatter yourself, Your Highness. Their suffering isn't entirely at your hands. If she's ashamed of anyone, it's my uncle."

Lucien falls quiet, and Fione snorts derisively, her hand resting on a small dagger at her waist. She pulls it out, inspecting the blade carefully. It's a beautiful thing—jeweled with rings of sapphires and pearls, the blade gold-kissed silver. A noble's dagger. No—a *royal's* dagger.

"I promised her, you know." Her blue eyes grow hard. "I promised her I'd never let him tear us apart."

The resolve in her words shakes me. I'm used to her playing stupid, shy, meek. Even when I first met her at Y'shennria's manor, her smiles were pervasive despite my attitude. She played happy, then. But now she burns, no careful calculations, no pretending. Only honesty. Only old wounds, still bleeding. Still bleeding...for Varia? Is that why she's betraying Gavik and risking so much?

Fione turns to me then. "You surprised me, Lady Zera. I'm sure you surprised my uncle, too. He's not used to people standing up to him who don't have d'Malvane as their family name."

"He should get used to it," I say. "Because I intend to do it as often as I can get away with."

She giggles. "Do you hear that, Your Highness? All that's

left is for either you or me to recruit her to our individual causes."

Lucien narrows his eyes. "No. That'd only put Lady Zera in more danger."

The locket on my chest gives a little shudder—he's worried about me? "I'm flattered," I start. "And simultaneously mystified."

Fione inhales. "His Highness and I have tried for years now to thwart my uncle. I've proposed we simply work together, but that never turns out well—neither of us especially enjoys the other's company." She stops, thinking. "But now that you're here, Lady Zera—"

"Absolutely not," Lucien says.

"I haven't even said it yet!" Fione stamps her foot.

"I know what you're thinking," he insists. "Gavik isn't to be toyed with, treated like some group project for our old tutors. I'm nearly immune to his influence because of my status, and you because of your blood ties to him, but Lady Zera has none of those things to hide behind. She'd be the perfect lamb for him to slaughter."

"Implying I wouldn't at least put up a fight?" I frown. "You give me far too little credit."

"No," Lucien presses. "I simply know the extent of Gavik's power. This isn't me underestimating you—this is a fact. He would rip you to pieces."

Just as I will to you, soon enough, the hunger sneers. Fione clears her throat.

"Listen, Your Highness, you saw how brave Lady Zera was. I've seen her in court—she's clever, too. Always has some witty thing to say. She isn't savvy like we are to the ways of Vetris, but she's something more important—neutral ground. For both you *and* I. I like her well enough, and you—" She looks between Lucien and me, a smile growing on her face, kitten-like. "Well. Let's just say I can tell you like her, too."

Lucien makes a noise in the back of his throat like a snarl cutting off a retort, but Fione presses on.

"I'm so close, Lucien." She uses his first name, sincerity and determination blazing across her face. "All these years, and it's almost complete. The cage for my uncle just needs the lock, and it's over. Everything will be over, and I can finally rest. I can finally visit her portrait holding my head high."

Lucien stares at Fione, and she stares back. And then the moment breaks, and her blue eyes find mine, a smile blossoming.

"What do you say, Lady Zera? The three of us against Gavik? With your wit, and my charm, and the prince's glowers, we might be able to actually do it."

"Do what?" I ask. Her smile only grows bigger.

"Destroy my uncle from the inside out, of course."

11

BLOODRULE

I EXPECT LUCIEN OF ALL PEOPLE to say no, to shoot it down like he's shot down everything else of Fione's. But after a long, strained silence, he nods.

"All right."

Even Fione seems wary of how fast he agreed. "Just like that?"

"The witchfire incident at the temple." He exhales. "And now this raid on the black market that kept the poor fed—Gavik's attempts at sowing fear and dissent to fuel his war aren't slowing. And my father will never stop him. Someone has to."

War—the same war I'm trying to stop, or at least delay. The war the witches are so terrified of—the whole reason they sent me here.

"I thought—" I bite my tongue before it can spill dangerous opinions. I hate that my opinions are at all dangerous. I'm used to saying whatever I want, whenever I want. But Lucien knits his eyebrows at me.

"What is it, Lady Zera? Ask, and I'll answer."

I glance to Fione, who pointedly won't meet my gaze. "I've heard you go on hunts. For witches and Heartless. Why are you trying to stop a war against them if you hunt them? Don't you hate them?"

Fione and Lucien share a look that, for once, isn't full of barbs.

"We should be getting home." Fione takes my arm and smiles. "It's awfully late, and I'm sure Lady Y'shennria is worried about you."

Prince Lucien clears his throat and bows to me. "Thank you, Lady Zera. For tonight. Take care to clean that wound properly, for my peace of mind, if nothing else."

I quickly bow to him, utterly bewildered as Fione forcefully leads me off—on any other night I'd be strong enough to rip away from her, but the buzz of alcohol and the fatigue of my wrist wound catches up to me. The prince watches us, and I watch him over my shoulder until he's a tiny speck in the distant streets.

"What—"

"He doesn't hunt witches, you silly girl," Fione interrupts me. "He pretends to. It's a cover."

"For what?"

Her eyes dart around. "Not now. Wait until we have four walls to hide us."

I squirm impatiently the whole walk to Y'shennria's manor. Reginall lets us in, offering Fione a glass of warm goat milk and hazelnut sweetrounds, but she declines both politely. When he gets the hint and leaves, she turns to me.

"Since Y'shennria obviously hasn't considered it important enough to tell you, I will." She inhales once, hugely, like what she's about to say takes strength from her very core. "I told you I grew up with Lucien. But I grew up with Varia, too. The three of us—" She swallows. "We were very close. Varia hated the witch-human tension, especially the aftermath the Sunless War caused. When she could escape the palace she'd head into the town, offering her labor to shelters, to the polymaths, to the veterans and the widows. To anyone who needed help. That's just the kind of person she was."

Fione looks around, going over to the drawing room door and closing it. She turns back to me, leaning against the door tiredly.

"I looked up to her more than anyone. But my uncle hated her more than anyone. She argued with him. Foiled his machinations where she could. She even turned King Sref against him, sometimes. She was a constant headache for him. If only I'd realized just how much of a headache, perhaps I could've saved her."

I dread what's coming next. Fione steadies herself, one hand against the back of a settee.

"Varia went off when she was sixteen to tour the country, meet the people she was going to rule. She'd always wanted to leave Vetris. King Sref couldn't stop her. We found out later he didn't stop her, because Gavik wanted her to go. Convinced him to let her go."

"You mean—"

Fione blurts out the next words, like they've been packed inside her for a long time. "I heard my uncle talk about it. Laugh about it. The courier came to him with the news, and he laughed and laughed. Drank half a bottle of Avellish brandy by himself in celebration. *She's dead*, he kept saying to the fireplace." She meets my eyes with her blue ones, sadness darkening them to gray sleet. "That was the night before her entourage returned to Vetris with her remains."

The night before. That means—

"Archduke Gavik killed Princess Varia?" I croak. Fione flinches but finds her voice.

"With mercenaries, I think. Or assassins. I've been trying to track down which branch but haven't found anything solid—" She stops herself. "Regardless, I told Lucien. I tried to tell the king, but my uncle got to him first. He blamed it on the Heartless."

"That…that unctuous bastard!" I grit my teeth. "How do you stand living with such a man?"

"I tell him I'm going to bed early a lot." She laughs, though it has a despairing edge to it. "And then sneak out to investigate, or do business with the people who might have information or proof of what he did."

"And he doesn't catch you?"

Fione taps her leg. "He thinks me incapable of anything but hobbling about and saying 'yes, uncle dearest.' I've spent my whole life since Varia died building that particular illusion."

Amazed at her grit, I struggle with my response. "I still don't get why Lucien hunts."

"I sneak out and investigate, probe the underbelly of Vetris for my uncle's rare mistakes. But Lucien takes a different route. It's a Vetrisian tradition to let an unmarried Crown Prince go on yearly hunts, which used to be just for simple fox or deer. But Prince Lucien requested from his father that he hunt witches, claiming he wanted revenge for Varia. He's using those hunts to scour the woodlands where she died."

"For what?"

Fione shakes her head. "I don't know. He won't tell me."

"I thought you two grew up together."

She exhales, a single curl flapping in her breath. "At first, Lucien and I worked together to bring my uncle down, but... our grief eventually tore us apart. It does that to people. He wanted to chase some imaginary tree, and I wanted concrete evidence against my uncle."

"Wait—what tree?"

She rolls her eyes. "I don't know. It's what he's said over the past few years whenever I ask him what he's doing on his hunts: 'Looking for a tree.' It's a terrible joke, if you ask me."

My mind flashes with an image of Y'shennria's rosary. "Old God worship involves a tree."

"I know that. But that's all it is—a symbol. It's no more real than the gods are."

I quirk a brow. "I don't know if I should be impressed that you talk like you know everything, or worried."

"You think the gods are real, then?" she fires back, and it catches me off guard. Where's the sweet, pink-clad thing that simpered at me in this very room not two days ago? Is this the real her?

I prefer this version—it's much harder to be jealous of.

"I'm not as certain as you are about anything," I say. "If they are real, then they're cruel, and if they aren't real, all this carnage and hate is for the sake of a lie. Either way, it's depressing. But have you ever stopped to consider why Lucien would be looking for a tree?"

"Because he can't deal with Varia's death," Fione insists. "Because he'd much rather pin it on some magical Old God tree than face the fact that we'll never—" Fione's voice catches, coming back scratchy. "That we'll never see her again."

I choose my next words very carefully. "Do you know

how a witch becomes, Lady Fione?"

"No. Witchlore isn't exactly the sort of thing you find poking around Vetris. Do you?"

I open my mouth, then close it. I'm Zera Y'shennria to her, not a Heartless. "Of course not."

Her blue eyes flash. "Then why bring it up?"

When I don't say anything, she approaches, looking me square in the face.

"I saw her, Lady Zera. I saw the parts of her, all that was left. I saw her blood, her fingers, her—" Fione winces. "She's dead. And no amount of chasing superstitious beliefs about the gods—Old or New—will bring her back."

There's a long, yawning abyss of silence as I take it all in, and Fione regains her poise. I misunderstood Lucien. I counted him a murderer. A part of me squirms with shame. Another part laments—he's untouched, unstained. He's not the kindred spirit drenched in blood I thought him. He merely pretended, just as Fione pretends. These nobles move in dances more complex than I've ever seen.

"This hunt thing of the prince's...it's such an elaborate farce."

Fione folds her arms, begrudging admiration in her voice. "He's maintained it flawlessly for six years now."

"You've both maintained facades," I say. Fione's grin is small.

"And now you do, too."

The sandclock ticks into the shadows between us.

"Why did you volunteer me for teaming up with you and Lucien?" I ask.

"I'm an archduke's niece—and Lucien is a prince. He has access to areas of the palace I can only dream of. And he likes you."

Something catches in my throat, and I cough wildly. Fione smirks, holding up a nearby jug of water.

"Would you like some?"

"I'm perfectly...capable..." I manage between breaths.

"Oh, I'm sure you are. That's why Y'shennria brought you in to marry the prince and restore status to her family, after all. I had plans in place to deal with you if you were dumb as rocks. But thankfully, you aren't—"

"You should see me before I've had my morning cup of chocolate drink."

"—which makes this whole thing much easier." She ignores my quip. "I need the prince on my side to access certain areas of the palace. He needs you to even consider helping me. You need me to carve out more time with the prince for you."

"Y'shennria's doing a stellar job of that, thanks."

"Without guards," Fione presses, a sly smile on her face. "Without being in public. Dozens of opportunities to be with him, just the two of you, in many secluded locations."

Her smile betrays her confidence—she's so certain she knows that's what I want. And she does. But not for the reasons she thinks.

"You'll be queen in no time," she asserts. "And as for me—four years of planning, gathering, waiting—it's all going to pay off in the next several days. If I can get into a few places that are off-limits, my uncle will lose everything. All the respect and power and fear he's accumulated—gone. And to him, that is worse than death."

I stare at my hands, at the faint smears of blood on my outfit from my long-healed wrist wound. Something stirs in me, uneasily. *You're not afraid of death*, Gavik had said to me.

"Isn't that what you want? Time with Prince Lucien?"

Fione presses. I look up quickly.

"More than the Red Twins want to dance with each other," I answer. "More than anything."

"Then why do you look so sad at the thought?"

Her words grip me in fingers of ice. I rub my eyes, worried she can see the truth in them. "I'm simply tired and in pain."

"I know the feeling." She taps her leg and flashes me a facetious lawguard salute. "I'll leave you, then. If you agree to this arrangement, do let me know through a watertell. Nothing detailed, just a 'yes' will do. Good night, Lady Zera."

When she's gone I stumble up to my room, the *yolshil* finally wearing off, and collapse into the feather bed. Reginall knocks on my door—I've memorized his knock, two short raps followed by a pause. I answer it wearily.

"There you are, miss." He bows. "Milady was looking for you. She asked me to send you to her room when you got home, but…" He trails off, looking at Y'shennria's closed door. "I'm afraid she fell asleep some time ago. She hasn't been sleeping well."

Of course she hasn't—with every day Verdance grows closer, we run out of more and more time. The stress must be killing her—even if she does have a plan for the Hunt.

"Let her sleep," I say softly. "I'll go to her first thing in the morning." Reginall bows, and as he turns to leave, I stop him. "How many people did you kill in the war, Reginall?"

He freezes, back turned to me, but he doesn't miss a beat. "Forty-seven, miss."

"Do you remember their faces?"

"Every night, miss."

The wind blows the spines of a cherry tree's branches across a nearby window. I'd told Peligli that sound was the forest's good night to us, once. I breathe deep.

"If I make the prince into a Heartless, he'll have to kill. He'll have the hunger. He'll have a number like we do."

Reginall doesn't say anything. I press on, my words clear in the setting moonlight.

"What do you think is worse, Reginall? Killing, or forcing others to kill? To make it bigger, worse? To take a heart, knowing full well you're condemning them to bear the chains of this horrible guilt, this horrible hunger?"

He is perfectly still, silent.

"What's worse, Reginall—to be a monster, or to make monsters?"

We both know the answer. But only one of us goes laughing like she's mad back into her bedroom, closing the door behind her.

Only one of us realizes how alone she is, and leaves her room to pause before Y'shennria's door.

Only one of us raises our hand to knock, saying a silent prayer for comfort, for an embrace from someone, anyone. Only one of us freezes just before, and realizes how futile such a prayer is for a monster.

It's when I'm lying on my canopied bed, counting the darkwood stars in the ceiling pattern and wondering, as always, what that strange embossed star in the corner of the ceiling is for (aesthetics? To hang something from?) that I realize something is wrong with me. Something has shifted, like an itch deep down where I can't reach. Something won't stop playing an endless loop of tonight's events on the back of my eyelids—all of them focused on Prince Lucien's face, the crook of his golden neck, the shadow of his collarbone, the look in his eyes as we danced, the smile on his lips, that fierce bravery of his facing down Gavik with his blade raised—

I throw myself out of bed and walk over to where the glass jar meant for Lucien sits on my dresser. The snake etched in it taunts me. I envision a heart inside, and in this vision I'm utterly free, my own chest filled, pulsing again with a true human heartbeat. I pack my things and leave over the Cavanos border, to Pendron, to Avel—Crav and Peligli in tow—to the farthest corners of the Mist Continent where I can find peace at last. *Peace.* That dance, his laugh, the heat of his skin, they made me feel at *peace*—

I shake my head and focus inward. I envision carving his heart out with my sword, but it cuts off the moment I plunge the blade into his chest, turns into his tensed arms wrapping around my waist ever so gently, hesitantly, as if he were afraid—

He should be very afraid, the hunger snarls. **I am coming for him.**

I could tell in your eyes; you weren't afraid. Of me. Of anyone. And that's the exact moment I knew you'd be a thorn in my side.

He's mine to destroy, mine to ravage, mine to sink my teeth into—

But now I'm not so sure. Are you a thorn? Or are you a flower?

Sunrise shatters the night-locked loop of my thoughts, and I make my way downstairs to eat. The livers in the kitchen taste like ash in my mouth, worse than usual. Raw meat might keep me alive, but now that I've tasted so much delightful human food, I long for herbs and spices and slow-cooked fats. I used to fear it, the pain that came after, and now it's the only thing I want to eat, the pain be godsdamned.

Halfway through my reluctant meal, Y'shennria joins me, lips pursed and hair perfectly fluffed.

"Sleep well?" she asks.

"You could say that."

"What is that bandage on your wrist?" she asks, brows knit in impossible concern. "Lady Himintell sent me a watertell about the raid, but not that you got injured."

"Ah, so you knew all along I didn't get any sleep."

"It's polite to inquire."

"Aren't we beyond politeness at this point? Can't we just—I dunno—loosen up a bit?"

"If we 'loosen up,' we risk mistakes. Mistakes mean you die. And our hopes die with you."

There's a quiet in which I stir the chocolate drink I made to cover the taste of the livers, and Y'shennria delicately begins to pick apart a nearby starfruit. *Our hopes*, she'd said. Not *the witches' hopes*. She considers herself one of them, even after what they did to her and her family.

"I'll repeat it only once," she says firmly. "How did you get that wound?"

I smirk. "It's nothing. A small trifle, and besides, I have the tendency to heal quickly, Auntie. Or did you forget?" When she stares me down unblinkingly, I heave a sigh. "The archduke had his men shoot me."

Her grip around her fork turns white, and I swear she mutters something under her breath that sounds like, "Bastard." Is she angry on my behalf—on behalf of a Heartless? How unlike her. She composes herself quickly, though.

"You will act wounded, then, for the rest of your time in Vetris. I'll invite several of the more palace-distanced polymaths over, to make it look like you're being intensely treated. The cover story is you fell and twisted it." She scoffs. "Don't give me that look. We need a cover story. Telling everyone Gavik had you shot would paint targets on both our backs."

We move upstairs to the dining room, Maeve hobbling about as she sets the table and brings breakfast around.

"You aren't angry with me?" I quirk a brow.

"Of course I am," she insists. "Becoming involved with one of Gavik's raids, getting shot—you're lucky he didn't discover what you are right then and there."

You're not afraid of death. Gavik's voice lingers between my ears. I shake him out and get up, closing the distance between our seats on the opposite ends of the long table. I sit beside her and lean in as close as I know she can stand.

"Fione thinks Gavik killed the princess."

"I know." Y'shennria nods. "She told me that a year ago."

"What do *you* think?"

The older woman sighs. "He was certainly capable of it at the time, and he truly did hate her. I think if Fione is right, and manages to prove it to the king, Vetris could change for the better. But I believe she's playing the most dangerous game of anyone in this city."

"Even more than me?"

Her mouth twists. "A game requires you to enter of your own free will. What you're doing is a battle."

"This is the first battle I've been in that requires so many silk dresses and faked smiles."

"Pray that it never requires more than that," she says softly. The whitish scar tissue on her neck is freed to the air, her dress uncharacteristically low-cut. She isn't bothered with hiding today. The urge to tell her about the uneasy alliance I've struck with Fione and the prince in taking Gavik down nags at me. Fione promised me time alone with the prince. It'd be the perfect opportunity. But then I remember how insistent Y'shennria is on the Hunt being the time I strike, and no other.

After breakfast, Reginall comes in and announces there's someone waiting for Y'shennria and me in her study. We shoot each other befuddled looks and head upstairs. I glance at the fire-calendar on the wall. Seven days? Is that really all I have left? Time is slipping from my fingers, slipping away the more I'm distracted by unimportant things like a parade dance or human food. I can't become one of those girls Y'shennria has no faith in—human girls. She values me for my monstrosity, after all. And yet I've changed since stepping foot into this city. I'm an insufferable jokester, but I'm not stupid. I can tell I've grown weaker. My resolve slips away like sand every moment I spend with the prince, with Y'shennria, with the human illusions of food and dances. Comfort, after so many years in the woods, has begun to soften my edges.

I can't surrender to it. But neither can I resist it. I have to act, the sooner the better. So I keep the secret of my alliance to myself, and pray to the gods I don't regret it.

I straighten my shoulders and walk into the study only to see Malachite there, legs splayed out as he slouches on a settee. His long ears nearly touch the headrest of the low cushions, silver hair mussed. The pupils of his bloodred eyes narrow as he sees me, smiles crookedly, and stands.

"There you are. I was beginning to think you hated me."

"How could I hate that face? Especially when it always looks as if it's swallowed a particularly fat canary."

"Are you calling me smug, Zera?"

"You will address her as 'milady,'" Y'shennria sniffs,

reaching for a scarf with which to cover her throat. Malachite laughs, then stops at the strict look on her face.

"Right. Sorry, ma'am."

"Milady," she corrects icily. He flinches, and I smother a laugh at how much he looks like a little kid being chastised.

"Uh, anyway—this is for you." He hands me a folded note, and I take it.

Our mutual acquaintance from last night has invited me to a watering party on the western lawn, and I'd hate to go alone. Blackmail me this time, won't you?

A watering party, Y'shennria explains, is when—during hot summer days—nobles gather to drink and play outdoor games in the shade. She approves my pale, primrose-green and primrose-petal-thin outdoors dress, laced with little seed pearls in hypnotizing spiral patterns. Malachite offers to ride with me in the carriage, and while Y'shennria insists it's improper, Malachite counters that it's for my safety. They stare each other down, his bloodred eyes just as stern as her hazel ones for a moment. Finally, she relents.

"Take care of her, Sir Malachite. She's very important to me." Hearing her say that has my unheart in my throat. Y'shennria leans into the carriage window as if to hide herself from Malachite's gaze. "Be careful. Ensure you act injured. The archduke will not soon overlook a missed flinch from your wrist."

"Don't worry. I learned from the best, didn't I?" I smile, and Y'shennria snorts, though it isn't a disapproving one at all.

"I suppose you did."

Malachite climbs into the carriage with me, and Fisher nicks the horses into a trot. Malachite's legs are so long I have to squeeze into the opposite corner to avoid touching him.

"Are all Beneathers as tall as you?" I grumble, not intending to say it so loud, but he hears it anyway and laughs.

"You'll be happy to know most of us are rather short," he says. "But once in a while a Beneather is born strangely. It doesn't pay to be my height underground. My forehead's gotten to be *great* friends with nearly every single rock in Pala Amna."

"Pala Amna?"

"The Final City," Malachite clarifies. "Our haven. Well, the last haven the Beneather empire has left. The valkerax chased us out of the rest hundreds of years ago."

"They liked the taste of you that much, did they?" I stop. "You know, that sounded less terrible in my head."

"I'm sure." He snorts. "But, no. It takes more than a bit of Beneather flesh to bring a thousand screeching valkerax out of the Dark Below." He pauses. "That's what we call the underground world, in case you didn't know."

"You're an excellent teacher of Beneather culture. Why, you should've seen the look on Archduke Gavik's face when I asked him if he had any *vachiayis* last night."

Malachite laughs, so loud a flock of startled sunbirds take off into the air. He watches the scenery of the noble quarter flash by, crimson eyes reflecting the metal of lawguard armor and the whitestone of the buildings. I can't imagine an entire empire below my feet—dozens of miles down. The thought of the cavities beneath the earth holding screeching, fang-laden valkerax is terrifying. The only thing I do know about Beneathers is what everyone seems to know—they keep the valkerax from escaping into the world above by becoming peerless warriors. The broadsword on Malachite's back gleams ominously. I'm utterly convinced that despite his carefree attitude and disrespect for authority, he'd be a monstrous challenge in a fight. It's no small wonder King Sref hired him to be Lucien's bodyguard.

"I was supposed to be there, you know," Malachite says. "With you and Luc, at that raid."

"No one begrudges you a vacation day, or twelve." *Least of all me.* It's never been a question—taking Lucien's heart will be possible only if Malachite is absent.

"Vacations be damned—there was a guy sneaking around Lucien's bedroom, so I had to do a bit of last-minute interrogation. With my sword to his throat."

"Get any good bits?" I inquire.

"Oh, you know: *The d'Malvanes have been in power too long, King Sref took my son from me, so I'm taking his from him, Prince Lucien stands for everything I hate about nobles.* The usual."

At least one of those sounded like something I used to catch myself thinking. "I find it hard to believe wanting to kill the Crown Prince is 'the usual.'"

Malachite shrugs. "King Sref isn't a popular guy. Assassins aren't uncommon, but this one—" He gnaws his pale thumb. "No. Never mind."

"You can tell me," I tease him. "My mouth might look big, but I assure you, I keep my words small."

He chuckles, then falls quiet. "It was just strange. All his lines sounded rehearsed. He was still scared, but he wouldn't crack, wouldn't deviate from his story. Just kept saying the same lines over and over. And his blade—"

Malachite fishes a dagger out of his armor. The smell

hits me instantly—white mercury. There, inside the handle, is a broken vial leaking a little white.

"It was this weird thing," Malachite presses. "That's white mercury, right?"

I nod. "As far as I know."

"The royal polymaths told me this stuff dulls magic if it gets inside a witch or Heartless. It isn't cheap or easy to come by. And the polymaths keep most of it under lock and key. So why was a common assassin trying to kill a human prince with a white mercury weapon? And who gave it to him?"

The celeon assassin who tried to kill me before I left Nightsinger floats to the surface of my mind. The witches said someone in Vetris was sending assassins out with those white mercury weapons to test them on Heartless and witches. The royal polymaths, maybe? No—I know better than that. I know who controls them.

"The d'Malvanes are a witch family, right?" I ask lightly, though my words carry deep shadow.

Malachite nods. "Supposedly."

"There's one person who really hates witches and has access to white mercury who comes immediately to mind," I try. "Archduke Gavik."

He goes still and exhales, putting the dagger away. "Dark Below—I hope it wasn't him."

"Don't think you can take him?" I ask.

Malachite snorts. "I'd cleave that genocidal old coot in two with one hand. I'm just worried what it means for Lucien. They've never been on great terms. White mercury or no, Gavik's never tried to kill him outright, though. If he is now, it means Gavik is confident in his total power. It means Lucien is in more danger than I thought."

"You'll be happy to know, then, that Lucien, Lady

Himintell, and I have formed sort of a...*coalition* against him. I like to call it the United Army of Kicking Gavik's Moldy Arsehole into the Afterlife. You're welcome to join."

He laughs and shakes his head. "I heard. Maybe I will. Just be careful, will you? That Himintell girl tends to let her desire for revenge block out the consequences of her actions, for both herself and others."

"Did Lady Himintell—did she care about Princess Varia that much?"

"Still does," Malachite agrees. "I wasn't there before Varia died, but I was there for the aftermath. Fione worshipped her. Loved her, if I had to guess. Revenge doesn't burn that hot unless you've lost the one you love."

Love. It makes sense, falls into place—why Fione is risking so much. A foggy tendril of sadness worms into my heart locket; a love unfulfilled. I hope Fione got to tell Varia how she felt, at the very least. The more I find out about her life, the harder and harder it gets to cling to my jealousy of her.

The carriage stops in front of the palace, and Malachite and I get out and head toward the watering party gathered on the lawn beneath the oaks. The sun is piercing today, the air thick and hot like steam. Inside a moving carriage it was bearable, but now it suffocates me. The shade is only mildly cooler, and when I draw into it I realize the nobles at this party are entirely my age—the only adults are handmaids fanning their charges and palace servants offering cups of chilled barley wine. The Priseless twins are here, though they can't meet my eyes with Malachite next to me. Charm and Grace are here, too, unfortunately, but both of them ignore me. Lucien sits beneath a tree surrounded by a few celeon royal guards. Malachite shoos them off, quickly retaking his place by Lucien's side. The prince seems relieved to have Malachite back, and I can understand why now—Gavik might not have control over the royal guards like he does the lawguards, but influencing them would be a simple matter of manipulating King Sref. And Gavik's proven he can do that—even if it means killing the Crown Princess.

Perhaps Gavik, too, knows that to get to Prince Lucien, Malachite has to be out of the picture. The thought sends a cold chill down my spine despite the summer heat.

Fione walks up to me in a beige off-shoulder dress, her ivory cane sinking into the grass and the curls in her high ponytail shuddering with her slightest head movement.

"Lady Zera!" she chimes. "So very good to see you. Have a walk with me, would you?"

I take her arm and we walk a little way from the party, the nobles absorbed in their game—something played with silver throwing sticks and triangular dice. When Fione's sure we're alone, she speaks softly.

"I've informed His Glowering Highness over there of my plan, but I haven't informed you. Let's correct that oversight." She turns us at a hydrangea bush, the brilliant magenta flowers temporarily hiding us from view of the other nobles.

"My ultimate goal is to provide King Sref with irrefutable evidence that my uncle had Princess Varia killed," Fione murmurs. "The king is my uncle's one check. Varia is the king's one weakness. If he knows my uncle killed her, he'll orchestrate his downfall swiftly and surely. But my uncle is nothing if not very good at covering his tracks."

"Better than you are?" I marvel at the path she leads me through—around trees, between bushes, and behind fountains, smiling at me all the while. To the outsider it must look like a perfectly innocent walk.

"Where do you think I learned it from?" She laughs. "But that isn't the point. My uncle might've relished—" She swallows anger. "Killing Varia. But there's one thing he relishes more than eliminating his enemies."

"Executing innocents?" I ask lightly. She shakes her head.

"*Acquiring technology*. You've seen the prince's sword, right?"

"Is that a dirty joke? And here I thought Y'shennria said you were the perfect lady." Fione mimes vomiting, and I can't help laughing. "The prince has Varia's sword, right?"

She bends and picks a water lily out of one of the man-made rivers. "He does now. But it's my belief my uncle had it first, before the court got news she'd been killed."

"You've lost me."

Fione buries her nose in the flower, the petals shading her mouth. "That sword is rare—a marvel of smithing expertise. There was only one polymath in the world capable of imbuing white mercury into metal seamlessly. He made four swords in the war at King Drevenis's deathbed request and then disappeared."

The prince's sword is white mercury? I make a note not to be cut by it anytime soon. Fione hands the water lily to me.

"Some say the polymath was overcome with guilt for making such powerful witch-killing weapons. He left behind no blueprints, no apprentice. The swords were destroyed in battles, or lost in the fog of the Sunless War. No one else has been able to replicate the technique since. And it drives my uncle mad to this day."

"I'm sure he'd love nothing more than to arm his lawguards with a thousand witch-killing swords," I muse.

Fione nods. "Exactly. Everything changed when King

Sref presented Varia with one of the swords. My uncle coveted it, tried to get Varia to give it to him to study, but she knew his devious ways and refused. He killed her for many reasons, but the sword is the only tangible reason—the only hard evidence left."

I furrow my brow, but she just smiles wider at me—one of her strong and insincere smiles.

"The night she was killed, I believe my uncle's people delivered the news she'd died, and her sword, to him first. He had a whole day to study the sword before he returned it to the lawguard reporting the news to the royal family. He must have some notes on it, somewhere. If I can find those notes, I can prove he had the sword—that he knew Varia had been killed before the rest of us. That he arranged it with his own two hands."

I'm silent. It's a sound line of thinking, but so convoluted and dangerous it sets me on edge.

"He's been trying to replicate Varia's blade for five years now, but his attempts are clumsy," Fione presses. "Yet every year, they get better. He *must* have notes."

I think back to the dagger with the vial in it that I was stabbed with, and the one Malachite found on the assassin. Clumsy indeed, but effective. I look up at her.

"So what do we do? I imagine walking up and asking him politely for these notes is out of the question."

She laughs softly. "Quite. I know how my uncle thinks— what places he'd keep something so precious to him. I've narrowed it down to two such locations. And if I have my way today, I'll finally get the clue I need to narrow it down to one."

"Do I get any details, or are you just going to point me at a crowd and tell me to do my thing?"

She claps her hands excitedly. "Oh Lady Zera, this is

what I like about you! Straight to the point. I need you to draw out my uncle from his study. The window of his office is on this side of the palace, so he can see us now, and he will definitely notice any ruckus you cause here at the party."

"You're the one who knows him. How do you suggest I go about it?"

"Hmm, let's see—he likes watching people suffer, and Pendronic milk scones, and displays of martial prowess—"

"Martial prowess," I repeat. "Like a fight? A duel?"

Her smile grows delighted. "Exactly like a duel." She looks around at the noble boys, then sighs. "Except he's seen everyone here duel, including the prince. It'll be nothing new, unless we raise the stakes or perhaps cause an injury to his favorite Priceless twins—"

"As much as I like the sound of that last one, he hasn't seen *me* duel."

Fione's eyes spark. "You duel?"

"Enough to know a parry from a riposte."

"A girl dueling—a Spring Bride, nonetheless..." Fione whispers to herself, then looks up at me. "It just might work."

"How much time do you need?"

"Ten minutes. Three to get in, five to undo his puzzle-locks, and two to get out."

"And you won't be caught?"

"If I am, it was nice knowing you, Lady Zera."

"You're willing to risk your life for this?" I press. "For revenge?" Fione just smiles wider.

"Revenge? No. Justice? Yes." She turns. "I'll leave you to it. If I see an opening, I'm gone. Thank you in advance."

She leaves me to hang at the edge of the nobles' dice game. Winded by all this new information, I approach Lucien at his spot under the trees. Malachite gives me a little wave, and Lucien's frown lightens as he observes his partying peers.

"Took you long enough," he says, an edge of imperiousness to his voice. Malachite nudges him roughly.

"Just tell her you're happy she's here, you grump."

A laugh bubbles up from me. "Not only do you have no sense of decorum, Malachite—you also have no grasp on reality. The day the prince is happy to see me is the day Vetris welcomes witches within its walls."

Malachite and I share a chuckle, but Lucien's face remains stone, his dark iron eyes on me. Our laughter peters out quickly, and I clear my throat to cover the awkward silence.

"I was wondering, Your Highness—"

"Lucien," he insists instantly.

"Lucien." I start again, a moth beating its wings against my empty chest. "Do you enjoy dueling?"

"Very much so—especially if there are new opponents."

I give him a smile and excuse myself, my hands trembling mildly. Nervousness. Why did he look so serious? Surely I was right—the prince is no happier to see me than any other loudmouth blackmailer. I expected him to agree, to throw out some biting retort in unison. But he'd said nothing.

The almost-kiss last night lingers in my mind, but I plaster a smile on and approach the party's game. It doesn't take long to plant the idea of a duel in their heads—a chance for the boys to impress the ladies, and a chance for the ladies to have the boys compete for their affection. The boys shed their heavy overcoats in anticipation of the sweat they'll work up, the girls tittering madly at one fewer layer than usual. Servants fetch swords and place brightly colored rice pouches on the ground to denote the dueling arena. Girls work out bets between them—the clear favorite to win is Lord Grat, a broad-shouldered Secondblood boy built like an ox, his neck thicker than my not-insubstantial thigh. He lunges against an invisible opponent as he warms up, his thrusts with his longsword impressively quick for his size. Grat sees me staring and waves, cupping his hands to his mouth.

"I'll win this duel for you, Lady Zera!"

The girls giggle, and I do my best to fake a flattered blush. Next to me, someone whistles. I turn to see Malachite watching Lord Grat with me.

"Not bad. A few more years of growing and he might be strong enough to take on a hatchling valkerax."

I look Malachite up and down. He's slenderer than Lucien by far, though they're equally broad. "How strong are *you*?"

Malachite laughs. "What, don't I look that beefy?"

"I was thinking more…chickeny."

He clucks his tongue. "You're the worst. All I do is look out for you, and you call me fowl." I gloss over the pun with a groan, but Malachite presses on. "Beneathers are stronger than we look. Not celeon strong, certainly, but strong enough. It helps too that we have certain…*resistances*."

"To fire?" I ask. "You said you walked through that fake witchfire, when we first introduced ourselves."

"Very good, *milady*." He claps sarcastically. "You've been paying attention."

I give him a rude gesture, but he just laughs again. Lucien joins us, red waistcoat standing out among all the coatless boys.

"A duel?" He quirks a midnight brow. "I hope you didn't start one intending for me to participate, Lady Zera. I've fought these idiots before—none of them are very good."

I glance up at the window Fione pointed to. Gavik's

window. Lucien's right—the prince fighting a bunch of nobles won't nearly be enough to drag the archduke from his office. But if Prince Lucien fights a girl, and his Spring Bride, besides—

"I'm entering," I say suddenly. Lucien and Malachite both gape at me.

"What?" Lucien hisses. "You aren't serious?"

I pat Father's sword at my side. "As serious as the grave. I could use the exercise."

"What about your wrist?" he snaps. "If you reopen the injury—"

"Y'shennria's polymath said it was fine," I lie. "She's more concerned about me submerging it in water than exercising it."

"You're certain?" Lucien's voice gets hard, and I sigh.

"Yes, and nothing you say will change my mind."

"Dark Below." Malachite chuckles. "And here I thought I was the one worried about your well-being—" Malachite squawks incredulously as Lucien's bright red coat is thrown into his arms. The prince stands there in his loose white undershirt, swinging his sister's sword this way and that in a warm-up motion. White mercury melded into the blade, Fione said. I have to do everything in my power not to be cut by that sword. He looks me up and down, clearly unimpressed.

"Surely you won't be fighting in a dress like that," he insists.

"I will be *winning* in a dress like this," I correct. Malachite cackles a bit until Lucien throws him a glare. I look to the dueling field—the servants have set up a traditional Cavanos square. I prefer an Endless Bog round arena myself, but monsters can't be choosers.

"Do you need me to explain how this works, Lady Zera?" Prince Lucien asks. "Or did they teach you with the pig sticks on your farm?"

There it is—the barbed half insults I'm used to from him, even if they are a little icier than normal. I know him well enough by now; he was inquiring if I knew the rules, ready to explain them should I need it. How twistedly helpful.

"Save your breath for your duels, Your Highness." I smile at him. "You'll need it."

Crav taught me all I know about dueling traditions on the Mist Continent, and I silently thank him for it now. Cavanos rules are simple; if you force your opponent to step out of the square, you win. Though, unlike most countries, there are strict bloodrules in a traditional Cavanos duel— no injuries. If you inflict one on your opponent, you're considered unskilled—unable to control your blade, and you lose. And that rule alone is the reason I agreed to this duel, even knowing Lucien's sword is white mercury. If he does cut me, he loses, no matter how much pain I'm in, or how long it takes for Nightsinger to heal me.

If the Prince loses, surely Gavik will come running to gloat.

The girls gather the stems of nearby moonflower plants and have us all draw one to determine the seed. The first match begins between Lord Grat and Prince Lucien. Grat looks utterly panicked. If he loses, he'll be seen as weak. If he wins, perhaps the prince will hate him. An unfair outcome, either way.

Crav used to tell me you could discern everything about a person from the way they fight, but I only half believed it until now. I see exactly why the prince is called the Black Eagle—he fights like a bird of prey, and it takes the breath from me. His blows are sharp and quick, and though he lingers over his next move like a tensed raptor, he spares not a single shred of mercy when striking. It's terrifying and awe-inducing all at once. This is what I love most about swordplay—watching each person fight differently, their very souls manifesting through every strike and parry. Grat moves powerfully, like a bear in battle armor, but the prince waits patiently for him to make a mistake. And he does—too long a lapse in a swing and Lucien jumps on it, knocking Grat's sword clean from his hand. Grat has to bend to pick it back up, eyeing the prince warily; will he knock him over while he's doing it? But Lucien merely holds a hand out for him to go ahead. My chest swells with pride—it's a small move, but it's something a dishonorable duelist would delightedly take advantage of. But the prince is nothing if not honorable.

Grat, getting desperate, swings wildly at the prince, locking their blades together. Grat says something to him, and Lucien's eyes flicker to me briefly. He pushes against Grat with a sudden burst of wild strength so different from his careful blows earlier, the two parting. The ladies cheer for the prince, the boys cheer for Grat—Lucien evidently not very popular among the boys. I wonder what Grat said to elicit such a forward response from a patient duelist like Lucien?

The duel continues, the heat of the day reaching its peak, and I sneak looks at Gavik's window every so often. He doesn't show his face yet, though that's to be expected—he's probably seen the prince duel with every noble his age. Prince Lucien and Lord Grat back off from each other after a failed riposte, Lucien letting out a frustrated breath and pulling his shirt off in one swift movement. The girls at the sideline shriek madly, and even I have to admit the sight of his sweat-sheened back, ribbed with faint but very real lines of muscle, catches my eye.

A blush floods me instantly. I've never seen a boy without his shirt, and it's stupid, gods, it's so *stupid* how warm my face is. I'm better than this—Y'shennria taught me to have a better lady's mask than this. The hunger grows loud, slavering for the flesh, his flesh, but I focus on the long, strong line of his spine, his shoulder blades like the wings of a bird. I squint—there, dark against his golden skin is a tattoo of an actual black bird, its talons outstretched around his biceps, the wings extending to the edge of his left shoulder. An eagle.

"I told him it was tacky," Malachite sighs. "But he just wouldn't listen."

"He— When did he get that?"

"He went to the Wildwatch one year, like nobles used to before the war. It was the king's idea—meant to help him after Varia's death, I guess. The Wildwatch all get tattoos of their first kill. His was a giant—"

"Black eagle," I breathe. "That's why they call him that?"

Malachite nods, grinning. "What, you thought it was because he looks like a bird?"

My nod is embarrassed, and Malachite cackles. The duel doesn't slow, Lucien lunging in again. Malachite's smile fades as he resumes watching the match with an intense focus.

"Who do you think will win?" I ask. He shakes his gray-haired head.

"Dunno. Grat is nowhere near as good as Luc. But Luc is...*distracted*."

"By what?"

He snorts. "For all your smart quips, you're awfully slow on the uptake." He looks at me meaningfully.

Me? That beautiful, severe, lonely creature, distracted by *me*?

That doomed creature, the hunger snarls. **Distracted by his predator?**

The crowd lets out a gasp, and we rivet our eyes back to the fight. Grat is on the ground, his body just over the line. Lucien holds his blade pointed at Grat, eyes narrowed and chest heaving. A girl waves her arms madly, calling the match in the prince's favor. The ladies cheer, the boys help Grat up from his place on the ground. Lucien strides toward Malachite and me, adrenaline and anger carving his face as he draws close.

"Grat is an opportunist," Lucien murmurs just above my shoulder, breathing ragged. He smells of an intoxicating mix of sweat and fresh grass. "Don't waste your time on him."

"Is that a concerned warning or a princely command?" I ask, willing the heat in my face to die down, willing the hunger to stop screaming for him. Is this about what Grat shouted to me? Why is he so worked up about it? When he doesn't say anything, I start: "Unfortunately, Your Highness, you don't get to tell me who I can and can't waste my time on."

I draw my blade and step up to the dueling ring. I smile when I realize I'm against one of the Priseless twins. Revenge will be sweeter than summer honey.

"I'm not used to dueling girls, milady," the twin sneers.

"I assure you, it's no different than fighting a man," I say, and launch an immediate strike to his left flank. He parries it just in time, staggering back with wide eyes. "Allow me to impart a bit of wisdom from my teacher; a blade is a blade—no matter who wields it, it can still cut."

I knock him down with a feint to his knees, and his shock begins to melt into irritation.

I should rip you to bits for thinking you could ever hurt me, the hunger snarls. I tame it, tame my growing teeth, and settle for the human emotion of utter satisfaction. The twin jumps to his feet and strikes at me—overhead, obvious. I keep my distance—a sword might equal a playing field, but if I engage him close, he could easily overwhelm me with strength. I have to zone him away from my body, keep him at maximum distance. That's where I'm strongest. That's where I have to fight, or I risk being cut—and healing rapidly in front of this audience.

There are two things men will always believe about a woman: that she's stupid, and that she's weak. Today, as every day, I am neither of these things. But I pretend to get tired quickly, anyway. I pant and droop my sword minutely. Priseless takes it as a sign to lunge for me, overextending. I deflect his blow and step aside, the redirected momentum carrying him past the line. A girl announces my win with a squealing flourish, the ladies going wild. It takes a moment for the twin to stand, never bothering to bow to me before stomping off to his brother to nurse his wounded pride. I glance around at the crowd for Fione and find her in the very back. We lock eyes, hers kept light and amused, though I know she must be nervous inside. Or maybe she isn't. Maybe she's truly that confident. Maybe five years of gathering information in the most illicit ways makes something like this seem like child's play.

"Where do you think you're going, Lord Priseless?" Lucien's deadly cool voice cuts across the grass. The twin's blond head shoots up, fear creeping into his gaze. "You will bow to Lady Zera as the winner. Unless you wish to shirk tradition."

Surely Malachite told Lucien about the Priseless twins'

thwarted attack on me. His eyes are sharper than the blade hanging at his side, as if he's trying to cut the twin in half with his gaze alone. This is more than a decorum demand. This holds weight. He's asking the boy to apologize to me, using his royalty as a weapon infinitely more deadly than Varia's sword. Priseless walks back over to me and bows stiffly, and I bow back. Our eyes meet on the way up, his narrowed and clearly furious. He storms away, the nobles speculating over the exchange in whispers, though it doesn't last long. Several ladies glom onto me as I move out of the arena and to the sidelines.

"That was amazing, Lady Zera!"

"I've never seen a woman duel before! You must teach me your style of the blade!"

Their touches to my arm, their smiles—all I can think is how quickly they'd turn to screams of horror if they knew the real me. The hunger hisses at them all, flashing images of their broken bodies before me. I force my grin and say little, lest the shadows eke from between my sharpening teeth. A crowd has gathered—nearly twice the size since we started, mostly comprised of interested nobles and passerby lawguards. But still no Gavik. Fione waits patiently. I manage to peel the girls off and return to Lucien and Malachite.

"So?" I ask cheerfully. "What did we think?"

"I think Luc has some competition in marrying you." Malachite smirks. "From Lord Grat, and now from several very infatuated ladies."

Lucien snorts. "Let them have her. She's nothing but a font of trouble and irritation."

I swallow my laugh. He uses his position as prince to force Priseless to apologize to me one moment, and then he turns around and insults me the next. Fione was right—he does like to play tough.

"You forgot 'beauty,'" I correct him sternly. "And 'elegance.'"

"I'll be sure to add those to the list when you attain them."

"Okay! That's it!" I throw my hands up. "I've decided you have exactly three seconds to start being nice to me."

"Three whole seconds." Malachite whistles. "You'd better get on it quick, Lucien."

Lucien rolls his eyes. "Shall I have her hanged for daring to tell me what to do?"

"You'd better bury me deep," I threaten playfully. "Or I'll haunt you for the rest of my life."

"Tempting," Lucien drawls. "But I'll pass. I can barely stand the way you haunt me now."

"Romantically haunt, like in a bard's tale," I ascertain.

"No."

"Yes," I correct.

"No."

"*Yes!*"

"Please, infants," Malachite groans. "Enough—Mother needs peace and quiet."

"So you can watch these lords duel sloppily?" Lucien scoffs. "And here I thought you enjoyed *quality* entertainment."

"They *are* fairly bad," I muse in agreement, watching two lords whiff each other's parries. "You don't teach the girls to think, and you don't teach the boys to duel. What *does* Vetris teach its children?"

"Sucking up," Malachite answers. "With a dash of binge drinking and a sprinkle of fashion sense."

Lucien and I laugh in tandem, our eyes catching and disengaging all in the same moment. No matter how I might've slighted his advances yesterday, it still feels good to laugh together like this.

Finally, after watching clumsy noble after clumsy noble strike each other down, the only two duelists left are Lucien and me. It's then I see a familiar face in the noble crowd, toward the very back. White hair and eyes like water. The archduke is here. *I did it.* I look around for Fione, but she's nowhere to be seen. She must be making her move.

A girl steps forward, waving her kerchief and announcing with a loud voice: "Esteemed guests, this is our final match! In the challenger's ring, we have our surprise contestant, Lady Zera Y'shennria!"

Applause rings out. The girl motions to the prince, still shirtless, his tattoo stark.

"And on the opposite side we have your future king, the Black Eagle of the West, Prince Lucien Drevenis d'Malvane!"

Amid the cheering, the prince and I face each other. We raise our swords and bow. I force myself to keep my eyes on his face, not his body. I won't let something as shallow as his skin distract me, no matter how loud the hunger keens.

"You fight well," he says softly. His gaze flickers to my wrist. The wound on the back of *his* hand is all but healed, only a scab left. "But I'm not going to hold back."

"What a relief. I was about to tell you the same thing."

He lashes out with a blow so quick I barely see it, but I raise my sword and parry with a half second to spare. Our blades grind against each other's, our steel screeching in tandem.

Slide your blade between his ribs, now, the hunger snarls. *Taste him, feel his blood on your hands.*

I slip beneath his guard and put distance between us before I lunge in again. My strikes aim true and fast, never letting him catch his breath. He refuses to strike out at me. No matter how hard I go for him, he hesitates. If I didn't know better, I'd think he was hesitating because I'm a girl in some misguided attempt at treating me "well." But then I lunge too far, my foot catching itself, and he jolts forward with a response. I reposition myself quickly, and he backs off.

"You won't win waiting for me to make a mistake like the others," I lilt.

"We all make mistakes," he insists.

"I've made only one in my life," I murmur under my breath. "And that was meeting you."

Just when I think he's going into defensive mode again, he thrusts in to me. The force behind his blow is enough to make my arms go numb, my father's sword crying out in pain as Varia's sword bites into it. He's good. Old God's eye—he's much better than I thought. I can't move an inch; I can't give him an inch.

"I will never consider meeting you a mistake," Lucien says, his midnight eyes flashing.

My heart locket seizes—he heard that? The pain in my locket is a burning inferno—*no*. I can't let him distract me. Not now, not ever. I lunge in once more. He meets me with a slick parry with his blade behind his back. My stomach dances, and even though his sword point is inches from my face, molten euphoria seeps through my veins. It's the same feeling I got when I chased him through the streets, when we danced together in the parade. There is no future right now, no taking his heart, no nobles and what they think of me, no Y'shennria or Fione or Crav or Peligli depending on me, no hole in my chest, no Cavanos gone to war—there is only him, and me.

This moment is what it feels like to be human. This is...
happiness.

I'm so enamored by the moment I feel the sword edge
digging into me too late—warm blood seeps down my slit
forearm. Lucien's eyes widen, and his pressure against me
goes slack. Panic lodges in my throat, bracing me for the
instant agony. We separate.

"Lady Zera wins by blood-rule!" the girl announces. The
nobles go wild, cheering and throwing handkerchiefs into
the arena. Even Gavik begrudgingly applauds. Lucien is
much less joyful.

"You're injured," he starts. I grit my teeth against the
white-hot mercury burning in my body. I have to get away
as soon as possible and heal where no one can see me.

"I hate to break it to you, Your Highness, but these things
occasionally happen in a fight."

"Your arm—" Lucien cuts off my thought and slides
gentle fingers beneath my forearm, lifting it to show the
angry red wound there. "This is my fault."

I remain silent, watching his long, graceful fingers on my
skin. It feels good to have someone touch me like this—gently.
But it can't last. I pull my arm from his.

"You choose now to be nice to me? I see how it is—bleed
a little and suddenly you're all kindness."

His midnight eyes don't once waver from mine, and
something deep inside me begins to crumble—a feeling I
detest and relish all at once.

"Well, Lucien?" Malachite's voice resounds as he walks
up to us. "Are we going to treat her wound or not?"

Lucien tears his gaze from mine. "Yes. Of course."

"That really isn't necessary," I say. "I can do it myself—"

"It could get infected," he interrupts me. "Come. I have

a wound kit."

He reaches out for my uninjured hand, his fingers rough yet warm. The nobles whisper and watch with intent, Gavik's gaze narrowed. I can hear the rumors already. I need his heart, not his genuine affection. I pull my hand away.

"Your Highness, doing this yourself might give the wrong impression—"

"Impressions be damned," Lucien snarls. "We must treat your wound."

Malachite pushes the small of my back toward the palace. "Don't make me pick you up and bring you there."

"I'd like to see you try," I tease, desperate to get out of this situation. "Even a Beneather would be hard-pressed to lift my weight—"

"Enough!" Lucien demands, brows furrowing sharply. "Come with me, *now*. This is an order from your prince."

The tittering of the nobles stops at his tone. I can't disobey an order, not from the Crown Prince, and not in front of so many people. Indignation eats at me—how dare he use his position to force me to come with him? Does he think he can just get away with that? Of course he does—no one dares disobey him. I swallow, standing my ground, making my gaze sing iron refusals. I won't let him have his way. Not like everyone else. Not like the others. I never want to be "like the others" in his eyes. But why? I don't know, there's just selfishness where reasons should be, and Lucien opens his mouth to say something, and suddenly the world spins, the prince becoming a blur in front of me. I faintly hear Malachite's voice, and then my eyes are plunged into darkness.

12

THE APPLE
AND THE TREE

WAKE TO WHITE WALLS, white curtains wafting in the gentle breeze from an open window. A soft bed beneath my body, soft blankets on top—a bedroom. But the ceiling is so high—so high that even in my foggy state I know it must be a bedroom in the palace.

I try to sit up, but a lightning headache splits me down the middle. I double over, the pain so intense I'm convinced someone's taken my locket, but my hand finds it on my chest, and with shaking fingers I open it. My shard of heart still beats there.

I'm safe. But for how long? What happened? Who saw me heal? The fact that I'm in a bedroom in the palace and not in a dungeon is the only thing keeping me from losing my usual flawless composure. My forearm is bandaged so perfectly, snug and clean, and Father's sword rests against one of the bedposts. I still wear the same primrose dress I did during the duel.

How many people saw me faint? My mind flashes with

the crowd, shadowy and huge. Too many—Gavik included. *Why* did I faint? And why do I feel like death warmed over? My whole body cries—my lungs struggling to breathe, my mouth drier than old cotton. I've felt this awfulness before: every time I died.

I must've died.

"Lady Zera, you're awake." Prince Lucien stands there, flanked by Malachite. Both their expressions are worried, but Lucien's is twisted. His long braid is a little undone, wisps of dark hair hanging around his shoulders. Dark bags rim his eyes—has he not slept?

I try to sit up, but the pain is excruciating. Lucien lunges for me, helping prop me up against the pillows.

"Go slow," he murmurs. "Do you need water? Are you hungry?"

"It hurts," I gasp. This isn't right. Pain doesn't linger for a Heartless—it comes and then it goes as quickly as it came. I keep hoping it'll stop, heal magically, but it doesn't abate in the slightest. "How long have I been out?"

"A day. The polymath Lady Y'shennria brought said it would hurt in the beginning," Lucien agrees. "It's an infection."

"Polymath?" A tremor clings to my voice, and I desperately try to peek beneath my bandage—did I heal all the way? Did this polymath *see* me heal? Lucien shakes his head.

"Don't worry—he's the only one who's looked at your wound. Gavik wanted to send his polymaths, but I refused him at Lady Y'shennria's request."

Relief spreads through me, tempered by wariness. Y'shennria let a polymath look at me? Why would she divulge my secret like that? And Gavik, sending his people to tend to me? He'd never do such a kind thing, unless there was something in it for him. Unless he suspected me of something. Did Fione even get what she was after, or was it all for nothing?

Unease adds to the pain, and I swallow.

"This polymath—what did he look like?"

"Tall, white mustache," Malachite offers from his place tucked against the wall. "Very stick-up-the-butt air about him."

Reginall. Without a doubt, that's Reginall. Y'shennria had him pose as a polymath to visit me—clever.

"What else did he say?" I ask. Lucien motions for a lurking maid to fetch water, and she scurries off.

"He said you'd be better off resting at the Y'shennria manor," the prince says. "I promised Lady Y'shennria we'd send you to her the moment you woke, and I intend to keep that promise. Malachite, call for her carriage."

Malachite shoots me a wink and leaves the room. It's only the prince and me, now, and the gentle breeze. It toys with his loose hair strands, and absently I reach for one, stroking it, the softness a welcome distraction from my pain.

"Like silk," I manage. Lucien's expression shadows.

"I was worried you'd never wake—" His voice breaks, and I break with it.

"You can't." I despise my pleading tone. "You *can't* worry about me."

"And you think I haven't tried not to?" he asks. "I tried, *gods* I tried, but every time I saw you it got more and more difficult, until—" He reaches for my hand, encapsulating it in his own warm one. "I'm so glad you're alive."

What's left of me fragments in his hands. His words are a hammer in the center of a web of cracks on my surface I didn't know I had. I look to Father's sword; every night for weeks after their deaths I held that blade and cried for him, for Mother, cried for the gods to take me, too, to free me from my monstrosity and reunite me with them—it all surfaces in my memory, like a storm cloud overcoming the sun. I feel a tear slip down my cheek, and he sees it, wiping it away with a confused look on his face.

"Why are you crying?" he asks. "Is it the pain? I can get some brandy—"

"N-No. I-I'm sorry. It's just—no one has ever said that to me before."

I want nothing more than to stay in this moment, my hand in his. But that's an impossibility. A weakness. I am a monster, and he's a human. I want his heart, and I want his other heart. His affection, his blood. I want it all.

But if I take one, I can't have the other.

Kill him, the hunger begs, its voice deafening and more distorted than I'm used to, like a thousand voices at once instead of just one. *Eat him. Kill hIm. EAt him. KiLL—*

Lucien gets up and leaves, returning with a glass of amber liquid. I greedily down it, ashamed he has to help me drink.

"This isn't how I imagined our first date going," I mutter. He laughs, the sound honey to my ears.

TaKe his hEaRt, now! The hunger is suddenly desperate, howling louder than a hurricane. *Kill hiM! KILL HIM!*

It blindsides me, the urge to rip his skin from his face rising like a tide, a moon, something inexorable and unstoppable. I know then, with a horrible pinpoint certainty, that if I don't leave at this very moment, I'll lash out and hurt him. The hunger is *so* much stronger—so much stronger than I've ever felt. It's like I haven't eaten for weeks, *months*, when I haven't eaten for only a day. What's wrong with me?

"Lady Zera? Is something the matter?"

—*KiLL hiM*—

"I-I'm fine." I suppress the terrible hunger with all my combined years of experience, but it resists, tears through me anew like a bladed whirlwind. "I just need to get home."

"Of course." Lucien nods. Malachite comes back then, and it's a blur of the hunger screaming at me as Lucien helps me out of bed. He insists on carrying me to the carriage, but when he reaches for me I thrust my hands out, pushing him away violently. Any closer and he's dead. Any closer and I'll reach into his chest and pull out that godsdamned vital organ of his. Lucien's stunned look evaporates when Malachite steps in, hoisting me into his arms. I don't protest, and Lucien follows us lamely with my sword, a look of helplessness on his face.

He can't learn what I am, or he'll hate me for the deception, for my nature. But he *must* learn what I am, and soon, if I want my freedom.

When I'm in the carriage, sword at my side and Fisher driving me home, when Lucien is so far from me I can't hurt him, only then do I let the hunger rampage through me unbidden.

Only then do I let my teeth show.

The pain that doesn't fade is the first thing to tell me something's wrong. The second is the blood that blossoms on my forearm bandage. Blood means only one thing.

I haven't healed.

A whole day has gone by, and Nightsinger's magic still hasn't healed me.

Y'shennria piles out from her manor so quickly when we pull up it's as if she'd been watching out the window for me. She's at my side in a flash, helping me down from the carriage. My legs nearly give out twice from the pain, but she hefts me higher on her hip, never once ordering me to stand straight or to collect myself. Reginall takes over for Y'shennria in supporting me as we enter the manor, Lord Y'shennria's portrait warmly welcoming me home. The first thing my eyes look for is the fire-calendar, an extra mark burned into it.

"Five days," I moan. "That's all I have left."

"Hush," Y'shennria chides. "Focus on getting better."

"I don't care"—I grunt, every step Reginall takes with me in his arms ricocheting magma pain through my bones—"about getting better. If I get his heart, I'll be fine. His heart. That's all that matters."

"You're delirious." Y'shennria sighs. "Quickly, Reginall, get her in bed."

"I'm going to the Hunt," I insist as he puts me on my bed, wrapping the blankets around me. "I'm still going... no matter what."

"Of course." Y'shennria nods. "Now stop worrying and get some rest."

"Speak for yourself," I snort. She looks utterly fatigued, her dress wrinkled as if she fell asleep in it. Her makeup is a little off, and that's how I know she's been...what, worrying about me? Nonsense. I look to Reginall. "You came as a polymath, right? Disguised."

Y'shennria nods. "When I'd heard you collapsed, I knew it couldn't be from a simple human cause. So I brought the one who knows Heartless best. What happened to you?"

"Prince Lucien and I dueled, and he cut me accidentally, and then I fainted. That sword is made of white mercury. The wound burns, all over my body now. I think it…killed me."

"Surely you're fine—you're lying here talking to us, after all."

"Look!" I offer her a view of my arm. "My wound isn't healed. And the hunger—gods, Y'shennria, it feels like the hunger wants to devour everyone I see. Controlling it is like… like trying to tie down a starving beast with thread."

YoU call us tHe beast, but yoU're the one whO's killed fIve meN. You'rE the onE who's goiNG to beTrAy the prince, the hunger screeches. *PiTiFul.*

Y'shennria pales and quickly leaves the room. Dismay crawls into my throat at her abandonment (still, after everything we've been through?), but Reginall smiles grimly at me.

"Lady Zera, you said it was the prince's sword that killed you? A white mercury weapon?"

I nod. Reginall lets out a breath.

"There were weapons like that, too, in the Sunless War. Blades made of pure white mercury. We knew they were hard to make for the humans, because there weren't many of them. A few generals had one." He pauses. "If it sliced you, the white mercury would linger in your system for days and days, making it hard for your witch to heal you, command you. Do you remember when I told you about the Weeping Heartless?"

"Why?"

"The weeping were always those who'd been killed by a white mercury blade before."

"What are you saying?"

"I'm not entirely sure myself. I'd see them in camp, after battles, suffering with wounds that refused to heal. Being cut by such a strong white mercury blade might weaken a witch's hold on a Heartless, or so we'd hear the witches whisper."

"That's…that's nothing bad," I say. Reginall holds up a hand.

"I didn't know this for many years, but the connection between a witch and Heartless does more than heal you. A witch's magic helps keep your hunger calm. Calm*er*, at least, than if you didn't have a steady stream of magic siphoning into you."

"What are you saying?"

"I'm saying to be cut by a white mercury blade so powerful weakens your connection to your witch. The hunger becomes louder. And the beast within hovers ever closer to assuming control. A few Heartless cut, as you were, transformed randomly—lashing out wildly at anyone and everyone. Eventually considered risks, they were shattered by their witches. Only a few ever mastered Weeping—a way to quiet their hunger out of necessity more than anything. It was that or die."

I swallow. It's already so hard to keep the monster at bay. Reginall pulls a nearby chair up to the side of my bed, staring at me intently. "Close your eyes."

I do as he says, my locket thumping nervously.

"Concentrate on the void in your chest." Reginall's voice is low, even. "Feel the weightlessness of it, the emptiness where a beat should be. You are in the silence. You are of the silence."

The blackness on the back of my eyelids becomes somehow deeper, free of light imprints or nerve strain. Is he teaching me how to weep?

"Place your hand over your unheart," Reginall continues. "And you'll find it there."

I wait, my fingers still against my chest. Find what?

There's nothing under my skin—nothing but darkness. I'm incomplete, inhuman. There's nothing but a girl made of mistakes and lies beneath my hand. The door opens, and Reginall startles, my eyes flinging open. Y'shennria walks in, a silver tray of livers in her hands. She wrinkles her nose and places them on my bedside table.

"Eat."

GlAdly, the hunger screams. **OfFer yoUr tHroaT so I caN finIsh whaT tHe oTheRs staRteD.**

I wolf the livers down so fast I gag. Y'shennria turns her back, watching outside the window. Even Reginall, no doubt used to the sight, turns away, straightening a sandclock on the shelf. When the plate is clean, I expect to feel full, for the voices to stop. But the hunger still screams in my ears, deafening.

"H-Have you heard from Fione?" I struggle. "Did she get what she needed?"

Y'shennria nods. "She asked you to visit her at the royal shooting range. I told her only when you get better. If you get better at all."

"I will," I insist, unsettled by how unsure my voice sounds.

"Do not help Lady Fione more than necessary, Zera. No amount of help she can give us is worth exposing you." Y'shennria won't meet my eyes as she lingers in the doorway. "Rest, for now. Reginall, come. Leave her."

Reginall goes to her, flashing me one last hesitant smile and bowing as he closes the door. My unheart sinks—does Y'shennria think me useless now? If I lose my Heartless abilities, will she find some replacement for me? Logic manages to claw its way through my fears; she doesn't have the time to train a human girl to get the prince's attention. She's stuck with me, no matter how useless I become.

ShE caN't abAnDon whaT sHe doeSn't lOve, the hunger sneers.

Even with a plateful of livers in my stomach, the hunger isn't satisfied in the slightest. It shrieks for more. I can't sleep to ignore it, either, its nasty, violent thoughts piling up and up, like rancid garbage, like rusted needles poking under my skin. Maeve walks by my cracked-open door, dusting the hall's paintings, and the hunger claws against my skull.

OLd, wEak, easY prEy, a wArMup foR tHe huNTing dAy—

The sight in the mirror across from me only makes it worse— my reflection pale and ragged, my teeth constantly long, no matter how hard I fight to hide them. How will I ever blend in at the court again—at the Hunt—if I can't control myself?

How will Lucien ever forgive me if I take his heart?

He wOn'T—

I put my left hand over my right, desperately trying to imitate the warmth of his palm, the silken feel of his fingers against mine.

ImpOssiBle, the hunger snarls. ***You cAn't haVe boTh his heArts, yoU paThEtic liTTle girl—***

Fed up with wallowing in my own pain and mental filth, I grab my sword and get out of bed. The sun set long ago, and as I venture downstairs I spot the remnants of Y'shennria's preparations for the Hunt—an open trunk of mine, filled with perfectly folded dresses. The fire-calendar mocks me relentlessly, its charred marks like black eyes watching me. Lucien's eyes. What is this awful obsession with him all of a sudden? Just because he touched my hand? Why can't I shake him from my mind?

I stumble, my legs giving way for a moment. I'm weak. I'm distracted.

YoU'll nEver geT HiS hEarT liKe thiS—yOu'll dIe liKe this—

The hunger's voice is like a dozen harps being dragged over broken glass, jagged, the strings snapping as they go. Determined for a moment of peace, I venture outside and grab a whetstone, a bowl of water, and a rag. On the steps of the manor, in the full red and blue moonlight, I sharpen Father's sword relentlessly—the repetitive movements just barely drowning the hunger. The hordes of black rosebushes sway in the midnight wind, thorns like fangs trying to pierce the sky.

HoW maNy more pEopLe do yOu haVE to maKe sUFfer beFore you'Re sAtiSfied?

I admire my work, Father's sword so sharp I entertain the thought of trying to cut the moonlight itself.

It'S a cYcle Of hATE anD paIn and you're jUSt anOtheR wheel keepiNg it going—

The hunger's doubts and fears are a cacophony, never-ending. I clutch my head and double over.

"Lady Zera?" Reginall's voice makes me turn, his bushy eyebrows drawn in concern. "Are you all right?"

"No," I admit, half laughing. "Something's wrong with me. I'm in pain. The hunger is so loud and distorted. And my wound—" I hold up my bloodstained bandage, fresh red overtaking the faded brassy blood. "It won't godsdamn heal."

Reginall tidies my whetting mess, putting the bowl and rag aside. He's quiet for a long while, the hunger eating away at me with every second that passes. Finally, he clears his throat.

"Some wounds never do. Not even with magic."

He looks up at the lit window of Y'shennria's room on the second floor, and I watch the light with him.

"I'm afraid," I say. "Afraid of failing her. Failing myself."

"I see."

"But I'm more afraid of doing the wrong thing."

I feel Reginall's eyes on me, as if he's trying to read my face. His voice is a bare murmur.

"I remember what it feels like, still—being weighed down by the enormous burden of taking others' lives. Of being haunted by our every mistake, every doubt, every hunger, unable to forget. People love to say Heartless aren't human." He nods. "But to this day, I still wonder if they're perhaps more human than the humans themselves."

The moons watch us quietly as they chase the stars across the sky. Reginall stares at the Red Twins.

"No matter how bad the hunger gets, milady, you must remember it is a passenger in your body. It can feel oppressive, but it does not own you. You are very much still the *you* you were before you were turned."

"I can't remember who that was anymore." I choke on my own voice.

"Then you must hold on for that day when you can remember again."

The laugh that erupts from me is hysterical. "What if I fail? What if I'm shattered into pieces like a toy, what if I die without ever getting my heart, the memories in it—"

Reginall grips my shoulder, his wrinkled face set hard.

"Please, milady. Don't lose faith in yourself. It is the only thing the hunger can't take from you."

"It's stolen everything," I snarl. "How am I supposed to hope, when it tries to steal even that from me?"

He takes my hands in his own, unafraid of who I am. What I am.

"Fight," he insists, voice like fire, so different from his usual modest tenor. "Fight with everything you have, everything you are. Everything that is left of you—battle with it. Fight by the moonlight, the starlight, whatever faded hope you can find at any moment—cling to it. Embrace the smallest of lights, and never stop fighting."

I go silent, and we watch the sunrise together. I'm the first to retreat into the house. I ascend the stairs, the pain begging me to stop moving, the hunger begging me to tear someone, anyone, apart. I stand in the middle of my room, fighting it. My body and mind are exhausted, assaulted on every side. If I take Lucien's heart, I'll be free. That rings in my head like a mantra, a prayer.

His heart. Freedom. His heart. *Freedom.*

I reach for a dress and my makeup.

When I walk into the dining room for breakfast, I'm perfectly outfitted in a blue velvet dress, perfectly primped in blush and blue lip tint and dark wax lines down my cheeks like banners of war. Y'shennria looks up from her book with a stunned expression.

"Y-You—" She stutters for the first time I've ever heard. "You shouldn't be walking."

I smile with my lady's mask at her, and sit at the table. "That's what they all say."

It takes much convincing, but Y'shennria relents and allows me to meet Fione at the royal shooting range only when I can prove my coherency by reciting everything I know back to her. Firstbloods, Secondbloods, Goldbloods. The small spoons for cold soups, the large spoons for hot ones. Never take the hand of a man unless offered to you—a hundred questions, and a hundred answers I know by heart now. Y'shennria pauses after the last one.

"Something wrong?" I inquire. She frowns.

"You've learned well."

"Then why do you look upset about it?"

"I'm not," she corrects. "It's just…so strange. To feel pride like this."

"For a Heartless," I finish for her. She meets my gaze with her own soft one.

"For anyone. After my family died I thought—" Her elegant, scarred throat bobs. "I thought I'd never feel this way again."

She fixes her eyes on Lord Y'shennria's painting. I look at him with her.

"If he were here, I'd bet he'd be proud of you, too," I dare. Y'shennria tears her eyes from him, and I swear I see wetness there, but I must be wrong. Y'shennria doesn't cry—not in front of me, not in front of anyone.

"He'd tell me I was a paranoid old woman," she starts with a little laugh. "And I'd tell him to shut up."

She laughs and laughs. Somehow, in this moment, she seems so much younger. I ball my fists.

"I promise you, Lady Y'shennria—I promise you I'll prevent this war."

Y'shennria calms at this, wiping her eyes with her kerchief softly. "You little fool—of course you will."

An insult to anyone else, from anyone else. But from her, her confidence in me, her certainty—it's as near to a compliment as I can imagine. And I hold it close as I get in the carriage, as I watch the Y'shennria manor grow smaller and smaller behind me.

The royal shooting range is little more than a perfectly manicured lawn on the outskirts of Vetris with a few straw targets and weary groundskeepers with green mantles wandering about. No other nobles are present, which leads me to believe archery isn't very popular in Vetris. Either that, or someone got a stray arrow lodged in their arse here very recently.

"Lady Zera!" Fione waves me over to the only occupied lane—a hefty crossbow cradled in her thin arms. "I was wondering if you'd show!"

I trot to her, her target in the distance riddled with bolts. She aims and shoots, the steel-tipped wood cleanly sinking near the center. I whistle, impressed.

"Remind me to add you to the list of 'people I should definitely never piss off.'"

"I wasn't on that list already?" Fione laughs, winding the crannequin for another shot. "I'm hurt."

"Allow me to throw myself a momentary pity party," I motion to my bandaged forearm and wrist. "You're not as hurt as me."

She laughs again. "True. Y'shennria said not to expect you well enough to stand for several days."

"Auntie tends to underestimate my prodigious willpower," I say. "Or as she likes to call it, my 'pig-headed stubbornness.'"

My eyes catch Fione's valkerax-head cane as it rests on a nearby railing. *ShE'd be sLoW tO rUn*, the hunger snarls, ravenous. *CoNsuMe heR doWn to hEr preTTy cUrLs.*

Fione smiles faintly as she aims and fires another arrow. This one lands even closer to the center of the target. A groundskeeper approaches and asks if I need anything, but she waves him away, and he retreats.

"You'd think they'd know by the giant crossbow in my arms that I want to be left alone," Fione jokes.

"You're a noble, they're servants. It's a bit difficult to leave someone alone when you know they hold your fate in the palm of their hand," I drawl. Fione freezes, then nocks the next bolt in her bow, thinking on this. She fires again, the bolt missing the target entirely. She frowns prettily.

"I suppose I've never thought of it that way."

She fires three more bolts, these all clustered together at the heart of the straw target. She's got a keen eye, but she's easily distracted by her own thoughts. The single missed bolt tells me that much.

"Did you get what you needed?" I ask quietly. Fione looks up at me and smiles.

"I might've opened a puzzle-locked safe in a certain office in the palace, and I might've seen the name of a tower in the noble quarter. Then again, I might've heard a lawguard coming down the hall and escaped before I could read everything thoroughly."

"You have a funny way of saying yes." I squint. She giggles, leaning on her hefty crossbow as she does her cane.

"Your...sacrifice, shall we call it? I assure you, it didn't go to waste. What exactly made you faint? Are you bloodshy?"

I'm quiet, flicking through my mind for some excuse. Fione picks the crossbow back up, winding a bolt carefully.

"Prince Lucien says it was an infection. But I overheard my uncle thinking aloud to a royal polymath that no infection spreads that quickly."

My mouth goes dry—the last thing I need is Gavik suspecting me more.

"I was—" I lean in to her. "You can't tell anyone."

"Your secret's safe with me. We're in this together, after all."

I take in her wide, waiting blue eyes. She's an expert at

sniffing out information, secrets. I have to lie convincingly to hide the bigger lies beneath. I gnaw my lip for effect.

"I'm...fasting. The other Brides are so slender, and I—"

"Oh gods, not you, too." Fione heaves a sigh. "Is that why you visited the bathroom so much during that banquet? I hate this godsdamned Avellish trend. Just eat, all right?"

"Thankfully, you aren't my mother," I say.

"I won't have a half-starved thing helping me bring my uncle down," she insists. "Eat, or I'm cutting you from the team, and you lose your time with the prince."

WhiCh pArt shoUld wE eaT first? The hunger slithers around her, resting my eyes on her neck, her wrists—the most tender parts. *YoUr soFt eyEs, or youR soFt hEart?*

"For all your hatred of your uncle, you certainly threaten as well as he does," I manage. Fione laughs and lets the bolt fly. It sinks into the center of the target with a wooden *thud*, and it's not until the wind picks up that I see the two thin pieces of bolt dancing in the breeze. That shot cut another of her bolts in half in perfect overlap. I know nothing about archery, but a shot like that seems nearly impossible.

She turns and grins at me. If Gavik's eyes are water, hers are sky.

"True. He and I are very similar. But so are you and your 'aunt'. Even Lucien is a little like his father, no matter how he denies it. That's the cruel thing about family, isn't it? No matter how we feel about them, we will always look like them, act like them. We were raised by them, after all."

Fione puts the crossbow down and picks up her cane.

"It's not a question of whether or not the apple falls far from the tree, because of course it doesn't." Her eyes fix in the distance. "It's whether or not the apple can grow taller than the tree."

13

A MAN WITHOUT
MERCY MUST FALL

"**P**LEASE LEAVE US, if you would," Fione asks the groundskeeper nearby. He bows and quickly shuffles off, his
hound at his heels. When she's sure he's gone, Fione glances
back to me. "I'm expecting guests."

No sooner has she said this than two figures emerge from
the tree line behind the shooting range—one dark-haired, the
other gray, both tall and broad. Prince Lucien and Malachite.
They stride across the grass, and every thief's instinct in me
screams they were waiting in the woods all along. Watching us.

When they approach close enough, I ask, "Do you enjoy
staring at people for extended periods of time without their
knowledge, Your Highness?"

"I'm no decorum expert," Malachite retorts. "But shouldn't
you at least curtsy before you start throwing around accusations?"

Fione bobs into a curtsy, and I begrudgingly do the same.
Lucien bows ever so slightly to us, as befitting a Firstblood to
two others. Malachite watches it all, highly amused. Lucien's
dark-iron eyes fix on me as he straightens.

"Surely your wounds haven't healed yet. Are you in pain?"

CoNsTantLy, the hunger snarls.

His concern is too soft. Too unguarded. Seeing it is like a starving wolf watching a lamb struggle. Tempting, and borderline pathetic. I counted him warier than this. I counted him smart. Maybe I misjudged him. Or maybe, despite his scars, his heart hasn't learned to stop yearning. I've warned him again and again. And still he worries for me. Still he looks at me gently.

WhAt a fOoL.

"It's nothing a little polymath medicine can't fix," I assure him. Malachite laughs.

"It was all I could do to keep him from rushing to you the second he saw you. But when he realized you could stand and breathe as well as the rest of us, he evened out."

"Mal," Lucien warns, a flush working up his neck. "Silence."

Malachite waves a hand at him. "Fine, fine. The usual then—I'll just shut up and watch."

Fione chimes in. "If the prince agrees to my proposition, you'll be doing much more than that, Sir Malachite."

This captures all of our attentions, our eyes riveting to her apple-cheeked smile. Sensing she has the floor, she places two bolts carefully on the nearby railing, standing them up to point at the sky. She touches the tip of one.

"This is the Crimson Lady, at the edge of the common district." She touches the other. "This is the East River Tower, on the edge of the noble district."

"Just the geography lesson I needed," I drawl. Fione smiles at me, forced.

"I've learned that the East River Tower holds the evidence I've previously spoken to you all about."

"The East River Tower is a granary storage," Malachite

says. "It has no exits or entrances."

"No windows, either," Lucien agrees. "If Gavik buried that evidence in ten tons of grain somehow, you'll have to blow through the stone to get it." He looks to me. "Do you know how to make a bomb by any chance, Lady Zera?"

"Why ask me, Your Highness?" I quirk a brow.

"You know how to duel, how to thieve, and how to sniff me out despite every hiding place I can think of," he says. "I thought you might have an explosive trick up your sleeve as well."

"If only." I sigh. "Maybe then those banquets wouldn't be so boring."

Malachite lets out a horrified gasp. "Don't you even *think* of detonating my favorite salmon cream puffs!"

Fione clears her throat. "All of you are terrible at staying on track."

"I'd try to stay on track if you weren't talking nonsense," Lucien grumbles. "Your evidence is in the East River Tower—and what? It's a sealed tower. No one can get in there."

"I don't want to get *in* there," she asserts. "I want to get *below* there."

Lucien and I exchange a look. Fione taps her nails on the railing connecting the two upright crossbow bolts.

"I think my uncle cleared out an old watertell pipe and is using it as a tunnel between the Crimson Lady, where he does most of his work with the polymaths, and the East River Tower, where I believe he keeps his sensitive research material."

"A watertell pipe?" Lucien wrinkles his nose. "I have a hard time imagining Gavik squeezing himself down such a tiny thing every time he wants to access research."

"You're right, Your Highness," Fione says cheerily. "The new ones, installed in the last decade, are very small. But the old ones—the prototype builds? They're huge, and they remain beneath the city."

"How can you be so sure?" I ask.

"I've seen the old maps—one of them goes directly from the Crimson Lady to the East River Tower."

"And you think he keeps the information lying around in the pipe below it?" I cock my head.

"I don't know, but all the evidence points below that tower. If we can get beneath it, I'm certain we'll find enough to incriminate him to the king."

Malachite holds up a hand like a patient schoolchild, and Fione nods to him.

"So you want the four of us to infiltrate the most powerful anti-witch weapon in the country—in the world—to find this pipe?"

There's a silence even Fione doesn't have an answer for. Malachite presses on.

"The Crimson Lady is guarded around the sandclock, in eight shifts of ten men apiece. The pipe's probably in the basement levels, where all the delicate water pumps are that keep the damned thing running. Which, of course, is guarded by two independent patrols made up of the largest and strongest celeon guards Vetris has to offer. And you want us to get in there without being seen."

"I didn't say it would be easy," Fione says slowly.

"You didn't say it would be impossible, either," Lucien snaps.

"Not to mention any locks we meet on the way," I muse.

"I have all the keys we need for the Crimson Lady," Fione insists. Malachite blinks rapidly.

"Do you, now? And how in your troublesome god's name did you get those?"

"That's none of your concern." She frowns. "I just need to know if you three are willing to come with me."

"I, personally, do not enjoy being killed for trespassing," I admit.

"It's not as if I don't have a plan," she insists. "Lucien—is it possible for you to borrow four polymath robes from the Star Hall in the palace?"

The prince thinks for a moment. "Yes. But they'd be missed in less than an hour."

"We won't need more time than that, if all goes well."

"And if it doesn't?" he asks. She meets his gaze squarely.

"Then we never discover the truth of who killed your sister. And my uncle's reign of terror continues, until your citizens are driven into the arms of war."

Fione's words ring powerfully in the echoing moment of quiet between us. The prince has already made up his mind—I can see it. Malachite can see it, too.

"Ugh." The Beneather sighs. "Fine. But if we get caught, I'm ratting you all out so my remains get sent back to Pala Amna, at the very least."

Lucien nods to Fione. "I'll do it."

They all look to me. A laugh tears through me—at the absurdity of it all, at the determination of these noble children, of their dedication to the memory of a princess long dead. I can't imagine being loved so well. Or ever. Jealousy rises in me again—a snake that adores emerging whenever the humans do wonderful and stupid things with their mortal lives.

They can risk so much, because they have so much. Their hearts. Futures. Freedoms.

And here I am, begging for their scraps. Begging for an opening to take what I want and run.

I smile. "When do we get started?"

ione tells each of us what to bring and where to meet tonight. She is a mastermind—she already has four polymath tool belts, each distinct and each used as a badge of passage within the Crimson Lady. How she got them I can only guess at—but I'm willing to bet it involves blackmail and abusing much of her uncle's connections. Lucien will provide the robes, and as long as we keep our hoods up, no one should be any the wiser. Malachite is the muscle, and I'm—according to Fione—the excuse.

"If something goes wrong and we get caught," she'd said, "you are to pretend you were curious about the Crimson Lady, and begged Prince Lucien to bring you here. He will say he agreed because he 'loves you so,' begging the guard's silence and forgiveness."

At that Lucien had gone stock-still, his proud jaw tightening, and Malachite chortled to himself like a choking snowhyena.

"You don't think that'll actually work?" I'd managed through my dry throat. Fione grinned at me—not falsely saccharine, but wide and confident.

"He's their prince. Their future king. My uncle might not hesitate to punish the prince, but everyone else in Vetris surely will."

As I ride home in the carriage, Fisher leading us slowly through a spate of traffic in the market, I realize with blinding clarity that Fione is using us. Lucien agrees to it out of his need to know his sister's true fate, Malachite agrees for Lucien, and I agree for my own heart. A pipe system, shadows, edges of the noble quarter, splitting up to cover ground—all things that could line up perfectly to take his heart.

A spasm of ravenous hunger runs through me, stabbing between my every breath. I clutch at my chest, praying for the pain to stop. My wounded forearm begins to ooze blood, the bandages crimson all at once.

All of Fione's smiles, all her insistences on getting us together—it's not to be friendly, or to get to know us as people. It's to use us, like pawns in a game. I suppose when you want something badly enough, when you lose the thing most precious to you, people just become toys, puppets to move around to achieve your goals.

I'm using Lucien the same way Fione is. He's just a puppet to me. A stepping stone.

LiAr, the hunger shrieks with a thousand glass-crash voices. *YoU'rE a tErriBle liAr.*

Shouts tear me out of my own head. I watch outside the carriage window as the market crowd points at something in the sky—no, something settled on a building high up. Crows. Their shiny black feathers catch the sunlight, all except one. One crow, stark white.

"A witch!"

"Someone get the lawguards!"

"Shoot it down!"

A fruit merchant with a small crossbow does the honors. He shakes as he lines up the shot, but when the bird hits the ground the market erupts into cheers. The lawguards quickly congregate and take the bird's body away, and I watch them pass my carriage window. Blood drips from between the lawguard's hands. White feathers work free of the bird's lifeless body, swirling in the crowd's wake. The glassy pink eyes watch me, unblinking. Not a witch—witch-crows have no color at all on them. An animal. An albino.

A beautiful thing born in the wrong era.

14

SIN AND SHADOW

IT'S BEEN ONLY TWO WEEKS and Y'shennria can already tell when I'm up to something. That's the double-bladed peril of getting to know someone—you learn them, but they learn you.

Y'shennria narrows her eyes at me. "You're preparing for something."

"Is it that obvious?" I chirp, throwing steel hairpins into the belt pouch on my bed. When she doesn't say anything, I add in some medical gauze, travel rations, and emergency gold coins.

"Yes," she deadpans. "Did Lady Himintell forget to tell me about whatever illegal scheme she's borrowed you for this time?"

"Scheme?" I gasp. "Auntie, please. It's just a night of innocent drinking among terribly rich and bored young adults."

She raises a fine eyebrow at the steel hairpins hanging out of the pouch. I clear my throat.

"All right, you got me—there *may* be some mild breaking and entering. But that's it." She stares pointedly at me. I add,

"Unless you count smooching as an illegal scheme. Which, just between you and me, I think it should be."

"Zera." She sweeps over and upends the pouch on the bed. "You must tell me what's going on."

"If I do, you'll try to stop me."

"I'm stopping you regardless—we are so *close* to the Hunt. I won't have you ruin everything we've been working for on one night of crusading for Lady Himintell's cause."

"I thought you liked her," I say. "Weren't you the one who asked me to get along with her? You said she'd help me."

"That was before I—" Y'shennria swallows. "That was before I realized what a clean opportunity the Hunt is. It's the ideal setting."

"For you," I fire back. "I was fine with it, too, for a while. But then the hunger—it just keeps getting worse and worse."

"Zera…" Her eyes soften.

"I can barely hear myself think anymore," I interject. "Eating helps, but for only a few minutes. Every time I look at you, or Maeve, or anyone with human blood in them, the hunger shows me perfect images of ripping them to shreds. It's gotten so loud. It's loud right now, screaming at me to kill you."

—teaR tHe sKIn frOm hEr faCe and dRink yOur fiLL—

Y'shennria's dark complexion pales, tingeing greenish. "Zera, you mustn't—"

"I know I mustn't. I've always known. But ever since Lucien's sword cut me, it's been unending hunger. Do you know what it's like? To want to rip the world to shreds?"

The Red Twins peek through the windows, over the Tollmount-Kilstead mountains in the distance, like two crimson eyes watching us unblinkingly. Finally, Y'shennria nods.

"I do. And it's an awful thing."

She slides one hand toward my own on the bed. She hesitates, pulling back once before forcing herself the rest of the way. Her hand over mine is cool, slender.

"You must not put yourself in unnecessary danger."

"That's the whole reason I'm here," I argue.

"No," she says, stone in her voice. "Danger, certainly. But not unnecessary danger. If you're caught, it's over. For you and for me. For many witches."

"We can't bank all our hopes on the Hunt," I snap. "If an opportunity presents itself, I want to be there—"

"As do I," she interrupts, voice inching louder. "To make sure I can get you back to the manor without being seen. To ensure you aren't wounded by the prince's bodyguard, or worse."

I start to laugh, the sound despairing. "None of those are the fiercely logical Y'shennria reasons I've grown to know and love. It sounds almost like you…" My throat swells up, unable to form the next few sounds. Y'shennria takes her hand from mine, staring at her palms with a pained gaze.

"I don't want another painting in my hall, Zera."

A painting. She means like Lord Y'shennria's—a portrait of the dead. She clears her throat and turns her head to me, fluffy hair catching the red moonlight.

"It began as make believe," she says. "As pretend. Playing house, with a new niece. Buying her things, teaching her things, watching her improve as a lady before my very eyes. I had hoped, a long time ago, to do such things with my own daughters. When they were taken from me, I—" Her scarred throat bobs. "I made myself give it all up. Locked the very thought of it away behind steel and glass."

Her eyes catch mine, and she smiles twistedly.

"But the Old God loves to test us," she presses on. "He loves to send us people who change our lives in great and terrible ways."

"When I become human again," I start, "then you can care about me. Not now. Not when I'm like this."

Y'shennria laughs. "You don't get to tell me when to care about you, Zera. That's not how being an auntie works."

My unheart clenches in my locket, so hard and sudden I skip a breath. Y'shennria recovers quicker than I do, always—she stands and makes her way to the door.

"You will not go tonight," she says, clipped. "I'll be ordering Reginall to lock all your windows from the outside, and he will be guarding your door for the rest of the night. If you leave, I will know."

"You can't stop me," I snarl.

"No. But this can." She holds up a dagger, a strange groove in the blade and a little latch at the base of the handle. A white mercury dagger.

"You—how'd you get one of those?"

"I may have asked the witches to give me one before you came to Vetris—a contingency required for me to agree to their proposition. I was quite worried about having a Heartless sleeping next to me. The difference now is I'll use it not out of fear, but for your own good."

"I warn you—I'm very good with a sword," I press.

Y'shennria's brows arch delicately. "And I've been wielding a dagger since long before you were born. You will not leave this room. You will not act on your own. You will attend the Hunt as we planned."

She closes the door behind me with a soft *thunk*, the volume of it somehow more enraging than if she'd slammed it violently. I pace on the rug, my fists clenched. I should've known better—Y'shennria is just as stubborn as I am. She can understand my pain but not my hunger. I can feel it worming its dark fingers deeper into my veins with every second. I ate livers earlier, but the relief lasted a bare few minutes. If I don't leave now, I'll be late to the meeting place, and too hungry to even talk to anyone without my teeth showing.

A glassy *clink* draws my attention—an iron rod clipping my window locks closed from the outside. Reginall. He does each one, daring an apologetic smile up at me when I glare down at him from the window. I can't break the glass, or Y'shennria would hear it. Besides, even if I jumped, I'd break my legs, and with my forearm still unhealed I seriously doubt my legs would heal either.

I bend three iron hairpins trying to pick open my door lock with no success. I shout to Reginall to let me out, pleading, but he doesn't answer back. The hunger dares me to break things, break them *(brEaK tHe foolS hOldiNg uS aGainsT oUr wiLL)*, but I rein in my jagged-growing teeth. Finally, I collapse on the bed, anger and effort exhausting me equally, my eyes skimming the black diamond pattern in the ceiling I've grown so used to.

Y'shennria is by no means an idiot. If anything, I'm one for daring to flaunt my intentions right in front of her. Then again, I couldn't have seen this little lockup coming, considering I didn't know at the time that she…cares for me. It's with a begrudging sort of gratitude that I realize this must be how all humans with parents and guardians feel: angry and yet finding it impossible to be truly angry with them. My memories of how it was with my parents are long gone, but this feels somehow familiar. Somehow…*right.*

"I'll care about her, too," I grumble. "Just as soon as I'm done being furious with her."

My eyes catch on the far left corner of the ceiling. There, the dark diamond tile is off—just a little more pronounced. I didn't notice it the first few days, but after a straight week of staring at a ceiling, one tends to spot differences. I don't make a habit of retaining every piece of useless noble gossip I hear, but my mind wanders to one:

It was a dinner party, one Y'shennria threw for me before I went to court. Baroness d'Goliev smiled at me with all her aging yellowed teeth over her cold fig custard.

"You should've met Lord Y'shennria, Lady Zera. A more brilliant man at court there'll never be again." She'd sighed.

"Oh?" I was genuinely curious. "Was he a polymath?"

"In his younger days, he aspired to be one. But his family was quite insistent he marry a Firstblood and bring honor to their name. And he always had a weak spot for family." The Baroness wipes a fleck of custard off her silk bosom. "But he never lost his spark. Why, as a young boy he'd bring all sorts of little contraptions to court—things that moved, things with secret doors, little boxes you couldn't open without puzzle solutions. He later refined the puzzle-locks, and sold the patent to Archduke Gavik, if you can believe it! That was the only invention of his that he pursued. Oh, and this manor, of course."

"This manor? Did he have a hand in building it?" I asked.

"Indeed! He invited me over during its construction, in fact. Showed me a wonderful little catwalk of his, in the upper levels. You had to get to it by this athletic hole in the ceiling—but it was so well hidden I never spotted it at all!"

The Baroness laughed, and I laughed with her.

But now, I'm not laughing. I stand beneath the strange tile. It's high up, but if I move furniture to reach it too loudly Y'shennria will definitely hear. Surely she'd know if my room had a secret catwalk made by her husband. Still, I carefully pile my trunks on top of one another—as wobbly as it is, it gets me high enough to touch the tile. I press on it, and like a tightly wound spring it gives, the tile opening on a hinge and revealing a dark hole just barely big enough for someone my size to fit through.

"Gods bless you, you clearly very skinny genius," I grunt, reaching for the hole. I pull myself up with difficulty, a dim corridor stretching ahead of me. I stay on my hands and knees, making my impacts with the wooden catwalk as gentle as possible. I must be passing over Y'shennria's room right now.

The corridor ends just above what I think is the bathroom. The spring-loaded tile gives way under my hands, and I lower myself off the edge carefully, my boots still making a resounding *thud*. I freeze, waiting for the inevitable uproar, but nothing happens. My hand reaches for the doorknob, only to find it locked. It's never locked! Count on Y'shennria to cover all her bases.

I wander to the windows; at least they're unlocked. And then I see it—a cherry tree, tall and proud and twisted just so. I *could* do it. I could also miss and shatter my entire spine, and it wouldn't heal this time.

"In the words of the very intelligent witch philosopher Erildan," I grunt as I open the window and perch myself on it, the night wind blowing my hair every which way. "*What is safe can never be satisfying.*"

I throw myself as far as I can, and for a split second, I feel like I'm flying. Then painful reality slams into me, my torso wrapping around a branch and knocking the wind from me. I scrabble to hold on, easing myself down to the ground and limping away into the night, far from the sight of the manor.

"In the deathbed words of the maybe not-so-intelligent witch philosopher Erildan," I pant. "*I shouldn't have done that.*"

I'm in so much pain from elsewhere on my body I don't notice the cut on my cheek until I enter the Tiger's Eye Pub, and Prince Lucien, sitting at a table in his dark leather cowl and armor, starts up from his chair. The windlutes playing in the corner go soft to my ears, the crowd drinking and singing all around us dulling as he approaches. His sharp, dark eyes over his cowl are the only things I can see of his expression.

"You're hurt," he murmurs, procuring a handkerchief from seemingly nowhere and pressing it to my face. He sighs. "I'm starting to hate this trend wherein you're always somehow bleeding when I lay eyes on you."

"I happen to be a girl of many talents, including expunging life force from all orifices," I chirp, then wince. "Oh gods. I didn't mean to make a monthly joke this early in our partnership."

Lucien smirks. From behind his broad shoulders I hear a loud, half-swallowed laugh. Malachite sits at the table watching us, though when I look his way he avoids my gaze. Fione sits next to him, tapping her fingers impatiently on the wood. Lucien looks at them, then to me.

"Don't egg Malachite on—he's got the humor of a ten-year-old."

"He heard that?" I marvel. Lucien leads me to the table.

"What? Did you think those things on the side of his head were just for show?"

Malachite's long ears bob in the lamplight as he nods to me.

Fione clears her throat. "Now that we're all finally assembled—"

"My apologies," I whisper frantically. "For having to escape *total familial lockdown.*"

"We can begin." She ignores me. "Let's go."

She stands, Malachite following suit, but Lucien asks, "Where will we change?"

"Not here. The streets are safer," Fione asserts.

"Where?" Lucien repeats. "What street?"

"I was thinking First and North."

"Butcher's Alley? That whole place is swarming with lawguards this time of night. Second and Fish is better."

"I'm sorry, Your Highness." Fione smiles sweetly at him. "But with all due respect, this is my operation."

"With all due respect," he retorts, stone and dark iron. "This is my city. I know it better than you. Of that, I'm certain."

There's a tense moment where they stare each other down, and Malachite rolls his eyes at me in a *this is how they always are* way.

"Not to be the bearer of bad news or anything." I cough. "But there's this pesky little thing called time, and it keeps moving forward whether or not we're moving with it."

The animosity between the nobles breaks, and Fione sniffs, standing with her cane. "Very well. Second and Fish. Quickly!"

The four of us depart the Tiger's Eye Pub, Lucien leading the way. He takes us through a dizzying series of sharp turns until he stops us in a disused alley filled with fish guts. I gag, the scent nearly as bad as my worst memories of death.

"Ugh." Fione winces. "This place reeks."

"Why do you think the lawguards avoid it?" Lucien says coolly.

"Is this the part where we all start stripping wantonly?" Malachite asks, utterly unaffected by the smell. "Because that's really the only reason I'm here."

Lucien hands us each a plain brown robe, and we pick four less-infested corners in which to throw the robes on over our clothes, much to Malachite's groaning dismay. Fione shows us how to fasten our copper tool-laden belts around our waists so they look natural. But then Fione and Lucien begin to argue about something called the "caliper axis," until Fione sharply reminds him we aren't trying to disguise ourselves as *royal* polymaths, after which he falls silent.

With our hoods up, the four of us step into the streets of Vetris and head for the looming obelisk of the Crimson Lady. Our nerves sizzle in the air—Lucien closing and opening his fist, Fione, cane close to her side but hidden beneath her robe's folds as my sword is, practicing what I remember her calling her "normie" walk. Even Malachite grinds his jaw anxiously. The closer we get to the Lady, the more and more lawguards begin to crop up. Most leave us be, uninterested in a few polymaths out for a stroll with their hoods up—a common enough occurrence. Finally we face down the front stairs of the tower herself.

Fione mutters to us, "I'll be the one talking. Follow my lead."

I give her a mock salute, and she flashes me a little smile—one of her real ones—before sinking farther into the shadows of her hood. We follow on her heels, the four lawguards flanking the stairs moving for us only when we reach for the door.

"Whoa, one minute." A lawguard holds up his hand. "Archduke Gavik said there were to be no further visitors tonight. We've got enough bodies working in here."

"There's been a leak in the storage units." Fione's voice is startlingly deep, different. "We must let our superiors know as soon as possible!"

The lawguard sniffs, his eyes roving up and down our tool belts like he's checking for something. "Sorry, not happening. The storage unit fellows can take care of it."

"The storage unit fellows are knocked out from the mercury's gasses," she says sharply. "All seventeen of them." The lawguard looks taken aback. Fione doesn't relent. "So unless you'd personally like to explain to Archduke Gavik why his entire supply of white mercury has gone up in smoke overnight, I suggest you let us through. Now."

"Y-Your hoods—"

"We inhaled the smoke, too. Our eyes are sensitive to even moonlight because of it. For Kavar's sake, let us in, before we pass out with the details of this leak still in our heads!"

The lawguard starts, saluting suddenly and pressing the door open. Fione darts through with all the alacrity of a house cat, and we follow. Her strides are huge and fast, never slowing as she leads us through stone corridors and rooms of hissing copper machinery over which scores of polymaths are bent. Finally, she slows in a stairwell, removing her hood and clipping the same copper rod I saw Gavik use to amplify his voice during the purge to her belt. Is that what made her voice sound so strange? She points to a steel hatch.

"That's it."

"Are you sure?" Lucien asks.

"Reasonably," she snarks. "I've pored over the blueprints for this place for only six months."

"How—" Malachite starts. "How do you know so much about white mercury containment and stuff?"

"Why are your eyes glowing red?" she fires back. "You first."

I peer just enough to see beneath his hood—Malachite's crimson eyes glow gently, as if lit up from within by some inner fire, his pupils thin.

"Beneather thing during full moons," he lilts. "What's your excuse?"

"My uncle's an arsehole."

Malachite nods, impressed. "Fair enough."

"If you're done, we should go," Lucien mutters, dagger-eyes darting about. "Standing in any one place for too long goes against my personal beliefs."

Fione fishes a ring of keys from her tool belt and looks up at Malachite and Lucien. "Keep watch."

She kneels at the hatch, fiddling with the lock as she tries each key.

Malachite suddenly hisses, "Bogey coming west. Get that thing open."

"I'm trying!" Fione grits out.

"Try faster," I singsong.

"Vetrisian blueprints don't exactly have key-to-lock ciphers on them," she argues, shoving a gold key in the lock.

Lucien never takes his eyes off the polymath approaching, his hand moving slowly to the hilt of his sword under his robe as he murmurs to Malachite, "Remind me to change that when I become king."

Malachite groans and fingers his serrated dagger on his hip. The droopy-eyed polymath is already shooting wary looks our way. Middle-aged, greasy-haired, and ready to blow the whistle on us. A danger.

"I'll catch up to you," I whisper to Lucien and Malachite. "Just make sure the rest of you get down there."

"What are you planning, Lady Zera?" Lucien narrows his eyes. I wink at him, and start down the hall. I peel my hood off slowly, using every trick I've learned since coming to court to make my smile irresistible. This guy's a polymath— not a royal one—so the chances he knows my face and the title that goes with it are slim. I pout my lips and bat my eyelashes at him, imagining for the briefest moment he's the prince behind me, instead. I know I've got him when he trips a little on the hem of his own robe. He's distracted—and now for the final touch. I stumble, thrusting my not-insignificant chest into the polymath's shoulder and catching myself on his arm. I smile up at him and fake being winded.

"Oh gods, I'm so sorry. This is my first week here, and I'm just not used to walking these halls quite yet."

The man goes red in the face, stammering, his eyes roving over me, over the soft *V* shape where his arm presses between my chest. "Y-You—I didn't—I'm sorry..."

"Don't be sorry," I simper. "It was my fault. I'm such a clumsy idiot."

Behind me I hear a half-choked protest and the closing of a metal hatch. Utter silence follows. Good. The others must've gone down. The polymath's eyes rove behind me, and I quickly tighten my grip on his arm.

"I'm still so lost in this place—could you show me where the washrooms are, by any chance?"

"W-washrooms," the man manages, clearly not experienced

at speaking to women. "Yes. This way!"

So enthusiastic is he that he strides off, quickly and furiously, and I laugh to myself before turning to the metal hatch and climbing down. Fione waits, locking it behind me the moment my foot reaches the ground. Lucien won't meet my gaze, instead ferociously staring at a nearby torch. Malachite smirks at me.

"So? Did you suck the poor man's soul out of him before or after he was done drooling on you?"

"*No one*," Lucien mutters, "is doing any *sucking*."

"I know your parental humans never told you this, Lucien," Malachite drawls. "But it's all right to be jealous. Perfectly natural, even."

I laugh, biting my lip when Lucien's dagger eyes meet mine for a split second. Fione clears her throat.

"If you're all done being severely adolescent, I'd like to get moving. Malachite, you'll be leading the way. Stay to the west of the room, and look for a door without a keyhole."

I squint, the darkness beyond the few torches nearly impenetrable. Malachite sighs, running a hand through his hair.

"That's why you brought me—not just for my outstanding muscles."

"Congratulations, you figured it out," Fione agrees. "Now let's go."

She instructs us to make a chain, Lucien holding on to the back of Malachite's robes, myself holding on to Lucien's, and Fione holding on to me. We move forward slowly, the gentle red glow from Malachite's eyes all I can see in the oppressive darkness. The hiss of distant, unseen machines echoes eerily.

"They keep it dark to dissuade intruders," Lucien

whispers softly to me. "The celeon guards see perfectly well in the dark. Gives them a distinct advantage."

"Cheaters," I whisper back, and even though it's dark I swear I see him smile, my heart locket skipping at it. He's so close I can feel his body heat seeping into me, keeping me warm. For a split second I wish it was only him and me, here, in the dark.

ThE beTTeR tO tEaR hiS heaRt fRoM hiS bEauTifuL chEst, the hunger sneers. For once, it's right. This darkness is so all-encompassing. If I could just get Lucien alone somehow, I could take his heart as swiftly as a mongoose ends a viper.

As we pass a torch, I faintly see Malachite's long, sharp ears. If he could hear me snipe in a crowded pub from thirty feet away, he can surely hear anything down here. Especially a blade being drawn on my end. Once again, he ruins everything. If he wasn't so charming, I might start to hate him for it.

"Hide," Malachite whispers, Lucien crouching as he does. I quickly bend my knee, the four of us taking shelter behind what feels like a large metal barrel. The sound of someone breathing heavily comes closer, a faint panther-like growl laced in between every breath. Heavy footsteps, a pause, the sound of huge amounts of air being taken in by a large nose. The heart shard in my locket goes cold—it won't matter if the celeon can't see us, they have an excellent sense of smell. We're done for. Surely we're done for—

"Baudur," a rough voice calls out, so close it makes me jump. "Did you eat livers again?"

Livers. Can he smell that on me? A second celeon voice echoes from a good distance away.

"They were cooked in goat butter. What do you want from me?"

The first voice near us grunts. "A friend who has better taste in Avellish food."

The second voice laughs, a half screech and half purr. The heavy footsteps pass us, growing faint. Lucien stands, and I stand with him, following Malachite along the wall.

Malachite hisses softly, "Here. The only door with no keyhole. Be quick about it—the celeon are patrolling clockwise."

I feel Fione's hand leave my back, the sound of her fingers fumbling against the wall, and then tiny clicks replacing it. Malachite's red glowing eyes dart around, the only thing I can see in the dark.

"Do you need light to solve that puzzle-lock?" Lucien murmurs.

"No," Fione answers. "It's a touch-sensitive one—bumps instead of numerals. Uncle wouldn't compromise the dark security down here just for his comfort."

"Can the celeon not see the light from your eyes?" I ask Malachite. He chuckles.

"I'm closing them most of the time."

"And you keep walking?"

"I can tell where I'm going without seeing. This is home for me," he insists. "The darkness, the stone. It's where we thrive."

"I guess that's why they call you Beneathers," I muse. He chuckles again.

"Bene-Thar."

"What?"

"Our word for our people, the Bene-Thar. It means *'the ones with blood-eyes.'*"

"But, we call you Beneathers—"

"Because when humans and Bene-Thar first met, that's

what they thought we were saying when they asked what we were," Malachite scoffs. "Hilarious, isn't it?"

"And you never bothered to correct them?"

"Oh, we tried," he assures me. "But it'd spread too far by then. The name has its uses; if an outsider says it the upworld way, foe. If they say it like we do, friend—Fione, not to rush you or anything, but you *really* have to hurry."

"There!" She quietly celebrates the sound of something heavy opening. Cold air rushes out to meet us, and we press into the enveloping chill. It's slightly less dark in here, in that I'm finally able to see my own hands in front of my face. The *thud* of the door closing behind us makes me jump.

"There may be booby traps," Fione says clearly, holding up a copper-and-crystal tube and clicking another nutcracker-like tool from her belt over it. Light flickers on the end of the tube, illuminating the crystal on the end with pure white brilliance. It reveals a long, mossy tunnel. "Malachite, you go first."

"I'm not exactly an expert on your uncle's traps," he points out. Fione shakes her head.

"You have the best reflexes of us."

Lucien's snort is loud. "No—that would be me."

"I haven't had the pleasure of fighting Malachite yet," I chime in. "But the prince speaks truth—he's very quick on his feet."

"Don't be stupid, Lucien," Malachite insists. "I'll go first."

"You told me that's what being young is all about," Lucien walks in front of us with all the careful calculation of the thief Whisper. "Being stupid, taking chances."

"Not when you're the last heir to the throne! Move behind me," Malachite barks, trying to shoulder him aside.

"*You* move behind *me!*" Lucien insists, doubling his

speed. Malachite easily catches up with him, and Fione and I desperately try to keep up with this war of pride.

"Slow down!" I call. "You're going to set something off—"

If they do, and Lucien dies to such a trap…

Yo**U** **c**o**uL**d **st**E**aL** **h**I**s** **h**E**a**r**T** **a**N**d** **v**A**ni**S**h** **in**T**o** **th**E **da**R**k** **wh**i**L**e **th**E**se** **p**A**theti**C **m**o**Rtal**S **m**O**urn**, the hunger cackles even as my heart locket squeezes at the thought of Lucien dead, of his handsome face lifeless…

There's a crunch beneath Malachite's boots, and the two boys look down slowly. Bones—the ground before them is littered with old, yellowed bones. Lucien bends and inspects them.

"I think these are cow," he announces. "Deer. Some dogs."

I swallow, hard. This is a familiar sight, something I'd seen in the woods near bear caves or wolf nests. "This—this is a den."

"Den?" Fione purses her lips at me. "What do you mean?"

"There!" Lucien points. Fione holds her crystal light up higher, and Malachite says something in Beneather none of us know, but all of us intrinsically understand. A swear. A prayer. There, in the pale white light are the massive, moss-chewed bones of a serpentlike creature curled around itself, crowding the tunnel. Each rib bone is bigger than an entire ox, each claw taller than me, each tooth the width of my thigh. It throws eerie, bladed shadows on the pipe's walls. It's wolflike skull lies on its crossed forearms, as if it put its head down to rest in its final moments.

"Valkerax," Malachite breathes.

15

BONES LIKE MEMORIES

MY MOUTH GOES DROUGHT-DRY, my hands shaking. A valkerax, here of all places?

"I'm not a religious person," Malachite confesses, his voice on the border of panic. "But what in Kavar's bleeding eye is your uncle doing with a valkerax skeleton?"

"It lived here, clearly." Fione swallows, jolting into motion. "Someone…fed it."

"Someone like your uncle?" I ask.

"The bones are old," Lucien muses, approaching it without a single ounce of fear. "Five—maybe six years? And the marks here—" He rests his hands on the ribs, where ragged indents carve through the bone. "Someone killed it with something sharp to the heart. A stab from a sword or a halberd."

He takes Varia's sword out experimentally and thrusts it into the grooves. To our surprise, the blade fits perfectly. Lucien sheathes his blade and retreats to me. I point at the skull.

"What's that, there?" In the bone of the forehead is carved a very distinct symbol—not accidentally done in the least. Malachite narrows his glowing blood-eyes.

"That's— But that's impossible."

"What is it?" Lucien barks.

"That's the Beneather method of marking a valkerax kill. Someone knew of our traditions, or a Beneather was here." He breathes, then begins looking around the walls of the pipe wildly, digging at the moss layer. "There have to be runes around here somewhere."

"Runes for what?" I ask. Lucien is so close, and Malachite is frenzied, distracted. My hand fondles my blade's hilt. I could do it now—*dO iT nOw*—carve out the prince's heart and retreat into the darkness before either Fione or Malachite could react. Follow the west wall out, quickly and quietly, the celeon guards be damned. No—they'd find me. It's too risky. I need to locate a better exit first.

"The runes hold the valkerax in—like a cage. They're the only things that can," Malachite insists, his scratching revealing jagged carvings in the metal pipe's walls. "Here! *'Torvanusin, first of his name, charged with guarding the valuables of the Man Without Mercy'*…there!" Malachite pulls more moss away, voice rapid, excited. "The runes begin incomplete, and etch themselves in with the cause of the valkerax's death when they die."

"That sounds like magic," I muse. Malachite nods.

"Old Vetrisian magic—from a thousand years ago, when humans and witches still worked together to seal the valkerax away." He points at the last few etchings. "There's his death; *'he was killed in an act of mercy by the Laughing Daughter.'*"

"Laughing Daughter?" I whisper. "Man Without Mercy? What are these odd names?"

"The valkerax aren't like us," Malachite insists. "They're old, older than anything else in the world. They can see a living thing's true self, and they call us by our true self names. It's....a hard concept to explain to an upworlder."

Beside me, Lucien goes stiff. Fione looks to him sharply.

"You know something, Your Highness." The prince knits his lips. Fione strides up to him, apple-cheeked face deadly serious. "The Laughing Daughter? You know who that is, don't you? Tell me."

"It's none of your concern," Lucien says softly.

"Of course it's my concern! Tell me!" Fione roars. All three of us step back at the tone of her voice, the fury echoing down the pipe. "It was Varia, wasn't it? She did this. She knew about this thing down here, and she killed it. To what, anger my uncle?"

Lucien keeps his face pure granite, Fione snarling—her eyes full to the brim with tears.

"She's dead, Lucien! I saw the pieces of her. *You* saw them. We buried her together. She's never coming back. The fact she killed this thing doesn't change that!"

"I'm aware," the prince manages tersely.

"Then stop. Just *stop*," Fione grits out, "with that hopeful look in your eyes."

Malachite meets my gaze over their shoulders, something like regret in his face. Fione whirls on her heel, holding the light higher as she picks her way through the valkerax's skeleton and makes it to the other side of the pipe.

Malachite calls after her. "Wait! What about those booby traps?"

His voice peters out as he runs after her, leaving only Lucien and me behind.

ThIs iS iT, the hunger sneers. ***It'S fInaLLy tIme.***

I can't do it. The celeon guards…

YoU caN cUT tHeM doWn, the hunger insists. *ThEy aRe onLy flEsh. He wiLL be yOurs. EvErythinG wiLL be yOurs—*

"Varia told me once," Lucien murmurs, shaking me out of my head, "that if she ever met a valkerax, she'd like to ask it some questions." His midnight eyes rest on the last runes. "Killed in an act of mercy, hmm? Perhaps that was the price it asked for its knowledge."

My hand tightens around my blade, and the prince laughs all of a sudden, a crippling sadness in his voice. I can't see his face in the darkness, but I can hear every inch of agony, every day of waiting, regretting, hating.

"Even when she's gone, I keep finding fragments of her."

My hand goes lax, paralyzed by the pain in his words. His body heat is so close, and I tentatively reach a hand out to his shoulder. He's trembling.

"Every fragment, every shadow of hers makes me hope again," he mutters. "And that's the worst part. Not that she's dead. But that she won't stay dead."

He leans in to me only slightly. I put my other arm around him, and like a dam breaking, that one motion collapses him, his full weight pressed against me, his arms around my waist, and his cheek resting against mine. The hunger salivates and keens in equal parts—my fingers itching, my teeth growing. But his warmth against me, the way my locket shudders with every breath we share—I do the only thing I can; I breathe. I remember.

You are in the silence, Reginall's voice. *You are of the silence.*

Slowly, achingly slowly, like a thorn being pulled from a wound, the hunger recedes. Not all the way, not even significantly, but enough that my head feels a little clearer, a little lighter, as I dare to stroke one hand comfortingly over Lucien's raven hair.

It's sick, and it's wrong, but for one moment in this strange pipe, in this strange city, embracing this not-so-strange boy, this monster feels happiness.

Lucien and I eventually part, though he snakes his hand in mine with a crooked smile that nearly stops my heart locket cold. He leads me down the pipe wordlessly after Fione and Malachite, and I follow, relishing the feel of his strong fingers intertwined with mine, the way he pauses to make sure the bones don't trip me. Care. Consideration. They etch his black eyes like streaks of fire, muted enough that I don't feel the full burn, but still very warm.

Uncomfortably warm.

I'm going to kill him, after all, and resurrect him as a thrall of a witch. A prisoner of war.

With gargantuan effort, I pull my hand from his, and he stops. "Is something wrong, Zera?"

Zera. Just Zera. It sounds like honey to my ears. "I'm worried," I force out. "If Lady Himintell sees us breaking decorum like this—"

"To the afterlife with decorum," Lucien asserts, offering me his hand again. I hesitate too long, and he exhales gently. "Perhaps you're right. You're less of a target for the court if this remains secret."

To the very end, caring about my well-being. Yet it doesn't make me feel good in the slightest—it twists my unheart around in my chest, stabs molten regret through my gut.

Before I can say anything, a muffled explosion rocks the pipe, coming from the end of it. Lucien and I dash ahead, where a doorway tinted with Fione's white light lies open, her frantic words echoing out.

"—you all right? Say something, Sir Malachite!"

There, sprawled on the floor between broken bookshelves and a flurry of torn paper fragments lies Malachite, motionless, his long leg twisted beneath his body. Lucien collapses at his side, shaking him by the shoulders.

"Malachite!" The prince rounds on Fione. "What happened to him?"

"I-I don't know! I found the safe behind the bookshelf, and I asked him to move it for me, and then—oh gods." She wrings her hands over each other. "I didn't check it for a trap! I was so angry I— Sir Malachite, *please*; wake up!"

Malachite doesn't stir, eyelids unmoving. I swallow the hard, toxic lump in my throat. I wasn't supposed to feel like this, ever. I wasn't supposed to care about anyone—not the prince, not his bodyguard. No one. This was all supposed to be faked. And yet here I am, my stomach roiling with very real dread.

Lucien slaps Malachite's face, hard. "Wake up, godsdamn you!"

Nothing. Lucien snarls, desperation edging his voice.

"You can't leave me here alone. You promised you'd be by my side until I took the throne. You *promised*!"

I kneel at Malachite's body, listening for a heartbeat in his chest. It's there, but very faint, his breathing shallow and ragged. I've died enough times to know a ragged breath is the worst sign—the sign your body is about to give out beneath you.

"We have to get him help." I look up. "Fione, is there an exit?"

She nods and points to the ceiling, where an iron trapdoor hangs. If we can get him out of here, just far away enough from the tower, finding a royal polymath to tend to him...

"Get up!" Lucien shouts. I put a hand on his arm, but he rips away, slamming his own hands on Malachite's chest. "I said *get up!*"

It happens in a blink—Malachite sits up instantly, pulling in air in a single massive gasp. The glow of his eyes flutters as his eyelashes do—he looks around at all of us blearily.

"What did I miss?" he manages. Lucien's posture eases, Fione going still.

"I'm sorry, Sir Malachite!" she blurts. "It was my fault—I didn't check the bookshelf for a trap before you—"

"*Vachiayis!*" Malachite snarls as he shifts, clutching at his leg. "What in the Dark Below happened to me?"

"You might be resistant to fire, but it turns out you're not immune to explosions," I joke softly. Malachite shoots me a pained smirk.

"Well that's good to know." He tries to stand, Lucien helping him up. "Sorry if I worried you, Luc. Sometimes a guy just has to take a dirt nap, you know?"

A torn laugh escapes Lucien's mouth, and even Fione lets out a small, strangled giggle. Relief is a heady drug, and it calms the humans down quickly. Malachite insists he's fine, and Fione points out the explosion was probably linked to an alert system, and that we need to move. With Lucien's help, she carefully approaches the safe and begins to work on its puzzle-lock, leaving me to splint Malachite's leg with shards of the broken bookshelf.

"You always carry around gauze?" Malachite asks as I

procure the roll from my pouch.

"Only when I know the most idiotic Beneather is tagging along," I quip. He snorts.

"In my defense, I was just trying to hurry things up. Hanging around those valkerax bones wasn't doing Lucien any favors. Or Fione."

"Memories are dangerous things," I murmur.

"They keep you prisoner sometimes," he agrees. "But just having them, being able to remember them, revisit them, live in them when life gets too rough—I think it's worth it."

We wOuLdn'T kNow. The hunger curls its lip. **We'Ve leFt thOse wEaK hUmaN meMoRies behiNd.**

I laugh, because I can do nothing else, and it's then I realize most of my laughter here in Vetris has been laced with utter despair.

Fione finds what she's looking for in the safe—a single aged parchment roll—and we all manage to pile out through the trapdoor just as the footsteps of the celeon guards echo down the pipe. I'm so glad to see triple moonlight again, smell the crisp night air. We shed our robes as we hike quickly away, eager to get out of the East River Tower's long shadow. Malachite struggles, and Fione and Lucien look exhausted, Fione leaning heavily on her cane. I'm perfectly fine, and I motion to a secluded bench, overgrown and hidden from the road by thick, red Avellish trees. Even Fione relents at the idea of rest, and we settle on the bench. "Just to catch our breath," she insists.

There's a peace before the storm, I've learned, and this

is it. Fione speaks first.

"I read it; it's detailed notes on Varia's sword, in my uncle's handwriting, dated a day before the court got the news she was killed. I was…I was right. This whole time, I was *right*."

Lucien's fists clench, and Fione presses on.

"I'm on a time limit now. He'll notice it's missing and start searching. I've got two days at most before he figures out it was me."

"What are you going to do?" I ask. She smiles faintly at the parchment roll in her hand.

"Turn it in to the king. And then run. Hide somewhere my uncle can't find me, until he's behind bars and stripped of his power."

"The day after tomorrow is the Hunt." Lucien wipes sweat from his brow. "You can hide there, wait it out."

Fione flashes him an exhausted smile. "I'd appreciate that."

There's an awkward silence, the first gentle sprays of the golden sunrise breaking over the horizon, over the four faces of a very strange group of young things.

"I'm sorry, Lucien," Fione murmurs. "For yelling."

Lucien stares at her, eyes roving up and down her tired frame. He puts his elbows on his knees and his chin in his hands, and says, "It's all right. I'm sorry for not believing you sooner about Gavik."

"Consider me officially heart-warmed," Malachite drawls. I nudge his not-broken leg with my own.

"Shut up."

He chuckles, Lucien rolling his eyes and Fione shaking her head minutely. The sunrise begins bleeding the night sky dry with vermilion wounds. Lawguards move toward the East River Tower, first in drops, then in trickles, then a steady stream. Their voices carry through the trees, though they don't see us.

"—*Crimson Lady reported magic in this vicinity.*"

"—*you sure the eggheads got the readings right?*"

"*The polymaths aren't idiots; of course the readings are right.*"

"—*a huge surge of magic belowground—*"

The four of us share a look. Malachite mutters first.

"It wasn't the runes. Those go inert when the valkerax dies."

"And the explosion was a white mercury trap," Fione clarifies. "Not magic."

"Then what was it?" Lucien frowns. I bite back the urge to tell them Malachite was well and truly on the verge of death. A simple chest-thumping from Lucien wouldn't have even been close enough to bring Malachite back. The way Malachite sat up so suddenly, so awake and cognizant again all at once, the way Lucien's dark eyes seemed to get even darker in that second...

It was like magic.

As we go our separate ways—the influx of lawguards forcing us to be careful and leave one at a time—I watch Lucien's back. The d'Malvanes are a witch family. Witches can be turned Heartless, but the books in Nightsinger's hut always read like it was the worst thing you could do to a witch, short of killing them. A shameful punishment. A torturous punishment.

Lucien looks back once at me, his smile reaching his midnight eyes.

A pUniShmEnt wE mUst inFlicT.

16

THE HUNT

WHEN I MAKE IT BACK to the Y'shennria manor, she's waiting for me on the front steps, drinking tea and reading. She puts her book down and stands with a ramrod-straight posture as I approach, her eyes sharper than any sword.

"You went," she says, cutting into me with just those two words.

"I had to try." I return her gaze unblinkingly. Readying myself for whatever consequences I've earned.

There's a beat, a lingering moment. The sunbirds cry to one another, and the noble children from the manor over scream as they play in the yard. The swords in Y'shennria's eyes slide back into their scabbards, and she reaches a hand out to me.

"I know," she finally says, soft and even, and for a second I swear an *I'm just glad you're back* lingers behind them. I take her warm hand slowly, hesitantly, but she never pulls away. We share a pot of tea together in the drawing room, wordlessly, the sort of comforting wordlessness that fills the gaps like goose down—gentle and easy.

We've decided, Y'shennria and I, to make peace with each other. Like a family might.

The Crown Prince, too, has decided.

Later that day, he sends me what Y'shennria calls "a traditional invitation to the Hunt"—a luxurious white fur cape. I finger the fox tail at the end of it, my mind whirlpooling.

Did he realize it, too, after that night in the parade, or during our duel? Or maybe it was our darkened embrace in the tunnel. Does his mind drown in memories of our moments together like mine does, still fresh and new and warm to the touch? I should be happy he's called me to the Hunt, chosen me. It means he'll pull me aside, privately, and ask me that question every Spring Bride has longed to hear. It means I'll have the perfect moment to slice his chest open and rip his heart from his ribs.

The thought of taking his heart—it used to fill me with determination. But now? The idea of losing him to the witches, the idea of betraying him by making him into the thing I hate most makes me ill. Why is this so sudden? Why can't I just be the girl I used to be—bent on earning my freedom back, regardless of the cost?

Why can't I just be the monster?

BeCausE it hUrts, the hunger screams.

The day of the Hunt comes too soon. I stare at the fire-calendar as I wait for Fisher to drive the carriage to the front door of Y'shennria's manor. This is the last day. A single day is all that's left between Verdance Day and me.

Between failure and me. I fidget with the white fox-fur cape.

"You have everything?" Y'shennria asks, and I could swear beneath her composed voice and flawless green silk dress, she's nervous. "Your nightdress, your sword, your makeup—"

"I was thinking I'd ditch the lip tint and use blood, instead. You know, go for a bit of that 'wild hunting' look."

"You're a true jester," she asserts.

"I prefer the term 'fashion pioneer.'"

"Do you have the jar?" she presses.

I finger my shoulder bag for personal travel effects. Against the silk fabric I can feel the glass of Lucien's heart jar, filled with sweets to avoid suspicion should any humans see it.

"Sword—check. Jar—check. Overwhelming fear of the unknown—check." I brush my bangs out of my eyes and smile at Y'shennria. "Anything else I should bring?"

"A healthy dose of optimism," she says. "We're close. I have every faith in you."

"Wrong move," I singsong. "The last person to have faith in me was my mother, and look what happened to her."

Y'shennria's gaze wanders out a window overlooking the black rosebushes, now in full bloom with a storm of fragrant, midnight petals. "My daughter's name was Alyserat."

Her daughter—the one she lost. I'd never once heard her talk about her before.

"It's Old Vetrisian," Y'shennria continues. "They liked to name their children after sayings—pretty warnings. Hers was one that always haunted me: 'Fear the past, not the future.' In my youth, my naiveté, I used to think I understood it. If you feared the past, you were incapable of moving toward a future."

She looks at me, not through me or around me as she used to, but right at me, the full force of her hazel eyes knocking the breath from me.

"If you fear the past, it becomes your future," Y'shennria says finally. "You're locked in the past, eternally, by your fear. There's no way to escape it. I think some part of me knew that—that's why I hired Reginall. That's why I agreed to shelter and train you. Even if it caused me pain."

I flinch. "I'm sorry, Y'shennria—"

DoN't apoLogizE to tHe pReY, the hunger cries.

"No. There's nothing to be sorry for. Because it was you, I learned to feel no fear."

I go still, and her graceful lips curl into a smile.

"Because it was the girl I knew, the girl I trained, the girl I'd watched blossom from an ungainly thing into a fine young woman—because it was you, Zera, I feel no fear at all."

Her smile shines with pride, and my unheart wrenches around violently in my chest. To think she could be proud of me after all the doubts I've had, all the mistakes. In this moment she feels like the mother I can't remember having. Someone who cares.

Y'shennria and I have gone over what she'll do after I take the prince's heart on the Hunt. We've gone over every detail of how she'll escape out to the woods, where the witches have promised her sanctuary. Reginall, Maeve, Fisher, her stableboy Perriot—all of them are coming with her. The instant I lash out at Lucien, they will be traitors to their people.

And I will be a traitor to the prince. To Fione and Malachite. A liar and a monster besides. A monster who made yet another monster, all for her own freedom.

"The carriage is here, Lady Y'shennria!" Reginall calls. I tamp the fear threatening to rampage up through my throat and smile at Y'shennria.

"It's time."

She nods and helps me into the carriage. "Be careful, Zera. There isn't much I can do for you beyond the city limits."

"Relax, Auntie." I make one last effort to tease her. "You've done enough for me. It's my turn to repay the favor."

With one last order from her to Fisher to get me there safely, the horses trot off. She waves good-bye to me from the stairs until she's nothing but a brilliantly green smudge on the horizon. Watching her shrink, watching the manor grow small, I start to miss her, miss the home she risked so much to give me.

My forearm wound has finally scabbed over for good—though it still aches. The bruise from escaping the bathroom via the tree throbs on my ribs. It's a small comfort, but I realize this is what humans feel—constant pain from a healing injury. This is me, lingering in the cool shade of being human again after so many years of unrelenting sun.

I watch the lawguards going through their drills on the lawn of the palace, their swords shining high as they stab them into training dummies. Do they joke that those dummies are witches? Heartless? How badly do they wish to kill me, and others like me? In a blink the dummies become flesh and blood—one of them has Nightsinger's face. One of the dummies becomes Crav, his little body limp and broken, the other Peligli's, scratched and bruised. Y'shennria's bleeding visage on the last dummy.

I won't let it come to pass. It's not just *my* heart that hangs in the balance. I'd forgotten that, gotten so absorbed in my own selfish desire for freedom.

For Lucien. For happiness.

The dummy with Y'shennria's face echoes her voice; *A Heartless only ever burns for one thing—their own heart. And those who burn don't easily blind.*

I want to be human. But what kind of human would I be, without anyone to love? What kind of human would I be, having betrayed so many? I clutch at my locket and speak softly to the floor of the carriage.

"What if I've been burning blindly this whole time, Auntie?"

Once we're out of the city, the beauty of the grasslands is a temporary salve on my wounds. We head in the opposite direction of the Bone Road—east instead of west. Farmers prune orchards exploding in sour cherries and pink plums; bulbous, lettuce-like heads of sugarleaf hang from branches. Storms of unseen cicadas in the grass click and groan at one another. I linger on the windowsill, eager for the wind to blow away the dark thoughts between my ears. We pass so close to a farm that one of children helping with the harvest runs up to the wire fence, handing me a sugarleaf.

ConsuMe her. SliT hEr throaT, mAke her bLEed, the hunger demands. Before I can thank her, she's gone, deep in the fields again, leaving me to peel the fruit apart and nibble at it. It doesn't do anything to quiet my hunger, but it helps soothe my nerves, even if I have to wipe away blood tears minutes later. I watch the land flash by—little villages and trading outposts full of dust and dogs, bleached ruins of settlements decimated during the war and abandoned after it. Mass graves stick out alongside the road, memorialized with moss-covered statues of Kavar's eye. The scars of the

Sunless War run deep here.

It's strange to think that everything I can see would've someday been Lucien's. The Vetrisian nobles and their court are so far removed from the soil, the orchards and grasslands and trees. They couldn't care less if harvests are hit with bugs, if the potholes of the roads out here get steep and dangerous. The lives of Cavanos's people are so totally different from the nobles' perfumed banquets. A single potato means life or death for these people. I said that, and I stick by it. I just wonder if anyone in a position of power in Cavanos will ever really know what that means. Archduke Gavik certainly doesn't know; King Sref definitely has no clue. Lucien tries. Gods know he tries. But even the suffering in metropolitan Vetris is a far cry from the hard lives of his rural citizens.

Lucien. I try not to think about him, but it's no use—every time I blink I can see his smiling face at the Verdance parade as I watched him dance.

He's OuRs, OURS, no oNe else's, oUrS for the eaTiNg, ours fOr the toUchiNg—

The demented hunger drags me so far down I barely notice when we slow pace. We begin to pass other silk-decked carriages rather than the humble wooden carts and wagons of farmers and tradesmen. The hunting grounds must be close. I spot Charm's vessel but not Grace's, and Lord Grat even waves to me as we pass. I find myself searching for Fione's silver carriage on the road, then chide myself; the time to play pretend is over. It's better if I stay away from her.

"There's the huntin' grounds, miss!" Fisher calls. I poke my head from the window—ahead of us on a flat grassy plain bordering a dark pine forest rests a circle of brightly colored tents. The biggest tent is of expensive gold-streaked flax and no doubt for Prince Lucien. The others are more modest, but made of luxurious material nonetheless. Of course the nobles would bring their finest cloth, even out in the wilderness. Servants decked in the colors and emblems of their respective families busy about the campground doing all the real work: mucking horse stalls, sharpening swords, preparing meals at a makeshift kitchen with a roaring fire—loaves of fresh bread rising over the heat and legs of lamb dripping with grease and herbs. This wasn't just erected—this camp has been put together painstakingly over the course of some time.

Fisher parks the carriage in a line with the others, and when I get out, none other than Ulla, Headkeeper of the palace, makes a curtsy to me.

"Lady Zera, welcome."

"Thank you." I nod to her. "Forgive me—why are you here? Is your domain not the palace?"

She smiles sweetly—and I've seen her do it to enough people to know it's a patronizing smile. "I took this opportunity to leave the palace in the hands of my apprentice. And besides—I'd trust no one but myself to ensure the prince's first public Hunt runs smoothly. Your tent is the dark purple one, Lady Zera, in the north of camp. Dinner is at sundown, and the purification will commence about a half after."

"Purification?"

She startles, then settles. "I apologize—I forget you know little of Vetrisian tradition. It was thought in Old Vetris, before the days of polymaths and their knowledge, that a Heartless could smell fear. Thus the Old Vetrisians invented a bathing ritual to mask it with a special blend of herbs and spices. We know better now, of course, but the tradition remains. All participating hunters will bathe in the spring nearby."

"All participating hunters," I echo. "Together?"

"Together," she asserts.

I exhale. "Fantastic."

Ulla instructs Fisher to take my luggage to my tent.

"Where is he sleeping?" I ask Ulla, but Fisher flashes me a smile.

"Don't worry about me, miss. I've got the carriage."

Unspoken words fly between our eyes—he'll be nearby for my getaway—but he breaks contact first and hefts my trunk easily despite his scarecrow frame, disappearing into the crowd. Ulla leads me to my tent, and I spot Fione settling into her gray tent not far from the entrance. She doesn't notice me, and I make a note to see her one last time before the end, to say good-bye.

Good-bye.

The word, the concept itself, frostbites the soft bits of my brain—the bits in which Fione was my almost-friend. Almosts, I'm starting to learn, are fuller of regret than absolutes—much sadder than certain yeses and nos. Yes and no mark ends and beginnings. But almosts cling, hovering on the boundary, never quite realized yet still there.

Ulla's words defrost me. "The prince hasn't arrived yet, but when he does a greeting will be expected."

"Right. When is the Hunt?"

"It begins tomorrow morning—but fear not. I'm sure Prince Lucien will call his hunters together to discuss tactics before then."

Morning. It's not an optimal time to take Lucien's heart—I'd much prefer the shadows of night. Ulla bids me farewell at the entrance of my tent. The tent is cooler, the deep violet cloth doing wonders to keep the sun out. The trunk Fisher brought in sits at the end of a fur-piled sleeping cot, though

Fisher himself is nowhere to be seen. A leather chair and a foldable desk sit in one corner of the tent, a wash basin in the other. It's simple, and it reminds me of Nightsinger's cabin. Yet I find myself longing for the dreary, stately dark wood of Y'shennria's manor, for the kind portrait of Lord Y'shennria, for the calming presence of Reginall and Maeve, for the darkwood diamonds on my ceiling, ready and waiting to be silently counted, soothing my inner turmoil.

I slip outside—Lord Grat's crimson tent is right next to mine, both of us situated directly in front of Lucien's golden one. Lord Grat, in a stiff brocaded vest and breeches, smiles and jogs up to me.

"Lady Zera! Look at us—our tents so close, as if fate itself is conspiring to bring us together."

He sounds ridiculous, and I laugh. "That's one way of putting it."

"It's strange, though," Lord Grat muses.

"What is? Not my dress, surely—my tailor told me it will look better covered in mud."

He laughs. "No, not that. It's just very odd that Prince Lucien chose this area for his Hunt, considering what this place is."

"This place?" I look around at the tall, velvety trees in the distance. "What's so special about it?"

The wind whistles between us, and then he says, "This is very close to where Princess Varia was killed."

I think back to his words in the dark pipe. Maybe he still wants to be as close as he can get to her, to the last place she was alive.

A bell rings throughout the hunting camp, signaling the prince's arrival. We make our way to the entrance as everyone does—servants and nobles alike. My mind takes inventory of how many guards are present—royal lawguards, huge celeon, the kind stationed at the throne of the king at all times. But there are only a handful of them—thirteen to be exact, their insect-like mirtas tied up in the stables. The rest of the guarding force precedes the prince, a block of two battalions shining in polished silver armor, light green banners with the d'Malvane serpent whipping in the wind. The thunder of their horses' hooves shakes the ground, tremors reverberating in my chest.

Prince Lucien rides in on a sleek black mare, his posture perfectly regal, his hawking coat a deep forest green stitched with winding silver leaves. His dark eyes fixate ahead, not once looking at the crowd as he trots the mare through, his long black braid woven with silver threads, and his golden skin flushed with the wind. He's so incredibly handsome in this moment—the sun glinting off him, only to be reabsorbed by his darkness. Malachite rides beside him, his red eyes hooded, and wearing heavy ceremonial armor, his leg still situated in my clumsy cast. The entire crowd bends the knee, and though I know I should, too, my body is stiff as I look at the prince's resplendent face. I must turn him into a Heartless if I want to be free. I must turn him Heartless to stall the impending war between witch and human. But the misery of being a Heartless, of reducing him to the witches' political hostage without any freedom of his own—inflicting that on Lucien, no longer just a spoiled noble boy, but *Lucien*, Lucien of the piercing gaze and gentle touch, Lucien as the thief Whisper, Lucien of the parade dance, his body pressed against my own, his arms wrapped around me—

"Bow before your Crown Prince!" the head of the prince's guard bellows, pointing his sword at me. But he sounds so far away, the glint of his sword completely eclipsed as I try to memorize Lucien's visage as it is now—ignorant, still fond of me.

"I said bow!" the head of the guard barks, his sword nearing as his horse does.

If I take Lucien's heart, he'll despise me. He'll learn what I really am, and he'll hate me for it, for shackling him to the same hunger-ridden fate.

He'll hate me.

Lucien's eyes find mine when the guard yells, his gaze going from carefully guarded to a splintered look of confusion. It isn't until the head guard dismounts and forces me roughly to my knees in a mockery of a bow do I realize the wetness dripping onto my dress are two silent streams of tears.

There's a moment that feels like eternity stretching between Lucien and me, in which he looks like he's going to descend his horse and come to me, but then someone ringing the camp bell breaks it. The peals are frantic. A lawguard sprints to the prince's head guard, and they share fevered words. The head guard turns to the battalions, raising his sword.

"Bandits seen to the east! Squad Falcon, secure the camp's perimeter! Squad Robin, ensure the safety of the nobility!"

The battalion splits instantly, weaving into the stunned crowd and ushering nobles and servants back into the camp. I wipe my tears hurriedly and follow the flow of the crowd. As the guards shuttle us to our tents, I spot the mousy, curled hair of Fione, and suddenly I'm shoulder to shoulder with her as the flow of the crowd bumps us together. Her rosy cheeks pale strangely when her eyes find mine.

"You'd think a few bandits would have a brain between them and know not to lurk around the Crown Prince's hunt," I joke. Fione smiles.

"I'm sure they'll learn quickly—one way or another."

I open and close my mouth in the silence between us so many times I feel like a fish. Fione smooths her curls.

"I'm rather excited to hunt—I've never done it before."

"I have a hard time believing a spymaster such as yourself has never lifted a sword."

She giggles. "I've made it a point to think faster than anyone who might stand against me with force. It's strange, but I've always seen resorting to force as a sort of…failure. A breakdown in my own intelligence, that I couldn't think of something to avoid such bloodshed."

"This is where Varia was killed, right?" I ask.

Fione's smile fades. "Indeed."

"It must be hard for you, being near this place."

Her gaze flits over the dark, serrated tops of the pine trees. "Perhaps this visit is long overdue."

One of the guards forks off, taking her arm abruptly and leading her to her tent. I duck into my own, closing the purple door flap tight behind me and waiting as the guard instructs for the bell to ring out the all clear. Worry festers in me—I can only hope by now they've locked Gavik up and thrown away the key.

ThEy'LL aLL diE sCreAming iN the enD, the hunger promises with a thousand voices of rusted razor.

I sit at my little desk, surrounded by people outside and yet feeling more alone than ever before. But I knew—I knew this was what awaited me. This was my fate from the beginning, so the sadness I feel clawing at my insides isn't justified. I should've been prepared for this. I had two weeks to prepare, to harden myself, and I frittered it away pretending to be human instead.

The shouts of the guards, the clank of their armor. Would it be better, I wonder, to turn myself in? I pick up a letter opener on the desk, turning the sharp silver blade over in my hand. Would it be better to walk out there, this blade driven through my heart, showing the guards, showing everyone I'm immortal, hungry, inhuman? Show them I'm a danger—always have been—to their beloved Crown Prince? To them all?

"Zera?"

The deep voice makes me drop the letter opener and turn. There, in the doorway, stands Lucien. He looks winded, as though he ran here. Before the tent door closes behind him, I spot the edge of Malachite's armor as he stands guard outside.

"Your Highness." I duck into a deep curtsy. "You should be in your tent. It's probably much nicer than this, and if the bandits' arrows find us, I'd much rather only one of us perish."

He draws close in an instant, his gloved hand reaching out to cup my cheek and his eyes terribly, frighteningly soft.

"If you think you can make me forget your tears with a few clever words, you're wrong."

He's giving me the perfect moment to take his heart—alone, the forest just behind me, the guards distracted, my sword thirsty and waiting, and my hunger thirstier.

TAKE HIS IGNORANT GIFT, the hunger scream-whispers, the distortion gone and in its place an earthshattering volume that makes my whole head throb. ***SLIT HIM OPEN ON YOUR BLADE AND END HIS MISERABLE EXISTENCE.***

My hand trembles toward my sword, but I stop it.

WHY DO YOU HESITATE? FEAR? YOU FEAR
NOTHING, ESPECIALLY NOT A SINGLE WEAK
HUMAN. HE COULDN'T STOP YOU IF HE WANTED
TO. TAKE HIS HEART, TAKE HIS LIFE, HE IS YOURS
FOR THE TAKING!

I pull my cheek from his hand, putting space between us. The less he touches me, the farther I am, the stronger my will.

"I was simply moved, seeing your cavalcade of guards. It was quite the beautiful sight in the full sunlight."

HE MAKES YOU WEAK. BE RID OF HIM.

Lucien narrows his eyes. "You expect me to believe that?"

I EXPECT YOU TO BLEED.

"I expect nothing of you." I steel my jaw. "Save for the common courtesy of trust."

"Why were you crying?" he presses.

"I told you the reason. Or did you think that was a joke? I take my appreciation of beauty very seriously, Your Highness."

"You're lying."

It should be so sinfully easy. The jar is sitting right there on my desk, full of deceptive sweets. One stab, one spurt of blood, and all this agony would be over. I drift toward him again, my hand resting on his chest where my prize beats in an erratic rhythm, speeding the closer I bring my face to his, our lips hovering inches from each other's. My hand tightens on my sword, ready to strike.

PIERCE, the hunger sneers. *PIERCE ONCE, AND THE PAIN IS OVER.*

Lucien's breath mixes hot with mine, his eyes strangely conflicted beneath his knitted brows. That same heady rush of adrenaline surges through me as when I first chased him through the streets of Vetris. *Happiness.*

It happens all at once, like a storm from nowhere. Lucien moves like a dark blur, cradling both sides of my face with his hands, resting his forehead against mine. My hand readying Father's sword droops, all the strength in my arm sapped.

"I'm not good at this," he admits softly.

"Playing the heartbreaker?" I laugh. "You seemed good enough at it during the Welcoming with the other Brides."

"It's easy to pretend, but the real thing is"—he sucks in a breath—"*dizzying*."

"It can't be real," I say, making my voice strong despite the aching tug at my locket. "You know that, right?"

"Why not?" His stare pierces, demands an answer.

BECAUSE I'M A MONSTER, the hunger admits with a delighted hiss.

"Because—because I'm barely a noble at all. I'm a step niece, I know nothing about the court compared to you—"

"Do your feelings not matter at all?" Lucien asks.

"I am terrified of my feelings," I admit, the only piece of truth I can admit. His face falls.

"Then—am I the only one who feels this way? Tell me you don't feel the same, and I swear to you I will never bring it up again."

I can't tell him anything. I can't even tell him who I really am, what I really came here to do. I scrabble for something to say, any scrap that will serve as a plausible lie.

"I told you when we first met—I'm after your heart. The prince of Cavanos's heart."

Lucien flinches, but a smile forces its way onto his face. "The throne, then. That's what you're after? I'll give it to you. It's a small price to pay, if it means having you at my side."

Even "knowing" I'm after him for the throne, he won't stop looking at me like I'm a feast for a starving man, water for a thirsty flower. He's willing to give me a seat of power in his kingdom, a precious and priceless thing, just to keep me at his side?

"Why?" My voice cracks. "Why me? What did I do to deserve your heart?"

The world can crumble in so many ways. I saw it crumble when Mother and Father died. I saw it crumble when I killed those five men. I saw it crumble when I had to say good-bye to Crav and Peligli to come here. I saw it crumble the first time I witnessed a purge.

But unlike those times, when my world crumbles now, it gets rebuilt, right in front of my eyes. In front of my lips; his on mine, soft and sweet, his mouth hungry and his hands hungrier—lacing in my hair, resting on my hips. For one golden moment, nothing matters. I can't think. The hunger is completely, totally silent as he kisses me. A kiss. This is a kiss—strange and tender and wonderful. So very human. If I had a heart, I think mine would've stopped completely.

Can he taste the things I've done? The things I'm about to do?

We part slowly, Lucien's expression deadly handsome, glowing from within with pure joy. The hunger rises with a vengeance, reaching its clawed fingers deep into my brain, grasping desperately for him to come close once more.

It's ready this time.

"I hope that's answer enough for you." Lucien finds his voice, hoarse on the edges. "Because I have no words. I can only show you."

It's then he sees something by my feet and kneels, picking it up. Father's sword. I must've been so shocked I let it fall.

"You dropped this." He smiles, offering the blade in outstretched hands. His smile is so innocent. So convinced

I'm a beautiful thing, a thing worth being kissed. A thing worth being loved. It almost spills from me, then; that very moment when I'm left raw, when my world has crumbled and been rebuilt in a span of seconds—I almost blurt everything. What I am. What I came here to do. What he means to me.

I take the sword gingerly. For a fraction of a second, I can see myself jamming the blade clean into his chest, right here and now. He'd bleed all over this floor. All over me. He'd bleed, and he wouldn't stop, not until I pulled his heart off his arteries and put it in the jar, the jar that gleams with an etched snake, the jar I had hoped I'd never see—

"I'm sorry." Lucien's face falls. "Was I hasty?"

Outside the tent, I see the long-eared outline of Malachite shift from one leg to another. I can't. I can't kill him here— Malachite will know. Malachite will turn on me. He's always been the problem, hasn't he? But there's a way, my rational self insists, pushing down the lovestruck girl deep inside that threatens to ruin everything.

"This is so sudden. I-I need time," I say. "An hour? Maybe two? That would be enough to get my thoughts in order."

Lucien nods. "Of course."

"Could we meet somewhere private, after that?" I dart my eyes to Malachite's figure to get the point across. "Just the two of us?"

The Crown Prince of Cavanos smiles at me, like a lamb smiles at a wolf.

"I'd like that."

SO WOULD I, the hunger leers.

ucien and I agree to meet at the gnarled yew near the eastern hunting trail of the forest at midnight. He leaves with that same golden smile on his face, and it feels like half my chest is trying to cave, the other half trying to swell. Torn. Every bit of me is torn in two.

I briefly overhear Malachite as he and the prince leave—the bandit sighting was a false alarm; the guards couldn't find any sign of a camp or a single bandit. Whatever, or whoever, the lookout glimpsed disappeared. Or never existed in the first place.

When the threat of the bandits has passed, dinner begins.

It's a strict affair underneath an open-faced white tent, a hardwood table hauled out here by who knows how many servants, lined with every silver utensil and dish afforded to the palace's banquets. We seat the same way—according to rank. Nothing is different from the court here, save for the fact that most of us are in more casual clothes. The boys wear breeches and loose shirts and vague airs of nervousness. The girls wear outdoor dresses of simple flax, cotton pants beneath, their makeup painstakingly made to look more natural, glossed lips and bright cheeks. The meal is boisterous—without their parents around, the noble children feel freer, I suppose. They drink and flirt with more vigor than ever before, though beneath Ulla's watchful eye nothing gets too out of hand. The heady musk of hormones and freedom is sweeter than any summer wildflower, lacing the suffocatingly warm night air. Fireflies flit about the oil lamps strung from the tents and poles of the camp, glittering off the guards' armor like earthly strings of stars.

Fione sits close to me, teasing me relentlessly every time the prince's and my eyes meet across the table. I don't eat much, my nerves dancing too fast, too hard. Y'shennria couldn't send me with fresh meat, so she packed dried livers in my trunk. It isn't ideal, but it has to last me only a day. Or less. Midnight is mere hours away.

I've set the perfect trap. I am the perfect bait. I've played the part of the perfect bait so well, Lucien fell in love with me for it. Or—was it myself he fell for? The monster beneath? The orphan girl with no heart?

IMPOSSIBLE, the hunger thunders.

Prince Lucien sits at the head of the table, barely touching his food, sneaking glances at me over his water glass. When our eyes meet he smiles, and my heart locket tears itself apart on the inside. He stands once, to make a toast, the table rapt at attention.

"You who are gathered here are the privileged few," Lucien says. "I've chosen you to be my witnesses as the future of Vetris and Cavanos is shaped in the next few days."

Some clap politely. Whispers move around the table; he's talking about his impending engagement, surely. The future of Vetris will rest with him, and his Princess Consort, who is no doubt seated at this very table. Eyes fall on me, but I concentrate on the bubbles of my sparkling wine. I know better. I know how this ends, and they don't.

Lucien especially doesn't know.

"You are the new blood of Vetris," the prince says. "My peers, who will come to power someday in your own right. But I, too, will come to power soon." His eyes tear from mine as he stares down Lord Grat, Fione, all of them one by one. "I am not my father," he continues. "I will not threaten you as my father threatens your parents with his approval, his power. In my Vetris, in the days to come as I rise to the throne, suffering will not be tolerated any longer."

Lucien sweeps his eyes beyond the nobles—to the

servants, to a shocked Ulla, to the guards.

"We all grew up in a world newly ravaged by war. We've seen the veterans, our parents and grandparents and uncles and aunts, the people who work our fields, drive our carriages—all of them scarred by the Sunless War. We've seen our elders force Vetris relentlessly down a road of hatred and pain—purge after purge."

The nobles murmur to one another, but Lucien raises his voice.

"I've seen a little girl crushed under the feet of a desperate crowd, left with only one eye. I've seen men and women die, all because a red tower in the center of Vetris told a certain archduke they deserved to. And I'm tired of it. I'm tired of seeing it. I'm tired of being a part of it. It has to end sometime, and that time will be sooner rather than later, if the blood of the d'Malvanes that runs through me has anything to say about it."

Lucien unsheathes Varia's sword. "I know it's hard to comprehend. But I know too that you have seen it—caught glimpses of the suffering from between the gilded bars separating you from reality. I know you have seen it, and I know your first instinct has been to turn a blind eye. But I don't blame you for it—our parents taught us only how to blind ourselves. They drowned us in tradition—tradition like these Hunts, the Spring Brides." He pulls his braid over his shoulder. "Even this hair of mine is a tradition, chaining me to the nest of suffering we call Cavanos.

"My Cavanos will be a new Cavanos. Humans and witches will live in peace. The Old God, the New—neither of them will stand in the way of mortal progress any longer."

Lord Grat grimaces, and Fione is pale, though she looks faintly proud. This is heresy. What he speaks of will certainly reach the ears of the adults, of the court where the power truly lies. Lucien stands.

"Your Highness?" Ulla clears her throat, clearly nervous. Malachite stands with him, putting a hand on his shoulder.

"Luc," he murmurs. "What are you doing?"

Lucien ignores him and takes his long braid in his other hand, placing the bite of the sword just beneath the midnight hair at the base of his skull. In one fell movement, he slices the braid from his head cleanly, his hair hanging short. It suits his sharp face even more than his long locks did. The nobles give an audible gasp, clutching at their mouths. The royal family's hair is their pride, a symbol of their utmost power and regality. He might as well be cutting off the very crown from his head. The guards and nobles are so quiet in the moments after, you can hear the buzz of the fireflies hanging in the stillness. Lucien drops the braid to the ground, the hair skittering across the grass with a faint wind. He sheathes his sword, lifting his water glass again.

"For a new Vetris," the prince says, voice clear. "A new Cavanos."

The stunned silence is deafening. Something clear and crisp breaks it—a slow, strong clap. Next to me, Fione applauds, standing tall, her cane forgotten and her blue eyes shining at the prince. He looks so incredibly determined, so perfectly poised and ready for anything. Admiration glows on my cheeks—admiration diluted with despair. He's ready for so much. But not for his heart to be gone by the morn.

Fione's clapping breaks the spell of silence over the camp, and the nobles echo her hesitantly, one by one rising to their feet and clapping, as if unsure this is what they're supposed to do. Following the flow. But wariness gives way to murmurs, then smiles, then a deafening racket as some nobles begin to cheer. Some remain seated, glowering into their plates, clearly unenthused by the prince's vision. But most are on their feet. I stand, and I clap with them.

"Long live Prince Lucien! Long live Prince Lucien!"

Lucien's stone face melts, and he grins at them. He raises his goblet in a toast, and the nobles clink their glasses together and drink. I bring my eyes to his, only to find him already staring at me with a streak of fierce joy—so hot it burns my skin.

17

T'RAGAN DHIM AF-ARTORA, AF-REYUN HORRA

THE EFFECT OF THE PRINCE'S SPEECH can be felt as ripples throughout the camp—from the highest noble to the youngest stableboy, wine flows and smiles abound. Everyone is talking. A Cavanos of peace? A Cavanos without hate, without fear? Without the threat of war? Guards chatter—eager to see a time of peace wherein the chances they'll die on the battlefield are slim. The cooks of the camp—women, mostly—titter excitedly about what they'd do if they could leave the safety of Vetris's walls, where they'd go, what new and exciting places they'd see.

Hope.

That's what drips from everyone's mouth. I can almost see it as a golden honey on their lips as Fione and I walk through camp toward my tent after dinner. With the cold steel curtain of fear lifted, humanity doesn't seem nearly so terrifying and strange. They have hopes and dreams, just like I do. Given the chance, they want peace just like I do.

"Never in a million years did I think our dour little prince would inspire so many," Fione muses with a little laugh. "He's barely been able to look at a noble without a sneer for ten years, and all of a sudden he's instilling courage in them! What's gotten into him?"

I touch my lips absently, the memory of his kiss lingering. I look up to see Fione's face very near mine, her blue eyes voraciously curious.

"Now that I think about it, you've been awfully quiet the whole night. You've snarked maybe two times total, and that's being generous. Do you have a fever? Is your brain addled?"

"If it is, you're going to have to teach me how to use a salad fork again."

A courier approaching us cuts off her laugh. He looks very young and thin compared to the royal couriers stabled at the Hunt—the same hungry thinness as that girl Lucien gave the gold watch to, the girl with one eye. He hands Fione a letter, and she unfolds it, reading quickly. Her whole posture changes in a moment—spine straight, skin draining to white so quickly it's as if she's made of paper.

"Fione—what's the matter?" I ask. She swallows, eyes riveted to the page. Finally she shoves the paper at me. The writing is sloppy, but dire:

Checked Gavik's cell. Guards tell me it's been empty since this morn—he bribed one of them. The king's been keeping it quiet. Last known location headed east from Vetris. Stay safe.

My stomach tumbles over itself. I look up from the letter, but Fione is already walking away from me, cane insistently thumping into the grass with great speed.

"Fione! Wait!" I finally catch up. "What are you going to do?"

"I don't know." Her knuckles gripping the cane are white, too. "There's only one reason he's headed this way—for me. I'm one of the scarce few he taught to solve puzzle-locks. He'd make his way down the list, I knew that. And now—" She swallows. "Now he's coming for me."

"I can help," I insist. "I can challenge him to a duel, stop him at the gates, and you can escape—"

Her laugh is fragile. "You think he'll stop to *duel* you? I took everything from him, Zera. And he's going to take everything from me. But the joke is on him. He already did, all those years ago. All that's left to take is my life."

"We can get the guards to watch for him—"

"The guards won't stop him. King Sref's kept it quiet— they don't know he's a traitor. He'll order them to bring me to him, and that will be the end of me."

"Then—the royal guards! They listen only to Lucien—"

"As skilled as they are, the lawguards outnumber them fifty to one. You don't think I haven't thought of every possible avenue of escape already?" she snaps. "Nothing you suggest is any better than what I can think of."

I flinch. Her venom is born of fear. But I deserve it anyway. She just doesn't know that yet.

"Let me help." I put a hand on her shoulder. "I'll do whatever you need."

"You'll remain quiet about this. You'll act like nothing's wrong. And if he shows his face, I'll tell him what I did—how I feel about him—once and for all. No masks. No facades. Only a niece who hates her uncle. Only a family argument that's been brewing for thirteen years."

Fione turns on her heel and enters her tent, never inviting me in. It's a clear sign she wants to be left alone, and I have to honor that. It's the least I can do. Or is it?

Ulla lets the dark settle in and the wine wear off before she announces that it's time for the purification. She's going on as if nothing has happened at all—the smartest move, and the one least likely to get her own skin in trouble later. Whatever repercussions ensue from Lucien's speech, she's staying far away from them. Despite Lucien's words about shirking Vetris's traditions, he obviously thinks the purification one is worth keeping—perhaps because it's an Old Vetrisian tradition, and not a new one?

The servants saddle the nobles' horses, Fisher preparing one of his gray mares for me.

"She's gentle as can be, miss," he insists. "You won't have any problems with her."

I warily place my hand on the mare's flank before I try to mount her. I haven't ridden a horse in years—I think the last time I did was before I became Heartless. Y'shennria never taught me, thinking the carriage enough to transport me for the short time I was with her. I slide off the mare's side quickly, the other nobles staring. It should be so easy for me—for a supposed farm girl. My whole face lights red; I won't let something this small make them suspect me this late in the game.

I feel a strong grip around my waist the next time I haul myself up, and that extra boost is just enough to get me in the saddle. Malachite smirks lazily up at me.

"You looked like you could use a hand, milady."

"And you look like you enjoyed giving one," I drawl.

"What can I say? I delight in my service."

"Then perhaps you'll do me another service," I say. He quirks a silver-gray brow.

"Name it, and I'll...well, I'll extensively consider it."

I lean in to make sure none of the guards are listening.

"Fione's gotten word the archduke's broken out of his cell and is coming east. And the king hasn't announced he's a traitor publicly yet."

Malachite narrows his eyes at Fione, who ascends a roan gelding with an ease only possible with years of training.

"To get the last stab in?" he asks.

"Most likely. You know him—he isn't the world's most *understanding* man."

Malachite snorts. "That's a mild way to put it. Did Lucien's kiss startle all the spunk out of you or something?"

I freeze. "Y-You know about that?"

"I know he hasn't stopped grinning like an idiot." Malachite sighs. "And I haven't spent most of my life with you, but you're easy to read. Something's bothering you real deep down. Is it your feelings for him?"

Easy to read? He has no idea what he's talking about. I force my laugh to sound light. "Not everything in life is about love, Malachite."

He fixes me with the most serious of crimson stares, a strange thing coming from him. "No. Only the things that matter."

His words ring wise, wiser than I've ever heard him sound. "Will you keep an eye on Fione? If Gavik shows, she's as good as gone. And I'm not ready to let someone die on my watch again."

"Again?" Malachite asks sharply, his black irises shrinking to pinpoints as they focus on my face. He's so quick on the uptake, or maybe I'm just dulled, slowed. I feel like I've been moving through quicksand, heavy molten iron, ever since Lucien kissed me.

This is the end—isn't it? Malachite's been nothing but a pleasant friend. Friend? *Acquaintance.* Much less intimate.

A more harmless secret of mine won't hurt anything.

"When I was younger, there were these five bandits," I start, the words like copper coins in my mouth—bringing up the scent and taste of blood. "And I killed them."

Malachite is quiet, looking up at me from the horse's side. He looks shorter from this height. Less capable of cleaving me in two with his broadsword.

"One old, one young, one with no left eye, one with a crooked smile, and one who wouldn't stop smiling, no matter what I did to him."

MURDERER GIRL. TERRIBLE GIRL.

"Ever since then," I talk over the hunger, "I've been averse to playing any role in someone's death."

"*T'ragan dhim af-artora, af-reyun horra*," Malachite says, his crimson eyes a little serious, for once.

"Translation?"

"As we all should be, but as we all cannot be."

I smile, the feel of it thin on my lips. It's a beautiful sentiment—a sad one, perhaps fitting for a people who've remained fighting the overwhelming valkerax for centuries. The horse trained for the purification ritual begins to move, led by Lucien. My mare is eager to go. I look down one last time at Malachite.

"I've always thought the moments you speak Beneather are when your voice sounds the loveliest," I admit.

And with that, I urge the horse into a trot, leaving him and his pretty words behind.

The ride isn't long, but it's fraught with dangers: low-hanging branches and steep dips in the old hunting trails. Dangers the nobility, who've barely set a foot outside Vetris in their lives, consider thrilling. Shrill gasps and shrieks of excitement punctuate the ride, Fione one of the few who remains looking straight ahead, focused. When Lucien finally stops at the edge of a black rock formation, we all descend our horses. Ulla and the servants who came with us see to the horses, tying them to nearby trees.

The rock formation seems to be the center of everyone's attention, and I approach the rocks and the little crowd of nobles gathered around it. There, nestled in the middle of the formation, is a perfect jewel of sapphire water. The Blue Giant is new in the sky, dark, but the Red Twins are full and engorged, shedding bloody light that plays purple across the water. A servant carries a basket of fragrant spices and flowers, throwing them into the pool, the petals rippling across the still surface. Lucien sees me and flashes a smile.

HOW MUCH LONGER WILL HIS HAPPINESS LAST? the hunger screeches.

I'm so wrapped up in tamping the hunger down I don't notice the flesh becoming more prominent around me until Lucien himself peels off his shirt, the dimpled muscles of his back shadowed in the moonlight and his shoulder blades sharp. I catch a glimpse of black ink eagle, feathers arcing around his shoulder and talons curling around his biceps. Fione stands there still fully clothed, unlike most of the nobles around us who are easing themselves into the water of the spring, giggling and admiring one another's bodies in less-than-subtle ways.

Ulla walks by us, demanding we strip and join the others in the spring. I expect Fione to be shy, but she immediately pulls her dress over her head, leaving her in only her underthings. She makes her way to the spring, leaning her cane against a nearby rock.

Ulla asks me to undress, harder this time. I unbutton my dress and step out of it, the warm air pillowing against my skin. I keep my locket on, hoping she won't make me take it off. My stomach, my thighs—everyone in the spring can see it all. I can feel Charm snickering at me, Lord Grat staring. Malachite, despite our tension earlier, gives me an approving wink. He isn't in the water, instead standing guard outside the spring. Prince Lucien looks me over once and then glances away, so quickly it's as if he's been burned. My underthings barely hide anything, and I hurriedly step into the spring, letting the warm water distort my body from their view. Fione sits alone in one corner, picking at the moss on a rock face. Lucien is intently studying the sky, the heat of the spring flushing his neck and jaw.

I look at my hands under the water, fracturing through the red moonlight. I'm so tired of maintaining this facade, of being a monster, of this hunger within me. Lucien's and Fione's wants are so straightforward. Fione wanted Gavik punished. Lucien wants to change his kingdom. He wants me. What do I want? I want him. I want *him*, the happiness he brings me, the crooked grins and soft embraces. He makes me feel human again. He's the only one who's ignited a spark of humanity inside me in three years.

But I want the whole of my humanity, and the cost is his.

"Does everyone understand what they're to do during tomorrow's hunt?" Lucien asks. I was so lost in my thoughts I didn't hear a word he said, but I pretend I did, nodding. The circle of nobles also agrees, some of them pale-faced. Of course they'd be—they think they're off to hunt witches.

They have no idea Lucien doesn't hunt them at all. They have no idea they won't have a prince, come tomorrow.

HE'LL BE OURS, the hunger hisses with joy. **_FOREVER._**

Iawait midnight like a doomed man awaits the gallows.

The little sandclock built into my desk ticks away happily, ignorant of my all-consuming terror. I try to make jokes for myself, try to convince myself things will be all right, normal, by changing dresses a dozen times. But the mirror reflects only a pale, haunted girl, with eyes too big and hair too faded, with an emptiness inside her too large to contain.

Even though I know they aren't, every dress I try looks bloodstained. Wrong.

One last dress—black. Black for mourning.

Part of me prays, to the Old God and the New, that Lucien will arrive at our meeting place with Malachite in tow. Surely Malachite's told him of Gavik's approach. Surely he'll bring along Malachite as an extra sword against the mysterious vanishing bandits the guards spotted earlier.

If he brings Malachite, I can do nothing to him. Even with a broken leg, Malachite's still a Beneather. I can't challenge him at all.

But if Lucien doesn't bring him—

The sandclock strikes midnight. I pick up the silk bag the glass jar rests in and strap Father's sword to my waist.

Every breath, every smile, every lie has led to this moment. Y'shennria has led me to this moment.

I take the first step outside.

18

THE STARVING WOLF
AND THE BLACK ROSE
BENEATH THE YEW

GETTING OUT OF CAMP is more difficult than it should be—only the nobles are asleep. Ulla directs the cooks in rising sweetrounds in preparation for breakfast tomorrow. The guards patrol relentlessly, perhaps still spooked by the bandit sighting earlier today. Thankfully, most of the patrols are centered around the prince's tent, giving me a window in which to escape toward the stables. Hiding among horses is far easier than hiding among people, their sheer bulk camouflaging me as I make it to the edge of camp where the forest begins. Only when I'm completely covered by shadow do I look back—the oil lamps and bonfires of the camp burn bright against the darkness.

The forest is more familiar than any home I've ever lived in—the smell of trees, the smell of lichen and rot and dry leaves. The scent is identical to Nightsinger's forest.

Nightsinger. I haven't seen her for two weeks, but it feels like two months. I know she'll keep her word about giving me my heart back, but only if I bring her the prince's. If I don't—

I squeeze my eyes shut and steel my shoulders. The east path is short but twisted, and I scale a hill to see the yew tree nestled in a rocky little gorge. The twisted branches stand out among the pines—the tree itself old and long stripped of bark, bleached by the sun. A dead tree.

A fitting place to end it all.

Lucien is nowhere to be seen, but he is and always will be Whisper, too. He's somewhere among these shadows, these rocks. Not the north ones—too exposed. Hiding behind the fallen log would be too obvious. That leaves only one place. I approach the trunk of the bleached yew tree slowly, leaning against it.

"If you aren't here, then I'm losing my touch," I say. Lucien emerges from behind the other side of the trunk, his short, raven's-wing hair ruffled by the wind and his smirk lopsided.

THERE YOU ARE, MY PRIZE. MY PREY. The hunger bursts into flame, licking at my insides.

"I have a hard time believing you'll ever lose that uncanny ability to find me," Lucien says. He wears the dark leather armor of Whisper that I first met him in. Varia's sword still hangs at his waist—if I can't get a surprise attack on him, he'll fight back, and a repeat of the duel would be disastrous: long, drawn out, messy. It needs to be clean, quick. I need to end this as fast as I can for my own sake—the longer it goes, the more time I have to hesitate.

The longer it goes, the more he'll despise me. ***THE MORE I'LL DESPISE MYSELF.***

"What did you think of my speech?" He bridges the silence. "The whole time I was giving it I could practically hear you laughing at me for being too serious. I know it's a little idealistic, but it's something I've always wanted to say. I just never had the courage to. But then I met you, and I learned—"

Lucien's midnight eyes skitter away from my face. "I apologize. I'm getting ahead of myself."

There's another long silence, fraught with tension so thick I feel like I'm breathing molten steel.

"Is Malachite here?" I ask. Lucien shakes his head.

"No. I told him I wanted to be left alone. He doesn't listen, usually, but when I told him you and I were meeting, he agreed. Not that I'll last long. I'm sure he's making his way toward us as we speak, broken leg and all."

Then I have to hurry.

"For what it's worth," I start. "I think you would've made a wonderful king."

His gaze narrows, but only barely, smile still golden on his lips. "Would've? What are you talking about?"

SO WILLING TO TRUST ME, the hunger practically salivates. I draw near him, unable to conjure up even a halfhearted sultry look. My skin begs to feel his again, to feel the humanity thrumming through his veins and mine in tandem. His fingers, so long and slender—

TAKE THEM OFF ONE BY ONE. MAKE HIM SUFFER AS IIE HAS MADE YOU SUFFER—

Lucien is perfectly still. "Lady Zera—"

"Just Zera," I insist softly, walking ever closer to him.

"Zera." He half swallows my name, and it sounds wonderful. "If you hate me for what I did—for that kiss—if you don't like me at all, please. Just tell me. The wait has been agonizing—"

I laugh darkly. "It has, hasn't it? Three years for me. Perhaps a few days for you."

His brows knit now, more the suspicious and bitter Lucien I'm used to. "Three years?"

I can practically hear my freedom beating in his chest. I can taste it—so sweet and light, so free of this terrible guilt I've been carrying around for so long. This terrible monster. His heart will absolve me. His heart the only thing I want—

PULL IT FROM HIS CHEST! The hunger screams dementedly, its voice drowning out everything else—Lucien's words, his face. All that swims sharply before my eyes is the exact patch of leather over his chest where his heart beats. The hunger maddens—I can feel my mind slipping from my fingers like muddy water. The dried livers did nothing to satiate me. I've hungered and hungered for so long—

"Zera? Are you all right?"

My eyes flicker up for just a moment to lock with his. His smile still rests on his face. He has no idea what dark, ugly thoughts race through me, and yet he's smiling at me. *Still.* A bitter fury runs through me.

"It doesn't matter if I'm all right," I grit.

"Don't speak nonsense—"

"I'm a tool," I interrupt him with a snarl. "A tool doesn't have to be all right. Everyone keeps asking it, as if they really care, as if the well-being of someone like me actually matters to them! They have no idea! They're ignorant little idiots, so willing to trust a girl in pretty dresses with pretty words. **DON'T YOU GET IT?** You were so clever and distrustful when we first met but now, now you just have that stupid smile on your face. What—did I break down your fragile, self-inflicted barriers? Did your sick infatuation with a monster of a girl blind you?"

I throw back my head and laugh at the look on Lucien's face—utter confusion. Hurt. I'm hurting him, but with every word I say I'm tearing myself to ribbons. Every word I say is meant for myself, for the past me who's being so cruel just by pretending to enjoy his presence. Pretending to love him. Because that's all it was, all it can be—pretend.

I expect him to shout back, to insult me in return. I don't expect his arms, rough and warm, to encircle me in a single sweeping motion too fast to avoid. He holds me close, the smell of rainwater filling my senses, and the heat of him pressing against every cold part of me.

"You're not," he murmurs into my hair. "You're not a monster of a girl. You're smart, and so very kind—"

How dare he. ***HOW DARE HE!*** The hunger amplifies my fury tenfold, stoking the fire inside me instantly into a blazing inferno.

I push him away as hard as I can, screaming, "What do you know? You've spent your entire life in that wretched city, wallowing in your pity and the shadow of your dead sister! You know nothing about me! You of all people don't get to judge my monstrosity!"

Lucien is stock-still, face frozen in the triple moonlight. And then he melts, a glare in his eyes and his smile gone.

"You— Why are you being like this? You're like a whole different person."

"I was never the person you thought you knew," I sneer. "That girl doesn't exist. She was there for one purpose, and now it's over. The girl you fell in love with—that smart, kind thing—is dead, ***AND I KILLED HER***. I'm killing her right now, in front of you, so you get just how badly you fell for a trick. An illusion. Something that isn't real. Gods help you if you ever do ascend the throne—if a backwoods tool like me could fool you, who knows what someone really good at acting could do."

"Zera—"

"Elizera, actually. No last name. Daughter of a merchant couple whose faces I can't remember anymore."

"—this isn't you," he says, hard. Almost imperious.

"This is me." I smile with all my teeth. "You were just too stupid to see that. Blinded by a nice chest and a nice dress. *PATHETIC*."

Lucien staggers back like I've physically hit him, and in that instant I nearly crumble. I want nothing more than to embrace him and tell him everything I'm saying is a lie—that I love him, and will marry him, and rule beside him as queen in his hopeful new land of Cavanos. A perfect ending. But that's not how this ends. Our happiness isn't what I came here for. It's mine, and mine alone. The more I make my words hurt, the better he learns his lesson. The smarter he'll be the next time a girl comes along. The harder I speak, the brighter the truth will shine. And he deserves the truth more than anyone.

Despair. I can feel it opening up beneath me, a yawning black chasm. He still hasn't reached for his sword. I reach for mine.

IT'S OVER, the hunger cackles, those two words ringing in my ears like a deafening cacophony of screams. *IT'S OVER! ALL THE PAIN. ALL MY SUFFERING— FINALLY OVER. FREE! FREE TO LIVE A HUMAN LIFE—* My feet move toward him, my teeth growing long as I smile at him. *FINALLY THIS WRETCHED HUNGER WILL BE GONE. I WON'T BE A MONSTER, I WON'T BE A MONSTER, I WON'T BE A MONSTER ANYMORE—*

The blind anger, the blind lust, it lifts for a scarce moment. My blade is straight out, pointed at Lucien's chest. He's staring right at me, betrayal burning dark in his eyes. I can see it—the seeds of hate starting to blossom in his irises. The old me—the dead me—cries out with regret, my blood curdling in cold, final horror.

The only person in this world who makes me truly happy despises me.

My hand holding the sword shakes so hard and so suddenly.

DO IT.

No. (I lifted my veil, and he looked at me like I meant something.)

HE WOULD DO IT TO YOU, HE WOULD DO IT TO YOU IN A HEARTBEAT—ALL HUMANS ARE SELFISH ANIMALS, ALL HUMANS HATE YOU—

No—not him. (He laces his hand in mine as we dance, his eyes like black embers.)

HE'S GOING TO KILL YOU—LOOK AT HIM. LOOK AT HIS FACE. HE HATES YOU. HE'S GOING TO TURN ON YOU. TURN ON HIM WHILE YOU HAVE THE UPPER HAND!

You're wrong. (He kisses me. He kisses me and the world ends.)

DO IT, YOU COWARD, HE'S RIGHT HERE! INCHES MORE—AN INCH MORE AND WE ARE FREE FOREVER—

"No!" I clutch my head, the hunger fighting me like it never has before—wrenching my innards around, clawing at my throat to let it out, let it complete what it wants. "I won't do it to him! I won't make him suffer! Not him!"

My teeth grow even longer, sharper as my screams grow sharper. I fling my arm back and throw my sword as far as I can, before the hunger moves my body again.

"I won't do it, you godsforsaken monster—"

The flash of searing pain and the cold steel through my chest cuts my words in half. Slowly, I arc my head down to look at the blade sticking from my unheart. Someone's run me through from behind. Blood drips from the blade, soaking from the wound into my dress, staining the black a dark, wet crimson. Streaks of white liquid, too. I touch the liquid, my fingertips coming away sizzling. White mercury.

Someone's killed me. Someone who knows I'm Heartless.

I look up, Lucien the only thing I see, his dark eyes unreadable, unmovable. Desperately, hopelessly, I reach out for him.

"Lucien—" I croak. "I'm sorry. I'm so...*so sorry.*"

My legs give out, the earth pulling me to it inescapably. The smell of pine in my nose, the smell of blood. This is so familiar—like so many days I spent in Nightsinger's forest, being killed by mercenaries. By hungry wildcats. Today it is neither. Today, from what little I can see out of my blurring eyes and unresponsive body, it's Gavik. A strange Gavik—disheveled and in a plain, tattered brown robe, his white hair and beard dusty as if he's been traveling, his cold blue eyes ever the same, two shards of ice that look down on me cruelly. I can hear him speaking to Lucien, only half of it audible.

"—made it in time. Your bodyguard told me where you were...Heartless appear to pass out after...struck with such a weapon, but in reality they die...she wasn't afraid to die in the black market...when I saw the duel, I had my suspicions...a traitor harlot, and a bitch besides..."

Faintly, my neck cracks as Gavik wrenches my head up by my hair. He's mocking me—I can hear it in the tone of his voice, even if my brain is dying too rapidly to understand much more.

"...this is ideal...though your father will be so distraught... that his son, too, was killed by a Heartless."

Lucien? Killed...by a Heartless? I haven't done that. He's still alive, I can see him just in front of me —

"...the entire country...mourning the loss of a Crown Prince...eager for revenge, don't you think? Another war will begin..."

I see a glimmer of Varia's sword as Lucien draws it. Gavik's laughter rumbles, and then the sound of a dozen footsteps—heavy, in metal armor. Lawguards? All around us.

The sound of a dozen swords drawing.

Lucien. They're going to kill Lucien! As my vision threatens to go dark once and for all I force my eyes open. No—not like this.

Weak, the hunger chortles, tiredly—as if it, too, is dying. *You were weak, and this is what you get. He dies because of you. You die because of him. How romantic.*

I can feel it; through even the darkness of death, I can feel the hunger still in me. It's stronger than anything that's left inside—any emotion, any energy. It's all I have. It's all I am, here, at death's door.

I've died a dozen times, and yet getting up now is the most pain I've ever felt. Blankets of needles beneath my skin, acid in my veins instead of blood—I can barely blink without spasms running through me. My knees buckle, my very fingernails throb in agony. My vision is just a blur of colors—of movements. A ring of silver, a figure of white, and a figure of raven's-wing black.

But there, on the wind, I smell it.

Human, the hunger rasps. *Fear!*

For the second time in my life, I give in to the hunger.

The world is darkness, but all of a sudden I can taste heat, see colors—my limbs give aching creaks, elongating until I'm much taller, much thinner. I feel my teeth extending beyond my lips, claws breaking through my fingertips. No thoughts—only desperation. Desperation to get at the source of the delicious heat surrounding me; I move like wind, like water, in leaps and bounds, only two steps needed to catch up with the screaming, shining humans in armor. They're so difficult to open, but they have soft spots between their armor—soft spots that bleed the sweetest honey. They stab at me, but it doesn't hurt anymore. Nothing hurts anymore.

There's screaming, shouting, but it dies away as the silver humans dwindle to nothing more than piles of bone and flesh. The bleached yew tree is red now. Only one other thing is unsullied white —Gavik, so very afraid. He's pissed himself, the smell acrid. I reach for him, stabbing deep with my claws into his chest and ripping him from navel to throat. Like the bandits did to me. What bandits? I can't remember anymore—there's only the man's agonized cries as I devour him, some other part of me delighting in his death as more than just a way to satisfy this hunger. I throw his body away when I'm done, like a doll's carcass.

There's one last blazing heat source behind me, and I whirl around, claws at the ready. He's dark, eyes and hair like midnight, his face a hawk's face, his sword stance a hawk's stance.

Not him.

HIM, the hunger keens a low, desperate cry. I reach for him with my claws, but the sharp pain in my head staggers me. *Not him. Nothimnothim!*

I'm so empty inside. I can feel it, aching there in my chest.

The wound remains, but the void where my heart should be bleeds more. It aches so badly—everything aches. I become small again, my claws retracting, my teeth growing inward. The hunger fights it, rakes itself across the coals of my mind in a last, desperate attempt to regain control.

You are in the silence. You are of the silence. Reginall's words. *Place your hand over your unheart. And you'll find it there.*

Find what there? I put my hand over my unheart, listening. Waiting for the illusion within a lie. Nothing will beat inside my chest. Nothing has, not for three whole years.

Not him. Not him. Not Lucien.

There! A heartbeat! It thuds against my rib cage, so strong I can't deny it even as an illusion. How? How is this possible? *Lucien,* I think. The name shines, a light in the bloodstained darkness. **Lucien.** My unheart—no, my heart thumps again. And again. Every time I think of his name, of what that name means to me, it beats. Lucien, who hates me now. Lucien, who kissed me. Lucien, who stands there with nothing but fear in his eyes for me.

Lucien, who makes my heart beat again.

The pain floods back in, deafening everything around me, but it's completely silent in my head. The hunger doesn't so much as stir inside me. My body feels lighter than it ever has, lighter than I can remember since I was first turned. I'm air, silk, and yet the cold void of my unheart is heavier than ever. There's a weight there—comforting and warm.

Two drips of something cascading down my face, something that splats red onto the leaves. Tears of blood. I'm weeping—weeping like Reginall described. Weeping, because in this moment, I'm free.

Around me is a red landscape, lumpy and scattered with

metal, and in the midst of it all stands Lucien, his face blood-flecked and utterly hollow. I stop weeping when I realize bodies surround me. The light feeling fades, replaced only by horror. Human bodies, ripped to pieces. Lawguards—how many of them? I can't tell—every part of them is scattered, serrated, Archduke Gavik's white hair the only thing standing out, soaking up his own blood slowly.

"No—" I choke. "No, no, no! Not again!" I whirl to Lucien, pleading. "Please, Lucien—"

I'm met with Varia's blade pointed right at me, square and firm, though trembling ever so slightly as Lucien's hand quavers. His dark eyes gleam empty, with something cold and all-consuming in the very pits of them.

Utter fear.

"Stay away from me," he says softly, with a deadly edge to it that strikes at my very core. I can see it in his eyes—he no longer faces down the girl he embraced mere hours ago.

He faces down a monster.

"Please—"

"If you move one more step..." Lucien grits his teeth. "I'll cut you down where you stand."

I freeze in my tracks. His eyes flit between me to the mound of corpses at my feet. I want to be sick, but I can't move for fear of him striking out at me. What do I say? What can I say? I'm disgusted, and terrified, and so confused. But so is he. Never again—I could never again feel this way, if I only had the heart in his chest.

TAKE IT, the hunger begins again, coming over the horizon of my mind. I look up at Lucien.

"Run," I beg him. "Leave me—run while you still can."

The Crown Prince of Cavanos struggles for only a moment with his thoughts. His pause is the sort born of regret, no doubt. One second is all he gives me—one last second to take in his face, to memorize the lines and planes and beauty of it before it's gone forever. One last second to relish the memories I have with him, before they shatter into a thousand irreparable pieces.

I should've known—woods like these are where I belong. It's where a thing like me is meant to stay. The witches made a mistake, sending one of their beastly puppets out to play. And now a dozen lawguards and an archduke have paid with their lives for it. Now Lucien pays with his heart for it.

OUR LAST CHANCE, the hunger slavers mindlessly. **GET HIM!**

Lucien won't run. I don't understand why not—he knows what I'm capable of now. He knows I'm not the girl he fell in love with. Why? Why does he insist on standing there, risking his life? I clutch my head, the hunger's voice dark and crescendoing again. It's so unstable, my body so weak from my wounds. I refuse to let the hunger turn me into that... *thing* again, but here it is, singing to me of long claws and teeth, of nothing but the urge to consume. I try to summon up the silence, Reginall's teachings of the weeping I'd managed in that one desperate instant, but the hunger is so much stronger.

"Lucien, please! I can't control it for long—you have to run, *now!*"

"You heard her," a girl's voice flits between us. "You really should run. Then again, you were never very good at that. Always had to stay and see things through to the end, like an idiot."

Lucien and I look to the bloodstained yew tree, where a girl no older than me stands on its roots. Her face is round, expression as calm as a lake on a winter's morn, a shapeless robe billowing about her body. Her skin is golden oakwood, eyes like onyx, long hair so incredibly dark—the color of a raven's wing. Unmistakable. Unforgettable. This can't be happening—this can't be real. I'm seeing double, or a hallucination. Lucien is the first to find strength enough for words, his voice cracking in on itself.

"*Varia.*"

The girl's smile shines despite the blood she stands in. "Hello, brother."

END OF BOOK ONE

ACKNOWLEDGMENTS

When I was thirteen, I realized my life dream was to write a fantasy trilogy—something grand and sweeping and unforgettable. While this book might not be any of the three to some people, it is everything to me, and consequently, I owe many people for making this dream come true. This sort of book doesn't come about unless you have a lot of people preserving your sanity as you take a very bloody and very delightful trip into another world entirely. Eternal thanks to my indomitable editors Stacy Abrams and Lydia Sharp, without whom I would be utterly adrift. To Jessica Faust, for having the patience and wisdom to weather me. To Griffin, for always being there for me and making the best quesadilla on planet Earth, to Deborah for being a constant source of inspiration, and to everyone at the Entangled family for supporting me and my dreams. A very hearty thanks goes to Yuming Yin, the wonderful cover artist who brought Zera to such stunning life.

A special thanks to you, reader, for following me down the rabbit hole. The journey has only begun, and I'm so excited to walk it with you. May your reading be ever pleasant and your life full of joy.

BRING ME THEIR HEARTS
by Sara Wolf

Prepared by Nancy Cantor, media specialist,
NSU University School

- Discuss the relationship of Zera and Lucien. Did you think she would go through with the killing? Why or why not? Are they a good match?

- Zera comments that "the people of Vetris are clearly very devout. Or very scared. Perhaps both, considering one feeds the other." (page 73) Does this ring true for the world we live in now? Discuss how religion affected past societies and influences our current times.

- The nobles chant this prayer: "His light of knowledge touches all who are true, his light of knowledge smites all who are false." How does this prayer align with your beliefs?

- Gavik states at the worship ceremony, "True peace is only an illusion, so long as a single witch remains alive in Cavanos!" (page 156) Discuss examples of how leaders use fear to control people.

- Do the people of Vetris have just cause to be frightened of or bigoted toward the witches?

- At the first noble banquet she attends, Zera considers how many common people one small piece of dessert could feed. Discuss the imbalance of food accessibility in our country and the world. What are some possible solutions?

- Lucien states the polymaths' motto is "Create the power, control the power." (page 167) Do you believe this is an appropriate motto for the scientists of our world? Are the weapons of today controllable?

• Zera is ridden with guilt over the murders she committed. The monster in her head told her that she paid death and suffering back with more death and suffering. (page 177) Do you agree with her? With the monster? Were the killings justified? Does she deal with her guilt in a healthy way?

• Zera's physical description hints that she is a bigger than average girl. What is the significance of this? Does the fact that she isn't "perfect" in the way our society judges appearance affect your opinion of her?

• Do you know girls like Grace and Charm? How do you deal with them?

• Fisher tells Zera that "Killing only makes more hate, and the world's got enough of that right now." (page 208) How can we overcome the hate (terrorism, mass killings, etc.) in the world today?

• King Sref is bent on revenge against the witches he believes killed his daughter. Are there alternatives to starting a war to obtain the revenge he seeks? Do you see King Sref as a weak or a strong leader?

• Discuss Zera's relationships with Y'shennria, Nightsinger, Crav and Peligli, Fione, and Malachite.

• The book ends rather abruptly, with the thwarted killing of Lucien and the sudden appearance of Varia. Were these a surprise to you? What might happen to Zera and Lucien in the next book?

GRAB THE ENTANGLED TEEN RELEASES READERS ARE TALKING ABOUT!

KISS OF THE ROYAL
BY LINDSEY DUGA

In the war against the Forces of Darkness, the Royals are losing. Princess Ivy is determined to end this centuries-long conflict once and for all, so her new battle partner must succeed where the others failed. Prince Zach's unparalleled skill with a sword, enhanced by Ivy's magic Kiss, should make them an unstoppable pair—but try convincing Zach of that.

Prince Zach has spent his life preparing for battle, but he would rather be branded a heretic than use his lips as nothing more than a way to transfer magic. A kiss is a symbol of love, and love is the most powerful weapon they have—but try convincing Ivy of that.

With the fate of their world on the line, the battlefield has become a testing ground, and only one of them can be right. Falling for each other wasn't part of the plan—but try convincing their hearts of that.

Pretty Dead Girls
by Monica Murphy

Beautiful. Perfect. Dead.

In the peaceful seaside town of Cape Bonita, wicked secrets and lies are hidden just beneath the surface. But all it takes is one tragedy for them to be exposed.

The most popular girls in school are turning up dead, and Penelope Malone is terrified she's next. All the victims so far have been linked to Penelope—and to a boy from her physics class. The one she's never really noticed before, with the rumored dark past and a brooding stare that cuts right through her.

There's something he isn't telling her. But there's something she's not telling him, either.

Everyone has secrets, and theirs might get them killed.

Haven
by Mary Lindsey

Rain Ryland has never belonged anywhere. He's used to people judging him for his rough background, his intimidating size, and now, his orphan status. He's always been on the outside, looking in, and he's fine with that. Until he moves to New Wurzburg and meets Friederike Burkhart.

Freddie isn't like normal teen girls, though. And someone wants her dead for it. Freddie warns he'd better stay far away if he wants to stay alive, but Rain's never been good at running from trouble. For the first time, Rain has something worth fighting for, worth living for. Worth dying for.

By a Charm and a Curse
By Jaime Questell

Le Grand's Carnival Fantastic isn't like other traveling circuses. It's bound by a charm, held together by a centuries-old curse, that protects its members from ever growing older or getting hurt. Emmaline King is drawn to the circus like a moth to a flame…and unwittingly recruited into its folds by a mysterious teen boy whose kiss is as cold as ice.

Forced to travel through Texas as the new Girl in the Box, Emmaline is completely trapped. Breaking the curse seems like her only chance at freedom, but with no curse, there's no charm, either—dooming everyone who calls the Carnival Fantastic home. Including the boy she's afraid she's falling for.

Everything—including his life—could end with just one kiss.

Black Bird of the Gallows
by Meg Kassel

A simple but forgotten truth: where harbingers of death appear, the morgues will soon be full.

Angie Dovage can tell there's more to Reece Fernandez than just the tall, brooding athlete who has her classmates swooning, but she can't imagine his presence signals a tragedy that will devastate her small town. When something supernatural tries to attack her, Angie is thrown into a battle between good and evil she never saw coming. Right in the center of it is Reece—and he's not human.

What's more, she knows something most don't. That the secrets her town holds could kill them all. But that's only half as dangerous as falling in love with a harbinger of death.

ZOMBIE ABBEY
BY LAUREN BARATZ-LOGSTED

1920, England

And the three teenage Clarke sisters thought what they'd wear to dinner was their biggest problem…

Lady Kate, the entitled eldest.

Lady Grace, lost in the middle and wishing she were braver.

Lady Lizzy, so endlessly sunny, it's easy to underestimate her.

Then there's Will Harvey, the proud, to-die-for—and possibly die with!—stable boy; Daniel Murray, the resourceful second footman with a secret; Raymond Allen, the unfortunate-looking young duke; and Fanny Rogers, the unsinkable kitchen maid.

Upstairs! Downstairs! Toss in some farmers and villagers! None of them ever expected to work together for any reason. But none of them had ever seen anything like this.

TRUE STORM
BY L.E. STERLING

All is not well in Plague-ravaged Dominion City. The Watchers have come out of hiding, spreading chaos and death throughout the city, and suddenly Lucy finds herself torn between three men with secrets of their own. Betrayal is a cruel lesson, and to survive this deadly game of politics, Lucy is manipulated into agreeing to a marriage of convenience. But DNA isn't the only thing they want from Lucy…or her sister.

entangled teen

an imprint of Entangled Publishing LLC